PRAISE FOR THE

44 SCOTLAND STREET SERIES

"A characteristically sly and eccentric portrait of Edinburgh society." —*Entertainment Weekly*

"[McCall Smith's] sense of gentle but pointed humor is once again afoot." —*The Seattle Times*

"Soulful [and] sweet. . . . Will make you feel as though you live in Edinburgh, if only for a short while, and it's a fine place to visit indeed. . . . Long live the folks on Scotland Street." —*The Times-Picayune* (New Orleans)

"It is McCall Smith's particular genius to be able to look on the brighter side of life, and he's seldom done so more enjoyably." —*The Scotsman*

"A lively new series." —*The Washington Post*

"Alexander McCall Smith is the most genial of writers and the most gentle of satirists. . . . [The] characters are great fun . . . [and] McCall Smith treats all of them with affection." —*Rocky Mountain News*

ALEXANDER McCALL SMITH

LOVE OVER SCOTLAND

Alexander McCall Smith is the author of the international phenomenon The No. 1 Ladies' Detective Agency series, the Isabel Dalhousie series, the Portuguese Irregular Verbs series, and the 44 Scotland Street series. He is Professor Emeritus of medical law at the University of Edinburgh in Scotland and has served on many national and international bodies concerned with bioethics. He was born in what is now known as Zimbabwe, and he was a law professor at the University of Botswana.

Visit his Web site at
www.alexandermccallsmith.com.

LOVE OVER SCOTLAND

ALEXANDER McCALL SMITH

Illustrations by
IAIN McINTOSH

ANCHOR BOOKS
A Division of Random House, Inc.
New York

FIRST ANCHOR BOOKS EDITION, NOVEMBER 2007

This book is excerpted from a series that originally
appeared in *The Scotsman* newspaper.

Library of Congress Cataloging-in-Publication Data
McCall Smith, Alexander, 1948–.
Love over Scotland / Alexander McCall Smith. —
1st Anchor Books ed.
p. cm.
ISBN 978-0-307-27598-1
1. Edinburgh (Scotland)—Fiction. 2. Apartment houses—
Fiction. I. Title.
PR6063.C326L68 2007
823'.914—dc22
2007022072

Author illustration © Iain McIntosh

www.anchorbooks.com

Printed in the United States of America
10 9 8 7 6 5 4 3 2 1

This book is for David and Joyce Robinson

44 Scotland Street: The Story So Far

At the end of the second series of 44 Scotland Street we saw Domenica leaving for the Malacca Straits for the purposes of anthropological research. We saw Bruce safely departed for London. Now Pat is about to start her course in history of art at the University of Edinburgh. She moves out of Scotland Street to the South Side, but this does not mean that she breaks off all connections with the New Town.

Poor Matthew. Even with the recent substantial gift which his father has given him, he is still restless and unfulfilled. Matthew, of course, would like to be fulfilled with Pat, but Pat does not wish to find fulfilment with Matthew.

In the second series, Angus Lordie got nowhere. He is missing Domenica, though, and hopes that the part which she played in his life will be taken by Antonia Collie, a friend whom Domenica has allowed to move into her flat in her absence. However, Antonia proves to be a somewhat difficult character.

We saw Bertie spending more time with his father, Stuart, who had managed to wring some concessions out of Irene, but some dawns, alas, are false. Irene does not change; to change her would be to deprive this story of the strong air of reality which has pervaded it thus far. For this is no fanciful picture of Edinburgh life, this is exactly as it is.

1. *Pat Distracted on a Tedious Art Course*

Pat let her gaze move slowly round the room, over the figures seated at the table in the seminar room. There were ten of them; eleven if one counted Dr Fantouse himself, although he was exactly the sort of person one wouldn't count. Dr Fantouse, reader in the history of art and author of *The Discerning Gaze in the Quattrocento* was a mild, rather mousy man, who for some reason invariably evoked the pity of students. It was not that they disliked him – he was too kind and courteous for that – they just felt a vague, inexpressible regret that he existed, with his shabby jacket and his dull Paisley ties; no discernment there, one of them had said, with some satisfaction at the wit of the remark. And then there was the name, which sounded so like that marvellous, but under-used, Scots word which Pat's father used to describe the overly flashy – fantoosh. Dr Fantouse was not fantoosh in any respect; but neither was . . . Pat's gaze had gone all the way round the table, over all ten, skipping over Dr Fantouse quickly, as in sympathy, and now returned to the boy sitting opposite her.

He was called Wolf, she had discovered. At the first meeting of the class they had all introduced themselves round the table, at the suggestion of Dr Fantouse himself ("I'm Geoffrey Fantouse, as you may know; I'm the Quattrocento really, but I have a strong interest in aesthetics, which, I hardly need to remind you, is what we shall be discussing in this course"). And then had come a succession of names: Ginny, Karen, Mark, Greg, Alice, and so on until, at the end, Wolf, looking down at the table in modesty, had said, "Wolf", and Pat had seen the barely disguised appreciative glances of Karen and Ginny.

Wolf. It was a very good name for a boy, thought Pat; ideal, in fact. Wolf was a name filled with promise. And this Wolf, sitting opposite her, fitted the name perfectly. He was tall, broad-shouldered, with a shock of golden hair and a broad smile. Boys like that could look – and be – vacuous – surfing types with a limited vocabulary and an off-putting empty-headedness. But not this Wolf. There was a lambent intelligence in his face, a light in the eyes that revealed the mind behind the appealing features.

Now, at the second meeting of the seminar group, Pat struggled to follow the debate which Dr Fantouse was trying to encourage. They had been invited to consider the contention of Joseph Beuys that the distinction between what is art in the products of our human activity and what is not art, is a pernicious and pointless one. The discussion, which could have been so passionate, had never risen above the bland; there had been long silences, even after the name of Damien Hirst had been raised and Dr Fantouse, in an attempt to provoke controversy, had expressed doubts over the display of half a cow in formaldehyde. "I am not sure," he had ventured, "whether an artist of another period, let us say Donatello, would have considered this art. Butchery, maybe, or even science, but perhaps not art."

This remark had been greeted with silence. Then the thin-faced girl sitting next to Pat had spoken. "Can Damien Hirst actually draw?" she asked. "I mean, if you asked him to draw a house, would he be able to do so? Would it look like a house?"

They stared at her. "I don't see what that . . ." began a young man.

"That raises an interesting issue of representation," interrupted Dr Fantouse. "I'm not sure that the essence of art is its ability to represent. May I suggest, perhaps, that we turn to the ideas of Benedetto Croce and see whether he can throw any light on the subject. As you know, Croce believed in the existence of an aesthetic function built into, so to speak, the human mind. This function . . ."

Pat looked up at the ceiling. At the beginning of the new semester she had been filled with enthusiasm at the thought of what lay ahead. The idea of studying the history of art seemed to her to be immensely exciting – an eagerly anticipated intellectual adventure – but somehow the actual experience had failed so far to live up to her expectations. She had not foreseen these dry sessions with Dr Fantouse and the arid wastes of Croce; the long silences in the seminars; the absence of sparkle.

Of course there had been numerous adjustments in her life. She had left the flat in Scotland Street, she had said goodbye to Bruce, who had gone to London, and she had also seen off her friend and neighbour, Domenica Macdonald, who had embarked on a train from Waverley Station on the first leg of her journey to the Straits of Malacca and her anthropological project. And she had moved, too, to the new flat in Spottiswoode Street, which she now shared with three other students, all female. Those were enough changes in any life, and the starting of the course had merely added to the stress.

"You'll feel better soon," her father had said when she had phoned him to complain of the blues that seemed to have descended on her. "Blues pass." And then he had hesitated, and she had known that he had been on the verge of saying: "Of course you could come home," but had refrained from doing so. For he knew, as well as she did, that she could not go home to the family house in the Grange, to her room, which was there exactly as she had left it, because that would be conceding defeat in the face of life before she had even embarked on it. So nothing more had been said.

And now, while Dr Fantouse said something more about Benedetto Croce – remarks that were met with complete silence by the group – Pat looked across the table to where Wolf was sitting and saw that he was looking at her.

They looked at one another for a few moments, and then Wolf, for his part, slowly raised a finger to his lips, and left it there for a few seconds, looking at her as he did so. Then he mouthed something which she could not make out exactly, of course, but which seemed to her to be this: Hey there, little Red Riding Hood!

2. *A Picture in a Magazine*

At the end of the seminar, when Dr Fantouse had shuffled off in what can only have been disappointment and defeat, back to the Quattrocento, the students snapped shut their notebooks, yawned, scratched their heads, and made their way out of the seminar room and into the corridor. Pat had deliberately avoided looking at Wolf, but she was aware of the fact that he was slow in leaving the seminar room, having dropped something on the floor, and was busy searching for it. There was a notice-board directly outside the door, and she stopped at this, looking at the untidy collection of posters which had been pinned up by a variety of student clubs and societies. None of these was of real interest to her. She did not wish to take up gliding and had only a passing interest in salsa classes. Nor was she interested in teaching at an American summer camp, for which no experience was necessary, although enthusiasm was helpful. But at least these notices gave her an excuse to wait until Wolf came out, which he did a few moments later.

She stood quite still, peering at the small print on the summer camp poster. There was something about an orientation weekend and insurance, and then a deposit would be necessary unless . . .

"Not a nice way to spend the summer," a voice behind her said. "Hundreds of brats. No time off. Real torture."

She turned round, affecting surprise. "Yes," she said. "I wasn't really thinking of doing it."

"I had a friend who did it once," said Wolf. "He ran away. He actually physically ran away to New York after two weeks." He looked at his watch and then nodded in the direction of the door at the end of the corridor. "Are you hungry?"

Pat was not, but said that she was. "Ravenous."

"We could go up to the Elephant House," Wolf said, glancing at his watch. "We could have coffee and a sandwich."

They walked through George Square and across the wide space in front of the McEwan Hall. In one corner, their skateboards at their feet, a group of teenage boys huddled against the world, caps worn backwards, baggy, low-crotched trousers half-way down their flanks. Pat had wondered what these youths talked about and had concluded that they talked about nothing, because to talk was uncool. Perhaps Domenica could do field work outside the McEwan Hall – once she had finished with her Malacca Straits pirates – living with the skateboarders, in a little tent in the rhododendrons at the edge of the square, observing the socio-dynamics of the group, the leadership struggles, the badges of status. Would they accept her, she wondered? Or would she be viewed with suspicion, as an unwanted visitor from the adult world, the world of speech?

She found out a little bit more about Wolf as they made their way to the Elephant House. As they crossed the road at Napier's Health Food Shop, Wolf told her that his mother was an enthusiast of vitamins and homeopathic medicine. He had been fed on vitamins as a boy and had been taken to a homeopathic doctor, who gave him small doses of carefully-chosen poison. The whole family took Echinacea against colds, regularly, although they still got them.

"It keeps her happy," he said. "You know how mothers are. And it's cool by me if my mother's unstressed. You know what I mean?"

Pat thought she did. "That's cool," she said.

And then he told her that he came from Aberdeen. His father, he said, was in the oil business. He had a company which supplied valves for off-shore wells. They sold valves all over the world, and his father was often away in places like Houston and Brunei. He collected air miles which he gave to Wolf.

"I can go anywhere I want," he said. "I could go to South America, if I wanted. Tomorrow. All on air miles."

"I haven't got any air miles," said Pat.

"None at all?"

"No."

Wolf shrugged. "No big deal," he said. "You don't really need them."

"Do you think that Dr Fantouse has any air miles?" asked Pat suddenly.

They both laughed. "Definitely not," said Wolf. "Poor guy. Bus miles maybe."

Inside the Elephant House it was beginning to get busy, and they had to wait to be served. Wolf suggested that Pat should find a table while he ordered the coffee and the sandwiches.

Pat, waiting for Wolf, paged through a glossy magazine which she found in a rack on the wall. It was one of those magazines which everyone affected to despise, but which equally everyone rather enjoyed – page after page of pictures of celebrities, lounging by the side of swimming pools, leaving expensive restaurants, arriving at parties. The locales, and the clothes, were redolent of luxury, even if luxury that was in very poor taste; and the people looked rather like waxworks – propped up, prompted into positions of movement, but made of wax. This was due to the fact that the photographers caked them with make-up, somebody had explained to her. That's why they looked so artificial.

She turned a page, and stopped. There had been a party, somebody's twenty-first, at Gleneagles. Elegant girls in glittering dresses were draped about young men in formal kilt outfits, dinner jackets and florid silk bow-ties. And there was Wolf, standing beside a girl with red hair, a glass of champagne in his hand. Pat stared at the photograph. Surely it could not be him. Nobody she knew was in *Hi!* magazine; this was another world. But it must have been him, because there was the smile, and the hair, and that look in the eyes.

She looked up. Wolf was standing at the table, holding a tray. He laid the tray down on the table, and glanced at the magazine.

"Is this you, Wolf?" Pat asked. "Look. I can't believe that I know somebody in *Hi!*"

Wolf glanced at the picture and frowned. "You don't," he said. "That's not me."

Pat looked again at the picture then transferred her gaze up to Wolf. If it was not him, then it was his double.

Wolf took the magazine from her and tossed it to the other end of the table.

"I can't bear those mags," he said. "Full of nothing. Airheads."

He turned to her and smiled, showing his teeth, which were very white, and even, and which for some rather disturbing reason she wanted to touch.

3. *Co-incidence in Spottiswoode Street*

"Your name," said Pat to Wolf, as they sat drinking coffee in the Elephant House. "Your name intrigues me. I don't think I've met anybody called Wolf before." She paused. Perhaps it was a sore point with him; people could be funny about their names, and perhaps Wolf was embarrassed about his. "Of course, there's nothing wrong with . . ."

Wolf smiled. "Don't worry," he said. "People are often surprised when I tell them what I'm called. There's a simple explanation. It's not the name I was given at the beginning. That's . . ."

Pat waited for him to finish the sentence, but he had raised his mug of coffee to his mouth and was looking at her over the rim. His eyes, she saw, were bright, as if he was teasing her about something.

"You don't have to tell me," she said quietly.

He put down his mug. "But you do want to know, don't you?"

Pat shrugged. "Only if you want to tell me."

"All right," said Wolf. "I started out as Wilfred."

Pat felt a sudden urge to laugh, and almost did. There were more embarrassing names than that, of course – Cuthbert, for instance – but she could not see Wolf as Wilfred. There was no panache about Wilfred; none of the slight threat that went with Wolf.

"I couldn't stand being called Wilfred," Wolf went on. "And it was worse when it was shortened to Wilf. So I decided when I was about ten that I would be Wolfred, and my parents went along with that. So I was Wolfred from then on. That's the name on my student card. At school they called me Wolf. You were Patricia, I suppose?"

"Yes," said Pat. "But I can't remember ever being called that, except by the headmistress at school, who called everybody by their full names. But, look, there's nothing all that wrong with Wilfred. There's . . ."

Wolf interrupted her. "Let's not talk about names," he said. He glanced at his sandwich. "I'm going to have to eat this quickly. I have to go and see somebody."

Pat felt a sudden stab of disappointment. She wanted to spend longer with him; just sitting there, in his company, made her forget that she had been feeling slightly dispirited. It was about being in the presence of beauty that seemed to charge the surrounding air; and Wolf, she had decided, was beautiful. They had been sitting in that seminar room, she reflected, talking about beauty – which is what she thought aesthetics was all about – and beauty was there before their eyes; assured, content with the space it occupied, as beauty always was.

She picked up her sandwich and bit into it. She could not let him leave her sitting there – that was such an admission of social failure – to be left sitting at a table when somebody goes off. It was the sort of thing that would happen to Dr Fantouse; he was the type who must often be left at the table by others; poor man, with his Quattrocento and his green Paisley ties, left alone at the table while all his colleagues, the Renaissance and Victorian people, pushed back their chairs and got up.

At the door, Wolf said: "Which way are you going?" and Pat replied: "Across the Meadows."

"That's cool," said Wolf. "I'll walk with you. I'm heading that way too."

They walked together, chatting comfortably as they did. They talked about the other members of the class, some of whom Wolf knew rather better than Pat did. Wolf was a member of the University Renaissance Singers and had been on a singing tour with one of the other young men. "He's hopeless," he said. "All he wants to do, you know, is go to bars and get drunk. And he keeps going on and on about some girl called Jean he met in Glasgow. Apparently she's got the most tremendous voice and is studying opera at the Academy there. He can't stop talking about her. You watch. He'll probably bring her name up in the seminar: 'Jean says that Benedetto Croce . . . '"

There were other snippets of gossip, and then he enquired about what Pat had been doing the previous year. She told him about the job in the Gallery, which she still had on a part-time basis, and about Scotland Street too.

"It's more interesting in the New Town," he said. "Up in Marchmont everybody's a student. There are no . . . well, no real people. The New Town's different. Who did you share with?"

Pat wondered how one might describe Bruce. It was difficult to know where to start. "A boy," she said. "Bruce Anderson. We weren't . . . you know, there was nothing between us." But there had been, she thought, blushing at the memory of her sudden infatuation. Was that nothing?

"Of course not," said Wolf. "People you share with are a no-no. If things get difficult, then you have to move out. Or they have to."

Pat agreed. "And I knew everybody else on the stair," she said. "There was this woman called Domenica Macdonald. She lived opposite. And a couple called Irene and Stuart who had a little boy called Bertie. He played the saxophone and I used to hear 'As Time Goes By' drifting up through the walls. And two guys on the first floor."

They had now crossed Melville Drive and, having walked up the brae past the towering stone edifice of Warrender Park Terrace, with its giddy attic windows breaking out of the steep slate roofs, they were at the beginning of Spottiswoode Street. A few doorways along was Pat's stair, with its communal door and list of names alongside the bell-pulls. She assumed that Wolf would be going on, perhaps to Thirlestane Road, where so many people seemed to live, but when she indicated that she had reached her destination, he stopped too, and smiled.

"But so have I," he said.

Her heart gave a leap. Was there some other meaning to this? Did he expect her to invite him upstairs? She would, of course. She did not want him to go. She wanted to be with him, to be beguiled.

"I live here," she said, hesitantly.

"What floor?"

"Second. Middle flat."

Wolf swept back the hair that the wind had blown across his brow. "But that's amazing," he said, his eyes wide with surprise. "So does my girlfriend, Tessie. You must be sharing with her."

4. *At Domenica's Flat*

Angus Lordie, portrait painter and occasional poet, walked slowly down Scotland Street, looking up at the windows. He liked to look into other people's houses, if he could. It was not nosiness, of course; artists were allowed to look, he thought – no artist could really be considered a voyeur. Looking was what an artist was trained to do, and if an artist did not look, then he would not see. The evening was the best time to inspect the domestic arrangements of others, as people often left their lights on and their curtains open, thus creating a stage for passers-by to see. And the New Town of Edinburgh provided rich theatre in that respect, especially along the more gracious Georgian streets where tall windows at ground floor allowed a fine view of drawing rooms and studies. Of course curtains could have been pulled across such windows, but often were not, and Angus Lordie was convinced that this was because those who lived within wanted people to see what they had, wanted them to see their grand pianos, their heavily-framed pictures, their clutters of chinoiserie. Heriot Row and Moray Place were good for this, although the decoration of most Moray Place flats was some-what dull. But there was a particularly fine grand piano in a window in Ainslie Place and a Ferguson picture of a woman in a hat in Great Stuart Street.

As he walked down Scotland Street, Angus Lordie reflected on the melancholy nature of his errand. So many times I have walked this way, he thought, to call on my old friend, Domenica Macdonald, and now I make my way to her empty flat. But then he reminded himself: Domenica is not dead, and I must not think of her in that way. She has simply gone to the Malacca Straits, and that is not the same thing as being dead. And yet he wondered how long it would be before he saw her again. She had not said anything about when she would return, but had hinted that it could be as much as a year, perhaps even longer. A year! He had wanted to say to her: "And what about me, Domenica? What am I to do in that year?"

Angus looked down at his dog, Cyril, and Cyril looked back up at him mournfully. Cyril was an intelligent dog – too intelligent for his own good, according to some – and he knew that this was a dull outing from the canine point of view. Cyril liked going for a walk up to Northumberland Street, where he could lift his leg against the railings at each doorway, and he also liked to go to the Cumberland Bar, where he was always given a small glass of beer and where there were people to look at. He was not so keen on Scotland Street, where he knew he would be tethered to a railing while Angus went upstairs. And there were cats in Scotland Street, too; outrageous cats who, understanding the restraint of his teth-ered lead, would saunter across the street with impunity, staring at him with that feline arrogance that no dog can stand.

Angus reached the front doorway of No 44 and was about to press Domenica's bell out of habit when he remembered that he had no need to do this, and that there was no point. He had the key to her flat up on the top landing and could let himself in. He sighed, and pushed open the outer door. Inside there was that familiar smell that he associated with her stairway: the chalky smell of the stone, the sweet smell of the nasturtiums that somebody on the first floor grew in a tub on the landing.

He made his way up the stair, pausing for a moment on one of the lower landings. Somebody was playing a musical instrument, a saxophone, he thought. He listened. Yes, it was unmistakable. 'As Time Goes By'. *Casablanca*. And then he remembered that this was the home of that little boy, the one Domenica had told him about, the one with that ghastly pushy mother whom Cyril had bitten on the ankle in Dundas Street. He smiled. She had made such a fuss about it and he had been obliged to wallop Cyril with a rolled up newspaper to show her that he was being punished. But it had been hard to suppress his laughter. That woman had insulted Cyril and he had bitten her: what could she expect? But dogs were always in the wrong when they bit somebody – it was part of the social contract between dogs and man. You can live with us, yes, but don't bite us.

He continued up the stair and stood before Domenica's doorway, slipping the key into the lock. There was mail to be picked up – a small pile of letters and some leaflets from local traders. He shuffled through these, tossing the leaflets into the bin and tucking the letters into the pocket of his jacket. He would place those in one of the large envelopes left him by Domenica and send them off to the address in the Malacca Straits. He was not sure whether her mail would ever reach her – the address she had given him seemed somewhat unlikely – but his duty was done once he posted them.

He walked through the hall and went into Domenica's study. She had left it scrupulously tidy and the surface of her desk was quite bare. They had spent so many hours there, with Domenica talking about all those things she liked to talk about, which was everything, he thought; everything. And now there was silence, and nobody to talk to.

"I come alone to this room," he said quietly.

"This room in which you sat
And filled my world with images.
I would reply, but cannot speak,
I would cry, but cannot weep."

He stopped himself, and looked at his watch. He would not allow himself to become maudlin. Domenica was just a friend – that and no more – and he would not pine for her. I am not here to think about her, he said to himself. I am here to let her new tenant into the flat and to tell her about the hot water system. Life is not about thoughts of loss and separation; it is about hot water systems and remembering to put out the rubbish, and making siccar in all the other little ways in which we must make siccar.

5. *The Judgement of Neuroaesthetics*

"Now then," said the woman on the doorstep of Domenica's flat. "You must be Angus Lordie. Thank you for letting me in. I hope I haven't kept you waiting."

"You have not," said Angus, looking at the woman standing before him. "Not at all." His portraitist's eye, from ancient habit, noted the high cheek bones and the slightly retroussé nose; noted with approval, and with understanding too, as he knew that a feminine face such as this was subliminally irresistible to men. Men liked women whose faces reminded them of babies – a heightened brow, a pert nose – these sent signals to men: protect me, I'm vulnerable. 'Neuroaesthetics' was the term he had seen for this new discipline; not that such a science could tell him anything that he did not already know as a painter and connoisseur of the human face. Regularity was good, but not too much regularity, which became tedious, almost nauseating.

Of course, there was far more that Angus was able to read into the physical appearance of Antonia Collie as she stood before him. They had barely introduced themselves, and yet he was confident as to her social background, her interests, and her availability. The clothes spoke to the provenance: a skirt of cashmere printed in a discreetly Peruvian pattern (or, certainly, South American; and Peru was very popular); a white linen blouse (only those with time on their hands to iron could wear linen); and then a navy-blue jacket with a gold brooch in the form of a running hare. The navy-blue jacket indicated attachment to the existing order, or even to an order which no longer existed, while the brooch announced that this was a person who had lived in the country, or at least one who knew what the country was all about. Of course, the fact that this Antonia Collie was a close friend of Domenica's would have told Angus Lordie all this, had he reflected on the fact that people's close friends are usually in their own mould. Antonia would thus be a blue stocking, a woman of intellectual interests and marked views.

Angus smiled at the thought, relishing the prospect of a replacement for Domenica. It was all most convenient; his visits to Domenica, his enjoyment of her conversation – and her wine – would now be replaced by the exact equivalent, provided by Antonia Collie. It was a very satisfactory prospect.

"Please let me take that for you," he said, pointing to the small brown case beside her. "Is this all you have?"

"Sufficient unto the day," said Antonia, stepping aside to allow Angus to pick up the suitcase. "I didn't need to bring much of my own stuff. Domenica and I are the same size, you see. She said I could just wear her clothes if I liked. And drive her car too. She's such a generous friend!"

Angus nodded. He did not show his surprise, but it seemed a very odd arrangement to him. Clothes were very personal and he could not imagine being happy in the knowledge that somebody else was wearing his clothes. He had once found himself wearing a pair of socks that he did not recognise and had been appalled at the thought that he had inadvertently taken his host's pair of socks when he had stayed with friends in Kelso. What a dreadful thought! For the next few days he examined his toes carefully for signs of fungal infection; or would a normal wash effectively rid socks of lurking fungus? His host had been a perfectly respectable person – a lawyer, no less – but athlete's foot was no respecter of professional position: it could strike even a WS. Of course, women were much more relaxed about these matters, he thought; they shared clothes quite willingly. Perhaps this was because they did not find one another physically disgusting. Men, in general, found one another vaguely repulsive; women were different.

With these thoughts in mind, Angus carried Antonia's small suitcase through to the study and laid it down near the fireplace. Antonia had moved to the window and was peering down to the street.

"It's a long time since I was in this flat," she mused, craning her neck to look. "I seem to remember Domenica having a slightly better view than this. Still, no matter. I doubt if I shall spend my time gazing out of the window."

She turned and looked at Angus. "Domenica often spoke of you," she said. "She enjoyed the conversations the two of you had."

"And I too," Angus said. "She was . . ." He looked at her, and she saw the sadness in his expression.

"Let's not use the past tense when speaking of her," said Antonia cheerfully. "She's not exactly dead yet, is she? She's in the Malacca Straits. That, I would have thought, amounts to being amongst the quick."

"Of course," said Angus hurriedly, but added: "That does seem a long way away. And it's going to be months and months before we see her again."

Antonia shot him a glance. Was this man Domenica's lover? It was difficult to imagine Domenica with a lover, and she had never seen her with him. But people such as Domenica liked a certain amount of mystery in their personal lives, and he may have been something special to her. Curious, though, that she should choose a man like this, with his intrusive stare and those disconcerting gold teeth; to have a lover with gold teeth was decidedly exotic. And yet he was a handsome man, she thought, with that wavy hair and those eyes. Dark hair and blue eyes were a dangerous combination in a man.

And Angus, returning her gaze, thought: she's younger than Domenica by a good few years; younger than me, too. And she's undoubtedly attractive. Does she have a husband? Presumably not, because a woman with a husband would not come to stay for six months in a friend's flat and not bring the husband with her. A lover, then? No. She had that look, that indefinable yet unmistakable look, of one who was alone in this world. And if she were alone, then how long would that last, with that concise nose of hers that would break ilka heart, but no the moudie man's? It was a play on a poem about the moudie and the moudie man, and it popped into his mind, just like that, as off-beat, poetic thoughts will break surface at the strangest moments, leaving us disturbed, puzzled, wondering. The mole's little eyes would break every heart, but not the molecatcher's.

6. *Gurus as Father Substitutes*

While Antonia went into the bedroom with her suitcase, Angus Lordie busied himself in the kitchen making coffee for the two of them. After coffee he would show her round the rest of the flat; there was a trick with the central-heating controls that he would need to explain (the timer went backwards for some reason, which required some calculation in the setting) and he would have to tell her about the fuse-box, too, which had idiosyncrasies of its own.

They would have to have black coffee, as there was no milk in the fridge. A woman would have thought of stocking the fridge with essentials for an arriving tenant: a loaf of bread, a pint or two of milk, some butter. But men did not think of these things, and Angus had brought nothing. His own fridge was usually empty, so there was no reason why he should think of replenishing Domenica's.

"Have you known Domenica for long?" he asked, as Antonia, returning from the bedroom, seated herself opposite him at the kitchen table.

"Twenty years," she said abruptly. "Although I feel I've known her forever. Don't you find that there are some friends who are like that? You feel that you've known them all your life."

Angus nodded. "I feel that I've known Domenica forever too. That's why . . ." He stopped himself. He was about to explain that this was why he felt her absence so keenly, but that would sound self-pitying and there was nothing less attractive than self-pity.

Antonia continued. "I met her when I was a student," she said. "I was twenty and she was . . . well, I suppose she must have been about forty then. She was my tutor in an anthropology course I took. It was not my main subject – that was Scottish history – but I found her fascinating. The professors thought her a bit of maverick. They forced her out in the end."

"Very unfair," said Angus. He could not imagine Domenica being forced out of anything, but perhaps when she was younger it might have been easier.

"Very stupid, more likely," said Antonia. "The problem was that she was far brighter than those particular professors. She frightened them because she could talk about anything and everything and their own knowledge was limited to a narrow little corner of the world. That disturbed them. And universities are still full of people like that, you know. People of broad culture may find it rather difficult in them. Timid, bureaucratic places. And very politically conformist."

"I don't know," said Angus. "Surely some of them . . ."

"Of course," said Antonia. "But, but . . . the trouble is that they're so busy with their social engineering that they've lost all notion of what it is to be a liberal-minded institution."

"I don't know," said Angus. "Surely things aren't that bad . . ."

"Not that I'm one of these people who goes round muttering '*O tempora, O mores*'," went on Antonia. "Mind you, I don't suppose many people in a university these days understand what that means."

Angus laughed. He had always enjoyed Domenica's wit and had been missing it already; but now it seemed that relief was in sight. Or, as Domenica might have it, relief was insight . . .

"Scottish history," Angus said.

Antonia nodded. "Indeed. I studied under Gordon Donaldson and then under that very great man, John Macqueen. Such an interesting scholar, Macqueen, with his books on numerology and the like. You never knew what he would turn to next. And his son writes too – Hector Macqueen. He came up with some very intriguing things and then for some reason wrote a history of Heriot's Cricket Club – a very strange book, but it must have been of interest to somebody. Can you imagine a cricketing history? Can you?"

"I suppose it has lists of who scored what," said Angus. "And who went in first, and things like that."

They were silent for a moment, both contemplating the full, arid implications of a cricketing history. Then Antonia broke the silence.

"I've never played cricket," she said. "Yet there are ladies' cricket teams. You hear about them from time to time. I can't imagine what they're like. But I suppose they enjoy themselves. It's the sort of thing that rather brisk women like to do. You know the sort."

Angus did. He was enjoying the conversation greatly and had decided that he very much approved of Domenica's new tenant. He wondered whether he might invite her for dinner that night, or whether it would be considered a little forward at this early stage in their acquaintanceship. He hesitated for a moment; why should he not? She had said nothing to indicate that she was spoken for, and even if she was, there was nothing wrong in a neighbourly supper à deux. So he asked her, suggesting that she might care to take pot luck in his kitchen as this was her first day in the flat and she would not have had time to get in supplies.

Antonia hesitated, but only for a moment. "How tempting," she said quietly. "You really have been too kind to me. And I would love to accept, but I think that this evening I must work. I really must."

"Work?"

Antonia sighed. "My poor book, you know. I'm writing a book and it's suffering from maternal deprivation. Bowlby syndrome, as they call it."

"Bowlby?"

"A psychologist. He was something of a guru once. He took the view that bad behaviour results from inadequate maternal attention."

Angus thought for a moment. I need a guru, he said to himself. Would Antonia be his guru? He blushed at the unspoken thought. It would be wonderful to have a guru; it would be like having a social worker or a personal trainer, not that people who had either of these necessarily appreciated the advice they received.

"Of course it's absurd, this search for gurus," Antonia said. "People who need gurus are really searching for something else altogether, don't you think? Fundamentally insecure people. Looking for father."

Angus looked at her. He was beginning to dislike Antonia. How strange, he thought, that our feelings can change so fast. Like that. Just like that. And he thought of how the sky over Edinburgh could change in an instant, between summer and winter, as the backdrop can be shifted in a theatre, curtains lowered from the heavens in each case, changing everything.

7. *Angus Goes Off Antonia, in a Big Way*

Angus Lordie was deep in thought as he walked home. At his side, Cyril, sensing his master's abstraction, had briefly tugged at his lead at the point where Dundonald Street joined Drummond Place; he had hoped that Angus might be persuaded to call in at the Cumberland Bar, but his promptings had been ignored. Cyril understood; he knew that his life was an adjunct life, lived in the shadow of his master, and that canine views counted for nothing; yet it would have been good, he thought, to sit on the bar's black-and-white chequered floor sipping from a bowl of Guinness and staring at the assorted ankles under the table. But this was not to be, and he was rapidly diverted from this agreeable fantasy to the real world of sounds and smells. It is a large room, the world of smells for a dog, and Drummond Place, though familiar territory, was rich in possibilities; each passer-by left a trail that spoke to where he had been and what he had been doing – a whole history might lie on the pavement, like song-lines across the Australian Outback, detectable only to those with the necessary nose. Other smells were like a palimpsest: odour laid upon odour, smells that could be peeled off to reveal the whiff below. Cyril quivered; a strange scent wafted from a doorway, a musty, inexplicable odour that reminded him of something that he had known somewhere before, in his previous life in Lochboisdale, a long time ago. He stopped, and tugged at his leash, but Angus ignored his concern, yanking him roughly to heel. Cyril had never bitten his master, not once, but there were times . . .

Angus was thinking about what Antonia had told him. He had steered the conversation swiftly away from gurus, and had asked her about her book. So many people in Edinburgh were writing a book – almost everyone, in fact – and Angus had ceased to be surprised when somebody mentioned an incipient literary project. So he had inquired politely about Antonia's book. She had looked at him sharply, as if to assess whether he was worthy of being told, whether he was serious in his inquiries; one could not tell everyone about one's book.

"It's nothing very much," she said, after some moments of hesitation. "Just a novel."

He had waited for further explanation, but she had merely continued to stare at him. At last he said: "A novel." And she had nodded.

"Well," he said, "may I ask what sort of novel it is?"

"Historical," she said. "Very early. It's set in early Scotland. Sixth century, actually."

Angus had smiled. "You're very wise to choose a period for which there is so little evidence," he said. "You can't go wrong if you write about a time that we don't really know about. When people start to write about the seventeenth and eighteenth centuries – or even the twenty-first, for that matter – they can get into awful trouble if they get it wrong. And they often get something wrong, don't they?"

"Writers can make mistakes like anybody else," said Antonia, rather peevishly. "We're human, you know." She looked at Angus, as if expecting a refutation, though none came. "For instance, was there not an American writer who described one of his characters on page one as unfortunately having only one arm? On page one hundred and forty the same character claps his hands together enthusiastically."

Angus smiled. "So funny," he said. "Although some people these days would think it wrong to laugh about something like that. Just as they don't find anything amusing in the story of the man who went to Lourdes and experienced a miracle. The poor chap couldn't walk, and the miracle was that he found new tyres on his wheelchair."

Antonia stared at him. "I don't find that funny, I'm afraid." She shook her head. "Not in the slightest. Anyway, if I may get back to the subject of what we know and what we don't know. We happen to have quite a lot of knowledge about early medieval Scotland. We have the records of various abbeys, and we can deduce a great deal from archeological evidence. We're not totally in the dark."

Angus looked thoughtful. "All right," he said. "Answer me this: were there handkerchiefs in medieval Scotland?"

Antonia frowned. "Handkerchiefs?"

"Yes," said Angus. "Did people have handkerchiefs to blow their noses on?"

Antonia was silent. It had not occurred to her to think about handkerchiefs in medieval Scotland, as the occasion had simply not arisen. I'm not that sort of writer, she thought; I'm not the sort of writer who describes her characters blowing their noses. But if I were, then what . . .

"I have not given the matter thought," she said at last. "But I cannot imagine that there were handkerchiefs – textiles were far too expensive to waste on handkerchiefs. I suspect that people merely resorted to informal means of clearing their noses."

"I read somewhere that they blew them on straw," said Angus. "Rather uncomfortable, I would have thought."

"I imagine that it was," said Antonia. "But I am writing mostly about the lives of the early saints. Noses and . . . and other protuberances have not really entered into the picture to any great degree.

"And anyway," she went on, "you should not expect fiction to be realistic. People who think that the role of fiction is merely to report on reality suffer from a fundamental misunderstanding of what it is all about."

Angus Lordie's nostrils flared slightly, even if imperceptibly. His conversations with Domenica had been conducted on a basis of equality, whereas Antonia's remarks implied that he did not know what fiction was about. Well . . .

"You see," went on Antonia, inspecting her nails as she spoke, "the novel distils. It takes the human experience, looks at it, shakes it up a bit, and then comes up with a portrayal of what it sees as the essential issue. That's the difference between pure description and art."

Angus looked at her. His nostrils had started to twitch more noticeably now, and he made an effort to control this unwanted sign of his irritation. He had entertained, and now abandoned, the notion that he might get to know Antonia better and that she would be a substitute for Domenica; indeed, as the lonely-hearts advertisements had it, perhaps there might have been "something more".

He imagined what he would say if he were reduced to advertising. "Artist, GSOH, wishes to meet congenial lady for conversation and perhaps something more. No historical novelists need apply."

8. Money Management

Matthew was crossing Dundas Street to that side of the road where Big Lou kept her coffee bar, at basement level, in the transformed premises of an old book shop. The Morning After Coffee Bar was different from the mass-produced coffee bars that had mushroomed on every street almost everywhere, a development which presaged the flattening effects of globalisation; the spreading, under a cheerful banner, of a sameness that threatened to weaken and destroy all sense of place. And while it would be possible, by walking into Stockbridge to get the authentic globalised experience, none of Big Lou's customers would have dreamed of being that oxymoronic. One feature of the chain coffee shops was the absence of conversation between staff and customer, and indeed between customer and customer. Nobody spoke in such places; the staff said nothing because they had nothing to say; the customers because they felt inhibited from talking in such standardised surroundings. There was something about plastic surroundings that subdued the spirits, that cudgelled one into silence.

Big Lou, of course, would speak to anybody who came into her coffee bar; indeed, she thought it would be rude not to do so. Conversation was a recognition of the other, the equivalent of the friendly greetings that people would give one another in the street, back in Arbroath. And people generally responded well to Big Lou's remarks, unburdening themselves of the sort of things that people unburden themselves of in the hairdresser's salon or indeed the dentist's chair in those few precious moments before the dentist's probing fingers make two-sided conversation impossible.

Matthew had something on his mind, and he hoped that nobody else would be in Big Lou's to prevent him from speaking frankly to his friend. Or if there were anybody else there, then he hoped that it would be one of the regulars, as he would not mind any of them hearing what he had to say. Indeed, it would be interesting to have Angus Lordie's perspective on things, even if he would have to discard it immediately. Matthew liked Angus, but found him so quirky in his view of the world that he could hardly imagine taking advice from him. But at least Angus Lordie was prepared to listen, and that was what Matthew needed now more than anything else.

Exactly two weeks earlier, Matthew's situation had changed profoundly. He was still the owner of the Something Special Gallery; he was still the only son of the wealthy and recently engaged entrepreneur, Gordon; he was still a young man with a disappointing business record and a somewhat low-key personality; all of this was unchanged. But in another, important respect, the Matthew of today was different from the Matthew of a short time ago. This was the fact that he now had slightly over four million pounds to his name, the gift of his father at the instance of Janice, his father's new, and badly misjudged fiancée.

His father's official disclosure of the transfer of the funds had come in a letter from his lawyer, a man who had always, although in private, been somewhat scathing of Matthew (whom he regarded as being weak and ineffectual). Now the tone was changed, subtly but unambiguously. Would it be possible for Matthew to call in at the office, at any time that was convenient to him, so that the modalities of the transfer could be discussed? Modalities was an expensive word, a Charlotte Square word; not a word one would catch a lesser firm of lawyers bandying about. Indeed, some lawyers would be required to reach for their dictionaries in the face of such a term.

Matthew had made his appointment and had been warmly received. And it had taken only fifteen minutes for the real agenda of the visit to be disclosed. It would be important to manage the funds that were coming his way in a prudent manner. This meant that professional advice on the handling of the port-folio would be needed, and, as it happened, they had a very successful investment department which would be able to come up with proposals for a balanced portfolio at very modest rates.

Sitting back in his chair Matthew allowed himself a smile. Let's work it out, he thought. A management fee of one per cent of the capital at his disposal was, what, forty thousand pounds a year? That was a great deal to earn merely from watching money grow. But this, of course, was capitalism, and Matthew now found himself at the polite, discreet dinner-party end of the whole process. There were plenty of people in Edinburgh who were trained to sniff out money, rather like those friendly little beagles that one saw at the airports who were trained to sniff out drugs. These people, urbane to a man, knew when their services were required and circled helpfully. Then it was mentioned, discreetly, that of course there were others in your position, in need of just a little help. That was good psychology. Those to whom good financial fortune comes are alone. Their money frightens them. They feel unsettled. To be told that there are others in exactly the same boat is reassuring.

So the lawyer said: "Of course, we have a number of clients who are pretty much in a similar position to yourself. They find . . . and I hope I don't speak out of turn here, but they find that there are advantages in keeping everything under one roof."

And here, unintentionally, he looked up at the ceiling, as if to emphasise that the roof under which they were sitting was quite capable of accommodating Matthew's new-found wealth.

Matthew looked at the lawyer. He knew this man from the parties that his father occasionally gave. He knew his son too, a tall boy called Jamie, who had been at school with him and who had once hit him with a cricket bat, across the shoulders, and who had once said to the others – within Matthew's hearing – that the reason why Matthew was then afflicted by a partic-ular rash of pimples was . . . It was so unfair. And now here was the father of the same persecutor offering to handle his money.

"Thanks," said Matthew. "But I propose to handle it myself. I enjoy reading the financial press and I think I'm perfectly capable."

The lawyer looked at Matthew. He thought: Jamie once used a rather uncomplimentary word to describe this young man. How apt that epithet! Boys may be cruel to one another, but they were often very good judges of character.

9. *The Warm Embrace of the Edinburgh Establishment*

Matthew had left the lawyer's office feeling slightly light-headed. He paused at the front door, and thought about what he had done; it would be easy to return, to go back to the man whom he had written off on the basis of his son's unpleasant behaviour all those years ago. It would be easy to say to him that mature reflection – or at least such reflection as could be engaged in while walking down the stairs and through the entrance hall – had led him to believe that it would be best, after all, to have the funds consigned to the colleague whom the lawyer had so unctuously mentioned. Presumably it would be easy to stop the transfer that he had asked for – the transfer from the firm's client account to Matthew's own account – and once that was done the serious business of putting four million pounds to work in the market could begin. But he did not do this. All his life, money had come from somebody else (his father) and had been doled out to him as one would give sweets to a child. Now he had the money at his own disposal, and he felt like an adult at last.

He walked along Queen Street, in the direction of Dundas Street and his gallery. This route took him past Stewart Christie, the outfitters, and that is where he paused, looking thoughtfully into the window. It was a shop that sold well-made clothes for men, not the expensive rubbish – as Matthew thought of it – produced by Italians, but finely-tailored jackets made of Scottish tweed; yellow-checked waistcoats for country wear; tight-fitting tartan trews for formal occasions.

On impulse, he went into the shop and began to examine a rack of ties. Many of them were striped, which would not suit him, as he would not like others to think that he was one of those people who was emotionally tied to an institution of some sort – an institution that gave you stripes by which to remember it. He picked out a spotted tie and set it aside without looking at the price. You don't have to ask the price any more, he told himself. It doesn't matter. You can afford anything you want. The thought, which he had not entertained to any extent since his fortunes had changed, was an intoxicating one. What did it entail? If he went down to London, then he could walk into John Lobb's shop in St James's Street and have himself measured for a pair of bespoke shoes. Matthew had read about that recently in a lifestyle supplement, and had remembered the price. Two thousand four hundred pounds that would cost, and that was without the shoe trees. Shoe trees made by John Lobb would cost an additional three hundred pounds.

Matthew reached for a box of lawn handkerchiefs. He would take that, as he did not have many handkerchiefs. And then he saw some socks, all wool with toes reinforced with a special fabric, described as revolutionary. Matthew pulled out three pairs of these and then a further two. One could never have enough socks, particularly in view of the tendency of socks to disappear in the laundry. No matter what precautions were taken, socks disappeared into a Bermuda Triangle for socks, a swirling vortex that swallowed one sock at a time, leaving its partner stranded.

He was now assisted by a solicitous young man who had appeared from the back of the shop. Together, they chose four shirts, an expensive cashmere sweater which cost one hundred and twenty pounds, a pair of crushed-strawberry corduroy trousers, and a covert coat in oatmeal drill.

"Very nice," said the assistant. "You can wear that for shooting."

Matthew frowned. He did not go shooting, but then it occurred to him that he could if he wanted to. I can do anything, he thought, and smiled. He closed one eye and swung up an imaginary shotgun. "Bang," he said.

"Quite," said the assistant. "Bang."

His purchases nestling in a copious carrier bag, Matthew left the outfitters and continued his walk along Queen Street. The spending of a large amount of money within a short space of time had been a strangely liberating experience. In a way which he found difficult to express, the whole process of shopping had made him feel better. The tie, the fine cashmere sweater, the covert coat – all of these had been added to him and had made him bigger. He felt more confident, more assured, and, critically, less vulnerable. Having money, he thought, means that the world cannot hurt you. You can lose things and just replace them. You can protect yourself against disappointment because you can get the best things available. Ordinary shoes might pinch; shoes made for you by John Lobb did not.

He reached Dundas Street and turned down the hill. There, at the end of the street, beyond the roofs of Canonmills, was Fife – a dark green hillside, clouds, a silver strip of sea. Passing Glass and Thompson, he decided to call in for a slice of quiche and a glass of melon juice. Big Lou's was just a little way down the street, but Big Lou did not make quiche and there was no melon juice to be had there.

Matthew perched on a stool at one of the tables. There were a few other customers in at the time – a woman in a dark trouser suit, engrossed in a file of papers; a thin man paging through an old copy of a design magazine, an architect, as Matthew knew.

He picked up a copy of a newspaper and turned the pages at random. Split trust victims seek compensation, a headline read. And then another: with-profits policies encounter painful shortfall. Matthew paused, his glass of melon juice half way to his lips.

Outside, he did not have to wait long for a taxi, and he was soon outside the lawyers' offices again, and then, within minutes, inside, seated opposite the lawyer himself.

"Very wise," said the lawyer. "Very wise to change your mind." And then he added: "You know, I seem to recollect that my boy

Jamie – he's quite different these days – was a bit tough on you when you were boys. Sorry about that, you know."

Matthew nodded. "It's fine," he said. And he thought: yes, it is fine, isn't it? You're back. Back where you came from. The solid, cautious, Scottish mercantile class; among your own people. But for a moment, a brief moment, you had been about to do something yourself.

10. Does He Wear Lederhosen?

That had been a Monday. Now it was Tuesday, and that, under the new arrangement with Pat, was one of the days on which she came into the gallery for three hours to help Matthew. He had hoped to have had more of her time, as he had grown accustomed to her presence, as she sat at her desk, or stacked paintings in the storeroom, and without her the gallery seemed strangely empty. But Pat was now a student and had the requirements of her course to consider – essays to write, pages of aesthetic theory and art history to plough through, although she skipped, she had to admit, rather than ploughed. With all these things to do, she was unable to get down to the gallery for more than nine hours a week, and these hours were divided between Tuesday, Thursday and Friday.

Of course, Matthew could have employed somebody full-time, had he wished to do so. Four million pounds is enough to finance a two-room gallery for which no rent had to be paid and which was not encumbered by any debt. But Matthew did not wish to have anybody else; he wanted Pat, because she knew the business, had a precociously good eye for art, and because . . . well, if he were to admit it to himself, Matthew wanted to have what one might call a closer relationship with Pat.

On that Tuesday, Matthew left his flat in India Street dressed in the new clothes he had bought from Stewart Christie the previous day. He wore one of the expensive shirts, the spotted silk tie, the crushed-strawberry trousers and the cashmere sweater. The sweater, which was an oatmeal colour ("distressed oatmeal" was the official description of the shade), went well with the trousers and the tie, which had a dark green background (the spots being light green). Over all this he donned the covert coat, then examined himself in the hall mirror and set off into the street.

By the time that Pat arrived in the gallery at ten o'clock, Matthew had dealt with the few letters that he had received that morning and had almost finished paging through a new auction catalogue. There were several paintings in this catalogue that he wanted to discuss with Pat – a Hornel study of a group of Japanese women making tea, a Blackadder of a bunch of peonies in a white vase, and a shockingly expensive Cadell portrait. Matthew reflected that he could afford any of these – indeed, he could afford them all – but he knew that he would have to be careful. The market had its price, and it was foolish to allow a personal enthusiasm for a painting to encourage one to pay more than the real market figure. What one paid in such circumstances was the market as far as that particular sale was concerned, but not the broader market. The real market was more fickle, and it was all very well having an expensive Cadell on one's walls, but what if nobody else wanted it? So he ticked the Blackadder and put a question mark next to the listing of the Cadell.

When Pat came in, he showed her the Cadell and she shook her head. "Not for us," she said. "Remember who comes into this place. Our clients don't have that sort of money."

"But if we had that sort of painting," Matthew objected, "then we'd get that sort of person. Word would get out."

"Too risky," said Pat. "Stick to the clients you have."

Matthew smiled. "But we have the means, Pat," he said. "We have money. Plenty of it."

Pat said nothing. She had noticed the new distressed-oatmeal cashmere sweater and the covert coat hung over the back of his chair. Was Matthew dressing for her benefit? And if he was, then had his feelings for her revived – the feelings that she had been so concerned to discourage, even if gently? She glanced at

Matthew, at the new shirt, the new tie, the crushed-strawberry trousers. These were all signs.

"Well," she said airily. "We can think about it later on. You don't have to reach any decisions just yet." She paused. A few words would be sufficient. "Do you mind if I make a telephone call, Matthew? I have to ring my boyfriend."

She saw his expression change. The human face was so transparent, she thought, so revealing of the feelings below; in this case, there was just a loss of light, so subtle that one would never be able to pinpoint how it occurred; but there was less light.

"So," he said. "You have a romance on the go."

Pat did not like to lie, but there were times when the only kind thing to do with men was to lie to them. If one did not lie to men, then they suffered all the more. And she was not sure that what she was telling was a lie anyway. She had met Wolf, and had taken to him. What she had felt on that first encounter and in the subsequent conversation in the Elephant House had everything to do with romance, she would have thought; certainly the physiological signs had been present – the feeling of lightness in the stomach, the slight racing of the heart, the prickling of the skin. So she would not be lying at all.

"Yes," she said, looking down at the ground. It is easier to lie to the ground, in general.

Matthew fiddled with the edge of his desk. His knuckles, she saw, were white.

"What's he called?" he asked.

She hesitated. It was none of Matthew's business to know the names of her friends, but she could not tell him this.

"Wolf," she said.

He stared at her for a moment. Then he laughed. "You're not serious! Wolf? Is he German by any chance? Wears lederhosen?"

Pat shut her eyes. She had been too gentle with him. How dare he talk of Wolf like that; gentle, kind Wolf. She paused. She knew nothing about Wolf. She had no idea whether he was gentle and kind, and there was at least some evidence that he was not – and had he not mouthed the predatory words: hey there, little Red Riding-Hood? What sort of boy said that? Only a wolf, she thought.

11. *The Bears of Sicily*

If there had been change on the top floor of 44 Scotland Street, with the departure of Domenica and the arrival of Antonia, then there had been change, too, elsewhere in the building.

On the top landing, opposite Domenica's flat, was the flat which had been owned by Bruce Anderson, who had now left Edinburgh to live in London, in the hope that Chelsea or Fulham might provide that which he felt to be missing from his life in Edinburgh. Pat had been his tenant, but had left when Bruce had placed the flat on the market and eventually sold it to a young architect turned property developer. On the floor below, Irene and Stuart Pollock had not moved, thus providing the continuity required if a building is to have a collective memory. That was one of the features which made those Edinburgh streets so special; in contrast with so many other cities, where people may come and go and leave no memory, the streets and houses of the Edinburgh New Town bore an oral history that might survive, thirty, forty, even fifty years. People remembered who lived where, what they did, and where they went. People wanted to belong. They wanted to be part of something that had a local feel, a local face.

Irene Pollock was the mother of that most talented of six-year-olds, Bertie Pollock, now of the Steiner School in Merchiston and sometime pupil (suspended) at the East New Town Advanced Nursery. Bertie was still in therapy with Dr Hugo Fairbairn, author of that seminal work on child analysis, *Shattered to Pieces: Ego Dissolution in a Three-Year-Old Tyrant*. He had been referred to Dr Fairbairn after he had set fire to his father's copy of *The Guardian*, while his father was reading it. This act of fire-raising might have alerted one familiar with the literature on juvenile psychopathology to that well-known but still puzzling triangular syndrome in which an interest in setting fire to things is accompanied by a tendency to be cruel to animals and to suffer from late bed-wetting. The literature in forensic psychiatry contains several reports on this curious combination of behaviours and symptoms, and any well-informed child psychiatrist encountering a youthful fire-raiser would do well to inquire along these lines. Dr Fairbairn, however, ruled this out immediately. Unlike Frederick in the *Struwelpeter*, who so persecuted the good dog Tray, Bertie was not a cruel little boy. He was not unkind to animals, nor did he suffer from nocturnal enuresis, having been dry and out of nappies (and into dungarees) at the remarkably early age of eight months. His mother, indeed, had been so proud of his achievements in that department that she had contacted the newspapers to find out whether they were interested in interviewing her (and possibly having a few words with Bertie too) about this, and had been surprised, and hurt, by their indifference.

Bertie had accomplished a great deal since his early and distinguished toilet training. He had become reasonably fluent in Italian and a more than competent saxophonist. Both of these were skills which had been forced upon him by his mother, who, in the case of Italian lessons, had started these shortly after his third birthday. While other children listened to tapes of nursery rhymes – almost all of which were, in Irene's view, patriarchal nonsense – Bertie listened to the complete set of *Buongiorno Italia!* tapes, playing and replaying the recorded conversations these featured. By the age of four, he was quite capable of asking the way to the railway station in faultless Italian, or engaging in a conversation with an Italian waiter about the most typical dishes of the various Italian regions. After this, he graduated to listening with perfect understanding to Buzzati's story of the invasion of Sicily by bears, a vaguely sinister story which was later to surface in his concerns over the possibility of encountering bears in the streets of Edinburgh. *Ma, Bertie, non ci sono orsi a Edimborgo!* Irene had said to him (But, Bertie, there are no bears in Edinburgh!) To which Bertie had replied: *Non ci sono orsi in Sicilia, Mama, ma ecco qui la storia di Buzzati in cui incontriamo orsi!* (There are no bears in Sicily, Mother, but here is this story of Buzzati's in which we meet bears!)

His progress in music was equally meteoric. At the age of four, he was playing the soprano recorder with some facility, and had made a start on rudimentary music theory. By five, he had embarked – or been embarked, perhaps – on the study of the saxophone, and on this instrument he made particularly rapid progress. He showed an early propensity for the playing of jazz, although Irene was slightly uneasy about this, as she was not convinced that jazz encouraged the same musical rigour as did classical music. Bertie's rendition of 'As Time Goes By', although hardly jazz, was easy on the ear, and indeed had been much appreciated by Pat, whose bedroom in 44 Scotland Street lay immediately above the room in which Bertie practised.

But all this hot-housing produced precisely that reaction which any reasonable parent might have foreseen: Bertie rebelled, first by minor acts of non-cooperation (occasionally refusing to talk Italian) and then by major gestures (burning his father's copy of *The Guardian*). Irene had responded by placing her trust in psychotherapy, but had gradually been persuaded to allow Bertie more freedom, and in particular, to do things with his father. This had improved the situation, but if leopards do not change their spots, neither does the *Weltanschauung* of people such as Irene change in the space of a few days. And pregnancy – the condition in which she now found herself – had a strange effect: it led to renewed vigour in her desire to impose her views on others. This was probably a result of the loss of control she felt of her body and world: as the sheer brute fact of carrying another life within her resulted in a diminution of her sense of personal autonomy, so her need to assert herself in other respects grew.

This manifested itself in a variety of ways, but most remarkably in an increase in the number of altercations in which she became involved. There was the famous campaign against Nurse Forbes of the National Childbirth Trust, and then there was the terrible row over the Pollock car, which once again had gone missing. It was Bertie who had precipitated the row over the car when he made an apparently innocent observation. "Mummy," he said. "You know how you left our car at the top of Scotland Street, outside Mr Demarco's house? Well, it's not there any-more."

12. *Quality Time with Irene*

"Nonsense!" expostulated Irene. "Of course it's there." She was replying to the question which Bertie had posed about the disappearance of the Pollock car. Of course the car was parked in Scotland Street – she herself had parked it there only two days earlier, when she had driven to Valvona and Crolla to stock up on sun-dried tomatoes and olives. She distinctly remembered parking it because she had almost run over one of the cats which sauntered about the street and which had narrowly escaped being crushed by the back wheels of Irene's reversing Volvo. For a moment or two, she thought that she had actually crushed the cat, as she felt a slight bump, which proved to be nothing more than a folded up newspaper which somebody had dropped and which had become a sodden mound in the gutter.

"You must have been looking in the wrong place, Bertie," she said. "Maybe you were looking at the other side of the street. Our car is on the left as you go up the hill. Did you look on the right?"

"No," said Bertie. "I looked on the left. And it wasn't there, Mummy. I promise you."

Irene frowned. Bertie was a very observant little boy and would normally not make a mistake about this sort of thing. But it was impossible that she had inadvertently parked the car somewhere else and forgotten about it. That was the sort of thing that Stuart was always doing; indeed, on one occasion he had parked the car in Glasgow and then returned to Edinburgh by train. That had been disastrous, as the car had sat across there for weeks, if not months. Perhaps Stuart had used the car since she had parked it. That would provide a rational explanation for its absence from the street, if it was absent; but then had Stuart driven the car over the past few days? He had not said anything about it, and he had hardly had the time to do much driving, as he and his colleagues were all working against a looming deadline on a report at his office in the Scottish Executive and he was not coming back home until after ten at night. It was unlikely, then, that such a simple explanation would be found.

"I tell you what, Bertie," she said. "We'll take a little walk and see whether the car is there or not. I need to take more exercise now that I'm pregnant."

"Is it good for the baby?" asked Bertie, reaching out to lay a hand against his mother's stomach.

"I'm sure it is," said Irene. "Babies thrive if the maternal circulation is good. And a healthy mother means a healthy baby, Bertie!"

Bertie looked up at his mother. There was so much he wanted to say to her, but his conversations with her never seemed to go the way he wanted them to go. What he wanted to ask about was whether the arrival of the baby would change things for him.

He decided to try. "When the new baby arrives, Mummy," he began, "will things be different?"

Irene smiled. "Oh yes," she said. "Oh yes, they will! Babies make a terrible noise, I'm afraid, Bertie – even well-behaved Edinburgh babies! So we must expect a few disturbed nights until the baby settles. But you shouldn't hear him at your end of the corridor. I'm sure you won't be woken up."

Bertie thought for a moment. "But what I was wondering about was whether you'll be very busy. Will you be very busy, Mummy?"

"Of course," said Irene. "New babies are very demanding creatures. Even you were demanding, Bertie. You sometimes became quite niggly for some reason. I used to play you Mozart to calm you down. It always worked. You loved '*Soave sia il vento*', you know. You loved that. *Così fan tutte*, as you'll recall. You adored Mozart when you were a baby. And you still do, of course."

"But if you're busy," said Bertie carefully, "then you might have less time for me, Mummy. Is that right? You'll have less time for me?"

Irene thought quickly. Poor little boy! Of course he was threatened; of course he felt insecure. He must be dreading the day when the new baby arrives and takes all my attention away from him. Oh poor Bertie!

"Bertie, *carissimo*," she said, leaning down to enfold him in her arms. "You mustn't think that for one moment. Not for one moment! Mummy will spend just as much time with you as before. Even more. I promise you that. Look, I'm crossing my heart. That's how serious I am. I really mean it. You will have just as much time with me as you do now."

Bertie struggled to release himself from his mother's embrace, but it proved impossible, and he became limp. Perhaps if I go all floppy and stop breathing she will think that she's smothered me, he thought. Then she'll let me go.

Irene did release him, but only to adjust her hair, which had fallen over her face. "So, no more worries about that, Bertie," she said, standing up.

Bertie nodded glumly. His real hope had been that the arrival of the new baby would so distract Irene that she would leave him, Bertie, alone. He wanted to spend less time with his mother, not more, and here she was telling him that the baby would make no difference. It was all very disappointing; a very bleak prospect indeed.

Irene went out of the room briefly to fetch her coat. Then they left the flat and began to walk up the street towards Drummond Place. It was a fine afternoon, with a gentle wind from the south-west. Although it was early autumn, the air was still warm, and there were still leaves on the trees in Drummond Place Gardens, even if many of them were now tinged with gold.

They reached the top of the road in complete silence.

"You see," said Bertie. "No car."

Irene shook her head. "I don't know what to think," she said.

"I do," said Bertie. "It's been stolen."

13. *An Average Scottish Face*

When Stuart returned home that evening, Irene was in the sitting room with Bertie, playing a complicated card game of Bertie's own invention, Running Dentist. The rules, which Bertie had explained at extreme length, and with great patience, seemed excessively complex to Irene and appeared to favour Bertie in an indefinable way, but the game was quick, and surprisingly enjoyable.

"Ah," said Stuart, as he put down his briefcase. "Running Dentist! I take it that you're winning, Bertie."

"Mummy is doing her best," said Bertie. "She's really trying."

Stuart glanced at Irene. He knew that she was a bad loser, and that it was hard for her when Bertie won a game, as he so often did.

"It's a very difficult game to win," observed Irene, "unless you happen to be the person who invented the rules."

She laid her cards down on the table and looked up at Stuart.

She had been thinking for some time of what she might say to him about the car. Although it was not Stuart's fault that the car had been stolen – she could hardly blame him for that – in some inexpressible way she felt that he was responsible for this situation. He had, after all, brought the car back from Glasgow after its long sojourn there, and had brought home the wrong car. She had every right to feel aggrieved, she told herself.

"The car," she said simply.

Stuart gave a start. She noticed his face cloud over; *guilt*, she thought. *Guilt*.

"What about it?" he said. He tried to sound unconcerned, but she could sense that he was worried.

"It's been stolen," chipped in Bertie. "Mummy left it at the top of the street, and it isn't there now. We checked."

"Yes," said Irene. "Bertie's probably right – it's been stolen."

Stuart shrugged. "These things happen. But there we are." He hesitated for a moment. "I'm not at all sure why anybody would want to steal a car like that, but I suppose an opportunistic thief . . ."

"Be that as it may," interrupted Irene, "the fact of the matter is that this puts us in a very tricky position." She paused. "I'm surprised that you don't realise what it is."

"I don't see what the problem is," Stuart countered. "The car is hardly worth anything. And we very rarely use it."

Bertie looked at his father in dismay. He was proud of their car, in the way all small boys are of their family cars, and he could not understand why his father should be so dismissive of it.

Irene sighed. It was a pointed sigh, as sighs sometimes are, not one cast into the air to evaporate, but one calculated to descend, precisely and with great effect, on a target.

"The problem," she said quietly, "is that the car had already been stolen. When you went through to Glasgow and found that the car was not where you had so carelessly left it – I shall pass over that, of course – your new friend, Fatty O'Whatever . . ."

"Lard O'Connor," interjected Stuart. "He's called Lard

O'Connor, and I wish you wouldn't keep referring to him as Fatty."

"That may be," said Irene in a steely tone, "but the fact is that this Lard character then arranged for a similar car to be stolen to order. You brought back a stolen car – one masquerading under our Edinburgh number plates, but at heart a stolen Glasgow car! Now the stolen car has been stolen again. And that means that we can hardly go to the police and report that our car has been re-stolen."

"But we don't have to tell them that we suspect it's a stolen car," he said. "As far as we're concerned, that's the car I left in Glasgow. The fact that it has only four gears rather than five is neither here nor there."

Irene stared at him. "I can't believe what I'm hearing," she said. "I really can't believe it . . ." She paused and threw a glance at Bertie. "Bertie, it's time for you to go to your space and finish your Italian exercises."

Bertie looked at his father, as if for confirmation of the order, but there was no support for him in that quarter and he picked up his playing cards and left.

"Now," said Irene. "Now we can get down to brass tacks. I can't believe that you openly encouraged deception in front of Bertie. Are you out of your mind, Stuart? Here I am, doing my utmost to bring Bertie up with the right set of values, and you go and torpedo the whole thing by suggesting that we lie to the police."

Stuart hesitated. The first few faltering steps he had taken to assert himself – steps which followed his successful completion of an assertiveness training workshop at the office – had somewhat petered out. Now, faced with Irene's accusations of delinquent behaviour, he was silenced. Sensing this, Irene continued.

"We are, unfortunately, in a position where we can do nothing at all," she said. "We can't go to the police. We can't claim the insurance. In fact, we have to forget that our car ever existed."

Stuart blinked. Forget you ever had a car. It sounded like the sort of thing that gangsters said when they threatened one another. And yet here was his wife saying it to him – and he had no answer. He turned away without saying anything to Irene and made his way into the bathroom. He took off his jacket. He took off his tie. Then he filled the basin with tepid water and washed his face. He looked up, into the mirror, and muttered to himself: "Statistician, middle-ranking, married, one son, one mortgage." He looked more closely at his face. "Average Scottish face," he continued. "Small lines beginning to appear around the eyes." He stopped, and thought. Who was having fun? Other people in the office were having fun. They went to bars and held parties. They went off on weekends to Paris and Amsterdam. He never went anywhere. They had girlfriends and boyfriends. The girlfriends and boyfriends went with them to Paris and Amsterdam. They all had fun there.

"It's about time you had some fun yourself," he murmured, almost mournfully. Then he brightened and said: "Well, it's possible, isn't it?"

14. *Distressed Oatmeal*

Matthew left Pat looking after the gallery while he went off to seek solace in coffee. Her disclosure of Wolf's existence had not only surprised him; he had always assumed that Pat had no boyfriend and that she would be available when he eventually got round to making up his mind about her. But added to this surprise was a stronger feeling, one which made him feel raw inside. This was jealousy. How could Pat have somebody else? And how could she spend time with this other person, this so-called Wolf (what a completely ridiculous name!), when she might spend time with him? He disliked Wolf, intensely, although he had not met him. He would be some awful braying type from somewhere in the south of England, the sort brought up to be completely self-confident, even arrogant. And the thought that Pat should waste herself on such a person was almost too much to bear.

When Matthew entered Big Lou's coffee bar, Big Lou herself

was standing in her accustomed position behind the stainless-steel service bar, reading a small book. It was evidently compelling reading, and she barely gave Matthew a glance as he came through the door. Matthew nodded to her and went to sit down in his usual place. Glumly, he opened the newspaper on the table in front of him and scanned the headlines. His state of distraction, though, was such that not even the headlines were taken in, let alone the reports.

Big Lou said something to him, which he missed. She looked at him sharply and repeated herself.

"I said that's an orra jumper you're wearing," she said.

Matthew stared at her. He was vaguely familiar with the Scots word "orra", but he thought it applied to tractormen, for some reason. An orra man was a farm worker, was he not? And why would Big Lou refer to his cashmere sweater in those terms? He felt flustered and annoyed.

"What's wrong with you this morning?" Big Lou went on. "You're looking awfie ill."

"I'm not ill," said Matthew curtly.

Big Lou seemed taken aback by the rebuff. "Of course by ill, I don't mean ill in the way in which you mean it," said Big Lou. "In Arbroath, when we say that somebody's ill-looking we just mean that they don't look themselves. That's all."

"I don't care what you say in Arbroath," said Matthew. And immediately regretted his rudeness. Matthew was, by nature, a courteous person and it was unlike him to speak in such a manner. Big Lou knew this and realised that something was amiss. But the way to deal with it, she thought, was not to barge in and ask him what was troubling him, but to allow him to bring it up in his own good time. So she said nothing, and busied herself with the preparation of his cappuccino.

Matthew sat in misery. I'm useless, he thought. Nobody likes me. I have no friends. I have no girlfriend. And who would want to go out with me? Name one person who has ever expressed an interest. Name just one. He thought. No names came to mind.

He looked down at the sleeves of his distressed-oatmeal cashmere sweater and then at the legs of his crushed-strawberry trousers. Perhaps Big Lou was right. Perhaps the sweater was really no more than an orra jumper, whatever that meant. And as for his trousers, who wore crushed strawberry these days? Matthew was not sure what the answer to that question was. Somebody wore them, obviously, but perhaps he was not that sort of person. Perhaps he had just succeeded in making himself look ridiculous.

He sipped at the coffee Big Lou had now brought him, and she, back behind the bar, had returned to her book. She sneaked a glance at Matthew. I should not have said that, she thought. Heaven knows what he spent on that jumper. And as for those trousers . . . Poor Matthew! There was not a nasty bone in his body, which was more than one could say about most men, Big Lou thought, but somehow Matthew just seemed to miss it.

Matthew drained the last dregs of coffee from his cup. He wanted another cup, but he felt so miserable that he could hardly bring himself to speak to Lou. Sensing this, Big Lou quietly prepared another cappuccino and brought it over to him. She sat down next to him.

"Matthew," she said. "I'm sorry. I didn't mean to be rude to you."

Matthew looked up from the table. "And I didn't mean to be rude to you either, Lou," he said.

"You're unhappy?" Big Lou's voice was gentle. "I can tell." Those who have known unhappiness, as Big Lou had, knew its face, knew its ways.

Matthew nodded.

"That girl?" asked Big Lou.

Matthew said nothing, but he did not need to speak. Big Lou could tell.

"I always liked her," said Big Lou. "And I can understand why you feel the way you do. She's very bonny."

"And we get on very well together," mumbled Matthew. "I thought that maybe . . . But now she's gone and got herself a boyfriend. Some student type."

Big Lou reached out and took his hand. "I was in love for

years with somebody who had somebody else," she said. "I know what it's like."

"It's such a strange feeling," mused Matthew. "Have you noticed, Lou, how it feels when you know that somebody doesn't like you? I'm not talking about love or anything like that – just somebody you know makes it clear that they don't like you. And you know that you've done nothing to deserve this. You've done them no wrong. They just don't like you. It's an odd feeling, isn't it?"

Big Lou looked up at the ceiling. Matthew was right. It was an odd feeling. One felt somehow that it was unfair that the other felt that way. But it was more than that. The unmerited dislike of another made one think less of oneself. We are enlarged by the love of others; we are diminished by their dislike.

"I'm sure that Pat likes you," said Big Lou. "And perhaps she would like you even more if she knew how you felt about her. Have you ever told her that?"

"Of course not," said Matthew. Big Lou should have known better than to ask that question. This was Edinburgh, after all. One did not go about the place declaring oneself like some lovesick Californian.

15. No Flowers Please

It may be that Big Lou would have urged Matthew to reveal his feelings to Pat – that would have been in keeping with her general tendency to speak directly – but if that is what she had been on the verge of doing, she was prevented from saying anything by the arrival of Eddie. Big Lou was now engaged to Eddie, the chef who had returned from Mobile, Alabama, with the intention of persuading Big Lou to marry him. She had readily agreed, as she loved Eddie, for all his inconsiderate treatment of her in the past, and an engagement notice had duly appeared in the personal columns of both *The Scotsman*, for the information of the general public, and *The Courier*, for the information of those who lived in Arbroath. The wording of this notice had been unfortunate, as Eddie had chosen it without consulting Big Lou. *Both families are relieved to announce*, it read, *the engagement of Miss Lou Brown to Mr Edward McDougall. No flowers please.*

When she had seen the notice, Big Lou's hand had shot to her mouth in a gesture of shock. She was aghast, and she had telephoned Eddie immediately, her fingers shaking as she dialled his number. Before he answered, though, she replaced the handset in its cradle. Eddie was not good with words, and he had probably not realised how ridiculous the notice sounded. And very few people read such notices, in Edinburgh at least; it was different, of course, in Arbroath, where the personal columns were scoured for social detail by virtually everybody.

Matthew, of course, had read it and had hooted with laughter. Relieved? Were they serious? And as for the *no flowers please*, perhaps that was a typographical migration from the neighbouring deaths column. Even so, it made for a wonderful engagement notice. Poor Big Lou! She deserved something better, Matthew thought; something better than this rather greasy chef.

And now here was Eddie coming in for his morning coffee, his lanky hair hanging about his collar, which was none too clean as far as Matthew could make out. Eddie nodded in the direction of Matthew before he crossed the floor to speak to Lou.

"Well," he announced proudly, "it's mine."

Big Lou looked at him uncomprehendingly and then burst into a broad smile. "The restaurant?"

"Aye," said Eddie. "As from the end of the month. A year's lease – and quite a bit cheaper than I had thought. They were keen to get me to take it. They lowered the price."

Matthew raised an eyebrow. When people were keen to sell things and get other people to take things, there was usually a reason. Eddie might think that he had found a bargain, but there could be a serious snag lurking in the small print.

"Where is this place, Eddie?" Matthew asked.

"Stockbridge," said Eddie. "Very close to Henderson Row."

Matthew nodded. Stockbridge was a popular place for cafés

and restaurants. But why had the owners been so keen to get Eddie to take the lease? "That's a good place to be," he said. "Was it a restaurant before?"

It was, Eddie said. He had spoken to the owner, who was retiring and going back to Sicily. He had been there for five years, he said, and was reluctant to leave.

"Have you looked at the books?" asked Matthew.

Eddie hesitated. "Books?"

Matthew glanced at Big Lou, who had picked up a cloth and had started to wipe the top of the bar, somewhat thoughtfully, Matthew felt.

"The accounts," said Matthew quietly. "They show how a business has been doing. You know, profit and loss."

Eddie turned to Big Lou, as if for support. She put down her cloth. "Eddie knows about restaurants, Matthew," she said. "He kens fine."

"But you should take a look at the books," Matthew insisted. "Before you put your money into anything, Eddie, you should ask to see the books. Just in case."

Big Lou turned round and slid the coffee drawer out of the large Italian coffee machine. Noisily, she banged the tray on the side of a bin to loosen the used grounds. "It's not Eddie's money," she said quietly. "It's mine. I'm subbing Eddie on this one."

Matthew glanced at Eddie, who was smiling encouragingly at Big Lou. "Well, you should look at the books, Lou," he said. "It's basic . . ."

"Basic nothing," said Big Lou firmly. "The real question is whether you know what you're doing. It's the same as farming. You can't teach somebody to be a farmer. You either know how to farm or you don't. You understand restaurants, don't you, Eddie?"

Eddie nodded gravely. "I do, Lou, doll."

Big Lou looked at Matthew. "See, Matthew?"

Matthew was not one to be defeated so easily. He winced when Eddie called Big Lou "doll". It was so condescending, so demeaning. And Big Lou was not doll-like; she was a large-boned woman, larger than Matthew, larger than Eddie himself, in fact. To call her "doll" was a travesty of the truth. And the thought that Eddie was going to take her money for his ill-advised restaurant venture was unbearable. Matthew knew that Big Lou had been exploited all her life. She had told him about how she had looked after that uncle in Arbroath and how she had worked all the hours of creation in that nursing home in Aberdeen. There had been no joy, no light in her life – only drudgery and service to others. And now here was Eddie about to take her money.

Matthew was on the point of saying something, but Eddie now addressed Big Lou. "And here's another thing," he said. "I've negotiated with the waitresses. They're going to stay on and work for me. Braw wee lassies."

Big Lou paused. Then she picked up a spoon and began to ladle coffee into the small metal container. "Oh yes?" She sounded nonchalant, as if inquiring about a minor detail. But it was not minor. "What age are they?"

Eddie looked down at the ground. "One's seventeen," he said. "Nice girl, called Annie."

Big Lou's tone was level. "Oh yes. And the other?"

"She's sixteen, I think," said Eddie.

Matthew watched Big Lou's expression carefully. He knew, as did Lou, that Matthew's bride in Mobile, Alabama – the one who had run away from him – had been sixteen. He would do anything to protect Big Lou from disappointment and sorrow. But there was a certain measure of these things from which we cannot be protected, no matter what the hopes and intentions of our friends may be.

16. *How To Let Down the Opposite Sex Gently*

While Matthew was at Big Lou's, Pat remained in the gallery. She regretted misleading Matthew about Wolf. It had been a lie, no matter how she might try to clothe it in the garb of kindness. There was something shoddy about lying, even if the motive for lying was concern for the feelings of another. She had wanted to protect Matthew from the disappointment of rebuff, but there was something else which had prompted her to lie, something else not so altruistic. Pat wanted to spare herself the embarrassment of telling Mathew that she did not want a deeper involvement with him. That was nothing to do with Matthew's susceptibilities; that was to do with her own feelings.

She watched Matthew cross the road to Big Lou's coffee bar. He had been so chirpy in his new distressed-oatmeal sweater, and now he walked with his head down, staring at the ground in front of him. He looked disconsolate, and no doubt was. And yet, did she really owe Matthew anything? One could not pretend to have feelings that one did not really have. That, surely, was unkinder still: lying about an imaginary boyfriend might be considered cruel, but a precautionary let-down was surely less hurtful than a let-down after one has been allowed to cherish hopes.

Friendship, thought Pat, was for the most part straightforward, but the moment that friendship was complicated by sex, then its course became beset by dangers. One did not have to see every member of the opposite sex in a sexual light; quite the opposite, in fact: she had plenty of friends of the opposite sex with whom her relationship was entirely platonic. Such friendships, which rather surprised people of her father's generation, were relaxed enough to allow sharing of tents on holiday or sleeping in the same room – on the sofa or the floor – without any suggestion of intimacy. That used not to be possible other than in exceptional conditions. She had heard from an aunt about the ethos of the Scottish mountaineering clubs in the past, when a form of purity allowed mixed bathing in Highland rivers without any suggestion of anything else. And she had read, too, that in Cambridge young men used to bathe in the river, naked, even when women passed sedately by in punts. Perhaps there was something about rivers that promoted this sense of purity; she was not sure.

But none of this helped her in her current predicament. She felt the opposite of pure; she felt dirtied by her lie to Matthew and now, as she saw him, walking back across the road, she resolved to tell him that Wolf was only a friend, and that there was no boyfriend. And then she would go on to the delicate issue of her feelings for him. She would tell him that while she valued him as a friend . . . No, that really was too clichéd. She simply could not bring herself to tell Matthew she did not think of him "in that way"; nobody wanted not to be thought of "in that way"; men, in particular, would prefer not to be thought of at all. And yet it was true that she did not think of Matthew "in that way". Matthew was safe; he provided comfortable, unthreatening company, like the company of an old school-friend one had not seen for many years.

Wolf was different. From the moment she had seen him, in that tutorial in which poor Dr Fantouse wittered on about Benedetto Croce, she had thought of Wolf "in that way". And he, looking at her across the table, had clearly reciprocated the perspective. He had that gaze which some people have of mentally undressing the person at whom they are looking, but Pat had not resented this. Rather, she had enjoyed it. And she had enjoyed, too, the short time she had spent with him in the Elephant House and walking across the Meadows until that moment of surprise that had occurred in Spottiswoode Street, when she had discovered that Wolf was heading for her flat, too, where his girlfriend, Tessie, lived.

They had gone upstairs together to the door of the flat on the third floor. Pat reached into her pocket for her key and let them both in.

"She may not be in," said Wolf. "I didn't tell her I was coming."

"That's her room," said Pat, pointing to a closed door off the hall.

Wolf smiled. "I know that," he said.

Of course he would, thought Pat, and looked sheepish. And at that moment, as Wolf knocked at the door, his back to her, she felt an intense, visceral jealousy. It hit somewhere inside her, in her stomach perhaps, with the force of a blow. For a few seconds she stood stock still, shocked by the emotion, rendered incapable of movement. But then, as the door opened slightly and she saw Tessie, half-framed within, she found it within herself to turn away and walk into her own room. There, she took a deep breath and closed her eyes. The force of the emotion had surprised her; it had been as if, on a dusty road to Damascus, she had been hurled to the ground. And the realisation that came to her this forcefully was that she had found in this boy, this Wolf, with his fair hair and his wide grin, one who touched her soul in the most profound way. Without him she was incomplete. Without him she . . .

But such thoughts were absurd. She had known him for a very short time. They had talked to one another for – what was it? – an hour or two at the most. She knew nothing about him other than that his mother had been an enthusiast for herbal remedies, that his father sold valves in the oil industry and had accumulated a vast number of air-miles, and that he had a girlfriend called Tessie. And that last piece of knowledge was the most difficult of all to confront. Wolf was not available. He was taken. And by one of her flatmates too! That horrid, horrid girl, Tessie, who even now, no doubt, was in Wolf's arms, her fingers running through his hair. "Spottiswoode!" wailed Pat, as if the word had curative power, a verbal scapegoat for her misery, her sense of utter loss. Its effect was mildly cathartic. "Spottiswoode!" she wailed again.

There was a knock at the door, hesitant, tentative.

"Pat?" came a voice. "Are you all right?"

It was Wolf.

17. *Anguish*

"Why were you shouting out 'Spottiswoode'?" asked Wolf, as he opened the door of Pat's room.

Pat looked at him with what she hoped was a blank expression.

"Spottiswoode?" she said.

Wolf nodded, allowing a fringe of hair to fall briefly across his brow. This was soon tossed back. "I heard you out in the hall. You shouted out 'Spottiswoode'. Twice."

Pat clenched her teeth. Rapidly she rehearsed a number of possibilities. She could deny it, of course, and suggest that he had experienced an auditory hallucination. She was, after all, a psychiatrist's daughter and she had heard her father talk about auditory hallucinations. He had treated a patient, she recalled, who complained that the roses in his garden recited Burns to him. That had seemed so strange to her at the time, but here she was shouting out Spottiswoode in her distress.

No, she would not resort to denial; that would only convince him that there was something odd about her, and he would be put off. That would be the worst possible outcome.

"Spottiswoode?" she said. "Did I?"

Wolf nodded again. "Yes," he said. "Spottiswoode. Very loudly. Spottiswoode."

Pat laughed, airily (she hoped). "Oh, Spottiswoode! Of course."

Wolf smiled. "Well?"

"Well, why not?" said Pat. She looked about the room and made a gesture with her hands. "I was just thinking – here I am in Spottiswoode Street at last. You know, I've always wanted to live in Spottiswoode Street, and now I do. I was just so happy, I shouted out Spottiswoode, I suppose."

Her explanation tailed off. She saw his eyes widen slightly, and with a sinking heart she realised that this meant that he did not believe her. Desperate now, she thought, I must do something to change the subject in a radical way.

She looked at her watch. "Look at the time!" she muttered. "I'm sorry, I'm going to have to have a bath."

She turned round and began to unbutton her top. Wolf did nothing. Turning her head slightly, she saw him staring at her, a bemused expression on his face. She stopped the unbuttoning.

"So you don't have to have a bath after all?" said Wolf.

"No," she said lamely. "I forgot. I don't."

Wolf smiled at her, his teeth white against his lips. "Oh well," he said. "I'd better be going. So long."

"So long."

He closed the door, and Pat sat down on her bed. She felt confused and raw; unhappy too. And in her unhappiness, as ever, she retrieved her mobile from her bag and pressed the button which would connect her immediately with her father.

He answered, as he always did, in the calm tones that she had always found so reassuring. He inquired where she was and asked her how she was settling in, and then there was a brief silence before she spoke again.

"Can you tell me something, Dad?" she asked. "Why do we utter words that don't mean anything?"

Dr MacGregor laughed. "Perhaps you should ask a politician that. They're the experts in the uttering of the meaningless."

"No, I don't mean that. I'm talking about when you murmur a word to yourself. A name perhaps. The name of a place." She did not say the name of a street, of course.

There was a moment's silence at the other end. Dr MacGregor realised that this was not theoretical inquiry; doctors were never asked theoretical questions. They were asked questions about things that were happening to real people, usually to the questioner.

"Why?" he asked gently. "Have you found yourself doing this?"

"Yes," said Pat. "I suppose I have."

"It's nothing too worrying," said Dr MacGregor. "It's usually an expression of agony. Something worries you, something haunts you, and you give verbal expression to your anguish. And what you say may have nothing to do with what you feel. It may be the name of somebody you know, it may be a totally meaningless word."

"Such as . . . such as Spottiswoode?"

"Yes. Spottiswoode would do." Dr MacGregor paused. So that was what his daughter had uttered. Well, Spottiswoode was as good as anything. "You're unhappy about something, aren't you? That's why you gave a cry of anguish. It's a perfectly normal response, you know. Lots of people do it. They don't admit it, but they do it. People don't admit things, you see, Pat."

"They don't?"

"No, they don't. And that's very sad, isn't it? We're all weak, human creatures, with all those foibles and troubles which make us human, and we all – or most of us – feel that we have to be strong and brave and in command of ourselves. But we can't be. The people with the strong, brave exteriors are just as weak and vulnerable as the rest of us. And of course they never admit to their childish practices, their moments of weakness or absurdity, and then the rest of us think that's how it should be. But it isn't, Pat. It isn't.

"And here is another thing, Pat. When you find yourself doing something like this – something which appears to have no meaning – remember that it might just be plain old superstitious behaviour. A lot of the things we do are superstitious. And although we don't know it, we do them because we think that our actions will protect us from things getting even worse."

Pat was intrigued. For the time being, she had forgotten about her misery and about Spottiswoode and its attendant embarrassments. It was so like her father to understand so completely. And it was so like him, too, to make it that much easier.

"Of course," went on Dr MacGregor, "this will all be about a boy, won't it?"

She drew in her breath. He always knew; he always knew.

"Yes, it is."

"In that case," he said, "your options are very clear, you know. You find out whether it's going to work out, or you forget him. If he's unattainable, or not interested in you, then you simply have to forget him. Forget he exists. Tell yourself that he's really nothing to you."

Their conversation continued for a few minutes after that. Then Pat went to the window and looked out. Wolf is nothing to me, she said to herself. Wolf is nothing to me.

She heard a noise outside the closed door, and she spun round. The thought occurred to her that she had said – actually articulated the words Wolf is nothing to me – rather than merely thinking them. She could not be sure. And if that was Wolf outside, then he would have heard her.

But it was not Wolf. It was Tessie.

18. Fibs

Irene had taken Stuart to task for suggesting in front of Bertie that they should report the theft of their car without mentioning their suspicions that the car was already a stolen car, passed on by the Glasgow businessman, Lard O'Connor. Her squeamishness, though, did not preclude her from reporting the matter herself; she had been shocked by the idea that Bertie might hear of the planned concealment rather than that Stuart should propose such a thing in the first place.

"It's not really a deception," she said to Stuart, once Bertie was out of earshot. "All we are doing is reporting the theft of a car which has a certain number plate. It makes no difference that the car in question is not the original vehicle which had that number. That's all there is to it."

Stuart was not sure that it was so simple. In his view, the difference between their positions was that while Irene was happy to employ half-truths, he was happy to achieve the same end by simple misstatement. The end result was the same – as far as he could see. But he felt disinclined to argue the point with Irene, who inevitably won any such debate between them. So he agreed with her that she should make the report to the police, and should do so at the Gayfield Square Police Station, which was only ten minutes' walk from Scotland Street, at the very eastern edge of the New Town.

Bertie was very keen to accompany his mother. He had never been in a police station, he pointed out, and this was the only chance he would have.

"Anyway, I can help you, Mummy," he said. "I can provide corroboration of what you say."

Irene glanced at her son. She was aware that Bertie had a wide vocabulary, but she had not heard him refer to "corroboration" before. It was very interesting; one day she would have to attempt to measure the extent of his vocabulary. She had seen a kit which enabled one to do just that: one asked the meaning of certain words and then extrapolated from the results. Extrapolation, she thought. Would Bertie know what extrapolation meant?

She decided to indulge Bertie. "Very well, Bertie," she said. "You can come to the police station with me. I don't think that there's much to be seen there, quite frankly. Police stations are rather boring places, I understand."

Bertie looked puzzled. "Then why do people like to read about them, if they're so boring?"

Irene laughed. "I suppose that's because the people who write about them – people like that Ian Rankin – have no idea what a real police station is like!"

"So they just make it up?" asked Bertie. "Does Mr Rankin just make everything up?"

"He has a very active imagination," said Irene. "He makes Edinburgh sound very exciting, with all those bodies and so on. But that's not at all what real life's like. Real life is what we do, Bertie. Real life is you and me. Valvona and Crolla. That sort of thing."

Bertie thought for a moment. "Poor Mr Rankin," he said after a while. "It's sad that he has to make things up. Do you think he's unhappy, Mummy? Do you think that having to tell so many fibs makes him unhappy?"

Irene reached down and patted Bertie on the head. It was a gesture which Bertie particularly disliked, and he dodged to avoid her hand. "Dear Bertie," she said. "Don't you worry about Ian Rankin! He'll be fine. I don't think he knows that he's making things up, I really don't. I think he probably believes it's all true." She paused. "But anyway, Bertie, let's not concern ourselves too much about all that. If we're going to Gayfield Square, then we should leave now. And then, afterwards, we can go and buy sundried tomatoes at Valvona and Crolla. Would you like that?"

Bertie said that he would, and a few minutes later they were making their way up Scotland Street to the Drummond Place corner. Irene walked slowly, while Bertie skipped ahead of her. Every so often he would turn round and run back to join his mother, before detaching himself from her again. She noticed that when he skipped, he kept his gaze carefully on the pavement in front of him. And his gait, too, was controlled, as if he was taking care to avoid putting his feet . . . It was that old business with the bears and the lines again, she thought, with irritation. It really was most vexing that Bertie, who appeared to know what corroboration was, who was able to speak Italian with such fluency, and who could reel off all the main scales, major and minor, should believe that if he put his foot on a line in the pavement, bears would materialise and eat him. She had no idea where he got such notions from. She had never encouraged magical thinking in her son; she had always pointed out that darkness was just the absence of light, not cover for all sorts of ghosts and bogles; she had never encouraged any of that nonsense, and yet here he was being irrational. Of course, he got it from other children; she was sure of that. There was even now a whole world of childish belief – lore and language – that survived the most determined rationalistic attempts to tame it. And those belief structures still seemed able to lay a claim to the juvenile mind, sending it off down ridiculous avenues of fantasy.

She called out to Bertie, who had skipped ahead and was just about to turn the corner. Hearing his mother's voice, Bertie stopped, turned round, and then began to run back to her.

"I want to talk to you, Bertie," said Irene. "We can talk as we walk along."

Bertie looked crestfallen. He had planned to keep some distance between himself and his mother, in case anybody should think that he belonged to her. Now this would be impossible. He sighed. What did she want to talk about? She would ask him questions, he was sure of that, and she would give him a lecture about bears. He would listen, of course, but if she was going to try to get him to tread on any lines, then the answer would be no. Bertie knew what happened if you trod on lines. Of course he understood that there was no question of bears; bears were just a metaphor for disaster, that's all they were. But try to explain that to an adult – just try.

19. Leerie, Leerie, Licht the Lamps

Irene looked down at Bertie as they walked slowly round the north-eastern sweep of Drummond Place.

"I'd like to ask you a few questions, if you don't mind, Bertie," she said. "You know how Mummy is, don't you, with her intellectual curiosity? Silly Mummy! But Mummy does like to know what's going on in her little boy's head, that's all."

"I don't mind," Bertie muttered, crossing his fingers as he spoke. It was well known that if you crossed your fingers, you could lie with impunity. Would his mother cross her fingers in the police station? he wondered. Perhaps he would suggest it to her closer to the time.

"I've been wondering where you get your ideas from," Irene began. "I know that you get a lot of things from Daddy or from me." (Mostly me, she thought. Thank heavens.) "And you learn a lot from your teacher at the Steiner School, of course. But you must also pick up some things from the other children. You do, don't you?"

Bertie shrugged his shoulders. "Maybe," he said. He thought of the other children he knew: Tofu, Hiawatha, Olive. He was not sure if he learned much from any of them. Tofu knew virtually nothing, as far as Bertie could ascertain. Hiawatha hardly ever said anything, and anyway he spoke with a curious accent that very few people could understand. And as for Olive, she was always imparting information to others, but it was almost always quite wrong. Bertie had been shocked to discover that Olive thought Glasgow was in Ireland. And she held this view although she had actually been there – "Well, it seemed like it was in Ireland," she had said in her own defence. And then she had said that a tiger was a cross between a lion and a zebra and had stuck to this position even after Bertie had pointed out that lions ate zebras and would therefore never get to know one another well enough to have offspring. Olive had simply stared at him and said: "What's that got to do with it?" And so they had left the subject where it stood.

"Perhaps you'll tell me some of the things you pick up from other children," coaxed Irene. "Do you know any counting rhymes, for example?"

"Counting rhymes?" asked Bertie.

"Yes," said Irene. "Here's one that I remember. Shall I tell it to you?"

"If you must," muttered Bertie.

"Very well," said Irene. "Here we go:
Bake a pudding, bake a pie,
Send it up to Lord Mackay,
Lord Mackay's not at home,
Send it to the man o' the moon.
The man o' the moon's making shoes,
Tippence a pair,
Eery, ary, biscuit, Mary,
Pim, pam, pot."

Bertie looked at his mother. Then he looked away again. In his astonishment, he had almost trodden on a line. He would have to be more careful in future.

"So," said Irene jauntily. "Do you know anything like that?"

Bertie stopped and looked up at his mother. "I know some rhymes, Mummy. Is that what you want to know?"

"Yes," said Irene. "You tell them to me, Bertie, and I'll tell you if I knew them when I was a little girl. A lot of these things are very old, you know."

"Postie, postie, number nine," said Bertie suddenly. "Tore his breeks on a railway line!"

"Well!" exclaimed Irene. "Poor postie! I don't believe I know that one, Bertie. How interesting!"

"Leerie, leerie, licht the lamps," continued Bertie. "Lang legs and crookit shanks."

"My goodness!" said Irene. "That's remarkable. I suspect that's a very old one. The leerie was the lamplighter, Bertie. We don't have lamplighters any more, and yet there you are still using that rhyme in the playground. Isn't that interesting, Bertie? It shows the persistence of these things."

Bertie nodded. "Here's another one, Mummy," he said.

"There was an old man called Michael Finigin
He grew whiskers on his chinigin
The wind came up and blew them inigin
Poor old Michael Finigin, begin igin."

Irene clapped her hands in delight. "Oh yes, Bertie! I remember that. And there's more!

There was an old man called Michael Finigin
Climbed a tree and hurt his shin igin
Tore off several yards of skin igin
Poor old Michael Finigin, begin igin."

Bertie frowned. "Poor Michael Finigin," he said. "Nothing went right for him, did it, Mummy?"

"No," said Irene. "A lot of these things are very cruel, Bertie? People laugh at cruelty, don't they? We think that we don't, but we do. Just listen to the jokes that people tell one another. They're all about misfortune of one sort or another. And people seem to find misfortune funny."

"And it wasn't funny for Michael Finigin," observed Bertie.

"No," said Irene. "There are lots of people for whom it's not funny. Not funny at all."

They had now reached the end of London Street and were not far from the East New Town Nursery School, where Bertie had once been enrolled. Irene had said nothing about the nursery school on this trip, hoping that Bertie had forgotten all about the trauma of his earlier suspension. But she noticed now that he was looking nervously in the direction of the school, and she feared that painful memories were rising in his mind.

"You used to go to nursery school there, Bertie," she said. "A long time ago. But we don't have to think about that any more. We've moved on."

Bertie looked down the road that led to the nursery school. He had been happy there, and he could never understand why they had suspended him. That woman, Miss MacFadzean, had encouraged them to express themselves, and that was all he had been doing. It was really rather unfair. He looked at his mother, and reached for her hand. Poor Mummy! he thought. She has such strange ideas in her head, but she really means well, in a funny sort of way. And here she was getting excited about a few peculiar old rhymes that he had seen in Iona and Peter Opie's book *The Lore and Language of Schoolchildren*. Bertie had found a copy in the house and had read it from cover to cover. There was so much in it. It was a pity all of that had been forgotten – such a pity! Perhaps he would try to teach some of them to Olive, and she could pass them on to the other girls. There was no point trying to teach Tofu any folklore – no point at all.

20. *Truth and Truth-Telling in Gayfield Square*

At Gayfield Square Police Station, Irene and Bertie were greeted by a policeman, who smiled warmly at Bertie. "Lost your bicycle, son?" the policeman asked. Bertie looked at the policeman blankly. "I don't have a bicycle," he said. "I wish I had a bicycle, but I don't. Mummy won't let me . . ."

"The officer is just being playful, Bertie," Irene interrupted. "It's his idea of a joke, you see."

The policeman looked at Irene sharply. "And what can we do for you, Madam?" he asked coldly.

"I've come to report the theft of a car," said Irene.

"I see," said the policeman. "And are we sure it's been stolen? It hasn't been towed, has it?"

Irene gave a start. Towed? It had not occurred to her that the car might have been legitimately removed. What sort of line was there on the road at that point? Was it residents' parking? It was residents' parking, surely . . .

"I don't think it will have been towed," she said. "It was parked in Scotland Street, where we always park it. Now it's gone."

The policeman nodded. "The most surprising cars get towed, you know. You'd be astonished at how many people come in here to report their car stolen and all the time it's down at the vehicle pound."

Irene gave the policeman the number of their car and he went away briefly to feed the details into a computer. While he was gone, Bertie looked around the room with interest. There were several notices pinned on a board and he sidled over to these and peered up at them. There was a notice about the depth of tread required on a car tyre and one about the closing of a road. And then there was a Wanted poster, complete with the photograph of the wanted person. Bertie peered at the photograph. It was very interesting. Surely not . . .

"Mummy," he whispered. "Come over here and look at this. Look at this Wanted poster."

"Not now, Bertie," said Irene. "We must deal with our car first."

"But I recognise the person in that photograph," Bertie persisted. "Look, Mummy! Look at the person in the photograph."

"Oh really, Bertie," said Irene, the exasperation rising in her voice. "I don't see what . . ." She stopped. Slowly she leant forward and studied the picture. "My goodness . . ." she began.

"You see," said Bertie. "It is him, isn't it?"

Irene stood up again and pulled Bertie away from the notice board. "Hush, Bertie," she said. "We haven't come here to look at Wanted posters. We're here to find our poor car . . ."

"But," said Bertie. "But the notice says that anybody who recognises . . ."

The policeman was now returning to the front desk.

"Your car has not been towed," he said. "So if you'd like to tell me when you last saw it and where it was when you last saw it."

"We've just see that pho . . ." Bertie began, but was interrupted by Irene.

"Now then," she said loudly. "When did we last see the car, Bertie? Can you put on your little thinking cap? When did Mummy park the car up at the top of Scotland Street?"

Bertie scratched his head. "Last week, I think. Yes, Mummy,

it was last week. Daddy was out drinking, remember, and you . . ."

"Last week," interrupted Irene. "Yes, last week. And, Bertie, Daddy does not go out drinking, as you put it. Daddy had gone to meet somebody from the office and it just so happened it was in the Cumberland Bar. It was a working meeting." She smiled at the policeman. "Honestly! Out of the mouths of babes . . ."

The policeman looked at Bertie and winked. "So it was last week some time?"

"Yes," said Irene. "I think it was Tuesday. Yes, it was Tuesday."

"So it was stolen some time after Tuesday but before the day on which you found it to be missing, which was . . ."

"Yesterday," said Bertie. "I took Mummy up the street to show her that it wasn't there. She was very cross. She said a rude word."

"Bertie!" exclaimed Irene. "I did not say a rude word. You're making it up."

"But you did, Mummy," said Bertie. "You said . . ."

"No need," said the policeman. "None of us is perfect. Let's proceed. I shall need to take all your details at this stage. Then we'll enter the particulars of the car on the national stolen-cars register. And we shall make inquiries."

"It might have been stolen before," said Bertie suddenly.

Irene spun round sharply and glared at him. Then she turned back to the policeman. "He has a very vivid imagination," she explained. "You know how children are. They construct these vivid imaginative worlds. Melanie Klein . . ."

The policeman looked at Bertie. "You said it was already stolen?" he asked. "Who stole it? This Melanie Klein? Your Dad?"

"No," said Bertie. "Daddy would never steal a car. He works for the Scottish Executive."

"So," the policeman continued. "Who stole it then?"

"Oh really!" Irene interrupted. "This is completely pointless. It was just a bit of childish fantasy. You were making things up, weren't you, Bertie?"

Bertie shook his head. "I think it might have been that friend of Mr O'Connor's. You remember, Mummy, I told you about him. Gerry. He might have . . ."

"I think we've had quite enough of this," said Irene, reaching out for Bertie's hand. Turning to the policeman, she explained that they had to do some shopping and that if there was anything further that the police needed to know they could telephone her. Then, pushing Bertie before her, she hurried towards the exit.

"But what about that poster?" Bertie said, as they made their way out.

"Later, Bertie," said Irene. "We'll talk about that later."

Outside now, and heading up the square in the direction of Valvona and Crolla, Irene pointedly refrained from meeting Bertie's gaze. The little boy, head down, was a picture of dejection.

"I'm sorry, Mummy," he said after a while. "Did I say something wrong?"

Irene pursed her lips. "There are times when it's best to leave things to grown-ups, Bertie," she said. "That was one of them."

"But I was just telling the truth," protested Bertie. "Do grown-ups not tell the truth?"

"They do," said Irene crossly. "They certainly do. It's just that grown-ups know how to handle the truth. You'll learn that in due course, Bertie. You'll learn."

Bertie said nothing. He was thinking of the poster and the photograph on it. Who would have guessed?

21. *Missing Domenica*

Angus Lordie knew immediately that the letter came from Domenica. When he picked it up, there it was – a brightly-coloured Malaysian stamp portraying local flora, and beneath it the address, written out in Domenica's characteristic script. She had learned that script at St Leonard's School, St Andrews, all those years ago, at the feet of the redoubtable Miss Powell, a teacher who, so Domenica had once informed Angus, believed that clarity of expression in handwriting and speech was the greatest of goods which an education could confer. "It does not matter, girls," she had said, "if you do not have the most profound thoughts to convey – and I suspect that you don't – as long as you convey them clearly." Miss Powell, Domenica explained, had been a teacher of great antiquity, and had died in office, in the staff room, with much dignity. They had found her with an open exercise book on her lap with two words written, in her own handwriting, on an otherwise unsullied page – "the end". Or so the story went – schoolgirls, put together, were notoriously prone to fancy and indeed to the exchange of wild rumour.

The letter Angus now extracted from the small bundle of mail. The brown envelopes and the unsolicited advertisements which the Post Office saw fit to inflict on him, he tossed to one side; the advertisements would be recycled and would no doubt be made into fresh advertisements, endlessly perhaps, while the brown envelopes would be opened after breakfast. Angus was not one to put off the opening of mail, a habit which he had heard was extremely common. Sometimes it took the form of leaving the letter unopened for a day or so – something which was in the range of normality – but the condition could become more serious and could lead to mail remaining unopened for weeks, even months. A friend of his had suffered from this and had sought the help of a clinical psychologist, who had revealed to him that the letters represented an emotional claim – one emotional claim too many – and he was simply denying this to protect himself.

But this did not afflict Angus, who slit Domenica's envelope open with relish and read it while seated at his kitchen table, a cup of coffee in front of him, the morning sun streaming in through his window. It was a delicious feeling, this anticipation of word from Domenica, and he thought for a moment that he would paint such a scene, a small, carefully-worked canvas in the style of . . . well, let us not be too modest about our abilities, Vermeer. Yes, that would be entirely appropriate. A small tribute to Vermeer: the reading of a letter in an Edinburgh kitchen, with all that stillness and quiet which Vermeer could put into his paintings, and which Angus Lordie could, too.

The letter began with the usual salutation. Then: "You will see from the postmark – and the stamp – that I have reached my destination safely. When I embarked on that questionable ship I confess that I began to doubt my decision to make the journey by sea, but I must say that I do not regret it for a moment. Air travel is completely artificial. One enters a gleaming metal tube and subjects oneself to the experience of being carried through the sky while breathing the recycled air of several hundred other people. And then they have the effrontery to suggest that one should settle back and 'enjoy the flight'! Of course, these airline people speak a different language altogether, a sort of debased mid-Atlantic English which is full of circumlocutions and cliché. The word 'now', such an honest, workmanlike word, has been replaced by 'at this time', as in 'please fasten your seat belts at this time', or 'we are commencing (anglice starting) our descent at this time'. Why can't they say 'now'?

"Well, as you know, I refrained from all that and took a passage on a merchant ship, a large Norwegian container vessel of no discernible character. They had twenty passengers – a motley crew – and indeed they had a motley crew too. But we were able to read and play bridge with the Captain (a most eccentric bidder, I might add), and there was a simply immense deck to walk about for exercise.

"It got hotter and hotter, of course, and several of the other passengers became very morose and low. I was comfortable enough; my cabin windows opened and the ship's movement made for a pleasant breeze. I lay about a lot, reading suitable books. I must confess, Angus, that I reread Somerset Maugham because it seemed to be just the thing in such circumstances. You know, Maugham really could write, unlike some novelists today, who go in for pretentiousness in a very big way. Maugham told marvellous stories, in the way in which nineteenth-century writers told stories. No artifice. No play with words. Just stories. I read *Rain* several times on board, because it's all about a voyage, as you know. What a story! And *The Painted Veil* too, because it's so refreshing to see a male writer having a go at a truly nasty woman; male writers don't dare do that these days, Angus. You wouldn't get a modern Flaubert punishing Madame Bovary as the real Flaubert did. Oh no. By the way, did you know that Flaubert wrote terribly slowly? He managed five words an hour, which meant that on a good day he wrote about thirty words. Now they were good words, of course, but even so . . ."

Angus put down the letter and rose to his feet. He looked out of the window. It was as if Domenica was in the room with him. He could hear her voice. Her laughter. She was there, and not there at the same time. He did not want the letter to end, and so he decided to go for a brief walk and return to savour the rest of the letter. This would give him something to look forward to.

He whistled for Cyril, who appeared from the other end of the flat, one ear cocked inquisitively.

"Do you miss Domenica too?" Angus asked as he attached the lead to Cyril's collar.

Cyril was silent. As a dog, he missed everything – intensely. He missed Lochboisdale. He missed favourite, remembered bones. He missed the tooth he had lost when he had bitten that other dog's tail. Everything – Cyril missed everything.

22. *An M.A. (Cantab.)*

Angus returned from his walk round Drummond Place. There were people about, and one or two greeted him, but he barely noticed them, so absorbed was he in thoughts of Domenica's letter. He began to compose his response mentally – he would tell her about Antonia and how he had let her in and how he had decided that she . . . no, he would not do that. He should remember that Antonia was, after all, Domenica's friend. I must make more of an effort in that direction, he told himself. I shall persist. I shall give her the chance to prove that she is as charming and good company as Domenica herself. At the very least, I shall be civil; I shall do the neighbourly thing and invite her in for a drink some evening, although perhaps it might be wise to dilute her. And not just to dilute her with alcohol, which has the power to transform difficult company into good, but dilute her with other guests, perhaps Matthew and that engaging girl, Pat – if they would come.

Now entering his kitchen, into which the slanting rays of sun still shone, Angus made himself another cup of coffee and sat down to read the rest of Domenica's letter.

"We eventually arrived in Malacca. I must confess that I had made no arrangements to speak of and had to find myself a hotel more or less on the spot. This proved to be remarkably easy and I was soon ensconced in a rather charming old building with a wide veranda and a garden full of frangipani trees. The hotel called itself the São Pedro and was run by a charming Malaccan Portuguese and his Indonesian-Dutch wife. They made me extremely comfortable, but were much alarmed when I disclosed that I proposed to find a pirate community in which to do anthropological observation. They felt, for some reason, that I had some kind of death-wish (the very thought!) and were completely unpersuaded by my attempts to reassure them. I told them that anthropologists were accustomed to putting themselves in dangerous situations. Look at the number of people who did their field work in New Guinea amongst people who still resorted to occasional head-hunting. Look at the people who did their research in the mountains of Corsica, which are pretty dangerous at the best of times. Very few anthropologists opt for the soft life when it comes to their field work. In fact, I know only two – one went to the Vatican to study the domestic economy of a male-dominated society, and the other went to Monaco to study sense of place and permanence amongst tax exiles. Both of these were rather condescended to by their peers later on – they were treated as if they had not really earned their spurs, so to speak, as anthropologists. There were sniffy remarks about doing one's research in a meadow rather than a field – that sort of thing. Not really funny, but very barbed.

"But do you think that my hosts would be reassured by any of this? They would not. Eventually, they shrugged their shoulders and said that if called upon they would be happy to identify my remains and have them shipped back to Scotland. I thanked them for this; the offer was genuinely meant.

"Of course, I had to find somebody who would give me the necessary introductions. The Royal Institute of Anthropology had given me the name of somebody who was in the business of arranging academic exchanges for students, and they said that this person had been very helpful to another anthropologist who had studied minority-group relations in several of the Malaysian states. He was called Edward Hong, and I eventually found his office near a row of old godowns by the river. It was in a charming old Chinese house, with red roof and pillars which had been painted light blue. On the front door there was a sign which announced that this was the office of the World Scholar Cultural Exchange, of which the proprietor and director was Edward Hong, M.A. (Cantab.).

"I do like to meet an M.A. (Cantab.) in a place like Malacca – it's so reassuring! Of course, one does come across one or two of them who might not be the real thing, but they are usually utterly charming and tremendously Anglophile (and remember, Angus, before you say anything: Anglophilia includes Scots in its generous embrace). Do you remember, by the way, that charming habit of putting letters behind one's name, even if one failed the degree in question? Did you ever meet a B.A. (Calcutta)

(Failed)? Or were they apocryphal? I certainly remember speaking to somebody who had seen a plate outside a dental surgery in the Yemen which said: Bachelor of Dental Surgery (Failed). I suppose that if one's toothache were severe enough, one might just take the risk.

"Edward Hong was very urbane. He was an impressive-looking man with a pencil moustache and elegant patent-leather shoes. He appeared terribly pleased to see me and summoned a maid to produce a tray of tea, which we drank out of Royal Doulton cups.

"'I do so miss good old John's,' he said, referring, I assumed, to St John's College, Cambridge. 'I had such a well-placed room in Second Court, and from time to time I took tea with the Master and his wife in the Lodge. He had a strong interest in Chinese ceramics, and I used to help him read the reign marks on the base of vases. We also used to discuss Waley's translations of Tang poetry. We discussed those for hours. Hours.'

"I listened to this talk about St John's and Cambridge for almost half an hour. At one point, he asked me if the Church clock continued to stand at ten to three, and I replied that there was, as far as I knew, honey still for tea. He was delighted with that, and at the end of our conversation I think that he would have done anything for me. So that was when I asked him whether it would be possible to arrange an introduction to some contemporary pirates.

"He hesitated for only the briefest of moments before he smiled and said that this could certainly be arranged. It would take a day or two, he said, and in the meantime would I care to meet his daughter, Mary, who was studying piano and French? 'She loves Chopin,' he said, 'and I love listening to her playing. I can listen to Chopin for hours – hours and hours.'"

"I had rather a lot of Chopin that morning, I must confess," wrote Domenica. "The Mazurka in C sharp minor, the Nocturne in E major, and so on, all interpreted sympathetically by Mary Hong, daughter of Edward Hong, M.A. (Cantab.). By lunchtime I was obliged to look discreetly at my watch and claim that, owing to jet lag, I needed to get back to the hotel for an afternoon nap.

"We parted the greatest of friends. If I came back for a midmorning tea a couple of days later, Edward Hong said, he would make sure that there would be a pirate contact for me to meet. 'He might be a little on the rough side,' he said. 'But we can have some Chopin afterwards to make up for it.'

"I returned to the hotel and spent an afternoon writing up my diary. I haven't done such a thing for years, but I have the feeling that my experiences here in Malacca are going to be somewhat unusual and should be recorded. I did a little pen and ink sketch of Edward Hong in the margins and one of his daughter playing Chopin. I was quite pleased with these, although you would regard them as mere amateur scratchings, Angus. Yes, you would, although you would be far too polite to say as much.

"I spent the next two days wandering around Malacca. It's a delightful place, a bit like Leith, in fact, but with totally different people and buildings, and climate, too, I suppose. I spent very pleasant hours reading in a chair in the garden of the hotel, under a very shady tree that looked remarkably like those Sea Grape trees you see in places such as Jamaica, but no doubt something quite different. I read about the history of this place – very colourful – and about all the different groups of people who have made their home here. This had implications for my study of the pirates. Because of the dearth of information on the subject, I had no idea whether they would be Malay, Chinese or Indian in their origin, and this had implications not only for how I would approach the study, but also for how we could communicate.

"I had envisaged that I might need an interpreter, but then it occurred to me that because of the . . . how shall I put it? . . . delicate nature of the research it could be difficult to find a local person who would be prepared to live amongst the pirates themselves. For this reason, I might need to speak to them directly.

"I telephoned Edward Hong about this. He said that the pirate bands were of mixed ethnicity and that I should expect to encounter all the main groups to be found in Malacca.

"'It's rather like the French Foreign Legion,' he explained. 'People join up if they want to get away. But what makes them different from the Legion is that they bring their wives and children with them. And as for languages, well, I would suggest that since you don't have any of the local Chinese dialects – and no Tamil, or Malay? No? Well, I'd use a pidgin of some sort.'

"As it happens, I know all about pidgin – I learned Tok Pisin in New Guinea and I became quite interested in the subject. It's amazing how far one can get with pidgin, Angus. And pidgin languages are so colourful! Wonderful creations! I suspect they'll be speaking pidgin down in Essex before too long – they're certainly heading in that direction.

"As you know, pidgins are a real mixture of this, that and the next thing. You get a bit of English, a bit of German, a bit of Dutch – everything. And the grammar is simple in the extreme. Do you know that when Prince Charles went to address the Papua New Guinea legislative assembly – where the official language is a pidgin – they introduced him formally as 'Nambawan pikinini bilong Mrs Kwin'? Isn't that marvellous? And it was quite accurate, of course. The word "bilong" does an awful lot of work in pidgin. And here's another little gem. In Neo-Melanesian pidgin, if I wanted to say: Why did you wreck that machine? I would say: Olsem onem yu buggerupim onefelo masin? You'll notice that the verb has an obvious etymology.

"My mind was set at rest by the thought that I would be able to speak directly to the people in the pirate band – not that I imagined I would be speaking too much to the pirates themselves. I imagined that I would be talking to their wives – or, I suppose pirates have partners these days rather than wives – and discussing social arrangements and the like. It's always very interesting to find out how decisions are made in these alternative communities. Often, you know, the power structure is fairly clearly delineated. Remember *Lord of the Flies*, Angus? Remember how the right to speak was determined by possession of the conch? Well, I rather suspected that I should find similar symbols of authority amongst my pirates.

"I was really rather excited by the whole prospect. And so, when I went in due course to Edward Hong's to meet my contact, I was filled with anticipation. Edward's manservant greeted me at the door and ushered me upstairs and into the room in which we had listened to the Chopin on my previous visit. My face fell, I'm afraid. Edward was by himself.

"'I've made inquiries,' he said. 'I've found somebody who's prepared to take you to them. But he wouldn't answer some of my questions, and frankly I'm not sure if I trust him. But don't worry; he's obtained the pirate chief's agreement to let you live with them for a few months in exchange for money. He asked for one thousand US dollars, and I beat him down to sixty. He'll take you there tomorrow.'

"I was very grateful, and thanked him profusely.

"'No need to thank me,' he said. 'The pleasure is all mine. But now, how about a bit of Chopin? Yes? Mary will be only too happy to oblige.' He leant forward and winked at me. 'Onefelo Chopin make nambawan good musik bilong piano!' he said, and laughed, most collusively. Such a charming man. (Note: Edward Hong should not have said 'piano' but 'bigfela bokis tut bilong em sam i blak, sam i waet – taem yu kilim emi singaot', which means: big box with some black, some white teeth – when you hit it, it cries out.)"

When Pat found Tessie standing outside her door, she was unsure whether she had heard her agonised muttering about how Wolf meant nothing to her. The other girl, however, gave nothing away: Tessie was impassive.

"Oh, hello," said Pat. "It's you."

Tessie nodded. "Yes. I thought I might drop in and offer to make you a cup of coffee. We haven't had the chance to chat very much since you moved in. In fact, we haven't really seen one another at all."

Pat looked over Tessie's shoulder, into the hall. "But your boyfriend," she began. "I thought that your boyfriend was here."

"He was," said Tessie. "But he had to go. He just popped in to ask me something."

Pat relaxed. It appeared that Tessie had not heard her muttering and had no idea of how she felt about Wolf. *If* she felt that way about Wolf; she was by no means sure about that yet, although all the signs had been there – the quickening of the pulse, that warm, butterfly-like feeling in the stomach, the slight dizziness. And then there had been that strange desire to touch his teeth; that was very peculiar and surely meant that something was happening between them.

She thought for a moment. She could not let this happen; she would have to stop it. There was no point in falling in love with somebody else's boyfriend, particularly a flatmate's boyfriend. And yet, and yet . . . people fell in love with those who belonged to others. It happened all the time in fiction, and presumably in real life, too. And even if it often led to tears and disaster, sometimes, at least, it worked.

She looked at Tessie. The other girl was shorter than Pat – appreciably shorter – and had rather fat calves, thought Pat. She looked at her hair. It was rather mousy-coloured, and was not, in Pat's view, in very good condition. Split ends probably. As for her face, well, that was pretty enough – in an odd, irregular sort of way. There was something strange about her nose, which had the slightly angled look of a nose that had been broken. Men were generally improved by broken noses, which added character to the masculine face, but a broken nose could be more difficult for a woman.

They looked at one another for several seconds, each lost in an assessment of the other. At length, Pat broke the silence.

"That's kind of you," she said. "I must meet the others, too. You shared with one of them last year, didn't you?"

"Yes," said Tessie, as they made their way through to the kitchen. "I was at school with Donna – I've known her for yonks and yonks. But I didn't know Jackie at all. She's new – like you. She only arrived yesterday. She's in her third year of medicine, I think. At least, I saw her with a stethoscope sticking out of her pocket."

They went into the kitchen, which was the largest room in the flat – and had the finest view, too, over the green and the rooftops towards Arthur's Seat in the distance. The original floor of large flagstones had been preserved here, and this added to the charm of the room. There was also an old Belfast sink, with high arched taps, and a wooden draining board.

"This kitchen's a bit of a museum," said Tessie. "But there's always enough hot water to do the washing-up. You will wash up, won't you, after you've done any cooking?" she added, looking over her shoulder at Pat.

Pat slightly resented this question, and there was a tetchiness in her voice when she replied. "Of course I will," she said. "I always do."

If Tessie picked up the irritation in Pat's voice, she did not reveal this. She looked at Pat over her shoulder as she filled the kettle. "That's just one of the rules about sharing a flat with other people," she said. "Naturally, there are others."

Pat stared at her. "But naturally."

"Noise, for example," went on Tessie. "Some people think that if they close their door, then other people can't hear them playing their music. They're wrong. Noise travels through wood quite easily. It also travels through stone walls."

"I know," said Pat. "In Scotland Street there was a saxophone that . . ."

"And then there's the telephone," said Tessie, cutting short the rest of Pat's sentence. "Some people are dishonest when it comes to the telephone. They use it and they don't write their calls down in the book. And then when the bill comes they say that it should just be split equally four ways or whatever it is. I hate that sort of thing."

Pat felt her irritation grow. This was unambiguously a lecture on how to behave, and she resented Tessie's assumption that she needed to be told these things. "I have shared before," she said. "I had quite a difficult flatmate, in fact, a boy . . ."

"And that's another thing," said Tessie. "Boys. If anybody has a boyfriend, then the rule is that the boy is off limits to others. That's the rule."

For a few moments there was complete silence. Pat looked at the floor. She tried to look at Tessie, but the sight of the other girl's eyes glaring at her from either side of the broken nose was too disconcerting. What on earth did Wolf see in her? she wondered. Did he not mind those fat calves? Was he indifferent to the broken nose – and the split ends? She decided to speak.

"Of course that could be a problem, couldn't it?"

Tessie gave a start. "A problem? Why?"

Pat took a deep breath. She thought that she might as well continue. She hadn't started this, after all. "Well," she said, "what if the boy in question fell for somebody else – and that somebody happened to live in the flat? What if the boy in question suddenly went off his girlfriend because . . . well, because he decided that she had fat calves or something silly like that – what then? Why should the other girl turn him down if she felt the same way as he did?"

Tessie reached for the kettle and began to pour the hot water into the coffee pot. "There's a very good reason why the other girl shouldn't allow that to happen," she said quietly. "And that is because the first girl would kill her if she did. She could kill her, you know. Really kill her."

25. *Matthew's Friends*

Matthew had not planned to go to the Cumberland Bar that evening, but when six o'clock came round, he realised that he had nothing else to do. He could go back to the flat in India Street and make a meal for himself, but what could he do after that? The crowd, as Matthew called his group of friends, had not met for at least two weeks. One member of the crowd was on holiday, another was on a course in Manchester, and one had recently become engaged to a woman who not only was not a member of the crowd but who had little time for it. It had never entered Matthew's head that the crowd would disintegrate, but that was precisely what it appeared to be doing.

Matthew had other friends, of course, but he had rather neglected them over the last year or so. There was Ben, with whom he had been at the Academy. Matthew saw him from time to time, but now found his company somewhat tiresome, as Ben had become an enthusiastic jogger and spent most of his spare time running. He had finished in fifty-second place in the previous year's Edinburgh Marathon and was now talking about competing in the next New York Marathon.

He had met Ben for a meal at Henderson's Salad Table, and the conversation had largely been about calories, energy levels and the benefits of Arnica cream for soft-tissue injuries.

"I've got a really interesting story to tell you," Ben said over their meal of mixed pastas and roasted red peppers. "I was running about two weeks ago – or was it three? Hang on, it was three because it was the week before I was due to do the Peebles Half-Marathon with Ted and the others. Anyway, I was doing a circular route up Colinton Road, past Redford Barracks, and then down into Colinton Village. You know how, if you turn right after the bridge, there's a path that goes down and follows the Water of Leith? There's an old Victorian railway tunnel there that you run through – they've lit it now; it used to be pitch dark and you just used to hope that you didn't run into a group of neds or anything like that!

"Anyway, I ran through there and then over the bridge that goes over the Lanark Road and then turned and ran along the canal. You know the aqueduct? Well, that's where it happened. The path along the side of the bridge has setts or whatever, and I should have walked, but I didn't and I twisted my ankle. I swear that I felt nothing right then – nothing at all. You know how you can tear things without feeling them? Except your Achilles' tendon. If you tear that, you feel it all right. Cuts you down. Just like that.

"I didn't feel it, and I carried on running, but I knew by the time that I reached the Polwarth section of the canal that there was something wrong. You know that place where the Canal Society has its boathouse and there's that guy who wears the kilt who looks after all the boats? You know the place? That's where I found that I had to slow right down and then walk.

"I said to myself : 'First thing you do when you get home is rub Arnica cream into it.' And I did. I put a lot on – really rubbed it in. You can also get it in homeopathic solution but, I'm sorry, I've never been convinced by homeopathic remedies. If you look at the dilution, how can such minute quantities have an effect? Right, so I rubbed it in, and you know what, Matthew? The very next day, I was running again. No trouble. And I didn't feel a single thing.

"And the next day I ran out to Auchendinny and back, and did it in a really good time. That's quite a run, as you know. No trouble with that ankle. That's Arnica for you."

There had been a silence after that. Matthew had looked at his pasta and at the ceiling, and tried to remember what it was that he saw in Ben all years ago. He had liked him. They had been friends, and now this thing – this running – had come between them.

There was another close friend from the Academy, Paul, whom he used to see and whom he now avoided. He had married young – they were both twenty-two at the time – and now had two young children. This friend now spoke only of issues relating to babies: of nappies, unguent creams, and feeding matters.

"Here's a tip for you, Matthew," Paul had said to him the last time he had seen him. "When you put a baby over your shoulder to wind it, make sure you put a cloth underneath it, just where its mouth is. No, I really mean it. It's important. I found that out the hard way when I was about to go to work when little Hamish was about four months old. He'd just had his feed and I put him over my shoulder and started to pat his little back. The wind came up very satisfactorily, but what I didn't realise was that half the feed came up too and went all the way down the back of my suit jacket! I didn't notice it and went off to the office. I went to a meeting – it was quite an important one – and I was standing next to one of our clients and I could see him sniffing and puckering his nose. And then one of the secretaries came and whispered in my ear and the penny dropped. So just you remember that, Matthew!

"And here's another thing. When you travel with a baby, make sure that you've got a good, strong bag to put the dirty disposables in. We went off to see some relatives of Ann's who live at St Andrews. Stuffy bunch. We had to change the kids on the way there and we put the disposables in the same bag that we had put the flowers for Ann's aunt. Now, you can imagine what happened when we took the flowers out of the bag and thrust them into her hand! Yes. So that's another bit of advice for you. You don't mind my giving you this advice, do you, Matthew? I know that you're not at that stage yet, but it'll come before too long and you'll thank me. I'm sure you will."

26. *Matthew Meets an Architect*

Depressed at the thought of his shortage of friends – or "viable friends", as he put it – Matthew made his way that evening into the Cumberland Bar. He looked about him: there were one or two people he recognised, but nobody he knew well enough to go and join. So he bought himself a drink and sat at a table on his own. Sad, he thought; how sad. Here I am sitting in a bar, by myself, drinking; a situation in which I never imagined I would find myself. What lies beyond this? Drinking by myself in the flat? Of course, people drank by themselves; there was nothing essentially wrong in that – a glass of wine at one's solitary table in the company of *The Scotsman* crossword or a book. There were worse things than that. It was hardly problem-drinking.

He looked at his watch. He would sit there for perhaps half an hour, and if nobody he knew had come in by then he would go out and buy himself a pizza and take it back to India Street and eat it in the flat. India Street was not the sort of place where people sat and ate pizzas by themselves; it was dinner-party territory. Now, that was an idea! He would plan a dinner party and invite a group of brilliant guests. The wit at the table would be coruscating; the exchange of ideas vital and exciting. There would be elegant women and clever men, and people would go off into the night buoyed by the stimulation of the evening . . .

But then he thought: where would I get the guests? Do I actually know any brilliant and witty people? He thought of his friends: none of the crowd by any stretch of the imagination could be described as brilliant company, and the crowd was breaking up now anyway. Then there was Ben, who would only talk about running – he had heard that Ben actually went to dinner parties in his running kit so that he could run there and run home again afterwards. There was Paul, who would only talk about babies, and who would only accept an invitation if it included the babies. So that ruled both of them out. Would Pat come? He would like it if she did, but now that she had that ridiculously-named boyfriend of hers, Wolf, she would probably not want to come without him, and Matthew could not face the prospect of entertaining that Wolf. What would one serve him? Raw venison? Wolves liked venison.

He sighed, and looked at his watch again. Ten minutes had passed. If he bought another half pint of lager, then that would last him until the thirty minutes was up and it was time to go and order the pizza. Thirty minutes of loneliness in a place of society, he thought; thirty minutes to himself while everyone else in the bar was with somebody. A sudden, vaguely shameful thought struck him. Nobody else in this bar has four million pounds – nor even one million pounds – and yet I am alone. It was an absurd, self-pitying thought, a thought which implied that money brought social success, brought happiness, which it patently does not; and yet he thought it.

He stood up and went to the bar, suddenly wondering whether his distressed-oatmeal cashmere sweater was right. Nobody else in the bar was in distressed oatmeal; in fact nobody else was in cashmere. Yet should it matter? Teenagers worried about whether their clothes were the same as everybody else's; when you were safely into your twenties, that was not so important. You could wear what you like . . . Or could you? Could you get your colours entirely wrong and wear a colour that nobody else would wear? The colour of failure?

When Matthew reached the bar, the barman was waiting for him. Matthew saw the man's glance move quickly to the distressed-oatmeal sweater and then slide back again, discreetly, professionally. Or had he imagined it? Barmen saw everything; it was all the same to them. He ordered another half pint of lager and then, half turning, he saw a young woman standing beside him. They looked at one another almost inadvertently and one of them – and it was Matthew – had to say something, or at least smile.

"It's quiet," he said. "I don't know where everybody is."

"Wherever they are," she replied, "it's not here."

Matthew laughed. "Actually, this place gets quite busy. I don't know . . ."

"Oh, people go home sometimes," she said, "if they're really stuck."

Matthew gestured towards the barman. "Could I get you a drink?"

He had expected a rebuff, but it did not come. Instead, there was ready acceptance, and after the barman had served him again they went together to the table which Matthew had occupied. She introduced herself, smiling at Matthew in a way which immediately lifted Matthew's depression. She likes me, he thought. I can see it in her eyes.

Her name, she revealed, was Leonie Marshall and she was an architect, barely qualified, but still an architect. Matthew listened carefully. The accent was difficult to place. "Australian?" he asked.

She nodded. "Melbourne – originally. Until I was ten. Then we moved to Canada, to Saskatoon, and I lived there until I was eighteen. Then, when my parents went to live in Japan, I went back to Melbourne to uni, did my architectural degree there, and my office years, and then came and did my diploma year at Newcastle." She paused and took a breath while Matthew, watching her, mentally compared their lives: Australia, Canada, Japan, England, Scotland (her); Scotland (him).

"I finished in Newcastle," she continued, "and had to decide what to do next. I could go back to boring old Melbourne, or I could get a job somewhere over here. There was a vacancy in a practice here in Edinburgh – a firm called Icarus Associates – and I applied and got it. So here I am." She took a sip of her drink and looked at Matthew. "What about you?"

Matthew stared at the table. Small rings of liquid had formed where the glasses had stood. He moved a beer mat sideways and mopped one up. Then, in the other, he traced a pattern with a finger.

"I run a gallery," he said. "I try to sell pictures. It's in Dundas Street, near . . ." He stopped.

"Yes?"

"Would you like to come and have a pizza in my flat?"

"Yes."

27. *Leonie Talks*

They walked back towards India Street along Cumberland Street. "I really like this street," said Leonie. "You see the windows? Look at those ones over there. Astragals. Perfect proportions. And the buildings themselves are not too big. A comfortable size."

Matthew had not paid much attention to Cumberland Street, but now, through Leonie's eyes, he did. "This street is not as impressive as the next one up," he said. "Great King Street has great big houses. It's much higher."

"Social distinctions revealed in architecture," said Leonie. "Big houses – big people. More modest houses – more modest people."

"Have you seen Moray Place?" asked Matthew. "It's just round the corner from me."

Leonie nodded. "Yes, I know it. One of the people from Icarus took me round and gave me the architectural tour of the New Town. We had a look at Moray Place."

"And what did you think?" asked Matthew.

"Well, I wondered who lived there," she said. "That's what I thought."

"Very grand people," said Matthew. "The very grandest people in town."

She made a gesture of acceptance. "I suppose that's no surprise," she said. "It's very classical. Grand people gravitate to the classical. I suppose one wouldn't find any funky people there?"

Matthew thought for a moment. Were there any funky people in Moray Place? He thought not. He was not at all sure whether there were any funky people in Edinburgh at all. Some towns were distinctly funky – San Francisco was an example – but Edinburgh was not one of them, he thought. He answered Leonie's question with a shake of the head.

"I thought not," she said. "Mind you, Edinburgh has its groovy side. There are some quite groovy places."

"Groovy?" asked Matthew.

"Yes," said Leonie. "I was in quite a groovy street the other day. I forget what it was called. But it was definitely groovy. The doors were all painted different colours and there was this strange old shop that sold the most amazing old clothes."

"Stockbridge," said Matthew. "It must have been in Stockbridge. St Stephen's Street, probably."

"I can't remember," said Leonie. "But it was just like one or two streets we have in Melbourne. In fact, there's a street there that has the same sort of old clothes shops. Vintage clothing, they call it. They sell all sorts of things. Old military uniforms. Flapper dresses. Sweaters just like yours . . ."

It slipped out. She had not thought about what she was saying, and the remark slipped out. And she knew immediately what she had done, and regretted it. For his part, Matthew was assailed by the remark. It came from the side, struck him, and lodged. His distressed-oatmeal cashmere sweater, which he had paid so much for at Stewart Christie in Queen Street . . .

She reached out and took his arm. "I'm sorry," she blurted out. "I didn't mean to say that."

He tried to smile. "My sweater? This thing? It's just an old . . ."

"I really didn't mean it. I promise you. Look . . . there's nothing wrong with it. There really isn't. I like beige."

Matthew bridled slightly. "Beige? It's not beige. It's distressed oatmeal."

She thought: porridge. It's a porridge-coloured sweater. They must like porridge-coloured clothes in Scotland, and I've gone and hurt this really gentle, nice man with my stupid Australian tactlessness.

"I really didn't mean . . ."

They had now reached the end of Cumberland Street and Matthew, who wanted to change the subject, pointed out St Vincent's Church and the beginning of St Stephen's Street. "And up on the corner there was where Madame Doubtfire had her shop," he said. "She was a real person whose name was used by Anne Fine in her book. My father knew the original Madame Doubtfire. She was an old lady who kept a large number of cats and claimed that she 'had danced before the Tsar'. That's what she told everybody. Danced before the Tsar."

"Who's the Tsar?" asked Leonie.

Matthew hesitated. Was it possible that there were people who did not know who the Tsar was? He was about to explain, when Leonie said, "Oh him! The president of Russia."

He burst out laughing, and immediately regretted it. The laughter had slipped out, as had her remark about his sweater. It just slipped out, as the best laughter will always do, in spontaneity, uncontrollable. He recovered himself quickly and looked grave. "I'm sorry. I didn't mean to laugh. It's just that the Tsar was not exactly a president."

Leonie did not seem offended. "I never learned much history," she explained. "I was always drawing in history lessons. I drew houses – all the time."

"And so you became an architect."

"Yes." She looked at him, and smiled. "What about you? I bet you knew that you were artistic when you were a little boy. Did you draw things too?"

Matthew felt flattered. Am I artistic? I suppose I am. I own a gallery. I can talk about art. "Yes," he said solemnly, "I knew. I always knew."

They continued their conversation easily. There was no further talk about sweaters or tsars. They moved on to the subject of where Leonie lived. She explained how she had a studio flat in a converted bonded warehouse in Leith. "It's very fashionable to live in a bonded warehouse," she said. "It's the same as living in a loft in New York. All the really fashionable people live in lofts in New York. Bonded warehouses and lofts provide very flexible space. You can put in moveable room dividers. Tent walls. Living curtains."

"What's a living curtain?" Matthew asked.

"It's a curtain you live behind," answered Leonie. "Curtains are replacing walls. Take your flat, for example. Do you really need your walls?"

Matthew thought that he did, but he decided it sounded rather stuffy, rather conventional, to say that one needed walls. People who lived in Moray Place were welcome to walls – they clearly needed them. India Street was far less psychologically dependent on walls.

"No," he said. "I'd like to get rid of some of my walls."

"Great," said Leonie. "When we get to your place, I'll take a look around. I can do some sketches. We can work out what walls can come out."

Matthew said nothing, but Leonie continued. "The thing about walls is that they hide things. Society is much more open now. Everything's more open. The old culture of walls is finished."

Matthew frowned. "But what about . . . what about bathrooms?"

"Open plan," said Leonie, adding: "these days."

28. The Boy in the Tree

Antonia Collie had settled into Domenica's flat rather more quickly than she had imagined would be the case. Antonia did not consider herself a city person; she had been born and brought up in St Andrews, the daughter of a professor of anatomy, and apart from her student years in Edinburgh had lived the rest of her life in the country or in small towns. She had always felt vaguely uncomfortable in large cities; in a metropolis it felt to her as if something unsettling was always on the point of happening, but never quite happened. She had spent two weeks in London once, researching in the British Library, and had felt confused and threatened by the crowds of people on the street ("All going somewhere," she had complained. "Nobody actually staying where they are.")

Antonia had married young. Her attractive looks and her amusing tongue had caught the attention of the son of a prosperous East Perthshire farmer, a man who was regarded by his father as a hopeless prospect, by virtue of his complete lack of interest in crops and cattle, but who had, nonetheless, a talent for dealing in stocks and bonds by telephone. This young man, Harry Collie, found in Antonia an easy companion. They set up home in a converted mill at the edge of his father's sprawling farm, and enjoyed the country life that such people might lead. This was an existence dominated by a social round that both of them came to regard as ultimately rather pointless, although diverting enough at the time.

Harry encouraged Antonia to pursue her interest in history. She enrolled for a Ph.D. at Edinburgh, and spent a great deal of time travelling to and from the National Library of Scotland and the Scottish Records Office. She found herself drawn ever deeper into the mysteries of medieval Scotland, and completing and submitting her doctoral thesis was, as she described it, like having, at last, a baby, which one then promptly gives away. Its publication by the Tuckwell Press was a matter of pride not only to her father, the now retired professor of anatomy, who had taken to writing monographs on silkworms, but also to her husband, who liked the idea that intellectual distinction might shine from a corner of Perthshire generally only associated with the cultivation of soft fruit.

Antonia and Harry had two children, a son and a daughter, Murdo and Antonia, known in the family as Little Antonia. When the children were ten and eight respectively, Harry started to see a woman in Perth who owned and ran a dress shop. Antonia became aware of this, and thought that his dalliance with this woman, whom she called the Dress Shop Assistant, would pass once he saw through what she imagined to be the other woman's intellectual vacuity. She was wrong. Although he was not by nature fickle in his affections, what developed between Harry and the Dress Shop Assistant was a deep mutual dependence which neither was capable of defeating. Antonia suggested that Harry should move into Perth, but he refused. His family had lived on that bit of land for several hundred years, and it was all he knew. So Antonia decided that she would move back to St Andrews, taking Murdo and Little Antonia with her, and would live in a corner of her father's house.

Then disaster struck. When she explained to Murdo and Little Antonia that they would be coming to live with her in St Andrews, they refused to go. Murdo, in particular, had a deep affection for the farm, and said that he would simply run straight back if taken to St Andrews. Little Antonia wept copious tears and said that she would not touch a morsel of food until the decision had been rescinded. She was as good as her word. She simply stopped eating, and in admiration for his sister's act of defiance, Murdo climbed a tree in the garden of the house and refused to come down.

"But if you stay here, then you'll be staying just with Daddy," shouted Antonia into the foliage.

"Exactly," came a disembodied voice from above. "That's what we want to do."

Antonia left him where he was. Those who climbed trees usually came down from them after a short while, although in the back of her mind she remembered Calvino's novel *The Baron in the Trees*, a favourite book of hers. Calvino's hero, the twelve-year-old Baron Cosimo Piavosco di Rondo, takes to the trees after a row at the dinner table over the eating of snails. He never comes down, and thereafter leads a full life in the treetops, covering considerable distances by moving from tree to tree; impossible, of course, but a very affecting story nonetheless. Murdo could hardly remain where he was for very long. Cosimo lived in a more forested age; Murdo had only the one tree, with sky on every side.

She returned to call him down an hour later. He was still

there, though uncommunicative, and an hour after that she returned with the eighteen-year-old son of the stockman. "I'll get him down for you," muttered this young man, and he promptly scaled the tree, worked his way out onto the bough on which Murdo sat, and grabbed at the young boy's shirt.

In his attempt to avoid capture, Murdo hung for a moment on the branch and then fell, crashing through lower branches on his descent. Antonia screamed and ran forward to attempt to catch him. She could not, of course, and the boy fell heavily on a grass-covered mound of earth at the base of the tree, winded and unable to cry, but otherwise unharmed. For the next five days, he refused to talk, and turned his face away from Antonia whenever she addressed him.

She had little alternative. The children stayed on the farm with their father and the Dress Shop Assistant. Antonia went to live in St Andrews, which made it possible for her to see the children regularly and also to look after her father. It was an arrangement that seemed to make everybody content, and Antonia, rather to her surprise, found that she was inordinately happy. Even the formal ending of the marriage was amicable, and she had the satisfaction of knowing that it was not her fault. In this state of blessedness, she began to write her novel.

29. On the Machair

The idea of spending several months in Edinburgh appealed to Antonia. Novels – and other works of the imagination – are sometimes best written in unfamiliar surroundings, where the mind can wander without being brought back to earth by the constant interruptions of one's normal life. In Domenica's flat in Scotland Street, separated from St Andrews by the green waters of the Firth of Forth, she felt quite free of distraction. She knew one or two people in Edinburgh, it was true, but she had not told them that she was there and there was no reason why they should find out. If she walked up Scotland Street, if she wandered about Dundas Street, which was about as far as she intended to go, nobody would know who she was nor have any reason to speculate. Of course there was Angus Lordie, who had let her into the flat. She was not sure about him: she had not encouraged him, but one never knew with men. They could become interested without receiving any invitation, and some of them were very slow to take the hint. Really, men were most tedious, she thought, and a life without them was so much simpler.

When Harry had first gone off with the Dress Shop Assistant she had missed him painfully; but that feeling of loss had faded remarkably quickly and had been replaced by a feeling of freedom. She felt somehow lighter – it was as if Harry had been a burden who had been lifted off her. And what was there to miss? His physical presence? Certainly not! His conversation? Hardly. And anyway, if one were to miss the sound of his voice, there was always Radio Four, with its comfortable chattiness. How many lonely women the length and breadth of Britain found Radio Four a very satisfactory substitute for a man? And Radio Four could so easily be turned off, just like that, whereas men . . .

Antonia's novel was set in that period which interested her most, the sixth century. This was a time when missionaries from the Celtic Church made their perilous journeys into the glens and straths of Scotland, brave Irishmen who lived in windswept settlements on the edge of Scottish islands and who shone the light of their teaching into the darkness. It was a moment of civilisation, she thought; it was as simple as that – a moment of civilisation.

Now, at the desk in Domenica's study, Domenica's papers pushed to the side, she sat before a sheet of lined paper, pen in hand, and closed her eyes. She was on the machair of a Hebridean island. The flowers of early summer grew amidst the grass, and there, to either side of her (the island was a narrow one), were waves coming in upon the shore; glassy walls of water which seemed higher than the land, toppling and crashing upon the rocks . . .

"Here, in this place," thought St Moluag, "I am under the sea. I am under the water just as surely as that Irish brother who lived under the river in a holy place, who could, miraculously, breathe and live under water as ordinary men live upon the land." He turned his head to the north. Another man, a man whom he recognised, was walking down the strand towards him, his crook in his hand.

Antonia wrote: "Oh dear," thought St Moluag. "Oh dear. Here comes St Columcille. And I've never really liked him."

She lifted her pen from the paper and looked at the sentence she had written. Was there something vaguely ridiculous about it? Would early saints have thought about one another in this way? Would they have harboured animosities? Of course they would. The point about the early saints – and possibly about all saints – is that they were human in their ways. They felt uncharitable thoughts in the same way as anybody else did. They had their moments of pettiness and their jealousies. Had not St Moluag and St Columcille been particularly at odds over who reached Lismore first? And had this not led to St Moluag cutting off his little finger and throwing it onto the land before St

Columcille could reach the shore? By virtue of the fact that his flesh had touched the land first, then it was his – or so the story went. These tales were often apocryphal, but there must have been some ill-feeling for the legend to take root and persist as it had.

Of course, part of the problem, thought Antonia, was that it was necessary to express the thoughts of the saints in English. If one were to put their thoughts into p-Celtic, or whatever it was they spoke (and Moluag was a sort of Pict, she thought, who probably spoke p-Celtic), then it would not sound so patently ridiculous. He would not have said "Oh dear," for instance, nor would he have said "I've never really liked him."

No, that was not the problem. It was the mundane nature of the thought; it was the fact that the thought was one which an ordinary person would have entertained, and not a saint. So she scored out the line she had penned and wrote instead:

"The tall man, his hodden skirts flapping about his legs in the wind from the sea, stood on the sand. Another man came towards him, a man familiar to him, a man with whom there had been strong words exchanged. And he reached out to this man, the wind about them, and he gave him his crook, his staff which he had brought with him from Whithorn. And the other man gave him his staff in exchange, and they embraced and then walked off together, and the tall man thought: We must not fight in these times of darkness; for if we fight, then the darkness comes into our hearts."

Antonia rose from her desk. She walked over to the window of Domenica's study and looked out. Above the grey slated roofs, the clouds moved high across the sky, clouds from the west, from those airy islands, from the world which she had just been trying to evoke. Somewhere out there was machair, and wild flowers, and the same darkness of the spirit against which those brave, now largely forgotten men had battled. Their enemy had been very real. And ours? she thought.

30. Schadenfreude

When Stuart returned from work that evening, his one thought was to finish the crossword which he had unwisely started in an idle moment at the office. Stuart was a skilled crossword solver, having cut his teeth on *The Scotsman* before progressing to the heady realms of the puzzles with which the Sunday newspapers tormented their readers. These crosswords relied on additional gimmicks to add a higher level of complexity. All the words might begin with a particular letter, for example, or, when lined up in reverse sequence might make up a perfect Shakespearian sonnet; there was nothing so simple as an ordinary clue. He conquers all, a nubile tram: Tamburlaine, of course, but far too simple for this sort of puzzle.

Irene was in the sitting room when he returned, a half-finished cup of coffee on the table at her side, an open book on her lap. From within the flat somewhere, the sounds of a saxophone could be heard; a difficult scale, by the sounds of it, with numerous sharps. And then, abruptly, the scale stopped, and there could be heard the first notes of 'Autumn Leaves', Bertie's new set-piece.

Irene looked up when Stuart entered the room.

"I'm reading an extremely interesting book on Schaden-freude," she remarked. "It's a very common emotion, you know – pleasure in the suffering of another."

Stuart glanced at the book on her lap. His mind was still on his unfinished crossword, and Schadenfreude was no more than a diversion. He wondered how one might conceal such a word in a crossword clue. It would lend itself to an anagram, of course; most German words were good candidates for that, and this was a gift: Freud had . . . No, that wouldn't work. Sacred feud hen? . . . Sudden face her?

"The question is this," went on Irene. "Why do we feel pleasure in the suffering of others?"

"Do we?" asked Stuart.

"Yes we do," snapped Irene. "Not you and I, of course. But ordinary people do. Look at the way they clap and cheer when somebody they don't like gets his come-uppance. Remember how the papers crowed when that man, that annoying person, was sent to prison. They loved it. Loved it. You could more or less hear the church bells in London ringing out."

"That's because he played such a great pantomime villain," said Stuart. "And anyway, that's simply justice, isn't it? We like to see people being punished for what they've done. Is that really Schadenfreude?"

Irene's answer came quickly. "Yes. If it weren't, then punishment would be handed out with regret."

"This hurts me more than it hurts you?" said Stuart. "That kind of thing?"

Irene nodded. "Precisely. It's interesting, you know. I've never felt the desire to punish anybody. And I've never felt any pleasure in the discomfort of others."

Stuart looked at her. Crossword clues were forming in his mind. All colours out on this monument, except one (whited sepulchre). Or, more simply: Sounds like one recumbent, teller of untruths (liar).

"Are you sure?" he said mildly.

"Of course I am," said Irene. "I, at least, know what I think."

Stuart thought for a moment. There was much he could say to this, but there was no point in engaging with Irene when he was tired after the office. His head was reeling with the statistics with which he had wrestled during his day's work, and there was an unfinished, and possibly unfinishable, crossword in his briefcase. He decided that he would have a shower and then he might play a card game with Bertie before dinner. Bertie always won the games because he had invented them, and the rules inevitably favoured him, but Stuart enjoyed these contests between a mind of thirty-six and one of six. The advantage, he thought, was with six.

There was to be no time for a shower.

"That's the bell," said Irene. "Would you answer it, Stuart? You're closest."

Stuart went to the front door and opened it. Two burly policemen, radios pinned to their jackets and belts weighed down by truncheons, stood on the doorstep. Stuart looked at them in surprise. Had Bertie been up to some sort of mischief? Surely not. Irene . . . ? For a brief moment he felt fear brush its wings against him. Yesterday was the day that Irene had gone to report the theft of their car, and she had lied. She had lied to the police. A quinquennium within, just punishment? he thought: five years inside.

"Mr Pollock?"

He felt the relief flood within him. They did not want her; they wanted him, and he had never lied to the police.

His voice sounded high-pitched when he answered. "Yes. That's me."

"Your car, sir," said the policeman. "We've found it."

Stuart smiled. "Really? That's very good of you. Quick work."

The policeman nodded. "Yes. We found it this morning, up in Oxgangs. It was parked by the side of a road. It would seem that whoever took it had abandoned it."

"I'm surprised," said Stuart. "It's a nice car . . ."

"Old cars like that are often abandoned," went on the policeman. "Not worth keeping."

"I see."

The senior policeman took out a notebook. "Perhaps you can explain, though, sir," he said. "Perhaps you can explain why, when we searched this vehicle, we found a firearm hidden under the driver's seat? Perhaps you have something to say about that?"

Stuart was vaguely conscious of the fact that Bertie had slipped into the corridor and was standing immediately behind him. Now Bertie stepped forward and tugged at his father's sleeve. "Tell him, Daddy," said Bertie. "Tell him about how we got that car from Mr O'Connor. Tell him about how we can tell that it's not really our car at all."

"Not now, Bertie," whispered Stuart. "Go and finish your scales."

The policemen looked keenly at Bertie. "What's that, son?" one asked. "What do you mean when you say that it wasn't your car?"

"It wasn't," said Bertie. "Our car had five gears. That one had four. It was a car which Mr O'Connor gave us."

"Interesting," said the senior policeman. "A Mr O'Connor gave you a car. Then a firearm is found in it which I imagine you're going to say you know nothing about."

"I don't," said Stuart. "I had no idea."

"It must have belonged to this Mr O'Connor then?" asked the policeman.

"Yes," said Bertie. "It must be his. Or his friend Gerry's."

The senior policeman smiled. "I think I'd like to ask a few questions," he said, adding, and looking at Bertie as he spoke, "from you first."

31. Bertie Makes His Statement

"Now then, Bertie," said the policeman, as he took his seat in the kitchen. "When we talk to youngsters we like to check up that they know the difference between the truth and . . ."

He was cut short by Irene. "Of course Bertie knows the difference," she snapped. "He's a very advanced . . ."

The policeman glowered at her. "Excuse me, Mrs Pollock," he said. "I'm talking to this young man, not to you."

Irene opened her mouth to say something more, but was gestured to by Stuart, who raised a finger to his lips.

"Thank you," said the policeman. "Now then, Bertie, do you know what I mean when I say that you must tell the truth?"

Bertie, perched on the edge of his chair, nodded gravely. "Yes," he said. "I know the difference. I know that you mustn't tell fibs, although Mummy . . ." He was about to point out that Irene told a whole series of fibs at the police station, but decided that it would be impolitic, and he stopped himself.

"Well," said the policeman. "Perhaps you'd care to tell us about your car. Is it your car, or is it somebody else's?"

"Well, really . . ." snorted Irene, only to be silenced by a warning look from the policeman.

"We used to have a car," said Bertie. "Mummy and Daddy were always arguing about it."

"Oh?" said the policeman. "Why was that? Was it anything to do with where it came from?"

"No," said Bertie. "It wasn't that. It was just that they used to forget where they parked it. Daddy left it in Tarbert once, and then he forgot that he had driven through to Glasgow and he came back by train."

"Leaving the car in Glasgow?" prompted the policeman.

Bertie glanced at Stuart. "He didn't mean to leave it there," he said. "He forgot. Maybe it's because he's forty. I think you begin to forget things when you're forty."

The two policemen exchanged a glance. Irene was staring at Bertie, as if she was willing him to stop, but Bertie had his eyes fixed on the buttons of the policeman's jacket. It was easier talking to this policeman, he thought, than to Dr Fairbairn. Perhaps that was because this policeman was not mad, unlike Dr Fairbairn. It was hard to talk to mad people, thought Bertie. You had to be very careful about what you said. By contrast, you could tell policemen everything, because you knew you were safe.

He wondered whether the policeman knew Mr O'Connor. He thought that the two of them would get on quite well if they met. In fact, he could just imagine the policeman and Mr O'Connor driving off together to the Burrell Collection in Mr O'Connor's green Mercedes-Benz, talking about football, perhaps. Would they support the same football team? he wondered. Perhaps they would.

"So you went off to Glasgow?" prompted the policeman.

"Yes," said Bertie. "Daddy and I went off to Glasgow together." And for a moment he remembered; and recalled how he had been happy in the train with his father, with the ploughed fields unfolding so quickly past the window and the rocking motion of the train upon its rails, and the hiss of the wind. And they had talked about friends, and how important friends were, and he had not wanted the journey to end.

"And you found the car where Daddy had left it in Glasgow?" asked the policeman.

Bertie shook his head. "No. Our car had gone. And that's when Gerry invited us into Mr O'Connor's house. And Mr O'Connor said . . ."

The policeman held up a hand. "Hold on," he said. "This Mr O'Connor – can you tell me a wee bit about him?"

"He's very fat," said Bertie. "Fatter even than you. And he was no good at cards. I won lots of money off him. But then he told Gerry to go and find our car, and Gerry did. He came back with our car. But it wasn't exactly the same car. It was another car just like ours, but a bit different."

The policeman looked thoughtful. "And did Daddy know it wasn't your car?"

Bertie hesitated. He was not sure about that. He knew that adults often knew things but tried to pretend that they did not, and he thought that this might be such a case. On the other hand, his father had asked him not to tell his mother, which suggested that he knew that the car was not theirs all along.

What should he say? He should not tell the policeman any fibs because that would be wrong, and, anyway, if you told lies it was well known that your pants went on fire. But his father had never actually said that he thought it was somebody else's car; he had never actually said that.

"No," said Bertie. "He didn't know that it wasn't our car. I was the only one who knew that. You see, the handles on the door . . ."

The policeman looked rather disappointed. Off the hook, he thought. It was typical. These types always get themselves off the hook. Reset – having stolen goods in one's possession – was a difficult crime to prove. You had to establish that the person knew that the goods were stolen (or should have known, perhaps), and it would be difficult to get anything to stick in this case. But there was still this O'Connor character to deal with, and this might just be a very good chance to sort him out. It was Lard O'Connor that this wee boy was talking about – that was pretty clear. Lard O'Connor, also known as Porky Sullivan. That was him. Strathclyde Police would love to get something on him, and they would be pretty sick if it came from Lothian and Borders! Hah!

"Well, Bertie," said the policeman, snapping shut his notebook. "You've been very helpful. This Mr O'Connor character, I'm afraid, is not a very nice man. I fear that he might have given your Daddy a stolen car."

Bertie swallowed. He liked Mr O'Connor and he was sure the policeman was wrong. It was Gerry who had stolen the car, not Lard. Surely if Mr O'Connor could be given the chance to explain then all would be made clear. Gerry is the fibber, thought Bertie. He's the one whose pants will go on fire.

"I've got Mr O'Connor's address," said Bertie brightly. "I wrote it down. You can go and talk to him."

The policeman reached out to shake Bertie's hand. "Well done, son," he said. "We'll do just that."

Stuart closed his eyes.

32. Sirens and Shipwrecks

Pat was worried. Her unnerving encounter with her flatmate Tessie – an encounter that had ended in a barely-veiled threat of dire consequences should Pat have anything to do with Wolf – had left her speechless. The threat, in fact, was the last thing that Tessie uttered before she walked out of the room, lips pursed, her expression calculated to leave Pat in no doubt of the seriousness of her intent.

For a few minutes after Tessie had left, Pat had contemplated following her into her room and asking her precisely what she meant by the threat. Yet it had been unambiguous enough, and Tessie might well merely have repeated it. Perhaps, then, she should assure her that she had in no sense encouraged Wolf and that she had no intention of doing so. That would, no doubt, reassure the other girl, but it would also amount to a complete capitulation in the face of aggression. It was rather like giving in to blackmail: if you did that, then it would simply come back again and again.

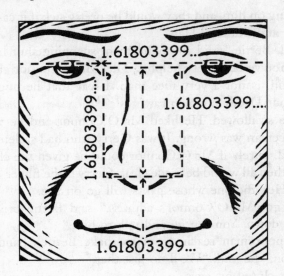

Her first instinct had been to telephone her father for advice. But then she decided that she could not go running to him over every setback. He would be supportive, of course, and patient too, but she could not burden him with this. What would he think of her if she confessed to him that she was attracted to a boy called Wolf who already had a girlfriend, and that girlfriend was her own flatmate? She could explain that she had not actually set out to attract Wolf (well she had, really: she had waited by the notice-board at the end of the seminar purely because he would walk past her). No, it would be better to talk to somebody else – somebody more her own age who would understand; somebody she knew reasonably well, but not too well; somebody like . . . Matthew.

There were several good reasons why she should talk to Matthew, not the least of these being that she had been feeling guilty about misleading him over Wolf. She wanted to make a clean breast of that to Matthew, and she could take the opportunity to talk to him about the awkward situation that had arisen in the flat. Matthew was a good listener. He had always been kind to her and had, on occasion, come up with useful advice. And if she told him the truth about Wolf, then she could also convincingly tell him that she thought of him as a confidant and not as anything else.

That day, following the confrontation with Tessie, she had a lecture to attend and planned to spend a couple of hours after that in the University Library. Matthew would be expecting her at twelve-thirty, so that she could look after the gallery while he went off for lunch, and she would stay there for several hours after he returned, as it was a Wednesday, and for some reason Wednesday afternoons in the gallery tended to be rather busy. She arrived in the lecture hall ten minutes early, and she was one of the first there. She picked a seat in the middle, behind a small group of students who were poring over a letter which one of them had received, and were laughing at the contents. She sat there, her pad of paper opened at the ready, as she paged through a photocopied article on proportion in the early Renaissance. It was a rather strange article, she thought, as the author was one of those people who believed that the ratio of phi would be found in every work of art of any significance. Even the human face could have lines superimposed on it in such a way as to come up with phi, and the more beautiful the face appeared, the more would the distance between the eyes and the length of the nose and such measurements all embody phi. Could this be true?

Suddenly, she became aware of somebody beside her and looked up from her article. Wolf. He had slipped into the seat beside her and had half-turned to smile at her.

"Phi," he said.

For a moment Pat was confused. Had Wolf said phi?

"What did you say?" she asked.

"I just said hi," said Wolf, smiling at her. And she thought: those teeth.

She tucked the article away in her bag. The hall was filling up now, and there was a hubbub of conversation.

"It's Fantouse again, isn't it?" said Wolf. "Wake me up if I fall asleep." He closed his eyes in imitation of sleep and Pat noticed that with his eyes shut he looked vulnerable, like a little boy. And his lips were slightly parted, and she thought

. . . this was very dangerous. It would be just too complicated if she became involved with Wolf. Tessie would be bound to find out, and if that happened the most appalling consequences could ensue. She would have to be strong. It was perfectly possible to be strong about these things, to tell oneself that the person in question meant nothing to one, that he was not all that good-looking and that one's stomach was not performing a somersault and one's pulse was not racing. That was what one could tell oneself, and Pat now did. But it did not work, and any private attempts at indifference which she might try to affect would be of even less use later on in the lecture, when Wolf's knee came to rest against hers under the writing surface which ran shelf-like in front of each seat. The knee moved naturally, not in a calculated nudge, but with that natural looseness of relaxation, casually, and this, for Pat, was the defining moment. If I leave my own knee where it is, she thought, then I send a signal to Wolf that I reciprocate, that I consent to this contact. And if I move it, then that will be an equally clear signal that I want to keep my distance. And I should want to do that . . . I have to.

Then she thought: there will be others. I don't need this boy. This room is full of boys and plenty of them are as attractive as this boy on my right . . . She looked up at the ceiling. She knew that she should not look at Wolf, because that would be to look into the face of the sirens and face inevitable shipwreck; but she did. "Phi," she muttered.

"Phi yourself," whispered Wolf. "Little Red Phiding Hood."

33. The Ethics of Dumping Others

In the corridor outside, in the midst of the post-Fantousian chatter, Pat turned to Wolf and addressed him in an urgent whisper.

"I'm really sorry," she said. "I've thought about it. I really have. But we can't . . ."

Wolf reached forward and placed a hand on her arm. "Listen," he said. "You don't know what's really happening. Just let me tell you."

Pat brushed his hand away. "I know exactly what's going on," she said. "You're seeing Tessie. That's it. You can't see both of us."

Wolf smiled. "But that's what I've been wanting to tell you about," he said. "Tessie and I are . . . Well, I'm about to break up with her."

Pat stared at him. He was taller than she was, but he was bending forward now, his face close to hers. She noticed that he had neglected to shave at the edge of his mouth and there was a small patch of blonde stubble. And his shirt was lacking a button at the top. The small details, the little signs of being human; and all the time this powerful, physical presence impressing itself upon her, weakening whatever resolve there had been before. How could she resist it? Why did beauty set such a beguiling trap? The answer to that lay in biology, of course – the imperative that none of us can fight against. In the presence of beauty we are utterly reduced, made to acknowledge our powerlessness.

"Does she know?" she asked.

Wolf dropped his gaze, and Pat knew that he was ashamed. "Yes," he said.

Pat had not expected this reply, and she doubted that it was true. If Wolf had told Tessie of his intentions, then he would not have felt ashamed.

"You've told her?" she pressed. "You've told her that's it over?"

Wolf looked up again. The bottom of his lip quivered as he spoke. "Not in so many words," he said. "Not specifically. But I have discussed with her the idea that we should have a trial separation. We did talk about that."

Pat raised an eyebrow. "A trial separation?"

"Yes," said Wolf. "We talked about that a few weeks ago. I suggested that we might not see one another for three or four weeks and then we could see how we felt."

"And she agreed to this?"

Wolf thought for a moment before he answered. "Not exactly."

Pat sighed. It was clear to her that Tessie was determined to keep hold of Wolf and that nothing had been agreed about their splitting up. Such cases, where one person was determined to keep the relationship alive, could only be brought to an end by brutality. He would have to dump Tessie, an action which, like the word itself, was unceremonious and unkind. It was not easy to dump somebody gently; and no wonder that somebody had started a service which involved other people doing the dumping for you. One contacted a company (the dumper) who then sent an e-mail to the dumpee that said, effectively: "You're dumped." In fact, the wording used was slightly more tactful. "The relationship between you and X is no longer in existence," it said. "We advise you that you should not contact X about this matter."

She looked at Wolf. He was, she realised, more beautiful than anybody she had seen for a long time. He could step into a Caravaggio, she thought, and go unnoticed, and for a moment her determination somehow to make herself immune to his charms faltered. Most girls confronted with an approach from Wolf would consider themselves blessed; and here she was spitting in the face of her luck. And yet, and yet . . . He was the property of another, and one did not trespass on the property of another unless one was prepared for conflict, which was exactly what Pat did not want.

A nun walked past. Pat had seen this woman before, and had been told by somebody that she was studying at the university and was in the second year of her degree. She did not wear a full habit, but had a modest black dress and white blouse, a uniform of sorts that set her apart from the run of female students, with their faded blue jeans and exposed flesh.

Pat looked up at Wolf. "No," she said. "And look, I have to go now. I really do. Let's talk some other time. Later."

Wolf opened his mouth to protest, but Pat had turned away and was already walking along the corridor, following the nun. Wolf took a step forward, but stopped himself. "I won't give up," he muttered. "I won't."

Pat followed the nun through the glass door and out into the purlieus of George Square. It had been raining when she had entered the lecture theatre that morning, but now the weather had cleared and the sun was bright on the stone of the buildings, on the glass of the windows. She saw the nun ahead of her, making her way towards Buccleuch Place, and she quickened her step to catch up with her.

"Excuse me."

The nun turned round. "Hello."

The response was friendly, and Pat continued. "I've seen you around," she said. "I mean, I've heard of you."

The nun smiled. "Gracious! Are people talking about me? What have I done to deserve that?"

Pat had already placed the voice. One half expected nuns to talk with an Irish accent – the stereotype, of course, but then stereotypes come from somewhere – and yet this nun was Glaswegian or from somewhere thereabouts – Paisley, perhaps, or Hamilton, or somewhere like that.

"Is it true you're a nun?" asked Pat, and added hurriedly: "I hope you don't think me rude."

"Not at all," said the nun. "I don't mind being asked. And, yes, it is true. I'm a member of a religious order."

The older woman – older by ten years, perhaps, if that – looked at Pat. She was due at a tutorial in five minutes, but something told her that she should not go, that she should talk to this rather innocent-looking young woman. At any time, in any place, a soul may be in need of help. She had been taught that, and she had learned, too, that the requests of those in need often came at the worst possible time.

"Would you like to have a cup of coffee with me?" she asked. "If you wanted to talk, then we could do that over coffee. It's easier that way, isn't it."

"The Elephant House? " said Pat. "Half an hour's time?"

"Yes," said the nun. "*Deo volente*."

34. In the Elephant House

They sat in the Elephant House, Pat and the nun, who had introduced herself simply as Sister Connie. They were at the very table which Pat had occupied with Wolf on their first proper meeting, and as Connie waited for the coffee at the counter, Pat thought about the strange turn of events that had brought her to this. One day I was here with a boy called Wolf, she said to herself, and now here I am with a nun called Connie. Why is that so strange?

Sister Connie brought over the coffee and set the two mugs down on the table. "I suppose you're wondering about me," she said. "I suppose you're asking yourself about how I can possibly be a nun." She paused, stirring her coffee with the tip of her spoon. "Am I right? Are you wondering that?"

"Yes," said Pat. "It had crossed my mind."

"And quite reasonably," said Sister Connie. "After all, how many members of religious orders do you see these days? Very few. I believe that it was very different not all that long ago. There were several convents in Edinburgh. More in Glasgow."

"I suppose it seems unusual," said Pat. "At least, it seems unusual to my generation."

Sister Connie nodded. "And why do you think that is?"

Pat shrugged. "Because . . ." She did not know how to say it. It was because of the me factor, she thought; because of the fact that nobody now was prepared to give anything up for the sake of . . . well, what was it for the sake of? For the sake of a God that most people no longer believed existed? Was that it?

She noticed that Sister Connie had blue eyes, and that these eyes were strangely translucent.

"Why don't I tell you what happened?" said Sister Connie. "Would you like me to do that?"

Pat nodded. Lifting her mug of coffee to her lips, she took a sip of the hot liquid. The feeling of strangeness was still there, but she felt comfortable in the company of Sister Connie, as one feels comfortable with one for whom the demands of ego are quiescent. "Please tell me," she said.

Sister Connie sat back in her chair. "I was a very ordinary schoolgirl," she said. "Just like everybody else. When I was fourteen, I wanted to be a dancer. I used to go to a modern dance class, and ballet too, and I was serious about dancing exams. I thought that it would be a wonderful thing to do. I imagined being picked for the Royal Academy of Dance, or somewhere like that, and appearing in London. I really thought that it would be that easy.

"But then something happened – something which changed the direction of my life – changed my life, actually. It's odd, isn't it, how one little incident, one conversation, one experience, one thing you see or hear, can change everything? That's odd, don't you think?"

Pat thought of her own life. Had there been something which had changed the whole course of her life? Yes. There had been. There had been something on that gap year, something which had happened in Australia, which had done that. If she had not gone to that particular interview, if she had not seen the notice in the *West Australian*, then she would not have met . . . Well, it would all have been so different.

"We were from Gourock," said Sister Connie. "We lived in a flat which looked out over the Firth. We were on the top floor, right up at the top, and there were one hundred and twenty-two steps from the ground floor up to our landing. I counted them. One hundred and twenty-two.

"On the floor below, there was a woman who lived by herself. She wasn't particularly old – I suppose she was hardly much more than sixty, but at the time, when I was a teenager, that seemed old enough. She was a nice woman, and I liked her. I used to get messages for her from time to time, as she had difficulty with those stairs. Her breathing wasn't very good, you see. People like that should live on the ground floor, but ground-floor flats are more expensive and I don't think she could manage it.

"She was frailer than I had imagined. She had given me a key to let myself in when I helped her, and one Saturday morning I used this key to let myself in when she did not answer my knock on the door. I went inside and found her on her bed, half in, half out. Her feet were on the floor, but her body was under the sheets. I thought that she was dead at first, but then I saw that she was watching me. Her eyes were open.

"I rushed over to her bedside and looked down at her. I saw then that she was still alive, and I reached out to take hold of her hand. It felt very dry. Very cold and very dry. Then she pointed to a piece of paper on the side of the table and whispered to me. She asked me to phone the number on the paper and . . ."

Sister Connie's narrative tailed off. She had noticed that Pat was no longer looking at her, but was staring in the direction of another table, one closer to the door.

"I don't want to bore you," said the nun. "Perhaps I should tell you the rest of the story some other time."

For a moment, Pat said nothing. Then she turned back to face her companion. "I'm sorry," she said. "I've just seen somebody I'm trying to . . . Well, I suppose I'm trying to avoid him."

Sister Connie looked in the direction in which Pat had been staring. "That young man over there?" she asked. "That handsome young man?"

Pat lowered her eyes. Wolf's presence could have been a coincidence, but that seemed unlikely to her. "Yes," she said.

Sister Connie frowned. "Is he bothering you?" she asked.

Pat hesitated. Was Wolf bothering her? Yes, he was. He must have followed her here and was presumably waiting until Sister Connie left so that he could talk to her. That was stalking, in her view, or something which was close enough to stalking.

Sister Connie leaned forward. "Troublesome men are easily defeated," she said. "Just give me five minutes. That's all I'll need."

35. Setting Off

Domenica had an early breakfast in the courtyard of her small hotel in Malacca. The couple who ran the hotel, the da Silvas, brought her a plate of freshly sliced tropical fruits – paw-paw, watermelon, star fruit – and this was followed by a fine white porridge, sweetened and flavoured with cinnamon, and after that by scrambled eggs in which chopped smoked fish had been mixed. She ate alone at her table; it seemed that she was the only guest in the hotel; she had seen nobody else since she had arrived, and the da Silvas had urged her to stay as long as possible. "There is plenty of room," they said, wistfully, she thought.

The courtyard suited her very well, as it had two frangipani trees in blossom and she could just pick up the delicate, rather sickly scent of their white flowers. She liked frangipani trees, and had planted several in her time in Kerala, all those years ago. But not everybody shared her enthusiasm; the Chinese often did not like them because they associated them with cemeteries, where they often grew. Tree associations interested Domenica. In Scotland, it was well known that rowan trees protected one against witches, just as buddleia attracts butterflies. And then there were the ancestor trees in Africa – a tree which one should not cut down, out of respect for the ancestor who might inhabit it. In India, the same rule applied to banyan trees, and she had once travelled on a highway where a banyan tree had been left growing in the middle of the road. Surprising as it was, that, she thought, demonstrated a proper sense of priorities. In her view, the car should give way to spiritual values, although it rarely did. And, of course, there were places where the car was even accorded an almost spiritual status. Had somebody in the United States not insisted on being buried in his car? It was so absurd.

Her breakfast over, Domenica returned to her room and packed her bags. In an hour's time, Edward Hong would be calling for her, as he had agreed to drive her to meet the contact who would lead her to the pirate village. He could not drive all the way, he explained, for reasons of security.

"I'm afraid that they're a little bit unwilling to let me go to the village itself," he said. "And you will be obliged to walk the last couple of miles. But everybody knows where it is, of course. I suppose they like to maintain at least some sense of clandestinity. Good for their self-image, I suspect."

When Domenica expressed astonishment that the location of the pirate stronghold should be widely known, Edward Hong waved a hand in the air. "But that's the way things are, you know. The police are probably rather frightened of these pirate fellows, I imagine. A policy of live-and-let-live is easiest."

Domenica had experience of this in India, where the law could be enforced sporadically, but surely piracy was different . . .

Edward Hong sighed. "They make an effort," he said. "They announced the hanging of a couple of pirates a few years ago, but nobody thought they were really hanged. Maybe just suspended." He glanced at her sideways and they both laughed. It was difficult to tell these days whether people still appreciated humour. He was pleased to find out that Domenica did; but of course she would, he thought – she is clearly a woman of discernment and wit.

"It's rather difficult for the authorities," he went on. "Poor fellows. They have so much to do, and it does get frightfully hot out here." He took a silk handkerchief out of his pocket and mopped his brow. Domenica noticed, with approval, the gold embroidered initials on the corner of the handkerchief: EH, worked in fancy script.

Edward Hong looked at his watch. "If you're ready," he said, "we can go. My driver will take us to pick up this reprobate, and then we shall take a little spin out to the village, or as close as we're allowed to get. Have you brought a good sun hat?"

Domenica nodded.

"And insect repellent?"

Again she nodded.

"I can see you've been in the field before," said Edward Hong appreciatively. He paused. "Are you absolutely sure that you want to go on with this? You know, I doubt if anybody would think the less of you if you decided to do something different. We have a very interesting set of Chinese secret societies here in Malacca; I'm sure we could fix you up to study those."

Domenica assured him that she was well aware of the risks and that she was determined to continue with her project.

"Oh, it's not the risk I'm thinking of," said Edward Hong quickly. "It's more the discomfort. You know these people have a pretty primitive cuisine – I gather that pirate cooking is just awful. And the boredom of the conversation. They're not brilliant conversationalists, you know, and you'll be talking pidgin into the bargain. I'm afraid that you're in for a rather thin time of it socially."

Domenica pointed to her trunk. "I have a good supply of books," she said. "I shall not want for reading matter."

Edward Hong inquired as to which books she had brought with her, and she told him of the last six volumes of Proust that she had tucked away in the trunk.

"Proust!" he exclaimed. "The ideal companion for a mangrove swamp! That sets my mind at rest. I shall picture you in that steamy swamp with your little notebooks and your Proust."

"I'm not so sure that Proust is the right choice," said

Domenica. "But at least it will fill the hours. And, of course, I shall be busy with my fieldwork. I have so many questions to ask these people. I doubt if I'll have all that much spare time."

They left the hotel and got into Edward Hong's waiting car. Then, negotiating a series of pothole-ridden backroads and alleyways, they arrived at a small café on the front of which was a block of Chinese script and a large sign in Baharsa Malay advertising the merits of Tiger Balm.

Edward Hong said something to the driver, who climbed out of the car and walked into the café. A few minutes later, Domenica saw him come out with a striking-looking young man with a blue headscarf tied across his brow. He was wearing a black T-shirt and a pair of denim jeans. His feet were in sandals.

The driver gestured to the passenger seat in the front and the young man got into it. He turned and gave Domenica a wide smile, exposing a brilliant set of teeth. Then he winked at her. She wondered if she had been mistaken, but then he winked again, and she realised that she had not. I cannot afford to have a romance with a pirate, she said to herself. Not at my stage of life. I just cannot.

36. Singapore Matters

As they drove out of Malacca, heading north, Edward Hong entertained Domenica with an account of his life. He had a strange way of talking – that style sometimes encountered which conveys the impression that the listener already knows what is being said and the narrator is merely adding detail.

"We're a Malacca family," he said. "My grandfather, Sir Percival Hong, was one of the first locals to be on the bench. He was a very popular man – everybody liked him, and he was the one who built our house, actually. He had a very good collection of early Chinese ceramics which he built up with the help of a dealer in Hong Kong. I remember that dealer coming to the house when I was a boy. I thought that he was the last word in sophistication back then. He had a pencil moustache and wore his handkerchief tucked into the sleeve of his jacket, which impressed me greatly, for some reason.

"Then, after my grandfather's death, when we had the appraisers in to value the collection, we discovered that virtually every piece was a fake. A clever fake, mind you, and an aesthetically-pleasing one, but a fake nonetheless. My grandfather simply had not known enough to tell what was genuine. And the dealer, it transpires, was a charming crook. And I must say it was better that my grandfather never found out, don't you agree?"

Domenica looked out of the window. They were on the outskirts of the town now and passing a small section of paddy field that abutted onto a warehouse of some sort. A group of children stood at the edge of the paddy field, throwing stones into the water. At the far end, a large white egret rose slowly into the air, circled, and headed off on some business of its own.

She answered Edward Hong's question. "I suppose it is better. It's never easy to discover one's been taken in."

Edward Hong nodded. "Then there was my father," he said. "He was destined for the law, too, but really couldn't knuckle down to his studies, and so he joined a cousin of his who had a business in Singapore. I was actually born in Singapore, you know, and spent my childhood there. We had a rather nice house just off Orchard Road, which wasn't so built up in those days. My father chose that in order to be close to the Tanglin Club, where he always went for a whisky after work. They had an arrangement whereby you could leave your own bottle of whisky in the club and be served from that if you wished.

"I felt a bit trapped in Singapore. I did not mind the government there, of course – it wasn't that. In fact, I rather liked Lee Kuan Yew. He used to come for dinner at the house from time to time and he would talk about things they were proposing to ban. Chewing gum, for example. You did know that chewing gum is illegal in Singapore?

"I must say that I happen to think that that is the most remarkably enlightened bit of legislation. I can't bear to see people chewing gum – they look so vacant, so bovine. I'm sorry, but when I see somebody chewing gum, I can't help but think that they look like a cow. It's such a moronic activity!"

Domenica thought of Edinburgh, and the chewing gum that had disfigured its pavements. In some parts of the city, the pavements had become covered in gum, which was difficult and expensive to remove. There was something to be said for a chewing-gum ban, she thought.

"You can say what you like about Singapore," went on Edward Hong, "but it's safe. They don't tolerate crime, and as a result they have very little. *Post hoc, propter hoc.* And they don't tolerate drug addiction, and again they don't have too much of that. Drug users, you see, are put into an institution at Changi and kept there for six months. They teach them a trade and they wean them off drugs."

Domenica looked doubtful. "And does it work?"

Edward Hong shrugged. "They claim a reasonable success rate, but . . ." He paused and looked at Domenica. "But tell me, what do you do for your drug addicts back in Scotland?"

Domenica thought. She was uncertain what was done, but she thought it was very little. Could we say, we leave them to get on with it, or would that imply a lack of concern? Or was the problem simply too big to be dealt with any more, with twelve-year-olds and the like starting drinking, with the connivance of adults? Where did one start?

"I can see that it's difficult," said Edward Hong sympathetically. "I understand. You have so much freedom, don't you, and then you find that freedom leads to complications. Would one rather live in London or Singapore, do you think?"

Domenica was about to laugh, as if the answer were so obvious, but she hesitated.

"Yes," said Edward Hong, shaking a finger. "You see, it's not quite as simple as one might imagine. In London, unless you're very fortunate, or rich, you have to worry a great deal about being mugged, or worse. You have to contend with crowded trains, and a lot of frustration. You have to struggle for everything. In Singapore, everything is tremendously clean. A woman can walk about anywhere in the city, anywhere, without fear of being molested or attacked. Children can play outside, on their own, wherever they like, in perfect safety. And there are no threatening beggars on the streets."

"But if there are no beggars on the streets," said Domenica. "Where are they?"

Edward Hong looked puzzled. "I don't understand," he said. "There are no beggars on the streets because nobody is allowed to beg. People can go about their business unmolested – it's as simple as that."

"So the beggars are gainfully employed?" asked Domenica. "They aren't just moved on?"

"Of course," said Edward Hong. "Besides, there's nowhere to move them on to. If you moved anybody on from Singapore they'd fall into the sea. So nobody is moved on."

"How interesting," said Domenica.

Both Edward Hong and Domenica were surprised to find out that the young man who was to act as her guide spoke passable English. This surprise, though, was accompanied by a great deal of relief. If Ling, as he was called, spoke English then the prospect of having to communicate in some form of pidgin, or to rely on gestures and body language, receded, and this meant that Domenica's fieldwork became all the easier. Of course, there was something to be said for studies in which no verbal communication took place between anthropologist and subject – such studies were free of the filtering effect of language and could therefore be more insightful than those in which language was used. There had been several well-known studies which had been completely compromised by the anthropologist's having accepted explanations given to him by the hardly disinterested subject. In a polygamous society, a man might lie, for example, as to the number of wives he had, a larger number being associated with greater wealth. Or he might exaggerate his position in the village hierarchy, thereby confusing the anthropologist's understanding of authority within the community. Such dangers disappeared completely if mutual incomprehension was the order of the day.

Ling explained that he was the son of a farmer who had gone bankrupt. Thanks to the efforts of a group of Catholic missionaries, he had received a good education, including a very good grounding in English, and had been planning to pursue a career in the United Bank of Penang, but had been distracted from this by having fallen in love with the daughter of one of the elders in the village towards which they were heading. He had decided to postpone the accountancy course he had enrolled in until his girlfriend was ready to leave her family and marry him. This would not be for a year or two yet, he explained, as a result of the illness of her grandmother, to whom she was particularly attached.

"The old lady does not have long to live," explained Ling. "The doctors doubt if she will last a year. My fiancée wishes to spend as much time as possible with her, and I support her in this decision."

"That is very considerate," said Edward Hong. "You will make a fine son-in-law." And then he added quietly: "Not for me, of course, but for this chap in the village."

Ling thanked him for the compliment. He then turned to Domenica. "Mrs Macdonald, may I ask you a question? What exactly do you want to find out in the village?"

"As you know," said Domenica, "I am an anthropologist. I was thinking of a new project, at the suggestion of my dear friend, Dilly Emslie, a few months ago, and it occurred to me that it would be interesting to do an anthropological study of one of these modern pirate communities. And so that is why I'm here."

Ling looked thoughtful. "Well, I suppose that you have come to the right place. There certainly are pirates operating in the Malacca Straits. It's quite dangerous for shipping these days."

Edward Hong had been studying Ling with care. Now he interrupted. "Tell me, young man," he asked, "are you involved in piracy yourself?"

Ling looked shocked. "Certainly not! I would never get involved in that sort of thing. It would hardly be a good start for my career, would it?"

"No," said Edward Hong. "But then you do live amongst these people, don't you?"

Ling sighed. "Some of us don't have much of a choice, Mr Hong. The fact of the matter is that my future father-in-law may know these people quite well, might even be slightly involved in their activities – I have no evidence of that, of course – but as far as I am concerned it is nothing whatsoever to do with me."

Edward Hong nodded. "Very well," he said. "I understand. But will you be able to ensure that Mrs Macdonald has adequate access to them? Will you be able to do that?"

"Of course I will," said Ling. "It's a small village, you know. Everybody knows everybody else's business."

Domenica looked reassured.

"I'm sure that Ling will be very good to me," she said to Edward Hong. Then, turning to Ling, she said: "And I really am very grateful to you for giving up your time to help me. It's very generous of you, you know."

"I have little else to do," confessed Ling. "Assisting the occasional anthropologist helps pass the time."

This remark was succeeded by complete silence. Domenica, who had been winding her watch, glanced up quickly. "You've had anthropologists before?" she asked.

Ling did not seem to notice the anxiety in her voice. "We've only had one."

Domenica looked at him searchingly. "And who was this person?"

"He was a Belgian," said Ling. "I never found out his surname. We all just called him André."

"And what happened?" Domenica pressed. She had visions of her study being rendered completely otiose by the imminent appearance, in one of the prestigious journals, perhaps *Mankind Quarterly*, of an extensive Belgian study of a pirate community on the Malacca Straits. It would be bitterly disappointing.

And what would they think of her when she returned to Edinburgh after only a few weeks and announced that there had been no point in proceeding? She would be a laughingstock, and everybody who made comments about the foolhardiness of the study would feel vindicated.

Ling, who had been looking out of the window, transferred his gaze to Domenica.

"He is still there," he said.

Domenica gasped. There was no situation more tense, more fraught with difficulty, than the unexpected encounter by one anthropologist of another – in the field.

If this Belgian were still in residence, then she would have to ask Edward Hong to instruct his driver to turn the car round without delay. There would be no point in proceeding, and they might as well return to Malacca and listen to Edward Hong's daughter playing Chopin.

Then Ling spoke again. "Yes," he repeated. "He's still there.

Down by the place where the fishing nets are hung out to dry."
Then he added: "Still there. In his grave."

38. At the Queen's Hall

"Hurry up now, Bertie," said Irene. "It's almost ten o'clock, and
if we don't get there in time you may not get your audition.
Now, you wouldn't want that, would you?"

Bertie sighed. To miss the audition was exactly what he would
want, but he realised that it was fruitless to protest. Once his
mother had seen a notice about the Edinburgh Teenage Orchestra,
she had immediately put his name down for an audition.

"Do you realise how exciting this is?" she said to Bertie. "This
orchestra is planning to do a concert in Paris in a couple of
weeks. Not much rehearsal time, but Paris, Bertie! Wouldn't
you just love that?"

Bertie frowned. The name of the orchestra suggested that it
was for teenagers, and he was barely six. "Couldn't I audition
in seven years' time?" he asked his mother. "I'll be a teenager
then."

"If you're worried about being the youngest one there," said
Irene reassuringly, "then you shouldn't! The fact that it's called
the Edinburgh Teenage Orchestra is neither here nor there. The
word "teenage" is there just to indicate what standard is required.
That's all it is!"

"But I'm not a teenager," protested Bertie, helplessly. "They'll
all be teenagers, Mummy. I promise you. I'll be the only one in
dungarees."

"There may well be others in dungarees," said Irene. "And
anyway, once you're sitting down behind your music stand,
nobody will notice what you're wearing."

Bertie was silent. It was no use; he would be forced to go,
just as she had forced him to go to yoga and to Italian lessons
and to all the rest of it. There was no use protesting. But he
thought he would try one final argument.

"Actually, I wouldn't mind being in it, Mummy," he said. "But the saxophone, you know, isn't an orchestral instrument. They won't want anybody to play the tenor sax."

"Nonsense," snapped Irene. "The tenor sax is in B flat. That's exactly the same as the clarinet or the euphonium. You see euphonia in orchestras, don't you? And other B flat instruments. You can just play one of those parts, or Lewis Morrison can arrange a part specially for you."

Bertie was silent. If he was unable to persuade his mother not to subject him to the humiliation of being the youngest member, by far, of an orchestra, then he would have to find some other means to ensure that he did not get in. He thought for a moment and then realised that there was a very obvious solution.

Irene saw Bertie's face break into a broad grin. He must have realised, she thought, what fun it would be to go to Paris. These little bursts of resistance were curious things; they could be quite intense and then suddenly evaporate and he would come round. Such a funny little boy, but so appealing!

"Why are you smiling, Bertissimo?" she asked. "Thinking of Paris? The Eiffel Tower – you know you can climb that right up to the top? And then there's the Louvre with the *Mona Lisa*. We'll have such fun in Paris, Bertie!"

Bertie, who had been smiling to himself over the prospects of escape which had just presented themselves, now became grave. We? Had his mother said we'd have such fun in Paris?

His voice was tiny when he asked the question. "Are you coming, too, Mummy? Are you coming to Paris, too?"

Irene laughed. "But of course, Bertie. Remember that you're only six. Mummy will come to look after you."

"But the teenagers won't have their mothers with them," pleaded Bertie. "I'll be the only one."

And it would be worse, he thought; the humiliation would be doubled and redoubled by the fact that Irene was now visibly pregnant. This would mean that the other boys would know what she had been doing. It was just too embarrassing. Tofu had already passed a comment on Irene's pregnancy when he had raised the subject in the playground.

"Your mum makes me sick," he said. "Do you know what she's been doing? It's gross! Yuk! Disgusting!"

Bertie had said nothing; one cannot defend the indefensible, but he had smarted with shame. And now he was to be subjected to yet further humiliation, unless, unless . . .

"I haven't been to Paris for years," said Irene. "There is really no other city like it."

Bertie nodded grimly. "Should I go and put my saxophone in its case?" he asked.

"Yes," said Irene, looking at her watch. "We will probably need to take a taxi now, as we'll never get up to the Queen's Hall in time if we have to wait for a bus."

They were soon in a taxi, rattling their way up Dundas Street and the Mound. Princes Street was *en fête*, with its lines of fluttering flags and its flowers. Bertie liked Princes Street Gardens, and had gone there once with his father, when they had climbed the hill beneath the Castle and watched the Glasgow train emerging from its tunnel beneath the gallery. He had also gone to the Gardens several times with his mother, but they had not climbed the hill. On the last occasion, she had insisted that they watch a display of Scottish country dancing at the Ross Bandstand.

"Why do people dance?" he had asked his mother.

"It's a form of deflection of the sexual impulse," explained Irene.

"Even at the Ross Bandstand?" asked Bertie.

Irene laughed. "Oh my goodness no, Bertie! Scottish country dancing is not like that at all. It's an expression of bourgeois obsession with time and order. That's what's going on there. Look at it! Absurd!"

Bertie looked at the dancers, who appeared to be enjoying themselves greatly. He did not understand why they should be absurd. "But aren't we bourgeois, Mummy?" asked Bertie.

Irene laughed. "Most certainly not," she said.

The journey to the Queen's Hall passed largely in silence, or at least on Bertie's part. Irene had various bits of advice for him, though, including tips on how to present himself at the audition.

"Don't feel nervous," she said.

"Remind yourself that there are not only strangers there – I'll be sitting there, too! Keep that in mind, Bertie."

Bertie reeled under the fresh blow. He had been hoping that his mother would wait outside. Now she was coming in! And that, he realised, would make his plan much more difficult to put into effect.

39. *Bertie's Agony*

The Queen's Hall was thronged that morning with a large crowd of ambitious parents and children. Bertie followed his mother down the corridor that led to the coffee room and bar at the end. He was aware of the fact that there were many people about, but he hardly dared look up to see who they were. His eyes were fixed on the floor, hoping to locate the geological flaw which would swallow him up and save him from his current embarrassment. But of course there was none; at no time is the earth more firm than when we wish that it were not.

Irene cast her eye about the room like a combatant assessing the field before joining the fray. Such gatherings held no terrors for her; this was the opposition of course, the other parents, but she knew that she had little to fear from any of them. In fact, she felt slightly sorry for them as she surveyed their offspring; that bespectacled teenage boy in the corner of the room, for example, standing with his mother – what an unhealthy specimen, with his sallow complexion and his jeans with holes in the knees. Irene knew how expensive such jeans could be. That boy, she thought, is a fashion victim and that mother of his does nothing to prevent it. Sad.

Her gaze moved on to the rather prim young girl seated at one of the tables, her oboe case balanced on her knee and her mother proudly sitting opposite her. Such a consummately middle-class pair, thought Irene: the daughter at St Margaret's, perhaps; the father – at the office, probably – a lawyer of some sort; their Volvo parked somewhere on the edge of the Meadows. Irene stopped. She had a Volvo, too, of course, or used to have one. Let those without Volvos make the first social judgment, she told herself, and smiled at her wit.

"You can sit down here, Bertie," she said, pointing to a chair beside one of the tables. "I shall go and get some coffee. But I won't get you a cup, Bertie, as we don't want you wanting to rush off to the little boys' room for a tinkle in the middle of the audition, do we?" Bertie felt his heart stop with embarrassment. It was bad enough for his mother to say such things in any circumstances, but for her to say it here, in the middle of the Queen's Hall, with the eyes of the world upon him, was horror itself. His face burning red, he looked about him quickly. A girl at a neighbouring table had clearly heard, and was giggling and whispering to her friend. And there, on the other side of their very table, was a boy who had also heard and was now staring at him.

The boy, who looked barely thirteen, glanced at Irene as she made towards the bar, and then turned to face Bertie. "Is that your mother?" he asked.

Bertie shook his head. "No," he said. And then added, for emphasis: "No, she's nothing to do with me."

"Who is she then?" asked the boy.

"She's just somebody I met on the bus," he said. "I talked to her and then she followed me in."

The boy looked surprised. "You have to be careful about talking to strangers," he said. "Haven't you been told that?"

Bertie nodded. "I know," he said. "It's just that I felt sorry for her." He racked his brains for a credible story, and then continued: "She's just been let out of a lunatic asylum, you see. They let them out every Saturday, and she had nobody to talk to her. So I did."

"Oh," said the boy. "Do you think she's dangerous?"

"Not really," said Bertie. "Or maybe just a little bit. But she's very strange, you know. She's pretending to be my mother, I think."

"Some grown-ups are really sad," said the boy.

"Yes," agreed Bertie. "It's really sad."

He looked at the boy. If he could make a friend here, then the ordeal of being the youngest person present, by far, would be lessened. And this boy, who had what looked like a trombone case with him, seemed to be friendly enough. "What's your name?" Bertie asked.

The boy smiled. "I'm called Harry," he said. "And you?"

Bertie swallowed. "I'm called Tom," he said.

"But she called you Bertie," said Harry. "That woman called you Bertie. I heard her."

Bertie shook his head. "Yes," he said. "It's sad, isn't it? I think she calls everybody Bertie. It's her illness talking."

Harry nodded. "Look," he said. "If you need to get away from her, I can help you. We can go and hide in the toilet while she's getting her coffee. I suppose she'll go away after a while. How about it?"

Bertie looked towards the bar. He had never run away from his mother before, although he had once managed to get as far as Dundas Street. He did not wish to run away, having decided that he would sit his childhood out until that magical date when he turned eighteen, but the humiliation he had just suffered at the hands of his mother seemed to him now to justify a strong response. But he was not sure whether hiding with Harry would solve anything. What if Irene panicked when she found him missing and started to scream? Or what if she saw him going into the toilets and came in after him to drag him out? She was quite capable of doing that, he thought, and he imagined the scene if Irene went into the men's room. He closed his eyes. He could not bear to think about it. "Too late," muttered Harry rising to his feet. "Look out, here she comes. I'm taking off. See you!"

Irene, reaching the table, put down her cup of coffee and lowered herself into the chair beside her son. "It's going to be very easy for you, Bertie," she said. "I was talking to one of the other mummies at the bar, and she said that the conductor is a good friend of Lewis Morrison. So I'm sure that he'll be kind to Mr Morrison's pupils."

"He may not know," muttered Bertie.

"Of course he'll know," said Irene. "Naturally, I'm going to have a word with him beforehand. I'll make sure that he knows just who you are."

Bertie looked at the ground in despair. "Mummy," he said. "Please take me home. That's all I'm asking you. Please just take me home."

Irene leaned forwards. "Later, Bertie, carissimo," she said. "I'll take you home after the audition. And that's a promise."

40. Bertie Plays the Blues

There were at least one hundred hopeful young musicians assembled in the hall for the orchestral audition. The young people ranged between the age of thirteen and eighteen, although there were one or two nineteen-year-olds and Bertie, of course, who was six. The teenagers had been instructed to sit in the first five rows of seats at the front and, in the case of those with large instruments, the cellists, bass players and bassoonists, in a cluster of seats to the side of the stage. The auditions were by section, and the aspirants were free to wander out of the hall until their section was called, as long as they kept their voices down and did not allow the door to bang shut when they left or came in.

To his horror, Bertie found that his mother insisted on sitting next to him in the fourth row. Nobody else's parents sat anywhere near them, he noted. Most of the parents sat at the back with their friends, or had remained in the bar. But Irene insisted, and Bertie sank down in his seat, trying to persuade himself that not only was she not there, but that neither was he. He had remembered reading somewhere that the best way of dealing with unpleasant moments was to try to imagine that one was somewhere else altogether. So he closed his eyes and conjured up a picture of himself in Waverley Station, watching the trains coming in, his friend Tofu at his side. Tofu had a large bar of chocolate and was breaking off a piece and handing it to him. And he felt happy, curiously happy, to be there with his friend, just by themselves.

He felt a nudge in his ribs. "We'll be next," whispered Irene. "It's woodwind next."

"Shouldn't I go on with the brass?" asked Bertie. "Maybe just after the trombones?"

"But you're woodwind, Bertie," said Irene reproachfully. "You know that the saxophone is technically woodwind."

Bertie bit his lip. His mother's insistence that he should audition even when there was no call for saxophones was perhaps the most embarrassing aspect of the entire experience. It was bad enough being six and trying to get into a teenage orchestra, but being six and a saxophonist, was even worse. Nobody else had brought a saxophone with them; everybody else, everyone, had a conventional orchestral instrument with them.

At a signal from a woman who was helping the conductor, a small knot of oboists made their way to the front of the hall.

"You get up now, Bertie," said Irene. "Woodwind now."

Bertie did nothing. His mother was giving him no alternative. He did not want to put his plan into effect, but she really left him with no choice.

"Come on," said Irene, rising to her feet and pulling Bertie up by the straps of his pink dungarees. "I'll come with you."

"Please, Mummy," pleaded Bertie. "Please . . ."

It was to no avail. Virtually frogmarched to the front, Bertie approached the conductor at his table.

"Tenor saxophone," said Irene, pushing Bertie forward. "Bertie Pollock."

The conductor looked up. "Saxophone?" he said. "Well, I'm afraid . . ."

"His sight-reading is excellent," said Irene. "And he can transpose very well, too. He can easily go from B flat to E flat, so you can let him play the tenor horn part. I don't see any tenor horns around. Bertie can fill that gap for you."

"Well," said the conductor. "It's a different timbre, you know. I'm not sure that . . ."

"Or the euphonium part," went on Irene. "I take it that you want a bit of slightly richer bass. I don't see any tuba players. You don't want to sound thin, do you?"

The conductor exchanged a glance with the woman beside him, who was smiling, lips pursed. Irene shot the woman a warning glance.

"He's a bit young, isn't he?" ventured the woman. "This is the Edinburgh Teenage Orchestra, after all. We've never had anybody that young . . ."

Irene's eyes flashed. "That, if I may say so, is a somewhat unhelpful remark," she said coldly. "Do you really want to stifle talent by discriminating against younger musicians?"

She waited for an answer, but none came. The conductor looked at the woman, as if seeking moral support. She shrugged.

"Oh, very well then," said the conductor wearily. "Go up on stage, Bertie. And just play us this piece, the first fifteen bars, that's all. Do you think you can manage?"

Bertie looked at the sheet of music. It was not all difficult. Grade five, he thought, or six perhaps; both of which examinations he had recently passed with distinction. It would be easy to play that piece. But no: he would now have to put his plan into operation. He would not play what was before him. Instead, he would play something quite different, something defiant. That would surely lead to his rejection; if one would not play what one was meant to play, then one should not be in an orchestra – that was obvious.

He mounted the stage and walked over to the music stand. He placed the sheet of music on the stand and hitched his saxophone onto its sling, at first ignoring the sea of faces in front of him. But then he saw that one or two were laughing. They were looking at him, and laughing at him; laughing at the fact that he had a saxophone, he thought; laughing at the fact that he was only six; laughing at the fact that he was wearing pink dungarees.

Bertie raised the mouthpiece to his lips and blew the first note. Closing his eyes, he continued and soon was well into a fine rendition of 'As Time Goes By' from *Casablanca*, the same piece that he practised so regularly directly below Pat's bedroom in Scotland Street; a fine rendition, perhaps, but a disobedient one, and one which would be bound to irritate the conductor. When he came to the end of the piece, he lowered the saxophone and glanced quickly at his mother. She would be angry with him, he knew, but it would be better to face her anger than to be forced into a teenage orchestra.

The conductor was silent for a moment. Then, rising to his feet, he clapped his hands together.

"Brilliant!" he exclaimed loudly. "What a brilliant performance, young man! You're in!"

41. *Delta of George Street*

"You clever little boy!" said Irene, as she bundled Bertie out of the Queen's Hall and into the street outside. "It was rather a risky thing to do, of course, but, my goodness, didn't it pay off!"

Bertie, his eyes downcast, said nothing. As far as he had been concerned, the audition had been a complete disaster. Not only was there that unfortunate episode in which his mother made that embarrassing comment within earshot of Harry, but then his playing and his deliberate disobedience had brought exactly the opposite result to that which he had intended. He was now a member of the Edinburgh Teenage Orchestra and would be obliged to go with the other players to Paris, with his mother in attendance. It would be bearable – just – if he went by himself, but that was not to be. Nobody else would have their mother with them; and none of them, he was sure, would be forced to go to bed at seven o'clock. Nobody went to bed at seven in Paris, even French children. *Les enfants* stayed up late at night, he had heard, eating with the adults, sipping red wine, and discussing the latest books and films. French mothers were obviously not like his own; French boys did not do yoga.

Irene glanced down at him. "Are you all right, Bertie?" she

asked. And then, answering her own question, she said: "Of course you are. You're as thrilled as I am. I can tell."

Bertie shook his head. "I don't want to be in it," he said. "I told you that a hundred times. You never listen, Mummy."

"Of course I listen," said Irene, pulling Bertie along. "I listen to you all the time, Bertie. Mummy is a listening mummy! It's just that sometimes mummies have to take decisions for their boys if their boys are not quite old enough to know what's good for them. You'll thank me, Bertie. You just wait. You'll thank me."

Bertie was not sure that he would, but he knew that there was no point in arguing with his mother. He sighed, and looked at his watch. It was a Saturday, and that meant yoga in Stockbridge, in the course entitled Bendy Fun for Tots. If Bertie felt that he was too young to be a member of the Edinburgh Teenage Orchestra, then he felt that he was far too old to go to Bendy Fun for Tots. In that class, he seemed to be the oldest by far; the other member of the class nearest in age to him was a four-year-old boy called Sigi, whose mother was friendly with Irene and discussed Melanie Klein with her. The other children seemed to be much younger still and had to be helped into the yoga position because they were unable to stand yet.

Bertie wished that after the excitement of the audition his mother would forget about yoga, and his hopes were considerably raised when she suggested that they get off the bus at George Street so that she could go to the bookshop. Although he wanted only to go home, Bertie felt that a visit to the bookshop, which would distract his mother from yoga, was worthwhile, and he would, if necessary, prolong the expedition by offering advice on what books were available.

"What are you looking for, Mummy?" asked Bertie, once they reached the bookshop. "More Melanie Klein?"

Irene laughed. "Dear Bertie!" she said. "No, I have rather a lot by Melanie Klein, you know. I'm after something different. I feel in the mood for something to entertain me."

Bertie stood on his tip-toes to look at the piles of books on a display table. "There are some nice books here, Mummy," he said. "Look. That one looks exciting. How about that one?"

Irene looked to where Bertie's small finger was pointing. "No dear," she said. "Anaïs Nin. I think not, somehow."

"But it looks like a nice book, Mummy," said Bertie. "There's a lady on the cover. Look."

Irene smiled. "Believe me, Bertie, that's not what I had in mind."

Bertie looked at the other books. There were several Patrick O'Brian novels, with pictures of sailing ships, their cannons blasting away at each other. The ships had sail upon sail, all the way up their towering masts, and the tiny figures of men, and boys too, it seemed, scaled the rigging.

"Look," said Bertie. "There's a book by Mr O'Brian, Mummy. Daddy has read some of those. Should we get one for Daddy?"

Irene looked disdainfully at the naval tale. "Pure masculine fantasy," she said. "Escape to sea, to a world without women. Rather sad, in a way."

Bertie looked puzzled. He did not see anything wrong with escaping to sea to escape women. He wondered if they still took cabin boys in the Navy. If they did, then perhaps he could enlist and go off to sea from Leith. They would not let his mother come with them – the Navy was fussy about things like that – and she would have to wave to him from the shore. But the other sailors would not know that she was his mother, and they might think that she was just a strange woman who liked to wave to ships. So that would not be too embarrassing. And perhaps Tofu could come with him, as a cabin boy too, and they could climb the rigging together and keep a look-out for other ships, up there, high on the mast, almost in the clouds. It would feel like flying, he thought, almost like flying.

Irene looked at her watch. "Bertie, dear," she began. And his spirits sank. Yoga. But no. "Bertie, dear," she said. "You'll never guess who I've just seen! Dr Fairbairn! I think I'll just pop up and have a quick chat with him in the coffee room upstairs. Would you mind? You could maybe look at some of the books in the children's section. They have a nice little chair through there."

Bertie did not mind in the least. He had no desire to see his therapist. It was bad enough seeing him in his consulting rooms. She was welcome to him. But then he thought: what does she want to chat to him about? Could it be about the baby? Bertie had had a dream in which he saw his future baby brother clad in a romper suit made of the same blue linen as Dr Fairbairn's jacket. It had been very strange, very disconcerting.

42. Empower Points

Pat had decided that she would have to do something about Wolf. It seemed to her that Wolf had far from broken off with Tessie, and this led to the conclusion that he envisaged having two girlfriends at the same time. Now, Pat knew that there were some men who liked the idea of such arrangements. On her ill-fated trip to Australia, she had read a novel in which an airline pilot had kept two wives, each in a different city. That was outrageous (although very clever), even if Bruce, to whom she had described the plot, had merely leered at her and said: "Lucky man." That was typical of Bruce, of course, and she shuddered at the memory of her unlamented landlord.

And yet, in spite of her distaste for Lotharios such as Bruce, she found herself wondering – and she did feel rather guilty about it – what it would be like to have two boyfriends. Did she, as a woman, disapprove as much of that as she did of the idea that a man might have two girlfriends? It was an interesting thought. What if she were to have Wolf as her exciting boyfriend (a sort of mistress, so to speak; perhaps the masculine term was master, but surely not) and Matthew as her solid, dependable boyfriend? That's exactly what men did when they kept a mistress, was it not? They had their wife, who was solid and dependable, and who kept the home going, and then they had a younger and more exciting woman tucked away in a flat somewhere, to be visited from time to time and indulged in expensive clothes and Belgian chocolates. Belgian chocolates had come to mind, but, she asked herself, did mistresses actually eat Belgian chocolates? It seemed likely that they did, sitting there on their pink sofas, in Moray Place perhaps. The image seemed somehow quite right, and she smiled at the thought.

She looked out of the window. She was sitting at her desk in the gallery, waiting for Matthew to return from his prolonged coffee-break at Big Lou's, paging through the catalogue of an impending sale. Women, she thought, were generally the victims of masculine bad behaviour largely because men, for all that they affected to have absorbed the lessons of equality, had steadfastly refused to change their ways. Men wanted to be in control; to take the initiative; to determine the pace and circumstances of a relationship. Many women, of course, were perfectly content that this should be so, and quietly allowed men to assert themselves, or at least enjoy the appearance of being the dominant sex. But others were determined that men should not get away with this and battled to assert themselves. The word for this, Pat knew, was empowerment. Every time a man was cut down to size, a woman was empowered.

In a sudden moment of stark self-appraisal, there in the gallery, Pat reflected on her position. What was she? A middle-class Edinburgh girl, attractive enough, intelligent enough, but amounting to . . . to nothing. I make nothing happen. I do nothing unusual. I have never challenged anything. I am an observer. I lack . . . What do I lack? And the answer seemed to her to be so immediately obvious. Power.

She was disempowered – completely disempowered.

She let the catalogue slip out of her hands and down onto the floor. It seemed to her that if she was going to change, to make something of her life, she should start getting what she wanted in life. She had never done this before. She had let other people decide for her; she had deferred to those who already had what they wanted and tried to get still more. Why should she be worried about what Tessie thought of her? If she wanted Wolf, then she should go out and get him. And if Tessie resented that, then let her do so. She would not be bullied by a girl like that, with her split ends and her broken nose. For all she knew, Tessie, who was definitely empowered, had herself taken Wolf from another girl. Well, whether or not that had happened, now she would find out what it was to come up against a newly-empowered woman.

Of course, there would have to be some reparative work. She had told Wolf in the lecture that she was not interested, and then, when he followed her to the Elephant House, she had thrown him to the mercy of her new friend, Sister Connie. It had been an eye-opener to see how the otherwise gentle nun had succeeded in dealing with Wolf. She had stridden across to his table, sat down opposite him, and spoken to him in an urgent and confidential way. Pat had noticed Wolf's reaction to this. He had listened intently and then, visibly backing off, he had risen to his feet and left the coffee house, barely looking back as he did so.

She had not managed to find out from Sister Connie what she had said to him. When the nun had returned to the table she had asked, but Sister Connie had merely smiled and raised a finger to her lips in a gesture of silence.

"Don't you worry," she said. "I warned him off. He won't be troubling you again."

She had not thought much more about it, but now that she might see Wolf again, she might have to undo Sister Connie's work, whatever that had been. She took out the small red diary that she always carried with her. Wolf had given her his mobile phone number, and she had written it down in the notebook. She found the number and picked up the telephone.

Wolf answered almost immediately, with the lupine howl that he gave to identify himself. It was very witty, very clever.

"It's Pat," she said.

There was complete silence at the other end of the line, or

almost complete, for Pat thought that she heard an intake of breath – not quite a gasp, but certainly an intake of breath.

Then Wolf spoke. "I'm sorry," he said. "I can't talk now. Goodbye."

"But Wolf . . ."

"I said that I can't talk."

There was a crackling sound, and Pat realised that somebody else had seized the phone.

"Is that you?" came Tessie's unmistakable voice. "Is that you? You listen to me. I warned you. I warned you. You leave my Wolfie alone. Understand?"

43. *Matthew Comforts Pat*

Pat was still upset when Matthew returned from Big Lou's. He noticed it immediately, and sat down beside her.

"There's something wrong," he said.

Pat shook her head; she could see that he was concerned, but she was not going to tell him.

"Yes, there is. There obviously is." He reached out and took her hand. "Come on. You're not very good at hiding things, you know. You're upset."

Pat felt the pressure of his hand upon hers. She had never had that degree of physical contact with Matthew, and it seemed strange to her. His hand felt warm and dry.

Matthew smiled. "That's better. Come on. What is it?" He paused, fixing her with a searching look. She noticed the grey flecks in his eyes, which she had often thought about before – they were so unusual, so unlikely; she noticed the slight stain on the front of his sweater. He was not wearing his new distressed-oatmeal cashmere today, but had on the sweater that she had seen him wear at weekends, an old, navy-blue garment that had lost its shape.

"I suppose I've just had a bit of a shock," she said. "I'll get over it."

Matthew raised an eyebrow. "It's that boy, isn't it?" he said gently. "That boy – the one with the name. Wolf. It's him, isn't it?"

Pat nodded miserably. "It's about him, I suppose. Although actually it's about his girlfriend."

If Matthew felt relief, he did not show it. "So he's let you down," he said evenly. This was very good news. Wolf was a two-timer; of course he was! "You know, I was worried that something like this would happen. I never liked him."

Pat looked up sharply. "You never met him," she pointed out.

He waved a hand in the air. "You know what I mean. You can dislike people you've never met. I sensed that he wasn't right for you. I sensed it."

Pat felt herself becoming irritated. She still felt defensive of Wolf, who had done nothing wrong as far as she was concerned – other than wanting to have two girlfriends at the same time. What worried her was Tessie, and the difficulty she would now face on going back to the flat. The animus in Tessie's voice, the sheer vitriol, was such that she simply could not see herself going back to Spottiswoode Street. She could not imagine how she could possibly face that unpleasant girl, and she could hardly live under the same roof and not see her. They each had their own room of course, but there was the bathroom and the kitchen, which were shared, and the front door and the stair too. She wondered what she should do if they both came back at the same time and had to climb the stair together. Would they do so in tight-lipped silence, or would one rush ahead to get away from the other? No, it was impossible. She would have to move out. She would have to find somewhere else to live.

She looked at Matthew. She should not be offended that he had taken against Wolf as he had. It was flattering, really, to have about her somebody like Matthew, who at least liked her enough to feel jealousy. And if his fondness for her was sometimes awkward, then perhaps indifference would have been more difficult.

She gave his hand a squeeze. "I'm sorry, Matthew," she said. "I'm sorry. I know that you . . . that you worry about me."

Matthew smiled reassuringly. "I suppose I do worry," he said. "I don't want you to get hurt. That's all."

Pat moved her hand away from his, but did so gently. She began to explain to him about Tessie and her hostility, and she told him about her snatching the telephone from Wolf.

"She's frightening," she said. "She really is. It seems that she'll do anything to keep him."

Matthew's expression was grim. "You can't go back there," he said. "Or you can't go back there by yourself. Why don't I go back with you and help you get your things?"

Pat looked relieved. Tessie would hardly try anything if Matthew were present, and then she could . . . She stopped. It was all very well planning to collect her possessions and move out of Spottiswoode Street, but where would she move to? She could not go back to Scotland Street, and she could think of no particular friends on whose floor she could ask to stay. She would have to go home, and that, in spite of the comfort and security which it represented, would be an unacceptable admission of failure. Her father would be nice about it, she thought, and her mother, if she was there, would hardly notice. But it would be so demeaning to have to go home after trying so hard to establish her independence.

"I don't know," she said. "I really don't know. I haven't got anywhere to go, you see. I can't think . . ." She looked around her, mentally sizing up the gallery for living purposes. She could have a bed in the back room – it was easily big enough – and she could keep her clothes in the walk-in cupboard they used to store paintings. It would be possible, just possible, particularly if one ate at Big Lou's and did not have to bother too much about cooking.

Matthew reached forward and took her hand again. "Now listen," he said. "I have a suggestion to make, and I want you to take it very seriously. I'm not just saying this – I'm not. You come and stay in India Street. I've got plenty of room and you can have the spare room at the back. It's nice there. It's very quiet."

Pat looked down at the floor. There was no doubt in her mind but that Matthew was trying to be helpful. There was no ulterior motive in this invitation – she was sure of that – but it would be a major step to share a flat with him. What if he wanted to be something more than her landlord, more than her flatmate? And he would want that – of course he would; she was sure of that.

But in spite of this conviction, this certainty, she thanked him for his offer – and accepted.

"Good girl," said Matthew, and closed his eyes at the thought.

44. *Angus Lordie Prepares to Entertain*

Angus Lordie felt disgruntled. He had woken early that morning – rather earlier than he had wanted to – and had found it difficult to get back to sleep. Now it was six o'clock, and still dark. In the summer, when the mornings were so bright and optimistic, he would sometimes make his way into his studio and paint for several hours. He loved those summer mornings, when the city was quiet and the air so fresh. Life seemed somehow richer in possibilities at that hour; it was like being young again; yes, that was what it was like, he thought. When you are young, the world is in better definition, clearer; it is a feeling not dissimilar to that which one had after the first sip of champagne, before the dulling effect of excess. But now, in the autumn, with the drawing in of days, the morning hours lacked all that, and painting could only begin much later on, after breakfast.

What produced this sense of disgruntlement on that particular day was the fact that Angus was due to entertain that night. He enjoyed dinner parties – in fact, he relished them – but in general, he preferred to be a guest rather than a host. It was such a bother, he thought, to have to cook everything and then to serve it. He found it difficult to relax and enjoy the conversation if he had to keep an eye on the needs of his guests. And at the end of it all, of course, there was the mess which had to be cleared up. Angus kept his flat tidy – it was rather like the galley of a well-run ship, in fact; somewhat Spartan, with everything neatly stacked and stored.

Of course, this preference for being entertained rather than entertaining had not escaped the notice of others. If records were kept of these things, in the same way in which certain denizens of London society kept lists of the season's parties – and that was never done in Edinburgh – then Angus Lordie's debit columns would heavily outweigh anything in his credit columns. In fact, his credit columns would be completely blank, unless one counted buying lunch for one or two friends in the Scottish Arts Club as a credit. And the friends for whom he had bought lunch were themselves noted more for the eating of meals than for paying for them. And as for those who had invited him to their large parties in places such as East Lothian, they did so in the sure and certain knowledge that their hospitality would never be repaid. Not that they minded, of course; Angus was witty and entertaining company, and nobody expected a bachelor to be much good at reciprocation.

"He's such a charming man," remarked one hostess to a friend. "Men like that are such fun."

"But he's absolutely no good," said the friend. "A convinced bachelor. No use at all."

"Such a waste," said the first woman.

"Criminal."

They were both silent. Then: "Remember when" – and here she mentioned the name of a prominent lawyer who, some years back, had become a widower – "Remember when he came on the market and there was that mad dash, and she got there first?"

The other thought for a moment. She shook her head. There were other cases too, though none as egregiously tragic for a number of hopefuls as that one.

"Of course, Angus is very friendly with that woman who lives in Scotland Street. That frightful blue-stocking . . ."

"Domenica Macdonald."

"Exactly. The one who went off somewhere on some madcap project."

"But there's nothing between them, surely?"

"No. They gossip together. That's all."

"So sad."

"Criminal."

But now Angus was cornered and found himself committed

to the holding of a dinner party in Drummond Place. This situation had come about as a result of an undertaking he had rashly given to Domenica shortly before her departure for the Malacca Straits. She had asked him to give her an assurance that he would invite to his flat Antonia Collie, her friend who was occupying her flat in her absence.

"She knows very few people in Edinburgh, Angus," Domenica had said. "And she is an old friend. I don't expect you to fall over yourself, but do at least have her round for a meal. Promise me that, will you?"

Angus felt that he could hardly refuse. He gave his word that he would invite her within a week of her arrival, and on the sixth day he had pushed an envelope through Antonia's letter-box and walked down the stairs quickly in case she should come out and invite him in. He did not want to see much of her. She's insufferably pleased with herself, he thought. And she has that arrogance of those whose modest amount of talent has gone to their head.

He considered how he might dilute her company. If he invited four other guests, then he could place her at the far end of the table, opposite his own seat at the head, and then he would have two guests on either side of the table between himself and Antonia. In this way, he would not have to listen to her at all and she would, in turn, find it difficult to condescend to him.

But it was not just the seating plan that Angus had been contemplating – there was also the menu to consider. His own taste tended towards uncomplicated fare – to lamb chops with mashed potatoes, to smoked salmon on brown bread, to venison stew with red cabbage. But he was aware that such dishes would not do for a dinner party of sophisticates – and Antonia would certainly consider herself a sophisticate. She may have drawn the conclusion that he knew little about fiction – but he would not allow her to draw a similar conclusion about his culinary ability. With this in mind, he had gone to some trouble to plan a meal of considerable complexity. He had consulted the book which he had received for his birthday from a female cousin some years previously, *Dear Francesca*, a book of memoirs and recipes, and had made a note of the ingredients he would need: pasta, extra virgin olive oil, anchovy fillets, Parmigiano Reggiano. His mouth watered.

"Come, Cyril," he announced. "Time to go shopping."

Cyril looked at his master. For some reason, he experienced a sudden sense of foreboding. But, being a dog, he had no means of articulating this, no means of warning.

45. *A Memory of Milanese Salami*

With Cyril trotting beside him, Angus Lordie made his way along London Street and turned up Broughton Street to complete his journey to Valvona & Crolla. Although he rarely bought anything more adventurous than a packet of dried pasta, he liked the authentic Italian feeling which he derived from browsing its shelves. On this visit, of course, there were more ambitious ingredients to be bought: fresh Parmesan cheese, for example; tagliatelle which were rich in eggs; olive oil from tiny, named estates in the Sienese hills; perhaps even a small jar of Moscatelli's grated truffles, as a treat. He would choose these ingredients with care, so that when that opinionated Antonia Collie came to dinner he could subtly put her in her place (what would she know about truffles, or vintage olive oil?) He thought of her condescension, and bristled. Who did she imagine she was? Breezing into Scotland Street like that from Perthshire and implying – or even doing more than that – stating, in fact, that he did not understand the nature of fiction. Domenica, for all her faults – and he thought that one day he might present her with a list of them, just to be of some assistance – never condescended to anybody. Indeed, she went to the opposite extreme, and assumed that those to whom she was talking shared her understanding, which was generous of her, as they usually did not. That was such a courtesy, and it was so refreshing to see it in operation. Such people made one feel better by just being with them. One was admitted to the presence of a liberal intelligence and made to feel welcome; made to feel at home.

Outside the shop, Angus looked down at Cyril, who gazed back up at him in expectation. Cyril loved going to Valvona & Crolla, but Angus had been reluctant to take him inside ever since Cyril had lost control of himself and snatched a small but expensive Milanese salami from the counter and gobbled it up before Angus had a chance to snatch it from his jaws. Nobody in the shop had noticed a thing, and Angus had felt torn over what to do in such circumstances. There were many different responses to such a situation. On the one hand, there were those who felt no compunction over eating in supermarkets and then walking out, replete, and not paying for what they had consumed. Angus himself had once witnessed a woman feeding processed cheese to her child in the dairy-products section of his local supermarket. He had stopped and stared at her in astonishment and their eyes, for a few instants, had met. What he had seen was not shame, as he had expected, but something quite else: the look of challenge of those who believe that they are doing nothing wrong.

Such a view was unconscionable – eating the food in a supermarket was simply theft, and could be distinguished from shoplifting only by virtue of the nature of the container used to remove the property. But in this case, when the salami had been eaten by Cyril, he had not intended to take any property that did not belong to him, and that made a difference. As he thought about it, he saw that there was a similarity with a situation where one mistakenly took the umbrella of another in the belief that the umbrella was one's own. That was not theft; that was a mistake. Of course then, when one discovered the error, the umbrella should be returned to the person to whom it belonged, or one might then become a thief by keeping. So, too, in this situation, although the salami could not be returned to its rightful owner, there was clearly a moral duty to report the incident at the cash desk and offer to pay.

Angus had ordered Cyril to desist, but for a short time the dog had completely ignored him, so lost was he in the pleasure of eating the salami. But then, the salami consumed and lingering only in the faint odour of garlic that hung about him, Cyril had been struck by the enormity of what he had done and had looked up at his master in trepidation. Angus rarely struck Cyril, and now he merely shook his head and spoke to him quietly and at length in a low voice that was every bit as effective as one that was raised. The words, of course, meant nothing to Cyril, apart from bad dog, which he recognised and which cut him to the quick. Cyril had no word for temptation, nor for irresistible, and could not explain that what had happened had been beyond his control. So he lay there and endured the shame.

Angus offered to pay, and when his offer was cheerfully declined on the grounds that such things happened – a most understanding response, he thought; but Italians, and this included Italo-Scots, always had a soft spot for dogs, and people too, for everything in fact – he had voluntarily offered to leave Cyril outside on his next visit to the shop. Now, standing outside the delicatessen, he looked about for a suitable place to tie Cyril's lead. The pavement at that point was broad and without railings, but the civic authorities had thoughtfully placed a bicycle rack nearby, and he thought that this would provide a handy tethering post for Cyril.

"I won't be long," he explained, as he fastened the leash to the rack. "Sorry, you can't come in. It's your record, you see. A small matter of a Milanese salami. Remember?"

He gave Cyril a pat on the head and entered the shop. A few minutes later, while Angus was examining a small bottle of olive oil, holding it up to the light to determine its clarity, a young man in a black T-shirt and jeans walked up to Cyril and bent down to ruffle his fur.

Cyril, always eager for human company, but particularly so when tied up on the street, licked at the young man's hand. His keen nose smelled tobacco, and something else, something he could not identify and which was unfamiliar, and sharp. He drew back a bit, and looked at the young man. He felt unsure, and he looked at the door of Valvona & Crolla. A bus passed, and Cyril smelled the fumes. He looked up;

there was a seagull hovering nearby, and he caught a slight smell of fish and bird.

The young man was undoing his lead. He was being dragged. He was confused. Was he being sent away? What had he done?

46. *A Conversation about Angels etc*

Inside the delicatessen, unaware of the drama being enacted outside, Angus Lordie carefully replaced on its shelf the bottle of olive oil he had been examining.

"That," said a voice behind him, "is a particularly good oil. We've been selling it for some time now. Poggio Lamentano. It's made from the Zyws' olives. Gorgeous stuff. This is the new vintage, which has just arrived – you can taste it, if you like."

Angus turned round and recognised Mary Contini. He had met her socially once or twice – and of course it was she who had written *Dear Francesca* – but he was not sure whether she remembered him. Her next comment, however, made it clear that she did. "You're a painter, aren't you? We met at . . ." She waved a hand in the air.

Angus nodded, although he, too, had forgotten the name of their host. He, too, waved a hand in the air – in the direction of the New Town. "It was somewhere over there," he said, and laughed. Then there was a brief silence. "I'm cooking a meal," he said lamely, as if to explain his presence. It was rather a trite thing to say, of course, but she did not seem to mind.

"They're a painting family too," she said, pointing at the bottle of oil. "They had a studio down in the Dean Village, overlooking the Water of Leith. But they have this place in Tuscany and they produce the most beautiful oil. I've visited it. Wonderful place."

"I would be very happy living in Italy," said Angus. "Tuscany in particular."

"What artist wouldn't be?" asked Mary Contini.

Angus gazed up at the ceiling. He knew of some artists who

would not like Italy; some artists, he thought, have no sense of the beautiful and would be ill at ease in a landscape like that. He was tempted to name them, but no, not amidst all this olive oil and Chianti. "In Tuscany, I have always thought one is in the presence of angels," he said. "In fact, I am sure of it."

Mary Contini looked intrigued. "Angels?" she said.

"Yes," said Angus, warming to his theme. "Have you come across that marvellous poem by Alfred Alvarez? 'Angels in Italy'. Written in Tuscany, of course, where Alvarez has a villa."

Mary Contini thought for a moment, and then shook her head.

"He describes how he is standing in his vineyard and suddenly he sees a choir of angels – that is the collective term for angels, I believe – or shall I say a flight of angels? – somehow that seems more appropriate for angels in motion; choirs are more static, aren't they? He sees this flight of angels crossing the sky, and it seems so natural, so right. Isn't that marvellous? And there they are, flying across the Tuscan sky while below them everybody is just carrying on with their day-to-day business. Somebody is cutting wood with a buzz-saw. The leaves of the vines rattle like dice. And so on."

"I can just see it," said Mary Contini.

Angus smiled. "Of course, angels are an intrinsically interesting subject. Especially if one has little else to do with one's time. Like those early practitioners of angelology who speculated about the number of angels who could stand on the head of a pin."

"I've always thought of angels as being rather big," said Mary Contini.

"Exactly," said Angus. "Mind you, there are an awful lot of them, I believe. The fourteenth-century cabalists said that there were precisely 301,655,722. Quite how they worked that out, I have no idea. But there we are." He sighed. He enjoyed a conversation of this sort – but ever since Domenica had gone away, there seemed to be so few people with whom to have it. And here he was taking up this busy person's time with talk of angels and the Tuscan countryside. "I must get on," he said. "One cannot stand about all day and talk about angels. Or olive oil, for that matter."

She laughed. "I am always happy to talk about either," she said, and she nodded to him politely and moved on. He reached for a bottle of olive oil and placed it in his shopping basket. Then, with his small collection of purchases selected, he made his way to the till, paid, and went out into the street.

He looked for Cyril, and saw that he was not there. He stopped, and stood quite still. Fumbling with the bag of purchases, he dropped it, and it fell onto the pavement, where the bottle of olive oil shattered. A slow green ooze trickled out of the crumpled bag. It soaked into his loaf of rosemary bread. It trickled down into a crack in the pavement.

Somebody passing by hesitated, about to ask what was wrong, but walked on. Angus looked about him frantically. He had tied Cyril's leash quite tightly – he always did. But even if Cyril had worked it loose, he would never leave the spot in which Angus had left him. He was good that way – it was something to do with his training in Lochboisdale, all those years ago. Cyril knew how to stay.

Angus saw a boy standing nearby. The boy was watching him; this boy with a pasty complexion and his shirt hanging out of his trousers was watching him. He walked over to him. The boy, suspicious, stiffened.

"My dog," he said. "My dog. He was over there. Now . . ."

The boy sniffed. "A boy took it," he said. "He untied him."

Angus gasped. "He took him? Where? Did you see?"

The boy shrugged. "He got on a bus. One of they buses." The boy pointed to a red bus lumbering past.

"You didn't see which one?"

"No," said the boy. He looked down at the packet on the ground and then back up at Angus. "I've got to go."

Angus nodded. Bending down, he picked up the oil-soaked bag and looked about him, hopelessly. Cyril had been stolen. That was the only conclusion he could reach. His friend, his companion, had been stolen. He had lost him. He was gone.

He walked back to Drummond Place slowly, almost oblivious to his surroundings. Worlds could end in many ways, but, as Eliot had observed, it was usually in little ways, like this.

The car in which Domenica Macdonald was travelling – the car belonging to Edward Hong M.A. (Cantab.) – came to a halt on the outskirts of a small settlement about an hour's drive from the city of Malacca. Ling, the young man who was to be Domenica's guide and mentor in the pirate community, had tapped Edward Hong on the shoulder as they neared the village.

"I'm sorry," Ling said. "We're going to have to walk from here. I'll find a boy to carry the suitcase."

"There are always boys to do these things," said Edward Hong to Domenica. "That's the charming thing about the Far East. I gather that in Europe these days one has run out of boys."

Domenica nodded. "Boys used to be willing to do little tasks," she said. "But no longer."

Edward Hong looked wistful. "When I was a boy," he said, "I was a Scout. Baden-Powell was much admired in these latitudes, you know. And we were taught: always do at least one good deed every day. That's what we believed in. And I did it. I did a good deed every day. Do you think that happens today?"

"Alas, no," said Domenica, as she prepared to get out of the car. "Most children have become very surly. That is because they are not taught to think about others any more. They are, quite simply, spoiled."

"I fear that what you say is right," said Edward Hong. "It is very sad."

They stood outside the car and stretched their legs while Ling went off to the village. Domenica, her head shaded by a large, floppy sun hat – for even with cloud cover, she could feel the weight of the noonday sun – stood on the roadside and gazed out over the surrounding landscape. The village, which seemed to consist of twenty or so houses, straddled the road, which had now narrowed to a single track. The houses were small square buildings, each raised a couple of feet above the ground on wooden pillars. This, she knew, provided both protection from floodwaters and allowed the air to circulate in the heat. The roofs, which were made of palm thatch, were untidy in their appearance, but everything else seemed neat and well-kept. A small group of children stood on the steps of the nearest house, staring at them, while a woman, wearing a red sarong, attended to some task on the veranda. On one side of the village stood a small shop, on the front of which was pinned a sign advertising Coca-Cola. The shop-keeper, standing outside, clad in a dirty vest and a pair of loose-fitting green trousers, seemed to be talking into a mobile telephone, gesticulating furiously with his free hand.

"Village life," said Edward Hong, pointing. "Children. Dogs. A shop-keeper in a dirty vest. It holds no romantic associations for me, I'm afraid."

Domenica laughed. "I don't romanticise these things either," she said. "Most anthropologists know too much about such places to romanticise them. I'm sure that life for these people is thoroughly tedious. They'd love to live in Malacca – I'm sure of it."

"And yet they are better off out here," said Edward Hong. "They may not know it, but they are. Wouldn't you rather live here, in relative comfort, than in some hovel in town – for the privilege of which you would be working all hours of the day in some sweatshop?"

"I don't know," said Domenica. "I just don't know."

Ling now reappeared, accompanied by a teenage boy, bare-shouldered, a printed cloth wound about his waist. He pointed to Domenica's large suitcase, which had been taken out of the car by the chauffeur, and the boy cheerfully picked it up.

"We must go," said Ling. "It's at least two hours' walk from here. Do you have your water bottle?"

Domenica answered by pointing to her small rucksack. Then she turned to Edward Hong and shook his hand. "You have been more than kind, dear Mr Hong," she said. Edward Hong lowered his head in a small bow. "I shall miss your company," he said. "And my daughter will too."

"I shall think of her playing Chopin," said Domenica. "If the company of the pirates becomes a trifle wearisome, I shall think of her playing her Chopin."

They said their final farewells, and then the small party set off, led by Ling, with Domenica in the middle, and the teenage boy bringing up the rear. Edward Hong waved from the car, and Domenica waved back. She knew that she would miss his urbane company; indeed she knew that there was a great deal that she was already missing, and would miss even more over the coming months. She missed her conversations with Angus Lordie. She missed looking out of her window onto Scotland Street. She missed her morning crossword in *The Scotsman*. And when would she next have a cup of foaming cappuccino and a freshly-baked croissant?

I shall not think of any of this, she told herself. I shall be thoroughly professional. I am an anthropologist, after all, heir to a long tradition of endurance in the field. If I had wanted a quiet and comfortable life, then I would have become something else. The furrow I have chosen to plough is a lonely one, involving hardship, deprivation, and danger. Danger! She had forgotten about Ling's almost throwaway comment about the Belgian anthropologist, the one who had preceded her to the village and who was now buried there. She had meant to ask Ling about this, but the direction of the conversation had changed and she had not had the opportunity. Besides, she did not want to give Edward the impression that she was frightened. If she did, then she knew that he would fret for her, and she did not want that.

She looked at Ling's back as he walked in front of her. A large patch of sweat had formed between his shoulder blades, making a dark stain on his shirt. Such circumstances as these, she thought, remind us of just what we are: salt and water, for the most part.

"Ling," she said. "That Belgian anthropologist you mentioned. Could you tell me more about him?"

Ling glanced back at her, but kept on walking. "We don't like to talk about him," he said. "Do you mind?"

Domenica was quick to say that she did not. But his comment puzzled her and, if she were to be honest about her level of anxiety, she would have to admit that it had grown. Considerably.

48. A View of a House

The small party followed a track that led away from the village. The track was narrow, but was wider than a footpath and had obviously been used by vehicles. There was white, sandy soil underfoot, and here and there this had been churned up by the wheels of a vehicle. There were other signs of human passage too – a discarded tin can, roughly opened and rusting; a fruit-juice carton, waxy and crumpled; the print of a sandal on the soil.

Trees grew on either side of the path. These, together with an undergrowth of creeping vines and thick-leaved shrubs, made for a barrier that was dense, if not entirely impenetrable. It would be easy to lose oneself in such surroundings, thought Domenica; one might wander about in circles for days, unable to see any reference points, unable even to work out the direction of the sun's movement. At moments such as this, she mused, dependence on one's guide reminded one of the mutual reliance of human existence. In large numbers, in towns and cities, we forget that without the help of others we are fragile, threatened creatures. But the moment that support is removed, then the reality of our condition becomes apparent. We are all one step from being lost.

After walking for half an hour, Ling called a halt and they sat down on the trunk of an uprooted tree. Domenica reached for her water bottle and took several swigs. The water, which had kept cool in the air-conditioned interior of Edward Hong's car, was now tepid – the temperature of the soupy air about them – and it bore the chemical taste of the purification tablets she had dropped into it. The boy, who had been uncomplainingly carrying Domenica's suitcase, shifting it from hand to hand every so often, was given a small sugared bun, which Ling had extracted from a packet secured to his belt. Domenica was offered one of these buns too, but declined.

"It must be very difficult living in such isolated conditions," she said to Ling. "I suppose they have to bring their supplies all the way down this track."

Ling shook his head. "This track is not used a great deal," he said. "The people in the village we are going to do not come this way very often. They have boats, you see."

Domenica nodded. Of course, the village for which they were heading was on the coast, or close enough to it.

"Where shall I be staying?" she asked. She had been told that accommodation would be arranged, but Edward Hong had not gone into details. All he had said was: "You will probably be somewhat uncomfortable, but I suppose that you anthropologists are used to that sort of thing." And then he had shuddered; not too noticeably, but he had shuddered.

Ling wiped his brow. "You will stay in the village guest house," he said. "It is a small place, just two rooms, which is used for any visitors to the village. It is clean and it is cool too. There is a big tree beside it. That will give you shade." He paused, and smiled. "You will be very happy there."

"Oh, I'm sure I shall," said Domenica. His description of her accommodation had cheered her slightly. A small, cool house in the shade sounded as if it would be perfect.

"And there is another house beside it," Ling went on. "The woman from that house will be your friend. She speaks a little English – not much – but a little. And she is making her sons learn English too. They are just boys, but they will speak to you too."

Domenica liked the sound of that. Ling made it seem no more than moving to a new suburb – a suburb with friendly neighbours.

"This woman," she asked. "She's married to . . ." She paused, unsure as to whether the term pirate seemed a bit extreme, ungenerous perhaps.

"To a pirate," said Ling. "Yes, her husband is a big pirate. He is called Ah, and her name is Zhi-Whei. They have called the boys after ships which . . . which he seized. The older one is called Freighter and the other is called Tanker. They have Chinese names, too, but that is what they are called in the village. They are a good family, and they will be kind to you."

They continued with their journey. As they progressed, the vegetation thinned. The trees, which had towered above them at the beginning, now became sparser. The dense undergrowth, too, was broken up by patches of grass and thinly-covered sand. And as the tree cover diminished, the light changed. There was open sky now, and the air seemed fresher. There was a smell of the sea.

"We're not far now," said Ling eventually. And as he spoke, Domenica heard a snatch of music somewhere in the distance; a radio playing. Then, a little later, she heard a voice – a woman's voice, calling to a child perhaps.

Suddenly the path turned sharply to the right and descended. Ling stopped and pointed ahead. "That is the village," he said.

Domenica looked at the place which was to be her home for the next few months. It was a small settlement – much the same as the village through which they had passed at the beginning of their journey. There was one difference, though: the houses in this village all faced a small bay, the blue waters of which now caught the early afternoon sun. It seemed to Domenica to be idyllic; the sort of place that Gauguin had found on his south sea islands; the sultry shores which he had painted in those rich colours of his; sexual, beguiling landscapes.

"That is your house just over there," said Ling. "You see that one? The one near that big tree? That is your place."

Domenica looked in the direction in which he was pointing. They were not far from the house, and she could make out the details clearly. It seemed to her that it was quite ideal. It was constructed of wooden planks, all painted off-white, and the windows were secured with green, slatted shutters. There was a veranda, too, with what looked like an old planter's chair on it, and a lithe young man in a sarong standing near the front door.

"Who is that young man?" asked Domenica.

Ling turned to look at her. "That is the young man who will be looking after you. He will cook for you and carry things. I will tell you what to pay him." He paused, and added: "He is utterly at your service. You will see."

49. The Story of Art

"Now," said Matthew firmly, as he opened the door of the taxi for Pat, "you've made your decision and you must stick to it! You're unhappy there. Of course you can't continue to live with that ghastly girl."

"You haven't met her," pointed out Pat, as she sat back against the cheerful Royal Stewart rug which the taxi driver had placed on the seat. It was a curious thing about Edinburgh taxis: insofar as they carried rugs, for some reason these were almost always Royal Stewart tartan.

She looked at Matthew, who was leaning forward to give instructions to the driver. It annoyed her that he seemed so ready to make judgments about people whom he had never met. He had done that with Wolf, whom he had disliked instantly, and now he was doing it with Tessie, her flatmate.

Matthew fastened his seat belt. "But of course she's ghastly," he said. "You yourself told me . . ."

"It doesn't matter," said Pat. "Let's change the subject."

Matthew nodded. "Yes," he said. "You have to look forward, Pat. Going to that awful flat was a mistake. A bad mistake. You should have stayed in Scotland Street."

He's doing it again, thought Pat. Matthew had never seen the flat in Spottiswoode Street, and yet he was calling it awful. There was actually nothing awful about it. It was a typical Marchmont student flat – rather nicer, in fact, than many, and she would miss it. But he was right about the need to move. Tessie was ghastly, whichever way one looked at her. She was aggressive. She was suspicious. And she had as good as threatened Pat with physical violence over Wolf.

They travelled up the Mound and made their way along George IV Bridge. On their right, just before they branched off beyond the Museum, they passed the Elephant House, the café where she had first talked to Wolf and where she had subsequently had that intriguing conversation with Sister Connie. "That place," said Matthew, as they drove past. "I had lunch there once."

It was the sort of inconsequential thing that Matthew sometimes said. When she had first gone to work for him, Pat had expected these remarks to lead somewhere, but they rarely did. In another taxi, a long time ago, he had once said to her: "The Churchill Theatre" as they had driven past it, but had said nothing more. Now, as the taxi shot past the little bronze statue of Greyfriars Bobby, Matthew simply said "Dog". Pat smiled to herself. There was something rather reassuring about Matthew. Wolf, and Tessie, and people like that were fundamentally unsettling; Wolf, for his physical attractiveness, and Tessie for her aggression. Matthew, by contrast, was utterly comfortable, and she felt for him a sudden affection. He might not be anything special, but he was a good friend and he was predictable. She would feel safe living with Matthew in India Street, although . . . There were doubts, but this was not the time to have them, just as she was about to leave Spottiswoode Street.

They reached their destination. Matthew insisted on paying the taxi fare, although Pat offered. Then, with Matthew behind her, Pat went up the common stair to the door of her flat.

"Is she likely to be in?" whispered Matthew, as Pat inserted the key.

She was unsure. Tessie kept strange hours; Pat had heard her going out in the early hours of the morning and had often found her in during the afternoons. And then, late at night, she had sometimes heard the sound of raised voices emanating from her room.

"She might be," she answered. "But I hope we don't see her."

Matthew shuddered. "Me too. Horrible girl." He paused. "What about him? Monsieur Loup? Will he be here?"

Pat shrugged. She did not want to see either of them at the moment, she thought, although when it came to Wolf – well . . .

They entered the hall. Tessie's door was closed, but there were faint sounds of music coming from within. She pointed to the door and raised a finger to her lips.

"Hers?" whispered Matthew.

"Yes."

Her own door was slightly ajar, which puzzled her. She always closed it when she left the flat and she thought that she must have done that morning. She hesitated. Could Tessie have done something to her room? The thought crossed her mind, but she tried to dismiss it immediately. That sort of thing did not happen in Edinburgh, in real life, in ordinary student flats in March-mont, in broad daylight.

She pushed the door open cautiously. Everything inside seemed to be as she had left it. There was Sir Ernst Gombrich's *The Story of Art* on the desk. There was her hairbrush and her sponge-bag. There was the picture of the family cat, Morris. There were the trainers she had been about to throw out, their frayed laces in a tangle.

Matthew pointed at the two suitcases balanced on the top of the wardrobe.

"Those?" he said.

Pat nodded and he reached up to retrieve the suitcases. She had fitted everything in those two cases when she had moved in, and so there was no reason why they should not do the move in a single trip. Matthew placed the suitcases on the bed and opened them. Then she began to bundle clothes from the drawers into the cases. She noticed that Matthew turned away and looked out of the window while she did so, and again she felt a rush of fondness for him. It was such a nice, old-fashioned thing to do, the sort of thing that a modern boy would not think of. Modern boys would stare.

Soon the suitcases were filled. It proved to be a tight fit, and the trainers, and one or two other items were ignominiously consigned to the wastepaper bin. Sir Ernst Gombrich would not fit in, but Matthew agreed that Pat should carry him under her arm; he would be able to manage both suitcases, he said, as they would balance one another out.

Pat looked about her. She was sorry to be leaving the room, which she liked, and in which she had been comfortable. But it was too late now to have second thoughts, as Matthew was manoeuvring the cases out of the door, as silently as he could, lest he attract the unwelcome attentions of Tessie. He need not have worried about being quiet, though, because there were now sounds coming from Tessie's room, strange sounds, rather like howls.

50. Bad Behaviour

When they heard the noise coming from behind Tessie's closed door, Pat and Matthew, on the point of leaving the flat, stopped. Lowering the two heavy suitcases to the floor, Matthew looked at Pat in astonishment.

"What on earth . . . ?" he began to whisper, but Pat, still holding Sir Ernst Gombrich's *The Story of Art* under her arm, did not reply. Creeping forward, she inclined an ear to the door. Matthew, embarrassed by such obvious eavesdropping, but curious nonetheless, quickly moved forward to join her at the door.

The howls which they had heard – if they were indeed howls, and it sounded like that to them – had now stopped, to be replaced by a peal of laughter. Then there was a voice, not raised at all, but still audible from outside.

"I wish you wouldn't howl quite so much." It was Tessie.

"Why not? If it makes me happy." There was a pause, and then: "And I know what makes you happy." That was Wolf.

Matthew glanced at Pat. There was something indecent in standing outside somebody's bedroom door and listening to what went on within. He was about to gesture to Pat that they should leave, but then Wolf could be heard again.

"And, as you know, I like to make girls happy. It's my role in life. We all need a hobby."

Tessie snorted. "You're lucky I'm not the jealous type. Most people wouldn't hack it, you know. You're lucky that I don't mind."

"That's because you know I don't mean it," said Wolf. "You know that you're the one. You know that."

"Yes," answered Tessie. "But how are you getting on with her over there? Pat. God, what a name! I'm fed up with acting jealous, by the way. All to keep you amused."

"I need another week. She's in lurve with me. Big time. But it'll be another week or so before . . ." There was laughter.

It was as if Pat had been given an electric shock. She moved back quickly from the door, reeling, nearly dropping Sir Ernst Gombrich from under her arm. Matthew, visibly appalled, made to support her, but she drew back, humiliated, ashamed.

"Quick," whispered Matthew, picking up the suitcases. "Quick. Open the door."

Out on the landing, the flat door closed firmly behind them, Matthew rested the suitcases on the floor and reached out for Pat's arm.

"Listen," he said. "Listen. I know how you must feel. But there's no reason for you to feel bad. It's not your . . ." He looked at her. She had turned her face away from him and he could see that she had begun to cry. He put down the suitcases and reached out to her.

"No," she mumbled, starting down the stairs. "I just want to go."

There were a few awkward moments at the front door, as they waited for the arrival of the taxi which Matthew had ordered. Matthew wanted to talk – he wanted to reassure Pat – but she told him that she did not want to discuss what they had heard.

"All right," he said. "We won't talk about it. Just forget him. Put him out of your mind."

They stood in silence. Matthew, looking up at the wispy clouds scudding across the sky, thought of something he had read in a magazine somewhere, or was it a newspaper? – he was unsure – of how Jean-Paul Sartre and Simone de Beauvoir had entertained themselves with stories of their conquests. He had been appalled by the story, and it had confirmed his prejudice against a certain sort of French intellectual, who deconstructed other people; who played games with people. One might expect bad behaviour from existentialists – indeed, that was what existentialism was all about, was it not? – but to find this happening on one's own doorstep was a shock.

Matthew looked down the street, which was quiet and taxi-less. A black and white cat was sauntering towards them and had now stopped a few yards away, staring at Matthew. An elderly woman, laden with shopping bags, was catching her breath a little distance away, holding onto a railing for support. It was a very ordinary street scene in that part of Edinburgh, and yet it seemed to Matthew that the moment was somehow special and that what it spoke to, this moment, was *agape*, the selfless love of the other.

Such moments can come at any time, and in unexpected circumstances, too. Those who travel to a place of pilgrimage, to a holy place, may hope to experience an epiphany of some sort, but may find only that the Ganges is dirty or that Iona is wet. And yet, on their journey, or on their return, disappointed, they may suddenly see something which vouchsafes them the insight they had wished to find; something glimpsed, not in a holy place, but in very ordinary surroundings; as Auden discovered when he sat with three colleagues on the lawn, out under the stars, on a balmy evening, and suddenly felt for the first time what it was like to love one's neighbour as oneself. The experience lasted in its intensity, he later wrote, for all of two hours, and then gradually faded.

Matthew felt this now, and it suppressed any urge he might have had to speak. He felt this for Pat – a gentleness, a cherishing – and for the cat and for the elderly woman under her burden. And he felt it, he thought, because he had just witnessed cruelty. He would not be cruel. He could not be cruel now. All that he wanted was to protect and comfort this girl beside him.

He looked at Pat. She had stopped crying and she no longer avoided his gaze.

"Thank you, Matthew," she said.

He smiled at her. "You'll be much happier in India Street. You really will."

"You must tell me how much rent I need to pay," said Pat.

Matthew raised his hands in protest. "None," he said. "Not a penny. You can live rent free."

Pat frowned. "But I have to pay something," she said. "I can't . . ."

"No," said Matthew. "No. No."

Pat was silent.

51. *Sun-Dried Tomatoes*

Cyril was not accustomed to travelling in a bus – nor indeed in any vehicle. Angus Lordie had no car, and so Cyril's experience of motor transport was limited to a few runs he had enjoyed in Domenica's custard-coloured Mercedes-Benz. From time to time, she invited Angus to accompany her on a drive into the country, to Peebles perhaps, or Gullane for lunch at the Golf Inn. Cyril was allowed to come on these outings, provided that he remained on a rug in the back, and he would stick his nose out of the window and revel in the bewildering range of scents borne in on the rushing air: sheep, hayfields, burning stubble, a startled pheasant in flight; so many things for a dog to think about.

But now he was on a bus, bundled under a seat amid unfamiliar ankles and shoes. He did not like the experience at all; he did not like the smell of the air, which was stale and acrid; he did not like the vibrations in the floor and the rumble of the diesel engine; he did not like the young man who had dragged him away from his tethering place. He looked up. The young man was holding the end of his leash lightly in his hand, twisting and untwisting it around his fingers. Cyril began to whimper, softly at first, but more loudly as he saw that the young man was not paying any attention to him.

As the whimpering increased in volume, the young man looked down at Cyril. For a few moments, dog and man looked at one another, and then, without any warning, the young man aimed a kick at the underside of Cyril's jaw. It was not a powerful kick, but it was enough to force Cyril's lower jaw up against the upper, causing him to bite his tongue.

"Haud yer wheesht," the young man muttered, adding: "Stupid dug."

Humiliated, Cyril shrank back under the seat. He knew that he did not deserve the kick, but it did not occur to him to retaliate. So he simply stared up at this person who now had control of him and tried to understand, but could not. After a few minutes, he closed his eyes and drifted off to sleep. It was at least warm in these strange surroundings and he was now becoming used to the throb of the engine. Perhaps things would be different when he woke up; perhaps Angus would be there to meet him wherever it was that they were going, and they would make their way back to Drummond Place by way of the Cumberland Bar.

He woke up sharply. The young man had tugged on his leash, and now tugged again, yanking Cyril's neck backwards as he did so. Cyril rose to his feet and looked expectantly at the young man, who now began to make his way towards the front of the bus, pulling him as he went. The bus slowed, and then stopped. The doors opened and there was a sudden rush of new smells as fresh air flooded in.

Cyril followed his captor outside, standing just behind him as the bus pulled away in a swirl of fumes: diesel, burnt oil, dust. The dog closed his eyes and then felt the pressure on his collar as the young man pulled him away from the side of the road. There were human voices; the sudden smell of a cat off to his right; the acrid odour of sweat from a passer-by; so much for a dog to take into account, and now hunger, too, and thirst. He opened his eyes and saw off to one side a building rising up against the sky. It made him dizzy to look at it. There were gulls wheeling in the air, white wings against the grey of the sky, tiny black eyes trained on him, a mewing sound.

He lunged away, pulling sharply on his leash. The young man cried out, a hostile yell which frightened him further, and, feeling the sudden freedom of the slipped collar, Cyril bolted. All he knew was that his collar was no longer around his neck, that he was free, and that he could run. There was a further shout, and a stone, hurled in blind anger, shot past him.

Cyril had no idea where he was going; all he wanted to do was to escape from the young man who had taken him away and put him in the bus. The young man was danger, was death, he thought, although Cyril had no idea what death was. All that he knew was that there was pain and something greater than pain – great cold and hunger, perhaps – which was death. Now, his heart thumping within him, the stones on the path cutting hard on his paws, he sought only to put as much distance as he could between himself and that death that was behind him, shouting. And it was easy to do so, because that death was slow and could not run as a dog could run.

Somewhere ahead of him – he could smell it – was water. His nose led him and soon it was before him, a thin body of water that snaked off to left and right, and beside it a path. He hesitated briefly and raised his nose into the air. Off to the right there was a confusion of smells, of other animals, of emptiness. And to the left there was a similar confusion, but somewhere, deep in the palette of odours, something familiar. He had no name for it, of course, no association – just familiarity. Sun-dried tomatoes. Somewhere in that direction there were sun-dried tomatoes.

Cyril chose the familiar. Aware now that there was nobody chasing him, he set off at a comfortable trot along the canal tow-path. There were many indications of the presence of other dogs, a tantalising array of territorial claims, of warnings left behind on bushes and trees, but he ignored these. He was going home, he thought, although he had no idea of where home might be, other than in this general direction. The hunger pains in his stomach were still present, but Cyril ignored these too. He felt calmer now, quite as calm as he would feel if he were going for a walk with Angus by his side. Angus. Cyril loved Angus with all his heart, and this sudden remembering of Angus, this knowledge that Angus was not with him, made the world as dark and cold as if the sun had dropped out of the sky.

52. Casting Issues

Bertie had told nobody at school about his unwelcome recruitment to the Edinburgh Teenage Orchestra. He had entertained hopes that the proposed orchestral tour to Paris would be cancelled; that war might break out between Britain and France, thereby curtailing all cultural exchange. But none of this happened. He scoured the columns of the newspapers in search of references to conflict, but none was to be found. Cultural relations, it seemed, were thriving and there was nothing on the horizon which would make it impossible for the Edinburgh Teenage Orchestra to venture to Paris.

It was not just the humiliation of being the youngest member of the orchestra which worried Bertie; it was the knowledge that his mother planned to come to Paris with him. He would be the only member to have his mother with him, and he could imagine how that would amuse the other players, the real teenagers. They might even make cruel jokes about it, asking him if his mother had brought his baby food with her. Bertie was under no illusions as to how unkind children could be to one another. Look at Tofu. Look at Olive. Look at the sorts of things they said about other people. Being down there, down among the children, was like living in a jungle teeming with predators.

But there was something else that worried Bertie. At the audition at the Queen's Hall, he had explained to Harry, the boy to whom he had chatted, that Irene was not really his mother at all but was a deluded madwoman who had followed him in off the bus. Harry had accepted this explanation, but what would he think if Irene came on the trip and was officially revealed as Bertie's mother? He would no doubt spread the story about, and Bertie would be exposed as a liar. So he would be doubly ostracised: both as the youngest member – not a real teenager – and as a liar, too.

These thoughts had preyed on Bertie's mind ever since the audition and now, a good week later, they were still there in the background, mixed up with all the other fears that can blight a six-year-old life. Bertie was conscious that not all was well in his world. He wanted so much to be like other boys, to play the games they played. He wanted to have a friend to share secrets with, a friend who would be an ally in the world and who would stand by him. Tofu was all very well – he was a sort of friend – but he left a great deal to be desired. Bertie did not think that Tofu would support him in a tight corner; in fact, quite the opposite. Tofu was your friend if you gave him presents, preferably money, but beyond that he really had little interest in anybody else. And as for Olive, she was completely unreliable in every respect. She had gone round the school telling everybody that Bertie was her boyfriend, and this had led to Bertie's being mercilessly teased, especially by Tofu, who found the idea particularly amusing. Olive had sent him a Valentine card, which she had tucked into his desk and which Bertie had rashly opened in the belief that it was a party invitation. He had been appalled to see the large red heart on the face of the card and, inside, the message 'My heart beats just for you'. It was unsigned, of course, but she had given a clue by drawing a large picture of an olive beneath the message. Bertie had quickly tried to tear it up, but had been seen doing this by Olive, who had snatched it back from him in a rage.

"If that's what you think of me," she spat out, "then . . . then you'll find out!"

She had left the threat vague, and this was another thing that Bertie had hanging over him. It was bad enough having his mother to worry about, but now here he was with Olive to think about, too. It was really hard being a boy, he thought, with all these women and girls making life difficult for one.

Such were Bertie's thoughts that morning at school when Miss Harmony, smiling broadly, announced that the class had been chosen to put on a play at the forthcoming concert in aid of the new school hall.

"This is, of course, a great responsibility, boys and girls," she said. "But it is also a challenge. I know that we are a very creative class, and that we have some very accomplished actors amongst us."

"Such as me," said Tofu.

Miss Harmony smiled tolerantly. "You can certainly act, Tofu, dear," she said. "But all of us can act, I think. Hiawatha, for example. You can act, can't you, Hiawatha?"

"He can act a stinky part," said Tofu. "He'd do that well."

"Tofu, dear," said Miss Harmony. "That is not very kind, is it? How would you like it if somebody said that about you."

"But my socks don't stink," said Tofu. "So they wouldn't say it."

Miss Harmony sighed. This was not an avenue of discussion down which she cared to go. It was certainly true that Hiawatha appeared to wear his socks for rather longer than might be desirable, but that was no excuse for the awful Tofu to say things like that. Tofu was a problem; she had to admit. But he would not be helped to develop by disparaging him, tempting though that might be. Love and attention would do its work eventually.

"Now then," she said brightly. "I have been thinking about what play we should do. And do you know, I think I've found just the thing. I've decided that we shall do *The Sound of Music*. What do you think of that, boys and girls? Don't you think that will be fun?"

The children looked at one another. They knew *The Sound of Music* and they knew that it would be fun. But the real issue, as they also knew, was this: who would be Maria? There were seven girls in the class and only one of them wanted Olive to be Maria. That one was Olive herself. And as for the boys, and the roles available to them, every girl in the class, but especially Olive, hoped that Tofu would not be Captain von Trapp. And yet that was the role that Tofu now set his heart on. He would do anything to get it, he decided. Anything.

53. *The Sybils of Edinburgh*

The effect of Miss Harmony's announcement that Bertie's class was to perform *The Sound of Music* was, in the first place, the descent of silence on the room. If the teacher had expected a buzz of excitement, then she must have been surprised, for no such reaction occurred. Nobody, in fact, spoke until a good two minutes had elapsed, but during that time a number of glances were exchanged.

Bertie, whose desk was next to Tofu's, looked sideways at his neighbour, trying to gauge his reaction. He knew that Tofu wished to dominate everything, and that the class play would be no exception. In the last play that they had performed, a truncated version of *Amahl and the Night-Visitors*, for which the music had been provided by the school orchestra, Tofu had resented being cast as a mere extra and had made several unscripted interventions in an attempt to raise the profile of the character whom he was playing (a sheep). This had caused even Miss Harmony, normally so mild, to raise her voice and threaten to write to Mr Menotti himself and inform him that the performance had been ruined by the misplaced ambition of one of the sheep.

When Bertie glanced at him, he saw that Tofu's expression gave everything away. He was smiling, his lips pressed tight together in what could only be pleasure at the thought of the dramatic triumphs that lay ahead. Bertie looked down at his desk. There was something else for him to think about now. Whereas all the other children had seen the film of *The Sound of Music*, he had not been allowed to do so by his mother, who disapproved of it on principle.

"Pure schmalz," she had explained to Bertie, when he had asked if they might borrow a tape of it and watch it one Saturday afternoon, after yoga. "Singing nuns and all the rest. I ask you, Bertie! Have you ever encountered a singing nun? And all those ghastly songs about lonely goatherds and raindrops on roses and the rest of it! No, Bertie, we don't want any of that, do we?"

It occurred to Bertie that it might be rather fun to listen to songs about goatherds, and that anyway his mother appeared to know rather a lot about the film. Had she seen it herself? In which case, was it fair that she should prevent him from seeing it? That, to his mind, sounded rather like hypocrisy, the definition of which he had recently looked up in *Chambers Dictionary*.

"But you must have seen it yourself, Mummy," he said. "If you know all that much about it, you must have seen it yourself."

Irene hesitated. "Yes," she said eventually. "I did see it. I saw it at the Dominion Cinema."

Bertie thought for a moment. "So you must have walked out," he said.

"Walked out? Why do you ask me whether I walked out, Bertie?"

"Because you disapproved of it so much," said Bertie. "If you hated it, then why did you stay to the end?"

Irene looked out of the window. Now that she came to think about it, she had seen *The Sound of Music* twice, but she could not possibly tell Bertie that, as he would hardly understand that one might see such a film in a spirit of irony. So the subject was dropped, and *The Sound of Music* was not mentioned again. Irene had, of course, attended the production of *Amahl* and had been very critical, both of the choice of the opera and the production itself. "I don't know why schools insist on choosing the same old thing time after time," she observed to Stuart as they drove back along Bruntsfield Place.

"I thought it was rather touching," said Stuart, but then added: "Or maybe not."

"Definitely not," said Irene. "Young children are perfectly capable of doing more taxing drama."

"Such as?" asked Stuart.

"*Who's Afraid of Virginia Woolf?*" said Irene lightly. "I've always liked Albee."

In the back seat, Bertie listened intently. He had heard his mother talk about Virginia Woolf before and he had looked her up in a book he had found on her shelves. Mrs Woolf, he read, had been married to Mr Woolf, and had written a number of books. Then she had filled her pockets with stones and had jumped into a river, which Bertie thought was very sad. He was not sure if he would enjoy a play about a person like that, and he was worried that his mother would suggest it to Miss Harmony. But then he had gone on to think what one should do if one saw a person with stones in his pockets jump into a river. Bertie was sure that he would try to rescue such a person, and that would raise the question of whether one should take the stones out of the pockets before trying to drag him or her to the shore. Perhaps it would depend on the depth of the river. If somebody filled his pockets with stones and jumped into the Water of Leith, it would be easy to save him, as the Water of Leith was a very shallow river and one would probably not sink very far, even with stones in one's pockets. One would just sit in the mud until help arrived.

Bertie knew about the Water of Leith because Irene had taken him for a walk along the river one day, after yoga, and they had stopped to look at the Temple of St Bernard's Well.

"That, Bertie," said Irene, "is a Doric temple. Nasmyth designed it after the Temple of the Sybil in Tivoli."

Bertie had looked at the stone columns and the statue of the woman within. "Who were the Sybils, Mummy?" he asked.

Irene smiled. "We'd call them pundits today," she said. "They were prophetesses who were associated with particular shrines. There was the Sybil of Delphi. She sat on a tripod over a sacred rock. Rather uncomfortable, I would have thought. And the Romans wanted their own Sybil – they were very envious of the Greeks, Bertie – so they appointed one at Tivoli. The Sybil of Tibur. They made pronouncements. On everything."

Bertie listened carefully. So a Sybil was a woman who made pronouncements on everything. A disturbing thought occurred. His mother was a Sybil!

It was yet another blow.

It was Olive who broke the silence in the classroom. Like Bertie, she had been staring at Tofu and had discerned, almost immediately, the look of determination that meant that he intended to play Captain von Trapp.

This conclusion required some quick thinking on her part. It would be intolerable for Tofu to be Captain von Trapp if, as she planned, she was going to play the part of Maria. She was confident about her acting ability, but it would surely test her talent to its absolute limit – and indeed beyond – if she had to pretend to be enchanted by Tofu. She could always close her eyes, of course, as actresses did in the films when they had to kiss somebody, but it would be difficult to act the entire play with her eyes closed. No, it would be impossible for her to be Maria and for Tofu to be Captain von Trapp in the same production.

It would be better, even, to have Hiawatha in the role; by a supreme effort of will she could probably ignore the problem of his socks. Yet it was unlikely that Hiawatha would be chosen, given the strange accent with which he spoke and which rendered him almost unintelligible, even to Miss Harmony. Nobody knew why Hiawatha spoke as he did – he was not foreign; he was not even from London, where they spoke in a very strange way. One of the other girls, Pansy, had suggested that it was something physical, and had put her fingers into his mouth to investigate it one morning while Miss Harmony was out of the room, but with inconclusive results.

Olive decided that the only possible strategy would be to claim the role of Maria before anybody else might ask for it. This pre-emptive move might then deter Tofu from suggesting himself as Captain von Trapp, on the grounds that he would not wish to play opposite her. This result could not be guaranteed, of course, but she felt that it was worth trying.

"I'll be Maria," she burst out. "Miss Harmony, is that all right, then? I know all the songs – you can test me."

Every eye in the room turned to Olive. While Olive had been thinking about the means of obtaining the role, every other girl in the class had been thinking similar thoughts, but each was consumed by her own version of despair when Olive volunteered herself. It was typical of Olive, thought Pansy: push, push, push. And Skye, who believed with utter conviction that she alone was qualified to play the role, felt a great surge of despair at the realisation that it might go to somebody else. For her part, Lakshmi, who was a quiet girl and rather given to defeatism, merely thought: Olive Oil, a soubriquet which she never openly uttered but which gave her great inner satisfaction and comfort.

Tofu, taken by surprise, was able only to glare at Olive, who returned his look with interest. She was now sure that her tactic had succeeded. Tofu would not dare to volunteer as Captain von Trapp while she was looking at him like this.

Miss Harmony, who believed in the innocence of children, pointedly ignored the undercurrents of ambition and hostility that flowed and eddied around the room. In her mind, Olive was not a suitable candidate for Maria because she had played a prominent role in the informal play they had performed in the classroom the previous week. She had also played a solo part in the class recorder consort's benchmark performance of 'Pease Pudding Hot', and it was a principle of Steiner educational theory that every child should be given a chance. No, it was definitely not Olive's turn.

"That's very kind of you, Olive," she said. "But we mustn't allow you to do all the work, must we? Your poor shoulders would buckle under the strain, wouldn't they? No, don't shake your head like that, Olive – they really would!" She looked around the class. "Now then, Skye. You haven't had a big part in any of the plays yet. Would you like to be Maria?"

Skye looked down at her desk. She had hardly dared hope, and yet it had happened. She began to cry.

Tofu turned to Bertie and smirked. "What a girlie!" he whispered.

Miss Harmony, who was comforting Skye, looked up sharply. "Did we say something, Tofu?"

Tofu looked sullen.

"I said: did we say something, Tofu?" repeated Miss Harmony.

"I said 'What a girl', Miss Harmony."

Miss Harmony smiled. "That's kind of you, Tofu. And yes, it is good of Skye to accept the part of Maria. These big parts are a lot of work, as I'm sure you know." She paused. "Now then, as you are all aware, boys and girls, the main part for a boy is Captain von Trapp. The Captain is a brave man, an Austrian patriot . . ."

"Me," said Tofu, raising his hand in the air.

Miss Harmony drew a deep breath. She had expected this, of course, and was ready with her response.

"Now then, Tofu," she began, "we're old enough to under-stand that we can't have all the things that we want in this life. If that happened, then what would we have to look forward to? So it's best to accept that we can't all be Captain von Trapp, much as we would like to be. And I'm sure that Captain von Trapp himself was very good at sharing. Yes, I'm sure he was. That's why they made him a captain. He knew when it was his turn and when it wasn't. And it's not your turn now, Tofu. So Captain von Trapp will be played by . . ."

There was complete silence.

"Bertie."

Bertie looked down at the floor. He did not dare look at Tofu, because he knew what expression would greet him if he did that.

He looked up at Miss Harmony. "I'm not sure . . ." he began.

"He's not sure," Tofu interjected. "Don't force him, Miss Harmony. Please don't force him."

"Bertie's a useless actor, Miss Harmony," said Larch.

Tofu, aware now of the threat that Larch might claim the role, spun round and glared at the other boy.

"And you're useless too, Larch," he said. "You know that you can't act for toffee."

"Toffee yourself!" said Larch, and everybody laughed, except Tofu, who fumed. He wanted to hit Larch, but he understood that principle which everybody, but particularly politicians and statesmen understand very well: you only ever hit weaker people.

55. *Domenica Settles In*

The arrival of a stranger in a remote village is usually something of an event. When Domenica Macdonald, though, arrived in the small pirate village on the coast of the Straits of Malacca, such interest as was shown by the villagers was discreet. As the party made its way down the path leading to Domenica's bungalow, a group of women standing under a tree looked in its direction, but only for a few moments. A couple of children, bare to the waist and dragging a small puppy on a string, drifted over to the side of the path to get a better view of the new arrivals. But that was all; nobody came to greet them, nobody appeared to challenge the arrival of the anthropologist with Ling, her guide and mentor, and the teenage boy recruited to carry her suitcase.

Ling led the way to Domenica's house. The young man whom they had spotted from afar now stood at the top of the steps. He was wearing a pair of loose-fitting linen trousers and a white open-necked shirt. His feet were bare, and Domenica's eyes were drawn to his toes. They were perfect, she thought. Perfect toes;

she had seen so many perfect toes in her times in the tropics – toes unrestrained by shoes, allowed to grow as nature intended them.

The young man lowered his head, his hands held together in traditional greeting. "I am very happy," he said.

Domenica returned his greeting.

Ling turned to Domenica. "He says he is happy," he announced.

"So I heard," said Domenica. "And I am happy too."

These niceties over, Domenica went up the steps that led to the veranda. Behind her, Ling took the suitcase from the boy who had carried it from the village at the end of the track. The boy was sweating profusely; it had been a long walk and the suitcase was heavy. Ling rested the suitcase on a step and fished into his pocket for a few coins. These he tossed at the boy, who caught them in the palm of his hand, looked at them, and then stared imploringly at Ling.

Domenica watched this, uncertain as to whether she should interfere. It was obvious to her that Ling had underpaid the boy. Of course, this is the East, she thought, and people work for very little, but it distressed her that she should be part of the process of exploitation. She looked at the boy; she had not paid much attention to his clothes, but now she saw them, as if for the first time. His shirt had been repaired several times, and his trousers were frayed about the pockets. He was obviously poor, and she, whose suitcase he carried, was by his standards, impossibly rich.

It would have been a simple matter for her to intervene. She had a pocketful of ringgits, and many more stashed away in her suitcase. It would have been easy for her to press a few notes into the boy's hand to make up for Ling's meanness, and she was on the point of doing this when she checked herself. One of the rules of anthropological fieldwork was: do not interfere. A well-meaning interference in the community which one was studying could change relationships and distort results. The anthropologist should be invisible, as far as possible; an observer. Of course, there were limits to this unobtrusiveness. One could not stand by in the face of an egregious crime if one could do something to help; this, though, was hardly that. The real bar to her intervention lay in the fact that if she now gave money to the boy, Ling would lose face. Her act would imply that he had acted meanly (which he had) and reveal her as the one who was really in charge (which she was), and that could amount to an unforgivable loss of face.

Domenica looked at the boy. He was still staring at Ling and it seemed to her that he was on the brink of tears.

She turned to Ling. "Such a helpful boy," she said. "And he has such a charming smile."

Ling glanced at the boy. "He is just riff-raff," he said. "The son of an assistant pirate."

"But such appealing riff-raff," persisted Domenica. "In fact, I really must photograph him – for my records."

She had been carrying a small camera in her rucksack, and she now rummaged in the bag to retrieve it.

"I do not think you should photograph him," said Ling, shooing the boy away with a gesture of his hand. "He must go away now."

"But I must!" exclaimed Domenica. "I must have a complete record."

Ignoring Ling, she moved towards the boy and led him gently away from the side of the veranda. At first he was perplexed, but when he realised what was happening his face broke into a grin and he stood co-operatively in front of a tree while Domenica took the photograph.

The picture taken, Domenica reached into her pocket and thrust a few banknotes into the boy's hand.

"Why are you giving him money?" Ling called out. "I have paid him. Take the money back."

"I'm not paying him for carrying the case," Domenica said lightly, indicating to the now delighted boy that he should leave. "That was for his photograph." She glanced at Ling and smiled. She felt pleased with herself. She had repaired the injustice without causing a loss of face to her guide. The natural order of things had not been disturbed, and the amount of happiness in the world had been discreetly augmented. It was a solution of which Mr Jeremy Bentham himself could only have approved. The young man who was to be Domenica's house-servant now picked up her suitcase and walked into the house. He moved, Domenica noticed, with that fluidity of motion that Malaysians seemed to manage so effortlessly. We walk so clumsily, she thought; they glide.

She followed him into the living room of the house. It was cool inside, and dark. Such light as there was filtered through a window which was largely screened by a broad-leafed plant of some sort. She suddenly thought of the Belgian anthropologist. Had he lived here? She looked about her. On one wall, secured by a couple of drawing pins, was a faded picture of le petit Julien, le Manneken Pis, symbol of everything that Brussels stood for, culturally and politically, or so the Belgians themselves claimed. I detect, she thought, a Belgian hand.

56. By the Light of the Tilley Lamp

There was no electricity in the village, of course, and when night descended – suddenly, as it does in the tropics – Domenica found herself fumbling with a small Tilley lamp which the house servant had set out on the kitchen table. It was a long time since she had used such a lamp, but the knack of adjusting it came back to her quickly – an old skill, deeply-ingrained, like riding a bicycle or doing an eightsome reel, the skills of childhood which never left one. As she pumped up the pressure and applied a match to the mantle, Domenica found herself wondering what scraps of the old knowledge would be known to the modern child. Would that curious little boy downstairs, Bertie, know how to operate an old-fashioned dial telephone? Or how to make a fire? Probably not. And there were people, and not just children, who did not know how to add or do long division, because they relied on calculators; all those people in shops who needed the till to tell them how much change to give because nobody had ever taught them how to do calculations like that in school. There were so many things that were just not being taught any more. Poetry, for example. Children were no longer made to learn poetry by heart. And so the deep rhythms of the language, its inner music, was lost to them, because they had never had it embedded in their minds. And geography had been abandoned too – the basic knowledge of how the world looked, simply never instilled; all in the name of educational theory and of the goal of teaching children how to think. But what, she wondered, was the point of teaching them how to think if they had nothing to think about? We were held together by our common culture, by our shared experience of literature and the arts, by scraps of song that we all knew, by bits of history half-remembered and half-understood but still making up what it was that we thought we were. If that was taken away, we were diminished, cut off from one another because we had nothing to share.

The light thrown out by the Tilley lamp was soft and forgiving, a light that did not fight with the darkness but nudged it aside gently, just for a few feet, and then allowed it back. Looking out through her open door, she saw that here and there in the village other lights had been lit. In one of the houses a kitchen was illuminated and she could make out the figures within: a woman standing, holding a child on her hip; a man in the act of drinking something from a cup or beaker; the moving shadow of fan-blades. She had yet to adjust to where she was, and it seemed to her to be strange that the people she was looking at through the window were outlaws – contemporary pirates. How peculiar it was that ordinary life should take place in spite of this sense of being beyond the law. She would get used to that, of course; anthropologists in New Guinea came to accept even head-hunting after a while.

The house servant, who had gone off to his hut shortly before dusk fell, had left a meal for her in the kitchen: a bowl of noodles, a plate of stewed vegetables and a pot containing pieces of grilled chicken. Domenica was not particularly hungry; she always lost her appetite in the heat, but now she tackled the meal almost for want of anything else to do. It was, she found, tastier than she had expected, and she ate virtually everything prepared for her. Then, sitting in an old planter's chair, she read for two hours by the light of her Tilley lamp.

It was nine o'clock when she went to bed. Taking the lamp with her, she made her way through to her bedroom, the only other room in the small house. Above her bed, suspended from an exposed rafter, hung a voluminous mosquito net. It was a comfort for her, a luxury, the only means of ensuring a night untroubled by stinging insects.

Sitting on the edge of her bed, she blew out the lamp's flame and slipped behind the net. The bed was narrow, but not uncomfortable, and it seemed to her that the sheets had been freshly laundered, for they were crisp and sweet-smelling. She wondered who had gone to all this trouble. It was unlikely that the pirates themselves – crude types, she suspected – would have bothered to ensure her comfort in this way, and if they had not done this, then it could only be Edward Hong who was behind it. In fact, the more she thought of it the clearer it became to her. In Edward Hong M.A. (Cantab.), she had a protector, a man who cared for her welfare. It was a reassuring feeling, a feeling that can normally be expected to induce in many single women a warm feeling of contentment. And Domenica, for all that she was a distinguished anthropologist, was a woman; and what woman would not be pleased to know that there was a lithe young man immediately at hand, at her beck and call, while, in the background, there was a more mature and urbane M.A. (Cantab.) who had her interests at heart?

With these pleasant thoughts in her mind, Domenica began to feel drowsy. It had been an unusual and demanding day. The walk down the track to the village had been physically tiring, and the change of surroundings had also had an effect.

As she lay there in this state of agreeable tiredness, Domenica allowed her mind to wander over what lay ahead. Tomorrow, she would introduce herself, with Ling's assistance, to the people of the village. She would introduce herself to the women first, as they would be the focus of her scientific inquiry, and then in due course she would meet the pirates themselves. For a moment she thought of pirates, and a few snatches of Gilbert and Sullivan came to her mind, faintly, as if from a distant, half-heard chorus: For he is a pirate king! Hurrah for the pirate king! And it is, it is a glorious thing, to be a pirate king . . . How absurd, thought Domenica sleepily; how completely inappropriate. It was not at all glorious; not at all.

57. *A Nocturnal Visitation*

Domenica was a sound sleeper, even if she had a tendency to awake somewhat early. In Scotland Street, in the summer, she would often find herself wide awake at five in the morning; it was, she felt, the finest part of the day, and she would often go out and walk round Drummond Place at that hour, enjoying the quiet of the morning. In Malaysia, where the day was divided into two roughly equal parts, it would still be dark at five and she imagined that if she woke up that early she would stay in bed for a while before getting up and starting the day. Once the sun rose, of course, it would be too hot to stay in bed anyway, and one might as well get up and begin by pouring a large jug full of tepid water over one's face and shoulders. She looked forward to that; bathing oneself in a place without running water was an almost sacramental act, underlining the preciousness of that water that one takes so much for granted when it flows from a tap.

However, she did not wake up at five that morning, but closer to two. She did not confirm that it was two o'clock; it just felt like that, when she suddenly became conscious of her surroundings and of the shafts of moonlight which came through the small window above her bed. The moonlight, soft and diffuse, fell half upon the folds of the mosquito net and half upon the floorboards.

Beyond it, the room was filled with dark shadows; the shape of the roughly-finished chest of drawers in which she had stacked her clothes before retiring; the form of the table and the small pile of books that she had piled there on retrieving them from her suitcase; the low hillock of the chair near the door. But then, between the bed and the chest of drawers, just touched in part by the moonlight, was the shape of a man, standing quite still.

The first thing that came to Domenica's mind was a literary reference. She had read somewhere, some time ago, that one of the most disturbing experiences in this life was to wake up and discover that one is not alone in a house in which one had gone to bed believing oneself to be alone. Who had said that? Who? It was John Fowles; yes, that was who it was; not in *The Magus*, but somewhere else. Or at least she thought it was him; and now the words, whatever their provenance, came back to her, and caught at her wildly palpitating heart.

She did not move. She lay there, her limbs heavy beneath the sheets, her eyelids the only part of her moving, and very slightly at that, as she watched the still figure at the end of her bed.

For a moment she wondered if she was imagining it, if this was just another shadow, a trick of the light; but it was not, and she knew that it was not. She thought: I can scream. I can wake people up. It's a small village and they will all hear me. People would come; Ling, the young man, the family in the house next door, which was not far away. And if I scream and this man comes for me, I can throw myself off the bed; there is a mosquito net between him and me, and he will have to fumble with that, which will give me the time to escape. She wondered if the man could see that her eyes were open. Probably not, she thought, for her head was in the shadows and he would not be able to see her face. That made her feel better. And the fact, too, that he was just standing there made her fear subside slightly. He was looking at her, just looking, and there was no sign that he was planning to attack her. And again, unbidden, there came to her mind another literary reference; this time its source quite clear. Carson McCullers, she thought. *Reflections in a Golden Eye.* The private soldier, the slow one, watches the Major's wife from outside her window; that is all he does, he watches her. And then he comes into the house and watches her there too. He is gentle, unthreatening, a watcher. Boo Radley, she thought; another gentle watcher; the man who watches Jem and Scout Finch; watches over them, really, and saves their lives eventually. I am being watched. That is all this man is doing. He is watching me.

She felt calmer now, and for a moment almost as if she would laugh, with the release of tension. The figure in the shadows had ceased to be threatening; it was as if he had become a companion. That is what she now thought, and it was at that moment that he stepped forward; not a great step, but just a small movement in her direction. And as he did so, the moon-light fell on his face, and she saw who it was. It was not a man at all. It was the boy, the teenage boy who had carried her suit-case and whose photograph she had taken.

She caught her breath in surprise, a gasp that he heard, for he turned round quickly and ran out of the room.

"What do you want?" Domenica called out. "Why are you here?"

Her voice was not loud at all, and the boy probably did not hear it. Or her words might have been lost in the sound of the outer door slamming behind him.

She reached for the box of matches on the table beside her bed and struck one to light the lamp. In the glow of the lamp, the shadows resolved and became solid, unthreatening objects. Domenica no longer felt alarmed, just curious. She had fright-ened the boy away, and in a strange way she was sorry about that. If he had not fled, she would have let him remain there, perhaps, and he would have been company for her. She had no idea why he had been there; it was curiosity, perhaps, on his part; she did not think it was anything more sinister than that. Perhaps she was something of a miracle in his mind; a woman from somewhere distant, who had given him money. It had been a small thing for her to do, but it was probably not small for him.

58. Moving In, Moving Out

"Here we are," said Matthew, as he fumbled for the key of his flat. "Home." Pat said nothing. It was evidently home for Matthew, but was it home for her? She had accepted his offer of a room, of course, but this had been only because of his persistence and the suddenness of her need to leave Spottiswoode Street. Home for her was her parents' house in the Grange, where her room was kept exactly as she had left it, as parents often will keep their child's room, as a museum. Home was not here in India Street; Matthew, she felt, should not make unwarranted assumptions.

She had never been in Matthew's flat before and she had not expected the spaciousness and grandeur which greeted her. The front door gave onto a large hall, perfectly square, topped by a sizeable cupola. There were flagstones on the floor and these were covered, in part, by dark oriental rugs. There were several paintings on the walls of this hall, one of which Pat recognised from the gallery – a gilt-framed but otherwise dreary view of the Falls of Clyde by a Victorian painter whom they had been unable to identify.

Matthew showed her to her room, which was at the back of the flat, next to the kitchen. It was considerably larger than the room she had occupied in Spottiswoode Street, and better provided with cupboards and drawers.

"I've always used this as a guest room," said Matthew. "Or, rather, I would have used it as a guest room if I'd had any guests." He looked out of the window, as if searching for guests who had never arrived.

Pat glanced at him. There was something inexplicably sad about Matthew; a sense of life having passed him by. There were some people who had that aura of sadness, often inexplicably so, she thought, and Matthew was one of them. Or was it loneliness rather than sadness? If it was, then it could be relieved by company. There was no reason why Matthew could not find somebody. He was presentable enough, quite good-looking in fact when viewed from a certain angle, and even if he required some gingering up there were plenty of girls in Edinburgh who would be prepared to see Matthew as a project.

Matthew dragged Pat's suitcase into her room and then left her to unpack. He would make coffee, he said, in half an hour, after she had sorted things out. He would then show her the kitchen and where things were.

"You can use everything," he said. "There's never much food in there, but you can help yourself to what there is. Feel free."

Pat thanked him, but thought that she would buy her own supplies. His insistence that she stay rent-free was difficult enough; to be fed by him too would have made her position impossible. I would be a kept woman, she thought; and smiled at the thought. It was a wonderful expression, she reflected; so exotic, so out-of-date, rather like the expression "a fallen woman". She knew somebody who lived in a house in Edinburgh that used to be a home for fallen women; after their fall, the women went there to have their babies before the babies were then given up for adoption. One of the rooms in the house had been a lecture room, where the women were lectured on the avoidance of further falls, perhaps.

After she had unpacked, she went through to the kitchen, where she found Matthew seated at the scrubbed-pine table, a coffee pot and two mugs in front of him.

"Don't you love the smell of freshly-brewed coffee?" he said brightly. "And the smell of the grounds before you make the coffee. That's even better." He sniffed at the air. "Lovely."

Pat sat down. She had resolved to talk to Matthew and decided that it would be best to do so now, right at the beginning. It would be easier that way.

"Matthew," she began. "I'm really grateful to you for letting me stay here. You know that, don't you?" He made a gesture with his hand, as if brushing aside, in embarrassment, an unwanted compliment. "I'm happy to be able to help," he said. "And I really don't mind. That room is never used."

The guests who never came, thought Pat; he was lonely – it was so obvious. She almost stopped herself there, but continued. She had to.

"Well, it's kind of you," said Pat.

"Don't think about it," said Matthew. "You'd do the same for me. I know you would."

Pat was silent. Would she? Perhaps.

"And it's not going to be for long," she went on. "No more than a couple of weeks. Until I find somewhere else."

Matthew was staring at the coffee pot. He reached out and picked it up, as if to start pouring, but then put it down. He reached for one of the mugs and peered inside it.

"Only a few weeks?"

She could tell that he was making an effort to keep his voice level, to hide his disappointment. But she had to go through with this; it would be far more difficult to say anything later on, when misunderstandings had already occurred.

"You see," she said, "I'm not sure if it's a good idea to share just with one person, particularly with a . . ." she hesitated for a moment before continuing, "with a man."

Matthew continued to stare into the mug. Then he looked up. "I hoped that you'd stay a bit longer than that," he said. "It gets very . . . very quiet around here. I just hoped . . ." He bit at his lip. "I would never make it awkward for you. Why would you think that? Why would you think I'd make it awkward for you?"

Pat reached out and took his hand. "Because it would be awkward," she said. "Because you're a man and I'm a girl, and . . . you know."

Matthew sighed. "But you don't fancy me. I know that. Nothing could ever happen, because you don't fancy me. Nobody does."

There was no self pity in his voice; he merely spoke with the air of one stating a fact.

"That isn't true," said Pat vehemently. "A lot of people fancy you."

"Name one," said Matthew flatly. "Name just one."

Pat did not have the time to answer the question, which she could not have answered anyway. But at that moment, with the question still hanging in the air, the doorbell rang and the conversation came to an end.

59. A Person from Porlock

The arrival of an unexpected visitor has ruined many an important conversation and at least one great poem. When Coleridge started to describe his vision of Kubla Khan's Xanadu, he had, we are told, the words in mind to describe what he saw. But then came the person from Porlock, who by chance knocked at the door at precisely the moment that the poet was committing his vision to paper, and it was lost. Thus began Porlock's long career as a symbol of that which interrupts the flow.

Pat might have been able to reassure Matthew that he was appreciated, had she had the chance to do so. But she was not to have that chance. As Matthew rose to his feet to answer the door, he gave her a look which said, very clearly, that what he said was irrefutable, and that she should not even bother to dispute it. Pat made a gesture of hopelessness, the meaning of which was similarly clear: if that's your view of yourself, then nothing will persuade you otherwise, will it?

While Matthew was answering the door, Pat poured herself a cup of coffee. She felt unhappy about the disappointment that she had caused Matthew; she liked him – she liked him a great deal, in fact, as he had always been kind to her. But there was no mistaking the difference between the affection she felt for Matthew – a rather sister-like affection – and the feelings which Wolf had aroused in her. She could hardly bear to think about Wolf now, but she had to admit that what she had previously felt for him was far from sisterly. The thought of that disturbed her, and she found herself wondering whether she was the sort of woman who was invariably attracted to the wrong sort of man. She had seen that behaviour in others, the stubborn refusal to acknowledge the worthlessness of some man. And it was always the same men who benefited from that; handsome, charming men who knew how to exploit women; men like . . . like Bruce and Wolf.

The solution to that problem was obvious: pick a man who was not handsome and not, on the face of it, charming; somebody like Matthew, somebody quiet and decent. But could she ever be attracted to somebody quiet and decent? And what, she wondered, had quiet and decent men to offer? They made good husbands, perhaps; they would wash the car and help with the children, but that was hardly what Pat, at her age, was interested in. She wanted romance, excitement, the sense of being swept away by something, and Matthew, for all his merits, would never be able to give her that. Matthew would never be able to sweep anybody away; it was impossible.

There was the sound of voices in the hall – Matthew was speaking to somebody, and now he walked into the kitchen with a young woman behind him.

"This is Leonie," said Matthew. "Leonie, this is Pat."

There was a moment of silence as the two young women looked at one another. Pat noticed Leonie's hair first of all, which was cut short, in an almost masculine style, and her black jeans, low on the hips. She's the type to have a tattoo, she thought, somewhere; somewhere hidden. And what is she to Matthew? Is she . . . ?

For her part, Leonie merely thought: interesting.

"Leonie's an architect," said Matthew as he pulled out a chair for the guest. "We met . . ."

"In the Cumberland Bar," supplied Leonie. "A few weeks ago, wasn't it, Matthew?"

Matthew nodded, and busied himself with pouring coffee.

"An architect," said Pat.

"Yes," said Leonie. She turned to Matthew. "I've done a few sketches for you, Matthew. Remember? You said that you might do something with this place?"

Matthew frowned. "Yes, well, I hadn't really decided. Not definitely."

"They're just sketches," said Leonie. "And I've made a card model. It gives you an idea of how things might feel."

Matthew looked at Pat. It was, she thought, a mute plea for help. "Is there anything wrong with this flat?" she said. "It seems pretty nice to me."

Leonie, who had addressed her remarks to Matthew, now

turned to Pat. "Oh, there's nothing wrong with it," she said. "But we can make much more of things, you know. Just about anywhere can be improved if you take a hard look at it. Made more user-friendly, if you see what I mean."

"But this isn't meant to be user-friendly," said Pat, gesturing towards the hall. "This is Georgian. This is what it's meant to be like."

Leonie smiled. "We don't have to live in museums," she said. "That's the trouble with this town. It's a museum."

"Maybe you could show me the sketches," Matthew interrupted. "Then we could see."

Leonie reached into the large black folder that she had brought with her. "Right," she said. "Here we are." She took out a large piece of paper and unfolded it. "Here's something."

They stared at the neatly-traced sketch, drawn on draughtsman's paper.

"Here's the hall," said Leonie, pointing to the sketch. "That's the welcoming space. At the moment, you come in and what do you see? Nothing. The hall leads nowhere."

"But is a hall meant to lead somewhere?" asked Matthew.

"Well, what else should it do?" asked Leonie. "You don't live in it, do you? Unused space." She tapped the paper. "You'll see that I suggest that we take down this wall here, which allows the hall to flow into this room here, to absorb it. You get a much better sense of being drawn into the living space, you see. The spaces will talk to one another."

Pat stared at the sketch. It was a short while before she established the orientation of the plan, but once she had done that she realised that the room which was being absorbed into the hall was her own. "My room," she said quietly.

"What was that?" asked Leonie.

"I said, my room," Pat replied.

Leonie looked to Matthew for an explanation.

"Pat's staying with me," he explained. "For the time being."

Leonie took her hands away from the plans. "I see." She looked at Pat in a curious way. There was something about her look which made the younger girl feel unsettled. It was not an unfriendly look, but it was not uncomplicated. The best word to describe it, she thought, was bemused.

"These are just ideas," said Leonie after a few moments.

60. An Invitation to Dinner

Feeling uncomfortable sitting in the kitchen with Matthew and Leonie, Pat retreated to her room with the excuse that she had more unpacking to do. Leonie smiled at her as she left, but it was a puzzling smile, and she found it hard to interpret.

"So," said Leonie after Pat had left. "So, Matthew, who's our young friend?"

Matthew blushed. "She works for me," he muttered. "In the gallery."

Leonie raised an eyebrow. "And the room goes with the job?"

Matthew did not reply immediately. He had not expected Leonie's visit and now he found himself resenting her arriving without warning. He had met her only once before, on that occasion when he had invited her back to India Street for a pizza. They had got on reasonably well on that occasion and had made a vague agreement to meet again. Telephone numbers had been exchanged, but he had not called her, and she had not called him. He had toyed with the idea of doing so once or twice, but had decided against it. He was just not sure that he liked her. Perhaps he did; perhaps not.

They had talked on that occasion about possible renovations to his flat, but he had not encouraged her in any way. And now here she was, with a set of unasked-for drawings, expounding about rooms talking to one another and fluid spaces. What business was it of hers who stayed in his flat? What precisely was she suggesting anyway? That he was taking advantage of a vulnerable young employee? It was all a bit too much.

"She had a bit of trouble in her last flat," he said evenly. "I'm helping her out."

Leonie took a sip of her coffee. Matthew noticed that she

was looking at him over the rim of her mug. Her expression, he thought, was one of scepticism.

She lowered her mug. "Nice for you," she said. "Very nice."

Matthew looked away with mounting irritation. "Look," he said. "I'm not sure that I'm all that keen on doing any structural alterations to this place. I didn't think that you were serious back then."

Leonie sighed. "They're just some ideas I had," she said. "Nothing more than that. I wouldn't want to force you to do anything."

"No," said Matthew. "Well, thanks anyway. Thanks for going to the trouble."

Leonie folded up the plan and slipped it into her case. Her manner was cool. "That's fine," she said. "I enjoyed doing it. You get a bit bored designing extensions for boring little houses in the suburbs. It's nice to imagine doing something more challenging."

She had abandoned her plan so readily that Matthew felt slightly sorry for her. Australians were direct speakers, and perhaps she had not meant to sound snide when she referred to Pat's presence. Perhaps there would be the possibility of a friendship here – nothing more than that, of course, at this stage.

"Have you been back to the Cumberland Bar?" he asked politely.

Leonie shook her head. "No. I had a long weekend in London and then a friend from Melbourne dropped by. She stayed for a week. You know how it is when you have friends staying. Busy."

"Yes, of course." Matthew hesitated. Leonie's visit had made him forget his disappointment over Pat's rebuff – for that is how he thought of it – and now the thought of asking Leonie out to dinner seemed attractive. It would make up, too, for any disappointment she might feel over the rejection of her drawings.

"I'm sorry about the plans," he said. "You must have spent a lot of time doing those. And then I . . ."

"Don't think about it," said Leonie reassuringly. "If you knew how many times drawings of mine have been torn up, you wouldn't think about it for a moment. It happens. Architects are used to it."

"Well, at least let me take you out to dinner," said Matthew. "As a thank-you."

Leonie laughed. "I thought you were never going to ask," she said. "Yes. Dinner would be nice."

Matthew rubbed his hands together. "I'll book a table for two somewhere," he said.

"Make it three," said Leonie. "Would you mind very much?"

"Three?" Matthew wondered whether she thought that Pat would be included, but why should she imagine that? Surely he had made it clear enough that although he and Pat were living together, that was all they were doing together.

"My friend," said Leonie quietly. "My friend, Babs."

Matthew was perplexed. "Your friend from Melbourne? Is she still staying with you?"

Leonie laughed. "No, not her. She's gone off to Denmark. Babs is my friend here. You know. My friend."

Matthew saw her bemused expression and realised that he had not been very perceptive. Mind you, how was one to tell? After all, she had accepted his invitation when they had met in the Cumberland Bar; she should have told him, or given him some indication, rather than relying on him to pick up the signals which were, anyway, non-existent as far as he could make out.

He made a quick recovery. That, at least, sorted that out. It would indeed remain a simple friendship. "Of course. That's fine. The three of us. Now where shall we go? What sort of place do you like?"

"I'm easy," said Leonie. "But Babs is wild about Italian. Do you think we could . . . ?"

"Of course. Italian."

Leonie seemed pleased. "Babs lived in Italy for a year, you see. She worked in Milan. She's a designer. Milan's the place for designers."

Matthew nodded. He had not thought that anyone called Babs would be artistic. Babs was a name full of old-fashioned briskness. What would somebody called Babs do? Perhaps work with horses.

Leonie looked thoughtful. "How about . . . Well, why don't you invite that girl through there? What's her name again?"

"You mean Pat?"

"Yes. Pat. Let's invite her too. You said that she had had a bit of trouble. An Italian restaurant would cheer her up."

Matthew looked out of the kitchen towards Pat's room. Her door was closed. "I'm not sure," he began. "She may not . . ."

"Just ask her," Leonie interrupted. "She may be keen to come."

Matthew felt that something odd was going on. A simple invitation to dinner, extended to Leonie, had been expanded to include her friend, Babs, and now was about to embrace Pat as well. Why was Leonie keen for Pat, whom she had barely met, to be included? Perhaps she was just being friendly, in the way in which Australians often are. Besides, they were, he remembered, inclusive people.

61. Beside the Canal

Cyril trotted along the canal, his head held high into the wind, his tail swinging jauntily behind him. On that section of the towpath, between the aqueduct and the turn-off for Colinton Village, there was nobody about, and the only sign of life was a family of eider ducks moving in and out of the reeds. Cyril stopped briefly to inspect the ducks, giving a low, warning bark. It would have been a fine thing to eat a duck, he thought; to sink his teeth into those soft breast-feathers and shake the annoying bird out of its complacency. But there was no time for that now. Scores like that could be settled once he had found Angus again, for that is what he yearned for, with all his heart. He had to find Angus.

After a few minutes, the path narrowed and now he felt hard stone beneath his feet. He slowed down and advanced cautiously.

There were railings to his left, like the railings he knew in Drummond Place, but through these he could make out an emptiness, a falling away, a current of cool air; and on the air there was the smell of water, different from the smell of the canal, a fresher, sharper smell. He stood still for a moment, his nose twitching. This was something he recognised, something he remembered from a past which now survived only in scraps of memory. This was a smell that he had encountered on the Hebridean island where he had started his life, the scent of running water, of burns that had flowed through peat. And the river carried other things on it, which were familiar; traces of sheep, of lanolin from their wool, and the acrid odour of rats that had scurried over stones.

He continued on his journey. The river had not helped; it had been too powerful, too evocative, and the distant smells that had been drawing him on were even fainter now. But they still lay somewhere ahead of him, layered into a hundred other smells, and he knew that this was the direction in which he should go.

A short distance further along, Cyril came upon a group of boys. There were three of them standing by the edge of the canal, under the shelter of a footbridge, fishing rods extended out over the water, the lines dropping optimistically into the unruffled surface. Cyril liked boys for several reasons. He liked the way they smelled, which was always a little bit off, like a bone that had been left out on the grass for a day or two. Then he liked them because they were always prepared to play with dogs.

The boys looked at Cyril.

"Here's a dug," said Eck, a small boy with a slightly pointed head.

"What's he doing?" asked Eck's older brother, Jimmy. "Is he running away, do you think?"

"No," said Bob. "There are some dugs just wander aboot. They dinnae belong to anybody. They're just dugs."

"I've always wanted a dug," said Eck. "But my dad says I cannae have one until I'm sixteen."

"You'll never be sixteen," said Bob. "You're too wee. And that pointy heid of yours too. All the lassies will have a good laugh, so they will."

The boys looked at Cyril, who sat down and wagged his tail encouragingly. He half-expected them to throw something for him, but they seemed unwilling to do this, and after a few minutes he decided that it was time to move on. He took a step forward, licked one of the boys on the hand, and continued with his journey.

There were more people now. A runner, panting with effort, came towards him and Cyril moved obediently to the side to let him past. Then a woman walking a small dog that cowered as Cyril approached. Cyril ignored the other dog; he had picked up that scent again, slightly stronger now, even if still distant. He began to move more quickly, ignoring the distractions that now crowded in upon him. He paid no attention to a practice scull that shot past him, the two rowers pulling at the oars in well-rehearsed harmony. He paid no attention to the swan that hissed at him from the water's edge, its eyes and beak turned towards him in hostility.

There was a bridge, and traffic. Cyril stuck to the path that led under the bridge. He saw trees up ahead, great towering trees in autumnal colours, and behind them the sky that Cyril saw as just another place, a blue place that was always there, far away, never reached.

He turned his nose into the wind. It was stronger now, the smell that he had been following. It was somewhere close, he thought, and he slowed to walking pace.

A long boat, the restaurant boat *Zazou*, was tied up at the edge of the canal, opposite the boating shed. Cyril saw the ramp that came down from the deck. He sniffed. There was a strong odour of food, of meat; and there was that familiar smell, the one that he had smelled in Valvona & Crolla that day – when was it? He had no idea whether it was a long time ago, for dogs have no sense of past time, but he had smelled it in that place. The smell of sun-dried tomatoes.

He began to make his way up the ramp onto the boat, stopping at the top, on the edge of the deck. Below him was the entry into a cabin in which there were tables and chairs. A group of four people sat at one of these tables. There was food before them, and glasses, and they were talking and laughing. Cyril jumped down and landed in front of the open door. As he did so, the people at the table stopped talking and turned to stare at him.

"Would you believe it?" said a man at the far side of the table. "That dog's got a gold tooth."

"You're right," said a woman beside him. "What an extraordinary sight."

A second man, who was sitting closest to the door, leaned forward to peer at Cyril.

"A gold tooth, did you say?" He stretched out a hand towards Cyril and clicked his fingers. "Come closer, boy."

Cyril advanced slowly into the galley. As he did so, the man who had called him leaned further forward and patted his head gently.

"I know who you are," he said quietly. "I've seen you in the Cumberland Bar, haven't I? You're Cyril, aren't you? Angus Lordie's dog. That's who you are."

62. Humiliation for Tofu

In Bertie's classroom at the Steiner School, the talk was almost entirely of the forthcoming production of *The Sound of Music*. Miss Harmony's casting decisions had not won universal approval; indeed, no choice of hers could possibly have secured that, given the fact that each of the girls wished to play the part of Maria and a good number of the boys had their heart set on being Captain von Trapp. The decision that Skye should be Maria at least forestalled an outcome that, by common consent, would have been disastrous – the casting of Olive in the principal role. Bertie's nomination as Captain von Trapp was, by contrast, approved of by the girls, who were generally relieved that the part had not gone to Tofu; among the girls, only Olive was hostile to this choice. Although she admired Bertie and considered herself to be his girlfriend (in spite of Bertie's vigorous denials of any such understanding), it was a bitter pill to swallow to see Bertie so favoured and herself relegated to a yet undisclosed minor role – possibly in the chorus of nuns. A better outcome, of course, would have been for her to be Liesl, the teenage girl who had a dalliance with Rolf, the telegram-delivery boy. That was a role she could have played with conviction and flair, but it had, for some inexplicable reason, been given to Pansy of all people. No boy, whether or not he delivered telegrams, would ever think of falling for Pansy, thought Olive. This was another example, in her view, of Miss Harmony's bad judgment. It was a good thing, she reflected, that Miss Harmony had become a teacher rather than a film director. Her career as a director would have been an utter failure, Olive imagined, and full of miscastings.

The one respect in which Olive felt that Miss Harmony had made a wise choice was the casting of Larch as a Nazi. That suited his personality very well, she thought, and she openly said as much.

"I'm glad that Larch is playing a Nazi," said Olive loudly. "He'll do that so well."

Miss Harmony looked at her severely. "Now, Olive, what do you mean by that, may I ask?"

The other children were silent. All eyes were now on Olive.

"Well," she said, "that's what he's like, isn't he? He's always threatening to hit people. And we all hate him. Even he knows that."

Miss Harmony pursed her lips. "Olive," she said, "Larch is a boy. Boys have different needs from girls. They sometimes need to assert themselves. We must be patient. Larch will learn in the fullness of time to control his aggressive urges, won't you Larch?"

Larch did not hear the question. He was wondering when the first opportunity to hit Olive would arise.

"He needs to get in touch with his feminine side," said Pansy suddenly. "My mother says that this helps boys."

Dramatis Personae
Skye......
Olive......
Bertie......
Pansy......
Larch......
Lakshmi......
Tofu......
Hiawatha....

Miss Harmony nodded her agreement. Larch was indeed a problem, but for the moment there were further decisions to be made. The role of the Mother Superior, a comparatively important part, had to be allocated, and this, she feared, would provide further cause for disappointment.

"Lakshmi," she said suddenly, "you shall be the Mother Superior. I'm sure that you will do that very well."

"No, she won't," said Olive. "Lakshmi is a Hindu, Miss Harmony. The Mother Superior is a Roman Catholic."

Miss Harmony sighed. "The fact that dear Lakshmi is a Hindu is neither here nor there, Olive," she said. "The whole point of acting is that you pretend to be something you're not. That's what acting is all about."

Olive was not to be so easily defeated. "But why are you getting girls to play the girls, and boys to play the boys? Why don't you make Larch or Tofu be nuns?"

Miss Harmony looked at Tofu. It was very tempting. Making him a nun would certainly help him to get in touch with his feminine side. What a good idea. "Thank you, Olive," she said quietly. "That's a most constructive suggestion. We do have rather a lot of nuns, of course, but there certainly are one or two other roles that might be suitable for Tofu. There's Baroness Schroeder. You may remember, children, that Captain von Trapp was engaged to a baroness when he first met Maria. Normally, when you are engaged to somebody that means you're going to marry that person. But an engagement also gives you time to change your mind if you need to. So it sometimes happens that an engaged person meets somebody more suitable and decides to marry him or her. That's what happened to Captain von Trapp. He realised that he preferred Maria to the Baroness and so he married Maria in the end. It was destined to be, boys and girls."

Miss Harmony stopped. It was very romantic, she thought. She herself would love to meet somebody like Captain von Trapp, who would sweep her off her feet and marry her. But were there any such men in Edinburgh? Or, indeed, in Salzburg? Somehow she thought not.

She looked at the children. "So we need a Baroness Schroeder." There was silence before she continued. Then: "And Tofu, dear, I think you could perhaps play that role."

This was a bombshell, and its target, without doubt, was Tofu. "You see, boys and girls," Miss Harmony went on, "there's a long tradition of male actors playing female roles. In Shakespeare's day, you know, all the parts were played by men and boys. So it's nothing at all unusual for Tofu to be playing the Baroness Schroeder. I'm sure he will do it very well, won't you, Tofu?"

Tofu opened his mouth to speak, but no words came.

"Good," said Miss Harmony, breezily. "So that's settled then. Now, boys and girls, we must get on with some other work. We shall start rehearsing the play tomorrow. There's no need to get costumes organised just yet. We'll start with a read-through."

Bertie felt acutely uncomfortable. He was not at all sure about being Captain von Trapp and he had his doubts about the read-through. Did Miss Harmony expect them actually to read their parts? Olive, he knew, was unable to read yet, as were Larch and Hiawatha. That was a problem. And then there was the question of Tofu's playing the Baroness Schroeder. Somehow, he found it difficult to see that. It was true, perhaps, that some boys had their feminine side, but he did not think that Tofu was one of them.

63. Irene Spoils Things

When Irene heard that Bertie had been cast as Captain von Trapp, her initial scorn at the choice of the play was replaced by enthusiasm. She had always thought that Bertie had acting ability, and this pleased her, as did any sign of talent in her son – and there were many such signs, and always had been. She herself had little time for actors and actresses, whom she regarded as brittle personalities with a tendency to both narcissism and egoism, and she would certainly not want Bertie to think of a stage career. But it was, she felt, only right that his talent in this direction should have been spotted and that he should have been given such a major part.

"I am very happy indeed, Bertie," she said as they walked down Scotland Street on the way back from school. "Not only did you do so well at that audition for the orchestra, but now here you are being given the lead role in the school play! Truly, your little cup doth run over, Bertie!"

Bertie looked at his mother. Everything she said, it seemed to him, was opaque or just wrong. He had told her that he did not want to be in the Edinburgh Teenage Orchestra, and for a very good reason, too. Bertie was six and everyone else would be at least thirteen. Why could his mother not understand that this would be a source of acute embarrassment for him? Why did she want him to do so many things, when all he wanted to do was to be allowed to play with other boys? And now here she was assuming that he was pleased to be Captain von Trapp in *The Sound of Music*, when all that this would do would be to bring down upon his head the undying hostility of Tofu, who believed the role to be his by right.

"Of course," went on Irene, "*The Sound of Music* is not the play I would personally choose, but there we are, the choice is made, and we must support Miss Harmony, mustn't we, Bertie? And, as it happens, Miss Harmony has made a very good choice in giving you the lead role. As long as you don't actually believe in anything in the play, that will be fine."

Bertie frowned. He was not sure of his mother's point. Miss Harmony had told the class that *The Sound of Music* was based on a real story; that there had been a Captain von Trapp and a Maria and all the rest. Now here was his mother saying that none of it should be believed. It was all very puzzling.

"I thought it was a true story, Mummy," said Bertie. "Miss Harmony said that the von Trapp family lived in America after they escaped from Austria. She said that they used to give concerts . . ."

"Oh yes," said Irene dismissively. "That's certainly so. But what I mean when I say that you shouldn't believe in it is that you should be able to see that the story is utterly meretricious, Bertie. *The Sound of Music* is all about patriarchy and the subservient role of women. It's a ghastly bit of romanticism. That's all that Mummy meant."

Bertie looked down at the pavement. He was not sure what meretricious meant, but it did not sound good. Melanie Klein, he assumed, would not have approved of *The Sound of Music*.

"I see that you're puzzled, Bertie," said Irene. "So let me explain. Captain von Trapp is an old-fashioned autocrat. That's a new word for you, Bertie! He was very strict with his family. He blew a whistle and made them line up in order of height."

"But maybe that was because he had been a sailor," interrupted Bertie. "Sailors love whistles. Daddy told me that. He says that Mr O'Brian . . ."

Irene raised an admonitory finger. "We can leave Patrick O'Brian out of this," she said. "I know that Daddy likes to read his books. Silly Daddy. Patrick O'Brian appeals to men because he makes them think that they can escape from their responsibilities by going to sea. That is what the Navy is all about. And Mr O'Brian told a lot of fibs about himself, you know, Bertie.

He told everybody that he was born in Ireland, whereas he wasn't.
He was an Englishman. Then he said that he went off to sea as
a sixteen-year-old or whatever age it was, and sailed a boat with
a friend. Such nonsense, Bertie! And it's significant – isn't it? –
that he then wrote all those novels about that ridiculous Jack
Aubrey sailing off with Dr Maturin, or whatever he was called.
Writers just play out their fantasies in their books. They are often
very unstable, tricky people, Bertie. Writers are usually very bad
at real life and feel that they have to create imaginary lives to
make up for it. And that was a bad case of it."

Bertie stared at his mother. She spoils things, he thought. All
she ever does is spoil things.

Irene stared back at Bertie. It was important that he should
understand, she thought. There was no reason why a bright
child like Bertie should not understand that all was not necessarily as it seemed. It was also important that he should be able
to see male posturing for what it was.

"Men often do that sort of thing," she continued. "You won't
have heard of him, Bertie, but there was another case in which
a writer pretended to be somebody else. There was a man called
Grey Owl, who lived in Canada. He pretended to be a North
American Indian and he wrote all sorts of books about living in
the forests. And he wore Red Indian outfits, too – feathers and
the like. He must have looked so ridiculous, silly man! He wrote
all these books which were about the customs of the Ojibwe
Indians and the like, but all the time he was really an Englishman
called Archie Belaney, or something like that!" She paused. "But
this is taking us rather far away from *The Sound of Music*, Bertie."

Bertie was silent. He had not started this conversation, and
it was not his fault that they were now talking about Grey Owl.
He sounded rather a nice man to Bertie. And why should he
not dress up in feathers and live in the forests if that was what
he wanted to do? It was typical of his mother to try to spoil
Grey Owl's fun.

64. Lederhosen

The conversation between Bertie and his mother on the subject of *The Sound of Music* had taken place as they walked down Scotland Street on their way home from school. The earlier part of the day had been unusually warm for autumn – indeed, the entire month had been more like late summer, with clear, sunny days that could be distinguished from June or July only by their diminishing length. Now, however, as they made their way up the stair that led to their second-floor flat at 44 Scotland Street, they both felt the chill that had crept into the afternoon.

"We must get your Shetland sweater out," said Irene, as she extracted her key from her pocket. "It's lovely and warm, and now that the weather is beginning to turn . . ." She stopped. The subject of clothing had made her think of possible costumes for the play. Maria, of course, had made the children wear clothes made out of curtain material, and that meant it would be simple enough for the mothers of the children playing those parts to run something up. Mind you, she thought, some of them probably already have clothes made out of curtains . . . She smiled. There was one of the mothers – who was it? Merlin's mother, was it not? – who wore the most peculiar clothing herself. She had a shapeless, tent-like dress made out of macramé that she had clearly run up herself, and yet she was so proud of it! She had no idea how ridiculous she looked, thought Irene, and of course that strange son of hers insisted on wearing a rainbow-coloured coat that his mother had obviously made out of . . . where on Earth had she got the material? It looked like one of those flags that they flew outside gay bars. Perhaps the silly woman had seized upon it at a gay jumble sale somewhere. What an idea! That boy, Merlin, must be so embarrassed by his mother, thought Irene. Some mothers, she reflected, are very insensitive.

She turned to Bertie as they entered the flat. "Bertie," she said, "we must fix up a costume for you for the play. Did Miss Harmony say what you should wear?"

Bertie stood quite still. The whole business of the play was enough of a minefield without his mother getting further involved. He would have to avert this, he thought.

He started to explain. "We aren't using costumes at the moment, Mummy," he said. "Miss Harmony says that we are just going to read through the play. I don't think you need bother about a costume."

"But I must," said Irene. "They always expect the mummies to make costumes. So I'll make you one, Bertie."

Bertie sighed. But then it occurred to him that Captain von Trapp probably wore a rather smart naval uniform. He would like to have such a uniform, with brass buttons down the front and one of those caps with an anchor on it.

"That's a good idea, Mummy," he said. "Why not start making it now, so that it's ready for when I need to take it to school?"

Irene was receptive to the suggestion. "Would you like me to do that?" she asked. "Well, why not? Daddy's not coming back until a bit later, so we have plenty of time. Now then, let me think. Yes, I know what I'll do."

"A Captain's outfit," said Bertie brightly. "Is that what you're thinking of?"

"Oh no," said Irene. "None of that. You know that I'm none too keen on uniforms. I think that it should be something Austrian. Yes, Captain von Trapp should wear something quintessentially Austrian."

Bertie was quiet. He was trying to remember what he had seen in a book he had which showed national dress of the world. What did the Austrians wear?

Irene answered Bertie's unspoken question. "Lederhosen, Bertie! That's what Captain von Trapp would wear."

Bertie's voice was small. "Lederhosen, Mummy?"

"Yes," said Irene. "Lederhosen, Bertie, are worn by people in southern Germany and in Austria. They're trousers that go up the front like this – a bit like dungarees, come to think of it – but they have short legs so that your knees show. And they're made of leather, of course. That's why they're called Lederhosen."

Bertie said nothing. His only hope, he thought, of averting this humiliation was an absence of leather. But again it was as if Irene had anticipated his thoughts. "Leather is a problem, of course," she said. "I have no idea where one would buy it, and it would probably be terribly expensive."

"Oh dear," said Bertie quickly. "But thank you, anyway, Mummy."

"However," said Irene. "Mummy has had an idea. Yet another one. You know that old chair which Daddy has? The one I've been meaning to get re-covered one of these days? The one where he sits and reads the paper?"

Bertie knew the old leather chair, but did not have the time to say so, as the doorbell sounded. Muttering something about not expecting anybody, Irene crossed the hallway and opened the door. A heavily-built man, out of breath from the effort of walking up the stairs, stood on the landing.

"Mrs Pollock?"

Irene nodded. She did not recognise the man, and she did not like the way that his glance shot into the hall behind her. Stewart had told her to use the chain when opening the door, but she never did. Perhaps . . .

"Bertie!" the man suddenly exclaimed. "So there you are, son!"

Irene gave a start as Bertie suddenly materialised from behind her. "Mr O'Connor!" he said.

The mention of the name made Irene freeze. So this was that man from Glasgow, Fatty O'Connor, or whatever he called himself. She looked at him coldly. "I suppose this is something to do with our car?" she said.

Lard O'Connor smiled at her. He was not easily intimidated, and he did not want to talk to her anyway. It was Stewie he was looking for. "I'd like to talk to your man," he said flatly. "And aye, it's about your motor."

"Well he's not here," said Irene, beginning to close the door. "You'll have to come back some other day. Very sorry."

Lard O'Connor glanced at Bertie. "You keeping well, son?" he asked. "Good. Well tell your Da that our man Gerry left something behind by mistake in the car. He'd like to have a wee look for it."

"But you can pick that up from the police, Mr O'Connor," said Bertie. "They found something in the car, you see."

Lard O'Connor took a step backwards. "Oh jings!" he said quietly.

65. *Reunited*

That evening, Angus Lordie went to the Cumberland Bar, as he did once or twice a week; but today there was no anticipation on his part of a couple of hours spent in pleasant company, conversing and catching up on the day's news. Rather there was a heart which was still numbed by loss. Cyril always accompanied him to the bar and was a popular canine figure there. Seated under a table, the dog would wait patiently until a dish of beer was placed before him, to be lapped at in contentment. Then Cyril would rest his head on the ground and sleep for a while before waking up and looking around the room with interest. It was a reassuring routine for both man and dog, but now it was over. Cyril was lost; he was stolen; he was, quite possibly, no more.

Angus sat alone at his table, teetering on the edge of self-pity. And then he fell in, closed his eyes, and gave himself over to thoughts of how pointless his life was. Here he was, fifty-ish, solitary, barely recognised as an artist, and then only by those who were themselves fifty-ish and unrecognised for anything very much. When had he last had a show? Two years ago, at least; and even then the paintings had hung on the walls unsold until Domenica – bless her – had out of loyalty bought one. Tom Wilson – bless him, too – had invited him to submit something for his small-scale Christmas show, and Angus, grateful for the invitation but worried that he had nothing small to offer, had simply cut a small portion out of the middle of one of his canvases and framed that. And later, when Angus had dropped in at the Open Eye Gallery to see the show and look at what others had submitted, he had noticed a couple standing in front

of his painting, peering at it. They had not noticed Angus, which was as well, for he knew them slightly – Humphrey and Jill Holmes – and he had heard Humphrey turn to Jill and say: "That's funny! I could swear that this is part of a larger painting. Don't you get that feeling?" And Angus had slipped out of the gallery in shame and had even contemplated withdrawing his painting, but had not done so. It would come back to him later on, he feared, unsold, and in this he had been proved right.

So now he sat in the Cumberland Bar and reflected on how bad was the hand of cards dealt him. If I died tomorrow, he asked himself, who would notice, or care? Now that Domenica had gone, there were few people he could drop in on; few people who were close friends. The people he knew in the Cumberland Bar went there to drink, not to see him, and if he were not there, they would carry on drinking just the same. Oh, life was dreadful, he told himself, just dreadful. And the words came back to him, the words of a song he had picked up in the Student Union bar, all those years ago, the bowdlerised words of a song sung at Irish wakes and which expressed so clearly what he now felt:

Let's not have a sniffle, boys,
Let's have a jolly good cry,

For always remember the longer you live,

The sooner you jolly well die . . .

"Angus?"

One of the barmen, the one he occasionally chatted with, had walked round the end of the bar and was standing at his table, drying his hands on a brewery towel. Angus looked up.

"You seemed very deep in thought," said the barman.

Angus tried to smile. "I suppose I was," he said. "An unhealthy state to be in. Sometimes."

The barman laughed. "Well, I wanted to tell you that that fellow who works down in the Royal Bank of Scotland – I forget his name – a nice guy. Comes in here from time to time. He phoned earlier today and left a message for you. I meant to tell you when you came in, but I forgot."

Angus looked confused. "I'm not sure if I know him," he said. "Which . . ."

The barman finished drying his hands and began to fold the towel neatly. "He said he found your dog. He found Cyril. He's bringing him in here this evening. He didn't know where you lived and he couldn't find you in the phone book . . ."

He did not finish, for at that moment the door opened and a man entered with Cyril on a lead. When Cyril saw Angus, he launched himself forward, as if picked up and propelled by a great gust of wind. The lead was pulled from the man's hand, but he did not try to stop it, as he had seen Angus at his table and he understood.

Cyril bounded over the floor of the bar, a strange sound coming from his mouth, a howl of a sort that one would not have thought a dog capable of, a whoop, an almost human wail of delight. Angus rose to his feet, and with a great leap Cyril was in his arms, licking his face, twisting his body this way and that in sheer delight, still howling in between gasps for air.

In a far corner of the bar, a young man sitting quietly at a table with a friend, turned and said: "You see that? You see that? That shows you – doesn't it? – how if you're looking for love in this life, you'd better buy yourself a dog."

The other said: "That's rather cynical, isn't it?"

"Realistic, you mean," said the first.

And they were silent for a moment, as were many in the bar who had witnessed the reunion, for they had all seen something which touched them to a greater or lesser extent. And at least some felt as if they had been vouchsafed a vision of an important truth: that we must love one another, whatever our condition in life, canine or otherwise, and that this love is a matter of joy, a privilege, that we might think about, weep over, when the moment is right.

66. Bathroom Issues

Matthew had become so accustomed to living on his own that when he arose that first morning of Pat's residence in his India Street flat he quite forgot that she was there. His morning routine was set in stone: he would pick up any post lying on the doormat, glance at the letters, and then he would take a shower in the very bathroom whose walls might have been knocked down had Leonie's plans progressed. Leonie, though, was not in his mind as he slipped out of the Macgregor-tartan jockey shorts in which he liked to sleep and stepped into the shower. Matthew was thinking of whether he should wear his new distressed-oatmeal sweater that day. He was not one to worry unduly about clothes, but he had recently realised that there was a uniform for art dealers and that if he wanted to be convincing in the role, then he had to look the part. And the one thing that art dealers in Edinburgh did not wear, it seemed, was distressed-oatmeal sweaters. That had been a mistake.

Many people in Edinburgh, it seemed to Matthew, had a uniform. Lawyers were most conspicuous in this respect, of course, with advocates in their strippit breeks striding up the Mound on their way to Parliament House each morning. India Street and its environs provided a good place for the more prosperous advocates to live, discreetly, of course, behind Georgian doors on which professional brass plates had been fixed, and

Matthew knew some of them sufficiently to nod to in the morning when he made his way to the gallery. What was their life like? he wondered: full of arguments and interpretation and the drafting of answers? His father, Gordon, had wanted him to study law, but Matthew had resisted. He had read – and quoted to his father – Stevenson's account of life in Parliament House, where the courts sat, and where advocates had to pace up and down the Hall deep in conversation with their instructing solicitors and their clients. They could make very incongruous groups, marching up and down, heads bowed in thought. Tall advocates were at an advantage, in that they could look down on their bread and butter trotting beside them – bread and butter that, by having to look, would be reminded just who was running the case. But height could work to the disadvantage of these tall advocates, who might not be instructed by short solicitors who did not like to be overshadowed in this way, whatever the realities of the professional relationship.

Matthew had heard of one very short advocate whose career had been built upon instructions given him by not-very-tall solicitors, who could walk in Parliament Hall with him and enjoy the – for them – rare experience of being able to look down on an advocate. He had done very well, even if the cases he received were small ones, with short hearings. That, thought Matthew, was an unkind story, typical of the unkind stories which lawyers told one another. The Bar, he had been told, was a strange place, given to the imposition of nicknames, which stuck. An acquaintance of Matthew's had once told him of some of these, and Matthew had listened in fascination. Who was the Pork Butcher? Who was the Tailor's Dummy? Who was the Head Prefect?

Stevenson, he pointed out to his father, had been forthright. He had been unhappy while training to be a lawyer and had called Parliament Hall *la Salle des Pas Perdus* of the Scottish Bar, where "intelligent men have been walking daily here for ten or twenty years without a rag of business or a shilling of reward . . ."

Matthew's father had sighed. "What Stevenson wrote is hardly anything to do with the law today," he said. "Think of what fun you could have, Matthew. Look at Joe Beltrami."

"Who's Joe Beltrami?" Matthew had asked.

"He's a very influential criminal lawyer," Matthew's father had replied. "A very great jurist, I believe. Glasgow, of course."

Matthew was silent. "I don't think it's really what I want to do," he had said. And his father had looked at him tight-lipped and the subject had been dropped.

That was the law. But now Matthew had found his vocation, which was in art dealing, although he had to sort out the appearance side of things. He had looked closely at what the other art dealers in Dundas Street wore and had decided that there was a distinct style. Denim was safe, but not blue denim. A black denim jacket on top of olive moleskin trousers was fine, and the shirt should be open-necked. In general, a slightly distressed look was appropriate, but this did not extend to distressed oatmeal.

Matthew finished his shower and had dried himself prior to getting dressed when Pat came into the bathroom. For a moment he stood stock-still, frozen in surprise. He had not locked the door because he never did so; people who lived by themselves rarely did. Pat was similarly motionless in the doorway. She had not heard the shower being run, and had just woken up. Seeing a light on in the kitchen – one which Matthew had, in fact, forgotten to switch off the previous night – she had assumed that he was in there having his breakfast. But he was not, as she now saw. He was standing before her in the nude, an expression of astonishment on his face.

Her eye ran down – to the pair of Macgregor undershorts lying on the chair. That was her family tartan.

"That's Macgregor tartan," she heard herself mutter.

Matthew looked down at the undershorts. It seemed to him that she was accusing him of something; that she was implying that he had no right to wear Macgregor tartan undershorts. Surely, he thought, that's no business of hers.

Pat recovered herself and turned away, closing the door behind her. Out in the hall, she looked up at the ceiling. This unexpected encounter with Matthew had unnerved her. It was not the embarrassment of the intrusion – anybody can burst in on anybody inadvertently – but it was that the memory of

Matthew standing there had affected her in a curious way.

The fact she had discovered was this: Matthew was very attractive. It was just a question of seeing him in the right light, so to speak, and now she had.

But at the same time, it irritated her to know that he wore Macgregor undershorts. What right had he to do that? she asked herself.

67. *Bathroom Issues (Continued)*

Matthew did not see Pat over breakfast that morning. When he emerged from the bathroom, fully clad, to have his breakfast, Pat's door was closed. And while he was eating his breakfast, which always consisted of a couple of slices of toast and an apple, he heard the bathroom door being opened and subsequently locked, almost demonstratively, and then the sound of a bath being run. He was glad to have the opportunity of creeping out of the flat without encountering his new flatmate. It would be embarrassing enough to appear naked to a flatmate with whom one had lived for some time; to do so on the very first morning of cohabitation was immeasurably worse. Of course, it was not his fault, unless one took the view that it was incumbent upon those within to prevent those from without from bursting in. And that was the precise question which he asked Big Lou when he crossed the road at ten-thirty for his morning cup of coffee in her coffee bar.

The coffee bar was empty when Matthew arrived – apart from the familiar figure of Big Lou, of course. The resourceful autodidact from Arbroath was standing behind the counter, a cloth on the polished surface to her left, a book open before her. As Matthew came in she looked up and smiled. She liked him, and being from a small town she had that natural courtesy which has in many larger places all but disappeared.

"Hello, Matthew," she said. "You're the first in today. Not a soul otherwise. Not even Angus and that dog of his."

Matthew leaned against the bar and peered at Big Lou's book. He reached out and flipped the book over to reveal its cover. "*A Pattern Language: Towns, Building, Construction?*" he said. "Interesting, Lou. You going to build something?"

Big Lou reclaimed her book. "You'll lose my place, you great gowk," she said affectionately. "It's a gey good book. All about how we should design things. Buildings. Rooms. Public parks. Everything. It sets out all the rules."

Matthew raised an eyebrow. "Such as?"

Big Lou turned to her coffee machine and extracted the cupped metal filter. Opening a battered white tin, she spooned coffee into the small metal cup and slotted it into place. "Such as always have two sources of light in a room," she said. "This Professor Alexander – he's the man who's written this book – says that if you have a group of people and let them choose which of two rooms they'll go into, they'll always choose the room with two windows – with light coming from more than one source. That's because they feel more comfortable in rooms like that."

Matthew looked around him. There was only one window in Big Lou's coffee bar, and a gloomy window at that. Did he feel uncomfortable as a result? Big Lou noticed his glance and frowned. "I know," she said. "I've only got one window. But sometimes one has no choice. I didn't design this place, you know."

"And what else does he say?" asked Matthew.

"Always put your door at the corner of the room," said Lou, leafing through the book to find the reference. "If you put the door in the middle, then he says that you divide the room into two."

For a moment Matthew visualised his flat in India Street. Like most flats in the Georgian New Town, it was designed with attention to classical principles, and in particular with an eye to symmetry. Palladio had understood what proportions made people feel comfortable, and so had Robert Adam and Playfair. Matthew's doors in India Street, he reflected, were all at the corner of a room, and the rooms certainly felt comfortable. This mention of doors made him remember the awkward event of earlier that morning. He would ask Big Lou about it, because it was just the sort of question which she relished and because he thought that in most matters she was intuitively right.

"Lou," he began. "You know how one locks the bathroom door when one . . . er . . . has a bath or shower or whatever."

Lou stared at him. "I believe I've heard of the custom," she said.

"Well, of course," said Matthew. "But the point is this, Lou. Do you have to lock it when you go in, or is it up to the person who is coming in to check and see if the bathroom's occupied? To knock, if the door is closed, for instance?"

Big Lou busied herself with her coffee machine. "You don't have to knock," she said. "You can assume that if there's somebody in there, then the door will be locked."

"I see," said Matthew. He paused. "But then why does the person who opens the door feel bad about it?"

The receptacle locked in place, Big Lou flicked a switch on her coffee machine. "Well now, Matthew," she said. "That's an interesting point. Why would that be? Is it because he – the person who's opened the door – has caused embarrassment to the person inside? Is that it, do you think? He has the advantage – he has his clothes on and the other person doesn't. And we don't always bother to think whether a person who causes something is at fault, do we? We say: 'You did it, you're in the wrong.' That's what we say."

The coffee machine hissed away while Matthew digested this observation. He had handled things badly, he thought. He should have stayed in the flat until Pat had come out of the bathroom and then he should have discussed it in a mature way. He should have said: "Look, Pat, I'm sorry. I totally forgot that you were there. That's why I didn't lock the door." And Pat, being reasonable, would have accepted the explanation and have laughed the incident off. But he had not done that, and the whole business had been allowed to become awkward, with the issue of his Macgregor tartan undershorts complicating matters.

"Lou," he said. "Here's another thing. Do you think that you should be able to wear clothes in another person's tartan? Do you really think it matters?"

Big Lou turned round with Matthew's cup of coffee. "Don't be so ridiculous," she said. "Here's your coffee. And anyway, here comes Eddie."

68. The Rootsie-Tootsie Club

Matthew had spent only a very short time in the company of Big Lou's fiancé, Eddie, but had decided that he did not like him. It was not one of those dislikes that develops with time, matures as more and more is learned of a person's irritating habits and faults; it was, rather, a dislike based on an immediate assessment of character, made on first meeting and never there-after doubted. We make such judgments all the time, often on the basis of appearance, bearing, and, most importantly, the look of the eyes. Matthew's father had instilled this habit in his son and had defended it vigorously.

"Take a look at the eyes, Matt," he had said. "The old adage that they are the windows of the soul is absolutely dead right. They tell the whole story."

"But how can eyes, just bits of tissue after all . . . ?"

Gordon had interrupted his son's protest. "They can. They just do. Shifty eyes – shifty chap. I've found it time after time in my business career. All the human failings are there – and the good qualities, too. You only have to . . . sorry, this is unin-tentional, keep your eyes open to pick it up."

"Give me some examples," said Matthew.

His father thought for a moment. "All right. Richard Nixon. President of the United States for a good long time. If the voters had looked at his eyes, they would have realised. Scheming. Untruthful."

"But that's because you knew what he was like," said Matthew. "If Nixon had been a saint, you would have thought his eyes looked saintly." He paused. "You've heard of phrenology, have you, Dad?"

Gordon frowned. "It sounds familiar, but . . ."

Matthew was accustomed to filling in the gaps in his father's knowledge. "They were the people who looked at the head. At the bumps. At the face, too." Gordon looked interested. "Well? What's wrong with that?"

"Because the shape of your head has nothing to do with what you're like inside," said Matthew. "Character comes from . . ." He hesitated. Where did character come from? The way you were brought up? Genes? Or a bit of both? "From the mind," he said. "That's where character comes from."

Gordon nodded. "And the mind shows itself physically, doesn't it? Well, don't shake your head like that – which, incidentally, proves my point. Your shaking head shows a state of mind within you. Yes, it does. It does."

Matthew sighed. "Nobody believes in phrenology any more, Dad. It's so . . . so nineteenth century."

"Oh is it?" challenged Gordon. "And you think they knew nothing in the nineteenth century? Is that what you're saying? Well, I'm telling you this: I judge a man by the cut of his jib. I can tell."

The argument had fizzled out, and later that day Matthew had stolen a glance at himself in the mirror, at his eyes. They had flecks of grey, of course, a feature which some girls had found interesting, and attractive, but which now seemed to Matthew to say something about his personality: he was a grey-flecked person. He knew that phrenology was nonsense, and yet, years later, he found himself making judgments similar to those made by his father; slippery people looked slippery; they really did. And how we become like our parents! How their scorned advice – based, we felt in our superiority, on prejudices and muddled folk wisdom – how their opinions are subsequently borne out by our own discoveries and sense of the world, one after one. And as this happens, we realise with increasing horror that proposition which we would never have entertained before: our mothers were right!

Had the scorned phrenologists got their hands on Eddie, they would have reached much the same conclusion as had Matthew. Eddie had a thin face – not in itself a matter for judgment – but a thin face combined with shifty, darting eyes and topped with greasy, unwashed hair conveyed an impression of seediness. It was, quite simply, not the face of an honest person – or so Matthew had concluded on first encountering Eddie.

And combined with this impression of unreliability – backed up, of course, by Matthew's knowledge of Eddie's past – was the conviction that Eddie was planning to take advantage of Big Lou by getting her to back his restaurant endeavour. Matthew had been horrified to discover that Big Lou was proposing to lend Eddie the money to buy a restaurant without anybody even looking at the accounts. Matthew may not have been a conspicuously successful businessman in the past, but his gallery now turned a profit and he knew the importance of keeping a good set of books.

When Eddie entered the coffee bar, Matthew was carrying his cup back from the counter to his accustomed seat by the wall.

"Good morning, Eddie," Matthew said politely.

Eddie nodded, but did not return the greeting. "Lou, doll," he said. "Big news!"

Big Lou leaned over the counter to plant a kiss on Eddie's sallow cheek. He smelled of tobacco and cooking oil and . . . She drew back. There had been another smell – that cheap, cloying perfume that teenage girls like to use. That was there too. "What's the news, Eddie?" she asked.

"We're going to be a club," Eddie announced. "Not a restaurant after all. This boy came round – this boy I know from the old days – and he's putting in a bit of money too, on top of what you're subbing me, and we're going to make it a club."

Big Lou was silent. A club for whom? she wondered.

"There's money in clubs," Eddie went on. "And it's less work just serving drinks. Less overheads. Although you have to pay the waitresses and the dancers."

Big Lou's voice was faint. "Dancers?"

Eddie reached for a stool and drew it up to the counter. Matthew, who had been listening while pretending to read the newspaper, glanced at him as he sat down. He's a funny shape, he thought.

"Aye," said Eddie. "Pole dancers. Not every day, but maybe once or twice a week. There's lassies very keen to develop a career as a pole dancer. We'll give them their chance."

Big Lou picked up her towel. "Well, that's nice for you, Eddie," she said. There was a sadness in her voice, a resignation, which Matthew picked up and which tugged at his heart. She does not deserve this, he thought. She does not deserve this man.

"What will you call the club, Eddie?" she asked.

"The Rootsie-Tootsie Club," said Eddie. "How's that for a name, Lou, hen? See yourself there?"

69. An Unfortunate Incident

Waking in her bungalow in the pirate settlement overlooking the Straits of Malacca, Domenica looked out at the world through the white folds of her mosquito net. Glancing at her watch, she saw that it was almost seven o'clock; the dawn had come some time earlier and already the sun was over the top of the trees around the village clearing.

Pushing aside the net, Domenica rose from her bed and stretched. The air was warm, but not excessively so. In fact, the temperature, she thought, was just perfect, although she knew that this would not last. If she felt fresh and exhilarated now, by the end of the day she would be feeling washed out, drained of all energy by the heat. So if anything had to be done, it would be best to do it in the first few hours before the sun made everything impossible and nobody could venture outside. That was the folk wisdom so neatly encapsulated by Noel Coward in 'Mad Dogs and Englishmen'; they were the only ones to be seen out in the midday sun. Well, Domenica knew better than to do that sort of thing.

She crossed the room to where her clothes were draped over a chair. She donned her blouse and her light-fitting white cotton trousers, and then, picking up her shoes – a pair of light moccasins which could be worn without socks – she slipped first her right foot in and then the left, and then . . . And then she screamed, as the sharp jab of pain shot into the toes of her left foot. Instinctively and violently, she tore the shoe off her foot and dashed it onto the floor. Out of it, half crushed and limping from the encounter, a dark black scorpion emerged and began to drag itself away across the boards.

Domenica stared in fascination at the creature that had stung her. It was so small by comparison with her foot; not much bigger than her large toe, and yet it had caused such pain. As it scuttled away, its curved stinging tail held up like a little question-mark, she felt an urge to throw a shoe at it, to crush it and destroy it, and she bent down to retrieve a shoe to do this. But then she stopped, shoe in hand. The scorpion, exhausted perhaps by its own injuries, had paused, and had turned round in a circle. Now it faced her, as if to stand up to the threatened onslaught, although it could not possibly have seen her with its tiny eyes.

If it had, she must have been a mountain to it, the backdrop to its minute, floor-level world.

She watched as it turned again and continued its limping escape. She did not have the heart to kill this little thing, this scrap of creation, which was, after all, no more predatory than anything else and considerably less so, when one thought about it, than we were ourselves. We, as homo sapiens, packed a mighty sting; a sting capable of blasting the miniature world of such arachnids into nothingness. And all it had done was to try to defend itself in its recently-discovered home against a great threatening toe. That was all.

And suddenly she remembered the lines of D.H. Lawrence about his encounter with a snake. A snake came to his water trough, a visitor, he said, from the bowels of the earth somewhere, and he threw a stone at it. Afterwards, he felt guilty, sensed that he had committed a pettiness. That was what she would feel if she crushed this small creature. She would feel petty.

She watched as the scorpion completed its retreat and disappeared over the edge of the veranda. That would have been a terrible tumble for it, falling three feet or so to the ground below, but arachnids did not seem to be injured by great falls. That was because they were so light; whereas, we, great leaden creatures, fell so heavily.

She looked down at her foot. The place where the scorpion had stung her was now inflamed and, she thought, had begun to swell. And it was painful too, the stinging having been augmented by a throbbing sensation. She bent down and felt that place. It was hot to the touch, the surface with that parchment-feel of damaged skin.

She stood up and gathered her thoughts. She had been stung by a scorpion once before, in Africa, but it had been a very small one and it had not been much worse than a bee sting. This had provoked a reaction of a completely different nature and it occurred to her that she might even need medical treatment. She remembered reading somewhere that scorpions' stings could be fatal, or could lead to the loss of a limb. Where had that been, and what sort of scorpions had they been talking about?

Domenica suddenly felt afraid. She was normally courageous, and accepted the risks of living and working in the field, but now she was frightened. It would take hours to get to a doctor, possibly a whole day, and how would she be able to walk up that path to the other village if she lost the use of her left leg?

Very tentatively, she put her weight on the affected foot. It was sore, but she could still stand, and now she walked slowly out onto the veranda. She would have to find Ling and get his help.

There was very little happening in the village. A few children were playing under a tree and a woman was washing clothes in a small plastic bucket outside her house. Domenica decided to walk over towards the woman. If she spoke English, then she could explain to her what had happened. If not, she could ask for Ling.

The woman watched Domenica approaching. As she got closer, she noticed that her visitor was limping, and she immediately dropped the clothes back into the bucket and ran over to Domenica's side.

"What's wrong?" she asked in English. "What's happened to you?"

"I've been stung by a scorpion," said Domenica. "Look."

The woman's eyes widened as Domenica pointed out the angry bite. "That is very sore," she said. "But you will not die. Don't worry. I was stung by one three weeks ago, and look, I am still alive."

She touched Domenica lightly on the shoulder, in a gesture of reassurance. "Come inside," she said. "You must not stand in the sun. Come inside and I will give you an antihistamine."

70. *Mrs Choo's Tale*

The woman to whom Domenica had gone in her pain and distress introduced herself as Rebecca Choo. Putting her arm around Domenica to help her limping neighbour up the steps, she led her into the front room of her house. There, Domenica lowered herself into the chair indicated by Mrs Choo and looked about her as her hostess went off into another room to find the promised antihistamine. The pain from the scorpion sting seemed to have abated somewhat, and when she looked down at her left foot she saw that the swelling also seemed to have subsided. She felt a strong surge of relief at this; obviously the scorpion was not too toxic, and she was not going to die, as she had feared earlier on.

The room in which she found herself sitting was plainly furnished and there was nothing on the walls – no pictures, no photographs, no religious symbols.

Domenica was still looking about her when Mrs Choo returned with a glass of water and a small white pill.

"This is an antihistamine," she said, dropping the pill into Domenica's outstretched hand. "It helps with stings and bites."

"It was my own fault," said Domenica, as she swallowed the pill. "One should never put on one's shoes without looking into them first. I completely forgot where I was."

Mrs Choo nodded her agreement. "You have to be careful," she said. "All sorts of things breed in the mangrove. Scorpions like it to be a bit drier, but we do get them from time to time."

Domenica finished the rest of the water and handed the glass back to Mrs Choo. "You have been very kind to me," she said.

"But you are our guest," said Mrs Choo. "We have a tradition of hospitality here. We look after our guests."

Domenica found herself wondering how many guests the pirate village received. She had assumed that not many people ended up here, but then she remembered the story of the Belgian anthropologist. He had been a guest too. She looked at Mrs Choo. Perhaps this was the time to start asking a few questions, now that she was seated comfortably and Mrs Choo was offering to make the two of them tea.

"Is your husband," she began. "Is Mr Choo a . . . a pirate?"

Mrs Choo laughed. "Yes, I suppose he is," she said. "It sounds very odd to say it, but I suppose he is."

Domenica frowned. It was a rather insouciant answer that she had been given and she wondered whether this was the right moment to begin her research, but Mrs Choo seemed happy to talk and it might be useful to clear the ground before she started to make detailed charts of relationship and social function.

"Has he always been a pirate?" she asked.

Mrs Choo shook her head. "Choo used to be a train driver," she said. "Then he met the headman of this village in a bar in Malacca and he invited him to come down and look at their business. That's how he became involved."

Domenica nodded her encouragement. "And you were married at the time?"

"Yes," said Mrs Choo. "Choo and I had been married for eight years."

"Were you not worried that he was going to be doing something illegal?" asked Domenica. "After all, it's a dangerous job."

"Not all that dangerous," said Mrs Choo. "I sometimes think that it's more dangerous to be a train driver or virtually anything else. Most jobs have their dangers." She paused. "We haven't lost any of the men over the last five years. Not one."

Domenica expressed surprise at this. Pursuing large ships on the high seas could hardly be a risk-free occupation, she thought. After all, some of the vessels would return fire these days. "But what about the illegality?" she pressed. "Aren't you worried that the men – and that would include your husband – may be arrested?"

Mrs Choo waved a hand in the air. "There's very little danger of that," she said. "Nobody has been arrested so far."

Domenica changed tack. "But do you approve?" she asked. "Do you think that piracy is right?"

The question did not appear to embarrass Mrs Choo. "I'm not entirely happy about it," she said. "After all, I come from a very law-abiding family. My father was the headmaster of a school. And my mother's people were a well-known mercantile family from Kuala Lumpur. But it's not as if Choo is involved in anything too serious. Just a little piracy."

Domenica decided that she would not press the matter at this stage. But she would return to it in future, she thought. There must be substantial dissonance of beliefs there; it would be fascinating to investigate that. There was, though, one question that she wanted to get out of the way now, and so she asked Mrs Choo about the Belgian anthropologist. Had she known him, and how had he died?

She asked the question and then sat back in her chair, awaiting the answer. But for a time there was none. Mrs Choo seemed to freeze at the mention of the Belgian. She had been sitting back in her chair before Domenica asked it; now she sat bolt upright, her hands folded primly at her waist. It was not body language which suggested readiness to talk.

There was silence for a good few moments before Mrs Choo eventually spoke. "That man," she said coldly, "went back to Belgium. He went back to where all those other Belgians live. That is what happened to him. More tea?"

Domenica, an astute woman, even in unfamiliar social circumstances, guessed that the conversation was an end. It had been a mistake to stray into matters of controversy so quickly, she thought. People did not appreciate that, she reminded herself. They liked subtlety. They liked discretion. They liked the circumlocutory question, not the brutal, direct one. So she immediately made a superficial remark about the attractive colour of the orchids on the veranda. Did Mrs Choo know that one could buy such orchids in Edinburgh? They were imported, she believed, from Thailand and Malaysia.

"They are very attractive flowers," said Mrs Choo, warming a bit. "I am glad that people in Scotland like orchids."

"Oh, they do," said Domenica. "They are always talking about them."

Mrs Choo looked surprised. "I'm astonished," she said. "Always talking about orchids? Even the vulgar people?"

Domenica smiled. It was such a strange expression, but she knew exactly what Mrs Choo meant. "Maybe not them," she conceded.

Domenica spent a further hour or so drinking green tea and talking to Mrs Choo. She did not wish to overstay her welcome, but it very soon became apparent to her that her hostess had very little to do. In fact she said as much at one point, when she referred to the heaviness with which time hung on her hands now that her children were at school. But apart from the occasional self-pitying remark, she was a light-hearted companion who made Domenica feel appreciably better about her situation. And her situation, of course, was that of having been the victim of a rather uncomfortable scorpion sting.

At the end of the hour, though, the swelling on the tip of Domenica's left foot had diminished considerably, and the stinging pain which had followed upon the initial encounter with the scorpion had all but disappeared. When she rose to leave, she found that it was perfectly possible to put her full weight on her left foot without feeling much discomfort, and her walk back to her own house was a proper walk rather than a hirple.

Ling was waiting for her on the veranda, seated on the planter's chair, a paperback book on his lap. Domenica did not see him until she had mounted the steps, and she gave a start when he rose to his feet to greet her.

"You frightened me," she said, "sitting there in the shadows."

"I'm very sorry," he said. "I saw you go across to Mrs Choo's house, and so I thought that I would just wait for you." He paused, and looked at her foot. "You were limping. I was worried that you had hurt yourself."

Domenica explained about the scorpion, and Ling bared his feet in sympathy and shared discomfort. "If you see another scorpion," he said, "you must ring this bell. You see, I have brought you a bell."

He fished into the pocket of the tunic top he was wearing and extracted a small brass bell. As he gave it to Domenica, he shook it and a penetrating, surprisingly loud sound rang out.

"If I hear that sound," he said, "then I shall come running over from my place."

Domenica thanked him and took the bell. "I shall only use it in a dire emergency," she said. "Only then."

Ling nodded. "If the Belgian had had a bell . . . " He tailed off, as if he had suddenly remembered that this was a subject that was not to be talked about. But Domenica had heard.

"This Belgian," she said quickly. "The anthropologist. Mrs Choo said to me . . ."

She did not have the chance to finish the sentence. "Now then," said Ling firmly, "we have much to do. Or rather, you have much to do." He looked about him. "Do you wish me to interpret?"

Domenica shrugged. "Well, I'll need to meet people," she said. "I've only spoken to Mrs Choo so far, and that was just a general conversation."

"Mrs Choo is not always accurate," said Ling, his voice lowered, as if Mrs Choo herself might hear. "She means well, but she is not an accurate person."

Domenica said nothing. If one was using an interpreter in an anthropological study, it was important that the translation be scrupulously correct. There was nothing worse than an interpreter who had his or her own view of what was what, and this, she feared, might be the case with Ling.

"It's very kind of you to be concerned about accuracy," she said gently. "But the important thing for me is that I hear exactly what people say. It doesn't matter if you think that they are wrong about something. I can work that out later. All I want to hear is what they say."

Ling frowned. "But what if they're telling lies?" he asked. "What if I know that what they are saying is just wrong? I cannot stand by and let people deceive you."

For a moment Domenica said nothing. This was going to be difficult, she feared, and a measure of tact was required. "Well, how about this, Ling?" she said. "You can tell me exactly what somebody says. Then, afterwards, you can tell me what you think they should have said. In that way we can keep the two things separate."

Ling smiled. "That is a very good idea," he said. "You can hear what the vulgar people say first; then you can get the truth from me."

Domenica nodded enthusiastically. But she had noted, again, the use of the term "vulgar people", the expression used by Mrs Choo earlier, when they had discussed orchids. This was obviously a literal translation from the local Chinese dialect. Unless, of course, Ling thought that the people of the village were truly vulgar. That was always a possibility.

"Tell me, Ling," she said. "What do you think of these local people?"

"I despise them, of course," he said evenly, as if that were the only possible answer. "Why do you ask?"

Domenica left it at that. She had talked enough that morning, and she told Ling that she would like to take a small walk around the village, just by herself, to get her bearings. He left her then, and after a refreshing drink of fruit juice, she set off for a stroll round the periphery of the village. After a while, she came to a path, and she followed this, assuming that it would lead to the sea.

Halfway down the path there was a small clearing off to one side, and in this clearing there was a large, solitary tree. Domenica hesitated. It was very still, and she felt vaguely uneasy, as if she were somewhere she should not be. She looked about her. On either side of her, the jungle rose, a high green wall, lush and impenetrable. One could not see far into that, she thought, and if one could, what would one see? She turned, and stared at the tree in its clearing. She had noticed something under it – a marker of some sort – and she went to investigate. It was a grave, a simple, untended grave, at the head of which a small board had been placed on a stake and fixed into the ground.

She bent to read the inscription on the wooden board. HERE LIES AN ANT, it said.

72. *Preparations for Paris*

"My goodness, Bertie!" said Irene. "Your little diary is very full these days. Let's think of what we have. In fact, let's play a little game. Mummy will list the things you have to do in Italian, and you can translate. How about that?"

Bertie, sitting at the kitchen table in the Pollock flat in Scotland Street, his legs not quite reaching the floor yet, sighed. "If you want to, Mummy."

"*Allora,*" said Irene. "*In primo luogo: Tutti insieme appassion-atamente!*"

Bertie looked puzzled. "*Cosa?*" he asked.

Irene smiled, and repeated herself carefully. "*Si, Bertie: Tutti insieme appassionatamente!* Do you know what that means? *Tutti* – we know that word, don't we, Bertie? *Tutti frutti!* You know what that means."

"All fruits," said Bertie.

"*Bravo! Allora,* if *tutti* means all, what about *insieme*? A nice little word that, Bertie. Very useful. No? Well, it means together, doesn't it, Bertie? You should have known that by now. But no matter. So . . ."

"All together passionately," said Bertie. "What's that got to do with me, Mummy?"

Irene raised a finger. "Well, Bertie," she said, "that's what *The Sound of Music* is called in Italian. Yes! That's what they call it. Isn't that interesting? But let's move on to the second thing."

Bertie was silent. He was thinking of the problems that lay ahead with the school production of *The Sound of Music*, in which he was to play Captain von Trapp. The fact that he had been chosen for this role was bound to lead to conflict with Tofu – he was sure of that – and Bertie had no desire for conflict, partic-ularly with a friend. Tofu was not much of a friend, but he was all that Bertie had.

"*In secondo luogo,*" said Irene brightly. "*In secondo luogo,* we have *L'Orchestra degli adolescenti di Edimburgo.* And we know what that is, don't we, Bertie?"

Bertie did, and the thought of playing in the Edinburgh Teenage Orchestra filled him with even more dread than did the prospect of being in *The Sound of Music*. They had already had one or two rehearsals, which Bertie had attended with some reluctance. Now it was almost time to go to France on the much-

L'Orchestra
degli
adolescenti
di Edimburgo

vaunted Parisian tour, and it seemed to him that there was no way out for him. He could try to feign illness, of course, but he very much doubted whether he would get away with that. So it looked as if he would have to go, in spite of being at least seven years younger than everybody else.

There was one consolation, though – the fact that his mother would not be coming after all. That prospect had truly appalled him, but had been eventually ruled out after the committee running the orchestra had refused point-blank to make an exception to their no-parents rule.

"It's not that we have any objection to parents *per se*," the chairman of the committee had told Irene. "It's just that it's difficult enough doing the logistics for the children themselves. If we have to start making arrangements for the parents too, then it would become a nightmare."

Irene had begun to protest. "But in my case . . ."

"And there's another thing," persisted the chairman, raising his voice. "If we allowed one parent to come, we'd have to allow all the others. And that would inhibit some of the children. We've found that they play better if they don't have parents breathing down their necks. It brings them out of themselves a bit."

Irene glared at the chairman. "Are you suggesting that I would actually inhibit Bertie?"

The chairman made a calming gesture. "Perish the thought! Naturally, this doesn't apply to you, Mrs Pollock. You wouldn't inhibit Bertie. But not every parent is as reasonable as you clearly are. You'd be surprised at some of the people I meet in this job. You really would. I meet some really pushy people, you know. Mothers who just won't let go, particularly of their sons."

The chairman looked at Irene as he spoke. He wondered what degree of insight she had into her behaviour. Probably none, he thought. These people smother their sons, poor boys, and then, the first opportunity the sons have, they distance themselves. It was rather sad, really. One boy who had been in the orchestra had actually emigrated to Australia to get away from his mother under the Australian government's Son Protection Scheme. And then she went to live there too.

Reluctantly, Irene had accepted that she would not be able to travel with Bertie. However, she had a list of things for Bertie to be reminded to do, and she asked the chairman to write these down and pass them on to one of the women who would be looking after the teenagers. There were instructions about Bertie's clothing, about his diet, and about the need for him to be given time to work on his Italian exercises.

"Bertie also does yoga," she went on. "It would be helpful if he were to be given a mat to do his yoga on. But please remind him to do it."

There were other things on the list, and these were all duly noted. Poor boy, thought the chairman, but did not say that. Instead, he said: "What a lucky little boy Bertie must be – to have all these things in his life."

"Thank you," said Irene. "My husband and I . . . well, we call it the Bertie Project."

The chairman said nothing. He had looked out of the window, where a bird had landed on a branch of the elm tree near his window. Birds are such an obvious metaphor for freedom, he thought.

And so now Irene had packed Bertie's case for him, neatly

folding and tucking in a spare pair of dungarees and an adequate supply of socks. It was a strange feeling for her, sending Bertie off to Paris like this, and she had more than one pang of doubt as to whether the whole thing was a good idea. But then she told herself that the people in charge of the orchestra would be experienced in looking after children on such trips, and that if they could look after teenagers, who were notoriously unruly and difficult, then looking after a compliant little boy such as Bertie would be simplicity itself. So she became reconciled to Bertie's imminent departure, as did Bertie himself. Paris, he thought, would just have to be endured, and three days would go quickly enough. And it would, after all, be three days without his mother. That was something.

73. *At the Airport*

By the time he arrived at Edinburgh Airport, Bertie's view of his impending trip to Paris had changed almost completely. Dread had been replaced by anticipation and the excited questioning of his father, who had driven his son out to the airport in their newly-recovered Volvo, the precise status of which remained an awkward issue. That it was not their original car was now beyond doubt, but Stuart felt – and in this he was backed up by Irene – that they now had some sort of prescriptive right to it. It was not as if they had acquired anything new; they had started with one Volvo and still had only one. Somewhere in between, presumably as a result of the helpful intervention of Mr Lard O'Connor, of Glasgow, the precise identity of the car had changed, but this still left them with only one car. Somebody else must have theirs, and so the overall number of cars in circulation had not changed. It was a rough calculation, but a just one nonetheless.

Stuart parked the car, taking careful note of which section it was in. Then, carrying the small brown suitcase that Irene had packed for Bertie, he accompanied his son into the terminal.

"Look, Daddy," shouted Bertie, pointing to the tail of a plane that could just be made out peeking over a covered walkway. "Look, that must be my plane."

"Perhaps," said Stuart, looking down at his son. This was Bertie's first flight; could he remember his own first time in the air? It was a remarkable moment for most people, a moment when the laws of gravity are for the first time ostensibly flouted, and for him this had been in Fife, he thought, during a brief time as an air cadet. He had been fifteen and had been taken, along with several other boys, on a flight from Leuchars. He had not thought about that for a long time, but now it came back to him. How young the world was in those days, how fresh.

They had been told that the members of the orchestra would all congregate just inside the terminal so that they might check in together. And there they were, all milling about near the foot of the escalator. Bertie spotted them first and tugged at his father's sleeve. Everybody was so tall, so grown-up, and this made his heart sink. Nobody was in dungarees, of course, except him.

Stuart would have wished to have remained with the group until they had gone through security, but he sensed that it would be important for Bertie that he should not.

"Well, that's it, Bertie," he said, passing the suitcase over. "That's you all set up. I'll let you get on with it now."

Bertie looked up at his father. "You're not staying, Daddy?"

"Well, I think you can look after yourself," said Stuart. "So I'll just say goodbye."

He wanted to pick this little boy up and hug him. But he could not do that, not with all these teenagers around, and so he put out his hand and Bertie took it in his.

"Good-bye, Bertie," he said. "Good luck in Paris, son!"

Bertie shook hands solemnly with his father and then Stuart turned round and walked off. He did not look back.

Left with the others, Bertie stood in silence. He imagined that people would be staring at him, but he soon realised that nobody was paying him any attention and he relaxed. One of the flautists, a girl of about sixteen, glanced at him at one point and smiled. Bertie smiled back. Then she said something to her friend, which Bertie did not hear, and the friend looked over in his direction and gave him a wave. Bertie waved back.

Bertie was fascinated by the whole process of checking in for the flight and going through the security search. The conductor seemed to be in charge of the party and Bertie decided to follow him closely, keeping a pace or two behind him. And then, on the other side of the barrier, he waited while the rest of the orchestra came through and they could go off to wait at the departure gate. Bertie looked about him; he felt very important.

"All right, Bertie?" asked the conductor. "You looking forward to Paris?"

"Yes, I am," said Bertie. "Thank you very much, sir."

The conductor laughed. "You don't have to call me sir," he said. "My name's Richard. Richard Neville Towle. But you can just call me Richard." He paused. "You checked your saxophone in, did you? I hope that you had a strong enough carrying case."

For a few moments, Bertie said nothing. Then, his voice barely audible, he said: "I'm sorry."

"Sorry about what?" asked Richard. "Do you think the case will break?"

"I didn't bring it," said Bertie, his voice small and broken. "Mummy just gave me my suitcase. That was all. I forgot my saxophone at home."

Richard sighed. Taking an orchestra anywhere was always a difficult business; taking a youth orchestra was even worse. This was not the first time that he had been obliged to deal with an instrument being left at home, and at least it would be easy to borrow a saxophone at the other end. It was not as if Bertie played the cor anglais or anything like that; that might have been a bit more problematic.

He reached down and patted Bertie on the shoulder. "Not to worry, old chap," he said. "Paris is full of tenor saxophones. We can very easily borrow one for the three days that we're there. In fact, I'll call ahead to a friend I have over there and get him to have it sorted out by the time we arrive at the hotel. No need to be upset."

Bertie had begun to cry, and so Richard knelt down and put

an arm around his shoulder. "Come on, Bertie," he said gently. "Worse things have happened."

Bertie made an effort to control his tears. This was a terrible start, he thought; to go off with a group of teenagers and then to start crying. It was just terrible. He looked about him furtively, half-covering his face with his hands so that the others might not see his tears. Fortunately, they all seemed to be busy talking to one another. They were smiling and laughing. As well they might, thought Bertie: they had their instruments with them.

74. *The Principles of Flight*

By the time they boarded the aircraft, Bertie's spirits had picked up again. He tried to give an impression of knowing what to do – an impression which would have been weakened if anybody had seen him turn left on the entrance to the plane, rather than right, and head purposefully towards the flight deck. But nobody saw this solecism, apart from a cabin attendant, who gently pointed him in the direction of the window seat that had been allocated him and into which he was shortly strapped, ready to depart.

Bertie had already seen, but not met, the boy who came and sat next to him. Now, turning to Bertie, this boy, who in Bertie's reckoning was at least fifteen, introduced himself. "I'm Max," he said. "And you're called Bertie, aren't you?"

Bertie nodded. "Yes," he said. "I play the saxophone, only . . ." He was about to explain that he did not actually have his saxophone with him, but he decided not to mention this. Max would think him rather stupid to have left his instrument behind, and Bertie wished to impress Max.

"Where do you go to school?" Max asked, as he adjusted his seat belt.

"The Steiner School," Bertie said.

"That's nice," said Max. "I go to the Academy. I play the cello there. And I'm in Mr Backhouse's chamber choir."

"I bet you're good at the cello," Bertie said generously.

"Quite good," said Max. "But not as good as somebody called Peter Gregson. He used to be at the Academy and now he's gone to study the cello in London. I'll never be as good as he is."

"But you do your best, don't you?" said Bertie seriously. He was enjoying this conversation and he wondered whether Max would be his friend. It would be grand to have a friend in Paris. Some people went to Paris without a friend, and that couldn't be much fun, thought Bertie. He looked at Max. He had a kind face, he thought, and he decided that it might be best to ask him directly.

"Will you be my friend?" Bertie asked. And then added: "Just for Paris. You don't have to be my friend forever – just for Paris."

Max looked at Bertie in surprise. Then he smiled, and Bertie noticed that his entire face lit up when this happened. "Of course I will," he said. "That's fine by me. I don't know many of the people in this orchestra and so it would be nice to have a friend."

Bertie sat back in his seat feeling quite elated. The forgetting of the saxophone was not really a problem, according to the conductor, and now here he was about to take off on his first flight and he was doing it in the company of a nice boy called Max. Really, he had everything he could possibly wish for.

The last preparations for the departure were completed and the plane began to taxi towards the end of the runway. Bertie stared out of the window, fascinated. And then, with a sudden, throaty roar the plane began to roll down the runway, slowly at first and then picking up speed. Bertie felt himself being pressed back into his seat by the force of the acceleration, and then, almost imperceptibly, they were airborne and he saw the ground drop away beneath him.

He watched as the plane banked round and began to head off towards Paris. He saw the motorway to Glasgow, with the cars moving on it like tiny models. By craning his neck, he saw the Pentland Hills and the Firth of Forth, a steel-grey band snaking up into the bosom of Scotland. And then, down below them, hills; green and brown folds, stretching off to the south and west.

Soon they were at altitude, and the plane settled down into even flight. The members of the orchestra made up the majority of the passengers and the cabin was filled with an excited buzz of conversation between them, restrained among the strings and woodwind, rowdy among the brass and percussion. Bertie looked over his shoulder and down the rows behind him. One of the girls who had waved to him earlier caught his eye and smiled. Bertie smiled back. He felt quite grown-up now, here with this group of which he was now a member, even if they were so much older. Somebody has to be the youngest, he thought, and they were all being very nice to him about it. Nobody had laughed at him, so far; nobody had suggested that he was too small.

After a while, Bertie slipped past Max and whispered something to one of the attendants. She smiled and told him to follow her to a small door near the galley. Bertie entered the cramped washroom and emerged shortly afterwards to find that the Captain of the aircraft was standing in the galley area, in conversation with one of the attendants. Bertie gazed in admiration at the Captain, who looked down at him and smiled.

"Hello, young man," said the Captain, winking at Bertie. "Is this your first flight?"

"Yes," said Bertie. "But I know how it works."

The Captain smiled. "Oh do you?" he said. "Well, you tell me then."

"Bernoulli's principle," said Bertie.

The Captain glanced at the attendant and then back at Bertie. "What did you say, young man?"

"You need lift to fly," explained Bertie. "Mr Bernoulli discovered that pressure goes down when the speed of flow of a fluid increases. That's what pushes the wing up. The air flows more quickly over the top than the bottom." He paused, and then added: "I think."

The Captain reached out and shook Bertie's hand. "Well, that's pretty much how it works. Well done! You carry on like that, son, and . . ."

Bertie waited for the Captain to say something else, but he did not, and so he went back to his seat.

"I saw you talking to the Captain there," said Max. "What did you say?"

"I was telling him about Bernoulli's principle," said Bertie. "But I think he knew already."

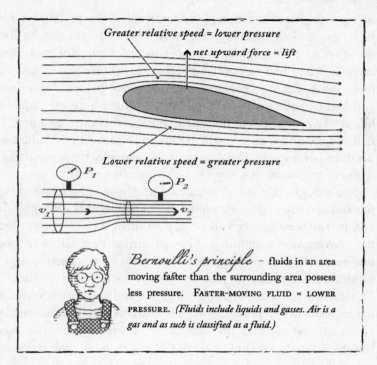

Greater relative speed = lower pressure

↑ net upward force = lift

Lower relative speed = greater pressure

P_1

P_2

v_1 v_2

Bernoulli's principle – fluids in an area moving faster than the surrounding area possess less pressure. FASTER-MOVING FLUID = LOWER PRESSURE. *(Fluids include liquids and gasses. Air is a gas and as such is classified as a fluid.)*

The flight was over far too quickly for Bertie. It seemed to him only a matter of a few minutes before the plane started to dip down through the clouds to Charles de Gaulle Airport.

"Charles de Gaulle was President of France," observed Bertie to Max, as they taxied up to the terminal.

"Ooh la la!" replied Max. "Paris! Boy, are we going to have fun, Bertie! Have you heard of a place called the Moulin Rouge, Bertie? You heard of it?"

75. *Scotland's Woes*

Antonia Collie, Domenica's tenant during her absence in the Malacca Straits, was uncertain what to do about Angus Lordie. The artist had invited her to dinner a few weeks previously and then, with very little notice, had cancelled the invitation. He had explained that his dog, Cyril, had been stolen, and he had said that he was, frankly, too upset to entertain. She had been surprised, and had wondered whether the excuse was a genuine one. She had been cancelled once or twice before, by others, and had herself occasionally had to call something off. But she had never encountered, nor used, a pretext relating to a dog. It had the air of the excuse which children use for their failure to produce homework: The dog ate it. Presumably there were dogs who really did eat homework, but they must be rare.

She thought that it had been kind of Angus to let her into the flat and make her welcome on the day of her arrival in Edinburgh, and it had been kinder still of him to invite her to dinner. But her conversation with him had been a curious one, full of tension just below the surface. It seemed to her as if he was keen to assert himself in her presence; that he was for some reason defensive. Of course there were men like that, she realised – men who felt inadequate in the presence of a woman who was intellectually confident, who could do something which perhaps the man himself wanted to do but could not. Some men only felt comfortable if they could condescend to women, or if they felt that women looked up to them. Her own husband had been a bit like that, she thought. He had found it necessary to take up with that empty-headed woman from Perth, a woman who could hardly sustain an intelligent conversation for more than five minutes, if that.

Or could it be envy? Antonia was very conscious of the corrosive power of envy and felt that it was this emotion, more than any other, which lay behind human unhappiness. People did not realise how widespread envy was. It was everywhere – in all sorts of relationships, insidiously poisoning the way in which people felt about one another. Antonia had been its victim. As a girl, she had been envied for her academic prowess, and she had been envied for her looks, too. She had no difficulty in attracting boys; girls who could not do this envied her and wished that something would happen to her hair, or that her skin would become oily.

Children, of course, knew no better. But she saw envy persisting into adult life. She saw it at work in her marriage,

and now she noticed it in public life too, now that she knew what to look for. Scotland was riddled with it, and it showed itself in numerous ways which everyone knew about but did not want to discuss. That was the problem, really: new ideas were not welcome – only the old orthodoxies; that, and the current of anti-intellectualism that made intelligent men (and she was thinking of men now) want to appear to be one of the lads. These men could talk and think about so much else, but were afraid to do so, because Scotsmen did not do that. They talked instead about football, trapped in that sterile macho culture which has so limited the horizons of men. Poor men.

Antonia moved to her window and looked out over Scotland Street. Our country, she thought, is such an extraordinary mixture. There is such beauty, and there is such feeling; but there is also that demeaning brutality of conduct and attitude that has blighted everything. Where did it come from? From oppression and economic exploitation over the centuries. Yes, it had. And that continued, of course, as it did in every society. There were blighted lives. There were people who had very little, who had been brutalised by poverty and who still were. But it was not just the material lack – it was an emptiness of the spirit. If things were to change, then the culture itself must look in the mirror and see what rearrangement was required in its own psyche. It had to become more feminine. It had to look at the national disgrace of alcoholic over-indulgence. It had to stop the self-congratulation and the smugness. It had to realise that we had almost entirely squandered our moral capital, built up by generations of people who had striven to lead good lives; capital so quickly lost to selfishness and discourtesy. It had to admit that we had failed badly in education and that this could only be cured by restoring the respect due to teachers and cajoling parents into doing their part to discipline and educate their ill-mannered children. It had to think sideways, and up and down, and round the corner. It had to open its mind.

This train of thought had started with Angus, who had re-issued his invitation for dinner for that evening. She had accepted, although she would rather have stayed at home and continued to write about her Scottish saints and their difficult lives. She did not think that the acquaintanceship with Angus would go anywhere. It was curious, was it not, that people expected those who were by themselves to be looking for somebody else. There were plenty of people – and she was one – who rather relished being on their own. If she met a man who interested her – and, thinking over the last year, she found it difficult to bring any such man to mind – then she might be prepared to contemplate an affair, or should she call it an involvement? The word "affair" was an odd one. It had suggestions of the illicit about it. And it implied the existence of a terminus: affairs were not meant to last. That, she thought, was why Graham Greene was right in that title of his, *The End of the Affair*. There was a sad inevitability about that.

Antonia turned away from the window and smiled. Graham Greene! That was Angus Lordie's problem. He was a Graham Greene-ish character, just like that dentist who had run out of gas and went down to the jetty every day to see if the boat would bring him new supplies. Dentists on jetties; whisky priests; seedy colonial officials; and now a failed portrait painter in the unfashionable end of the Edinburgh New Town. *C'est ça!* Greeneland.

76. Brunello di Montalcino

Had he known that Antonia was mentally comparing him to a character from a Graham Greene novel, Angus Lordie's existing dislike of his prospective guest would have doubled, or quadrupled perhaps. And had he known that a literary comparison was being made, he would himself have sought comparisons of his own. There she was, writing her novel in Domenica's flat, not doing anything of importance really. And the novel – if it existed at all – might never be published anyway. Plenty of people were writing novels; in fact, if one did a survey in the street, half of Edinburgh was writing a novel, and this meant that there really weren't enough characters to go round. Unless, of course, one wrote about people who were themselves writing novels. And what would the novels that these fictional characters were writing be about? Well, they would be novels about people writing novels.

Angus Lordie stood in his kitchen, his blue and white striped apron tied about his waist, contemplating the appetising collection of ingredients he had bought from Valvona & Crolla. Even if he was not looking forward to receiving Antonia, he was certainly looking forward to the experience of cooking the meal. He glanced at his watch; it was now five o'clock, which meant that it would be roughly three hours before Antonia arrived (provided, he thought, that she knew that an invitation for seven-thirty meant ten to eight). There were always people who did not understand this, and who arrived on time, but he did not think Antonia would be one of these. So he had his three hours to prepare the meal.

He had planned the menu carefully. They would start with ravioli Caprese, ravioli stuffed with a mixture of parmesan and goat's milk cheese. Angus had decided against using sheep's milk *caciotta*, the sort used in Tuscany, on the grounds that in Capri itself he had read that *caciotta* was made of goat's milk. That is something that he thought he might raise with Antonia, telling her, perhaps, that he had assumed that she would want the Caprian version rather than the Tuscan. That would catch her out, because she would not know anything about that. They would then move on, for their main course, to sogliole alla Veneziana, sole with Venetian sauce. That would involve a white wine sauce in which he would put a lot of garlic, and with it he would serve carciofi ripieni alla Mafalda, stuffed artichokes which he had learned to make by reading Elizabeth David's *Italian Food*. That was quite a complex recipe, involving more garlic and some anchovies, but he had plenty of time to get everything ready; and what was the time now that he had laid out all the ingredients? – five-thirty, which was time, perhaps, for a drink. He had obtained two bottles of a southern wine, a Cirò Bianco from Calabria, and he already had a supply of Biondi-Santi Brunello di Montalcino, which a friend had given him in payment for a portrait a few months ago.

Antonia would know nothing about Brunello, of course. He might mention Montalcino and ask her whether she thought it had been spoilt. "You don't know Montalcino? Oh, you should go there. But maybe it's a bit late, now that it's become so popular. That's the trouble with Tuscany. Terribly busy."

He had opened one of the bottles of Brunello to let it breathe, and while he was thinking these delicious thoughts involving the putting of Antonia in her place, he decided to allow himself a glass of the elegant Italian wine. He raised the glass to the light and stared at it lovingly. It would be wonderful to be back in Montalcino, perhaps walking in the woods with Cyril. Would Cyril have a good nose for truffles? he wondered. It would be interesting to take him there now that dogs could get a passport.

The Brunello slipped down very easily and Angus decided to refill his glass. The second helping would be more subtle, he felt, and he could savour it as he prepared the stuffed artichokes. He took a sip and closed his eyes. It was delicious. But what he needed now was some music, and this is where Cyril came in.

Angus had taught Cyril very few tricks. There were some dogs who were trained to carry the newspaper back from the paper shop, walking obediently behind their master, the day's news clamped in their jaws.

That, thought Angus, was a rather pointless trick. Like Mr Warburton in Somerset Maugham's *The Outstation*, a pristine newspaper was one of Angus Lordie's main delights, and it would not do to have canine toothmarks all over the front page.

But Cyril's inability to perform such standard tricks did not mean that he could do nothing useful. In fact, Cyril had been trained to perform a trick of which he was inordinately proud and which Angus Lordie felt was positively useful. On the command "Cyril! Music!" the obedient dog would bound through to the drawing room and press the on/off button of the CD player with his nose.

That would activate the disc, one of which Angus always kept in the player, and music would be heard. And in anticipation of the Italian cuisine planned for Antonia, Angus had loaded a disc of Florentine music of the sixteenth century.

On his master's command, Cyril dashed off to perform his trick. In the kitchen, Angus called out his thanks and cut off a small piece of anchovy to feed to Cyril as a reward. Then, into the white enamel bowl from which Cyril was given liquid treats, he poured a small quantity of Brunello di Montalcino.

It was far too good a wine to give to a dog in normal circumstances, but Angus was still enjoying the euphoria of being re-united with Cyril after his recent kidnap, and felt that an exception should be made.

Cyril wolfed down the anchovy fragment and then turned to the Brunello, which he sniffed at appreciatively before licking it quickly from the bowl. By this time, Angus had poured himself a third glass of the Brunello.

It's extraordinary how the level of a good wine in the bottle sinks so quickly, he said to himself as he lifted the bottle to the light.

Oh well, that was a gorgeous piece of early Florentine music playing: *Ecco la Primavera*, a favourite song of his. Spring has arrived. At last, at last. And here, Cyril my boy, is a toast to spring! *La Primavera!*

Cyril gazed at his master. There was much that he did not understand.

Antonia Collie, bound for dinner in Angus Lordie's Drummond Place flat, but none too enthusiastic about the prospect, left Domenica's flat shortly before twenty-to-eight that evening. She imagined that it would take her not much more than five minutes to walk up the street and round the corner, which would mean that she would arrive at about the right time for a seven-thirty invitation. In the event, it took her only two minutes to reach the top of Scotland Street, from which point the walk to Angus Lordie's front door would require only another forty-five seconds. So, rather than arrive too early, she decided to walk round the square once before ringing his doorbell. These things might not seem important, but Antonia thought that they were, and she was right, and Immanuel Kant, famous for the utter regularity of his walks around Königsberg, would doubtlessly have agreed with her.

Unknown to Antonia, her host was at that moment peering out of the window of his drawing room, which looked over the gardens in the middle of the square. He had finished his preparations in the kitchen, and had moved into the drawing room, taking with him Cyril and the second bottle of Brunello di Montalcino. Angus had not intended to have more than one or two glasses of wine while cooking the dinner, but he had found that the sheer quality of the Brunello had dictated otherwise. The contents of the first bottle had slipped down almost unnoticed, and now the second bottle was seriously broached.

He was now in an extremely good mood. The sinking feeling which he had experienced earlier on at the thought of entertaining Antonia had been replaced by a rather more positive attitude. In fact, now he was looking forward to her arrival, as he hoped to show her a recently-acquired Alberto Morrocco still-life, a present from an old friend. It had been a handsome gift, and Angus had given the painting pride of place on his walls. Antonia, he thought, was bound to like it, just as he imagined that she would in due course approve of the portrait he was planning of the retired lawyer Ramsey Dunbarton. Angus Lordie knew Ramsey Dunbarton from the Scottish Arts Club, where they occasionally had lunch at the same table. He found Ramsey's conversation somewhat dull – in fact, extremely dull, for most of the time – but he was a tolerant man and was prepared to put up with long-winded stories about Morningside as he ate his lunch, provided that the subject could be changed by the time they went upstairs for coffee. In a rash moment, Angus had offered to paint Ramsey's portrait, and the offer had been immediately accepted. Ramsey had taken out his diary and said: "When? Will next week do? Monday morning?"

Now, looking out of his window, he saw the figure of a woman come up from the top of Scotland Street and hesitate. He thought that it might be Antonia, but then his long vision was not very good at night and he could not make out the woman's features. He saw her hesitate, look about her, and then start to stroll around the square. That was interesting, he thought. "That woman has an agenda," he said to Cyril, who was sitting on the carpet in the middle of the room looking up at the light. Cyril cocked his head in his master's direction in acknowledgement of the comment addressed to him, and then resumed his contemplation of the light. Angus poured himself another glass of Brunello.

Angus was still at his window when Antonia completed her walk round the square and arrived outside his door. He was now very interested in the behaviour of this woman, but when the doorbell rang shortly thereafter he realised that it was, after all, Antonia. But why would she have gone for a walk round the square? Killing time, of course. He looked at his watch. Yes, that was it. How considerate of her.

He went into his hall to operate the buzzer that would open the door onto the street. Then, going out onto the landing, he looked down into the stairwell.

"Come on up!" he called out, and added: "Yoo hoo!" His voice echoed rather satisfactorily against the stone walls and stairway and so he decided to call out again. "Hoots toots!" he shouted, using the exact phrase which David Balfour's uncle used when he received his nephew in the House of Shaws. Would Antonia get the reference, he wondered? Did she know her Robert Louis Stevenson? Of course, this stair was considerably safer than that up which Balfour's uncle had sent him; there were no voids here into which one might step. So Angus shouted out to Antonia as she began her climb up to his floor: "No voids! Don't worry! This is not the House of Shaws!" Unfortunately, his voice was slightly slurred and he ended up shouting something which sounded rather like "This is not a house of whores". Or so it seemed to Antonia, who paused and looked up in puzzlement.

Angus met her at his doorway. "Antonia, my dear," he said, reaching out to kiss her on the cheek. "You are very welcome. Totally welcome."

She glanced at him sideways as she took off her coat. "I hope that I'm not late," she said.

"But not at all," said Angus, taking the coat. "My mother had a coat like this, you know. Virtually identical. In fact, this could be the very coat. Remarkable. Hers was in slightly better condition, I believe, but otherwise pretty similar. Amazing. Shows that fashion doesn't change, does it?" He paused. "My mother's dead, you see."

Antonia smiled, but said nothing.

"*On y va*," said Angus. "Let's go through to the drawing room. You've met Cyril, of course. He's my dog. Got a gold tooth, you know. Do you mind dogs, Antonia? Because if you do, I can send him out. Or should I say: Do you mind men? Because if you do, I can be sent out and Cyril can stay! Hah!"

Antonia smiled again, but more weakly.

"By the way," said Angus, "I saw you walking round the square. I didn't know it was you. And you know what? – I thought you were a streetwalker. I really did! Shows how wrong one can be – at a distance."

"Purely a social call," said Irene as she put her head round Dr Fairbairn's door. "I was passing by, you see, and they said downstairs that you had no patients until twelve o'clock. So I thought . . ."

Dr Hugo Fairbairn, seated behind his desk and absorbed, until then, in an unbound copy of *The International Journal of Psychoanalysis*, greeted her warmly.

"But there's no need to justify yourself," he said. "Not that you entered apologetically, of course. You're not one of those people who announces themselves with: 'It's only me'."

Irene slipped, uninvited, into the chair in front of the psychotherapist's desk. "But does anybody really say that?" she asked.

Dr Fairbairn nodded. "They certainly do. And it shows a fairly profound lack of self-esteem. If one says: 'It's me', then one is merely stating a fact. It is, indeed, you. But if you qualify it by saying that it's only you, then you're saying that it could be somebody more significant. Wouldn't you agree?"

Irene did agree. She agreed with most of Dr Fairbairn's pronouncements, and wished, in fact, that she herself had made them.

"You see," went on Dr Fairbairn, "how we announce ourselves is very revealing. J.M. Barrie, you know, used to enter his mother's room saying: 'It's not him, it's me'. He was referring, of course, to David, his brother who died. And that shaped, and indeed explained, everything about his later life. All the psychopathology. The creation of Peter Pan. Everything."

"Very sad," said Irene.

"Yes," said Dr Fairbairn. "Very. And then there's the interesting question of those who use the third person about themselves."

"Oh," said Irene, vaguely. It occurred to her that she used the third person on occasion when talking to Bertie. She said things such as: "Mummy is watching, Bertie. Mummy is watching Bertie very closely." That was using the third person, was it not? In fact, it was a double use of the third person; first (I, mother figure) became third, as did second (you, son). What did this reveal about Irene? she asked herself. No, deliberate play; what does that reveal about me?

"Yes," said Dr Fairbairn. "I knew somebody once who did this all the time. He was called George, and he said things like: 'George is very much hoping to see you tomorrow.' Or: 'George had a very good time yesterday.' It was very strange."

"Why did he do it?" Irene asked.

Dr Fairbairn looked up at the ceiling, which was a sign, Irene had noted, of an impending insight. "It's a form of dissociative splitting of the self," he said. "Or that's what it is in the most extreme cases. It's as if a decision has been taken that there are two persons – the person whose actions and thoughts are reported and the person who does the reporting. So if you're George and you say that George has done something, then it's as if you're speaking from the perspective of another person altogether, an observer."

Irene thought about that for a moment. "I can see that," she said. "But this self-bifurcation?"

Dr Fairbairn leaned forward and made an emphatic gesture with his right hand. "Ah!" he said. "Two possibilities. One is that it's a defensive withdrawal from a threatening social reality. I don't like what I see in the world and so I stand back for a while and let the alter ego get on with it. I take a breather, so to speak."

"And the other possibility?" asked Irene.

"Smugness," said Dr Fairbairn. "Have you noticed something about the people who do it? Well, I have. They're often smug."

Irene hesitated. She had been about to say that she sometimes referred to herself in the third person when talking to Bertie, but she was going to suggest that it was different with children. Adults spoke to children in the third person because it provided the child with a key to the understanding of a social world which would otherwise be too subjective. The extraction of the subjective element in the situation conveyed to the child the understanding that the social world involved impersonal, objectified transactions between people. In other words, we were all role players, and the child may as well get used to that fact.

That was what she was going to say, but she could not say it now. Smug? Was she smug? Of course not.

Dr Fairbairn leaned back in his chair, pulling at the cuffs of his blue linen jacket. "Smugness is a very interesting concept," he said slowly. "You may know that there's a fascinating literature on it. Not a very extensive one, but very, very interesting."

He reached for the journal which he had been reading when Irene entered the room. "Right here," he said. "As it happens. Much of this issue is devoted to the topic. Fascinating stuff."

Irene listened attentively. She knew that it was disloyal, but she could not help but compare Dr Fairbairn with Stuart. The worlds of the two men were surely about as different as one could imagine. Indeed, there were so few men like Dr Fairbairn – so few men who could talk with such ease and insight about matters such as these. It was like being with an artist who simply saw the world in a different way; saw colours and shades that others just did not see. Proust must have been like that too. He saw everything, and then everything behind everything. Behind the simplest thing, even inanimate objects, there was a wealth of associations that only somebody like Proust could see. So it was with Dr Fairbairn, and for a moment it made Irene feel a great sense of regret. Had she married somebody like this, then her daily lot would have been so different. She would have been able to explore the world with him in a way in which she would never be able to do with Stuart. Stuart lived in a world of statistics and brute facts. Dr Fairbairn inhabited a realm of emotions and human possibilities. They were so utterly different – two sides of a mountain range, she thought, and I am on the wrong one.

She told herself that she should not waste these precious minutes with Dr Fairbairn in thinking about what might be, but which was not. So she said to him: "Do tell me about smugness."

79. *Smugness Explained*

"Have you ever encountered a really smug person?" asked Dr Fairbairn, fixing his gaze on Irene as she sat before him in his consulting room. Not that this was a consultation; this was a conversation, and a rather enjoyable one, with no therapeutic purpose.

Irene thought for a moment. Who, in her circle, was smug? But then, she thought, do I really have a circle? She was not at all sure that she did.

"Plenty," she said. "This city is full of smug people. Always has been."

Dr Fairbairn laughed. "Of course it is," he said. "But can you think of anybody in particular?"

Irene's mind had now alighted on one or two examples. Yes, he was smug all right. And as for her . . . "Well, there's a certain facial expression," began Irene.

Dr Fairbairn cut her short. "There might be, but not always. If there is, it's the expression of oral satiety. The smug person has what he really wants, the good object, which is the . . . Of course, you know all about that. So he has it and he feels utterly fulfilled. He isn't really interested in anything else – not really. That's why smug people never talk about you – they talk about themselves. Have you noticed that?"

Irene had. She was now thinking of a cousin of hers, a man whom it had never occurred to her to label as smug, but that is what he was. He was insufferably smug, now that one came to think about it. And it was quite true; when they met, which was relatively infrequently, he never once asked her about herself but spoke only of himself and his plans.

"I have a cousin," she said. "He's extremely smug." She paused. "And do you know, he makes me want to prick him with a pin. Yes, I have this terrible pin urge."

Dr Fairbairn stared at his friend. Pin envy. He had been about to tell her of the common pathology of those who reacted with violent antipathy towards smug people. A lot of people were like that; the mere presence of a smug person made them livid. But he decided that it was perhaps best not to mention that aspect of it just at that moment.

"Smug people are completely satisfied with themselves," said Dr Fairbairn. "In that respect they are similar to narcissists. The narcissist is incapable of feeling bad about anything that he does because he is, in his own estimation, so obviously perfect. Smug people don't necessarily feel that way about themselves. They are very contented with what they have, and they may appear self-righteous, but the really salient feature of smugness is its sense of being satisfied and complete."

Dr Fairbairn paused. One day, he thought, he would write a paper on smugness. He would need, though, to find a few more patients to write about, but the problem with smug people was that they never sought analysis. And why should they? They had everything they wanted. So perhaps he should write about something else altogether; he should look for another patient, one undergoing regular treatment. He thought for a moment . . .

"Would you mind . . . ?" he suddenly asked Irene. "Would you mind if one of these days I wrote about Bertie? I would change his name, of course, so that nobody would know it was him. But he is a rather interesting case, you know."

Irene gave a little squeal of delight. "Of course I wouldn't mind," she exclaimed. "It would be wonderful to be able to share Bertie with the world. Just as Little Hans's father allowed us to hear about Little Hans's castration anxieties and all that business with the dray horses and the giraffe. Imagine if he had refused Freud permission to write about his son. Imagine that."

Dr Fairbairn agreed. It would have been a terrible loss. But at the same time, there was always the danger that a famous analysand might find himself discovered much later on. Irene should be aware of that.

"I should warn you," he said, "that sometimes people track down these famous patients, even after years have passed. Remember what happened to the Wolf Man." He paused. "And of course, Little Hans himself visited Freud later, when he was nineteen."

"And?" prompted Irene.

"He – Little Hans – had forgotten everything. Horses. Giraffe. All forgotten. Indeed, he recognised nothing in the analysis."

"How interesting," said Irene. "Of course you already have at least one famous patient. You have Wee Fraser." She paused; Wee Fraser was dangerous territory. "You were going to track him down, weren't you? Did you ever find him?"

Dr Fairbairn stiffened. Up to this point he had been fiddling with the cuffs of his blue linen jacket; now his hands dropped to his sides and he stared fixedly ahead. He had located his famous patient, now fifteen or so, and had risen to his feet to make amends for having smacked him in the early analysis (when Wee Fraser had put the toy pigs upside down), only to be head-butted for his pains by the unpleasant adolescent. But then, to his profound shame, he had responded by striking Wee Fraser on the chin, breaking his jaw.

"I found him," he said. " I found him, and then . . ."

Irene leaned forward. "You asked his forgiveness?"

Dr Fairbairn looked miserable. "I wish I could say that I had. Alas, the truth is the rather to the contrary."

"How much to the contrary?" pressed Irene.

"Completely," said Dr Fairbairn.

Irene held up a hand. "I do not want to hear what happened," she said. "We can all make mistakes. We can all do things that we didn't plan to do."

Dr Fairbairn looked at her with gratitude. Here was absolution – of a sort. "Yes," he said. "We all do things that we didn't plan to do. How right you are." He paused, and stood up. Moving to the window behind his desk, he looked out over the Queen Street Gardens. "Yes, I have done many things I did not intend to do. That is the human condition."

"Many things?" asked Irene.

"Yes," said Dr Fairbairn, turning round again. "Such as . . ." But then he stopped.

Irene waited for him to continue, but Dr Fairbairn had become silent. He looked up at the ceiling, and Irene followed his gaze. But there was nothing to be seen there, and so they both lowered their eyes.

He is so unhappy, thought Irene. He is so unresolved.

80. An Evening of Scottish Art

Neither Matthew nor Pat said anything about the unfortunate incident in the bathroom, although neither of them was quick to forget it. Both learned something from the experience. Matthew now knew to lock the door and to remember that he was no longer alone in the flat. This meant that he should be careful about breaking out into song – as he occasionally liked to do – or uttering the odd mild expletive if he stubbed his toe on the corner of the kitchen dresser or if he dropped part of an egg shell into the omelette mixture. For her part, Pat learned to assume that a closed door meant that the bathroom was not free, and she learned, too, that Matthew was a sensitive person, easily embarrassed and not always able to articulate the causes of his embarrassment. And for both of them, there was also the lesson that living together, even merely as flatmates, was a process of discovery. For although we are at our most secure – in one sense – in our own homes, we are also at our most vulnerable, for the social persona, the one we carry with us out into the world, cannot be worn at home all the time. That is where resides the real self, the self that can be so easily hurt.

There were things about Matthew that Pat had not suspected. She had not imagined that he was a member of the Scotch Malt Whisky Society and received its newsletters with all those curious descriptions of the flavour of whiskies. She had paged through one of these which she found lying on the kitchen table and had been astonished by the terms used by the tasting panel. One whisky was described as smelling of school jotters; another smelled like a doctor's bag (or what doctor's bags used to smell like). She had never seen Matthew drink whisky, but he later explained to her that he had been given the membership by his father, who was an enthusiast of whisky.

And then she had never seen Matthew reading *Scottish Field* before, but that is what he liked to do, sitting in a chair in the corner of the drawing room, paging through the glossy magazine. He liked the social pages, he said, with their pictures of people looking into the camera, smiling, happy to be included.

"I've never been in," he said to Pat. "Or never been in properly. My left shoulder was, once, when there was a photograph of a charity ball down in Ayrshire. I was standing just to the side of a group who were being photographed and you could see my shoulder. It was definitely me. I have a green formal kilt jacket, you see, and that was shown. It was quite clear, actually."

"That was bad luck," said Pat.

"Yes," said Matthew. "You have to be somebody like Timothy Clifford to get into *Scottish Field*. Either that, or you have to know the photographers who take these things. I don't."

Pat thought for a moment. "We could have an opening at the gallery. We could have a big event and ask all these people. Then, when they came, the photographers could hardly cut you out of your own party."

Matthew thought for a moment. "Yes, that's quite a good idea." He paused. "I hope that you don't think I sit here and worry about not being in *Scottish Field*. I have got better things to think about, you know."

"Of course you have," said Pat. "But should we do that? Should we have an opening?"

"Yes," said Matthew. "We could call it An Evening of Scottish Art. Let's start drawing up the guest list soon. Who should we have?"

"Well, we could invite Duncan Macmillan," said Pat. "He's written that book on Scottish art. He could come."

"Good idea," said Matthew. "He's very interesting. And then there's James Holloway from the Scottish National Portrait Gallery. He lives near here, you know. And Richard and Francesca Calvocoressi. And Roddy Martine. Are you writing this down, Pat?"

They spent the next half hour composing the guest list, which eventually included two hundred names. "They won't all come," said Matthew, surveying the glittering list. "In fact, I bet that hardly anyone comes."

Pat looked at Matthew. There was a certain defeatism about him, which came out at odd moments. Defeatism can be a frustrating, unattractive quality, but in Matthew she found it to be rather different. The fact that Matthew thought that his ventures were destined to fail made her feel protective of him. He was such a nice person, she thought.

He is never unkind; he never makes sharp comments about others. And there he is trying to be a bit more fashionable in that awful distressed-oatmeal cashmere sweater, and all the time he just misses it. Nobody wears distressed oatmeal, these days; it's so . . . it's so yesterday. It's so golf club.

Matthew needed taking in hand, Pat thought. He needed somebody to sit down with him who could tell him not to try so hard, who could tell him that all that was required was a little help with one or two matters and that for the rest he was perfectly all right. But who could do that? Could she?

Pat was thinking of that possibility when Matthew looked at his watch, rose to his feet, and remarked that they only had half an hour to get ready for dinner. Pat had forgotten, but now she remembered.

That night they were due to go out for dinner with Leonie, the architect, and her friend, Babs. She had been invited as well, on the insistence of Leonie, although Matthew seemed a little bit doubtful about this.

"She's a rather unusual person," he said hesitantly. "She has all these ideas about knocking down walls and open spaces. You know what architects are like. But I suspect that she's a bit . . . well, I suspect that she's a bit intense."

He paused, and looked up at the ceiling. "You may find that she's a bit intense towards you. I don't know. Maybe not. But you may find that."

"Intense, in what way?" asked Pat.

"Just intense," said Matthew. "You know what I mean."

Pat shook her head.

"Well, anyway," said Matthew. "I'm going to go and have a shower."

Pat blushed.

81. *At the Sardi*

The Caffe Sardi, an Italian restaurant on Forrest Road, was already quite busy when Pat and Matthew arrived for dinner. He had chosen the restaurant, which he particularly liked, and had left a message on Leonie's answering machine telling her where they would meet.

"I hope that she picked it up," he said. "Some people don't listen to their answering machines, you know."

"I do," said Pat. "I listen to my voicemail every day. Once in the morning and then again at night."

Matthew looked thoughtful. "And do you get many messages?" he asked.

"Quite a few," said Pat. "Most of them aren't very important, you know. 'Meet me at six.' That sort of thing."

"Meet whom?" he asked.

Pat shrugged. "Oh, nobody in particular. That's just a for instance."

"But sometimes there will be a message saying 'Meet me' or something like that?" persisted Matthew.

Pat thought that there was no real point to Matthew's questions. Sometimes he surprised her, with his opaque remarks, or with those Macgregor undershorts. That was odd. She wondered whether he was wearing them now; it was a disconcerting thought. "Yes," said Pat. "Sometimes people ask me to meet them."

Matthew looked down at the tablecloth. He was about to say "Who?" but at that moment they were joined by Leonie and her friend Babs.

"Have you guys been waiting long?" asked Leonie, as she

took off her jacket and hung it over the back of a chair. "Babs and me walked."

Matthew thought: why can't people distinguish between nominative and accusative any more? He wanted to say to Leonie: "Would you say me walked?" But he realised that he could not. People did not like being corrected, even when they were obviously wrong.

He looked at Babs, who was now being introduced by Leonie. She was about the same age as Leonie, perhaps slightly older, but was more heavily-built. She had an open, rather flat face, but she was still attractive in an odd sort of way.

Babs shook hands with Matthew and Pat. "How are you doing?" she said, glancing first at Matthew and then at Pat. She was thinking of something, thought Matthew. She's wondering whether Pat and I are together. That's what people do when they meet others, he thought. There's an instant judgment, an instant assessment. In this case, the question was: is he? Is she? Perhaps I should say to her right now: "I'm not and she isn't either." What would be the result of that?

The waitress gave them menus and they looked at them closely.

"Babs doesn't like anything with garlic in it," said Leonie.

"And Leo doesn't like anything with capers," said Babs, staring at the menu as if scrutinising it for offending items. "Nor mashed potato nor veal. In fact, little Miss Fussy is just a little on the picky side."

"Picky yourself," retorted Leonie. "Oh, I like the look of that! That's what I'm going to have."

Babs stared over Leonie's shoulder. "Me too. Well spotted, Leo. And no garlic! No! No! No! Naughty garlic!"

"What about you, Pat?" asked Matthew. "Why don't you have one of those nice pizzas?"

Leonie and Babs looked at Pat. Then Leonie turned to Matthew. "Let the poor girl choose," she said in a mock-reproachful tone.

"But she likes pizza," said Matthew. "She always has."

"Okay," said Babs. "But she can say that herself, can't she?"

Leonie nodded her agreement. "Men sometimes think that women can't make their own choices in life. I've noticed that quite a lot, actually. Particularly in this country." Matthew felt his face becoming warm. "Why do you say that?" he asked. "And why this country?"

Leonie smiled. "It's just what I've picked up," she said. "I see a lot of men giving orders to women – telling them what to do."

"And you didn't see that in Australia?" asked Matthew. He was aware that Babs was watching him as he spoke. She seemed vaguely amused by his response, as if he was behaving exactly as she had imagined he would.

"Oh, bits of Australia are like that," said Leonie. "There are places out in the boondocks where you get the real ockers, but things are very different in Melbourne and Sydney."

"I see," said Matthew.

"I haven't found that many men have tried to tell me what to do," said Pat suddenly. "And Matthew certainly doesn't. Even though he's my boss, he doesn't do that."

Babs turned her gaze from Matthew to Pat. "Well, that's very good to hear," she said.

"Yes," said Pat. "And actually, if you come to think of it, there are plenty of women who tell men what to do. I think it's men who have got the problem these days."

"You can say that again," said Leonie. "Or, rather, you can say the last bit again."

Matthew now decided that it was time to move the conversation forward. He turned to Babs. "Are you an architect too?" he asked.

Babs shook her head. "I used to be a designer," she said. "I was a designer when I lived in Milan. But I was one of those people whose hobby rather took over and became their job. So I changed."

"Babs has always been good with cars," said Leonie. "She has a real talent."

Babs acknowledged the compliment with an inclination of the head. "Well, put it this way, I can talk to cars," she said. "Cars and me – we're on the same wavelength."

Cars and I, thought Matthew.

"So now I've opened a new business," Babs went on. "I've started a small panel-beating shop – you know, car bodywork repair. I fix cars up."

Leonie raised a finger in the air. "But it's a very special business, this one," she said. "It's just for women who have dented their car. They can take it to Babs for confidential repair. Men needn't even know about it."

"Yes," said Babs. "It's called Ladies who Crash. And I can tell you something – I'm busy. Boy, am I kept busy!"

Matthew was very wary. "But this implies that women are worse drivers than men," he said. "Whereas all the evidence goes the other way. Women are safer drivers than men. All the accident statistics show that."

"But they can't reverse," said Babs. She spoke in a matter-of-fact way, as if enunciating an uncontroversial truth. But then she added: "Well, I suppose, neither can Jim."

"Who's Jim?" asked Matthew.

"My husband," said Babs. "Bless him!"

82. Misunderstandings

Dinner that evening at the Caffe Sardi was not a protracted event. Matthew tried valiantly to keep the conversation going into a second cup of post-prandial coffee, but Leonie announced that she had an important site meeting the next day with a demanding client and she wanted an early night. And Jim, Babs announced, did not like her to be too late.

"He worries about me," she explained, looking at her watch. "He worries when I go out."

"I'm sorry," said Matthew apologetically. "I would have asked him, too. It's just that I thought . . ." He left the sentence unfinished. Both Leonie and Babs were staring at him, and Pat, embarrassed, was looking up at the ceiling.

"You thought what?" asked Babs.

Matthew swallowed. "I thought that you and Leonie were . . . were friends."

"But we are," said Babs. "We've been friends for ages, haven't we Leo?"

"Yes," said Leonie, still glaring at Matthew. "Did you think . . ."

"You didn't!" said Babs, seemingly amused.

Matthew laughed nervously. "I'm sorry," he said. "I suppose I did rather assume that. It's just that when you came into the restaurant . . ." He glanced at Pat, but she was still looking up at the ceiling.

"Yes," pressed Babs. "We came in. So what?"

"Perhaps he thought that you looked a bit . . ." offered Leonie.

Babs leaned forward and pointed a finger at Matthew's chest. It was an aggressive gesture, but she was smiling as she spoke. "It's because I fix cars. Is that it? Well, you work in a gallery, don't you? That's a job for a sensitive man. And you don't get many sensitive men playing rugby, do you?" She laughed, and was quickly echoed by Leonie.

"No," said Leonie. "Can you imagine it?"

Matthew bit his lip. "Plenty of sensitive men play rugby," he said wildly. "Plenty."

"Oh yes?" challenged Babs. "Name one."

Matthew thought. He could not think of any sensitive men who played rugby – not a single one. "Oh well," he said. "I don't think we should speak about stereotypes. Men who work in the arts are just the same as anybody else. Some play rugby, some don't."

"None play rugby," said Leonie. "I'm telling you."

"Does it matter?" interrupted Pat. "Does anybody really care any more at all who plays rugby and who doesn't?"

"Is rugby some sort of metaphor?" asked Babs.

Matthew shook his head. "It's a game."

"Which is not played frequently by sensitive men," interjected Leonie.

There was a silence. Then: "Let's not argue," said Babs pleasantly. "It's been such a nice evening and it would be a pity to ruin it with an argument, wouldn't it? I suppose that I am a bit of a direct speaker. And I know that these days you can't speak freely about anything. I'll try to be a little bit more politically correct, I really will."

"Good girl!" said Leonie, putting an arm around her friend's shoulder.

They sat together for a few moments, with nobody saying anything. Then Matthew signalled to the waitress for the bill and the party began to break up.

"You don't have to pay just because you're a man," said Babs. "Leo and I can pay our share."

"Well . . . ." Matthew began.

"But thanks anyway," said Leonie hurriedly. "Thanks very much for the evening, Matthew."

Afterwards, when Babs and Leonie had disappeared together in a taxi, Matthew and Pat walked over the road to the pub on the opposite side of the road. Sandy Bells Bar was known for its folk music, and as they made their way to the broad mahogany bar they saw a fiddler at the other end of the bar rise to his feet.

Matthew stopped where he stood. "Listen," he said. " 'Lochaber No More'."

The long, drawn-out passages of the heart-rending lament largely silenced the drinkers present. An elderly man, seated by the window, clutching a small glass of whisky in both hands, started to sway gently in time with the music. The fiddler, glancing up, saw him and smiled.

"I love that tune," Matthew whispered to Pat. "It makes me so sad."

Pat stole a glance at Matthew. It had been a confusing evening. She had not known how to take their fellow-guests over dinner; things were not as they seemed, she realised, but then, it still seemed a bit strange.

"Leonie and Babs," she said quietly to Matthew. "Do you think that . . ."

"That they're an item?" whispered Matthew. "No, I don't. And anyway, it doesn't matter."

He looked at Pat, and suddenly, with complete clarity of understanding, he realised that he was in love with her and that he had to tell her that. He had not been in love with her half an hour ago. He had liked her then. He felt a bit jealous of her. But now he loved her. He simply loved her.

He moved very slightly towards Pat, who was standing a few inches away from him. Now they were touching one another, his right leg against hers. She did not move away. Emboldened, he reached out and took her hand in his, squeezing it gently. She returned the pressure. "Let's sit down," she said. "Over at the table. Over there. I want to talk to you, Matthew."

Matthew followed Pat to the table. He felt that he had misjudged the situation, and now his fears were to be confirmed. She would tell him that she thought of him as a brother; he had heard that sort of thing before. Or, worse, she might say that she thought of him as an employer.

"Matthew," she said. "We're friends, aren't we? No, don't look so down-in-the-mouth. We're friends, aren't we?"

"Yes," said Matthew, flatly. "We're friends."

"And friends can speak their minds to one another?"

Matthew sighed. "Yes, I suppose they can."

Pat lowered her voice. "I feel very awkward about this," she said. "But I think that I know you well enough to talk about it."

Matthew said nothing. It was all so predictable.

Pat reached out and took his hand. "I'm rather keen on Babs," she said.

Matthew remained quite immobile. He opened his mouth, and then closed it. His mouth felt dry.

"Only joking," said Pat. "But the point is this, Matthew. I know that you want to find somebody. I know that you want to find a girlfriend. But you don't seem to be able to do it, do you?"

Matthew looked down at his feet. He said nothing.

"Well, why don't you let me help you?" said Pat quietly. "Let me help you find somebody."

83. *Mothercraft*

With Bertie away in Paris, Irene felt at something of a loose end. She had enjoyed her recent visit to Dr Fairbairn, and they had agreed to meet again for coffee later that week. She felt slightly guilty about this, because she had not mentioned to Stuart that she was seeing the psychotherapist in this way, but on subsequent reflection she concluded that it was perfectly appropriate for the two of them to meet, on the grounds that Bertie almost always cropped up in their conversation. Her meetings with Dr Fairbairn could therefore be justified as directly related to the therapy that Bertie so clearly needed.

And Bertie really did need therapy – at least in his mother's view. The original incident which triggered the first visit to Dr Fairbairn – Bertie's setting fire to his father's copy of *The Guardian* (while he was reading it) – had not been followed by any acts of quite so dramatic a nature. But even if that was so, it was obvious that Bertie was still puzzled by life and uncertain about himself and who he was. And there was also an outstanding question about his dreams. Bertie had vivid dreams, and it was not uncommon for Irene to go into his bedroom early in the morning and find Bertie lying in his little bed with a puzzled frown on his face. That, thought Irene, was an indication of a confusing or threatening dream.

If she could visit Dr Fairbairn, then there was at least something to take her mind off her situation. And that situation was this: she was pregnant, she had very little to do, and she found the behaviour of her husband increasingly irritating. The only salience in this otherwise dull existence was the Bertie Project, and for a large part of the day Bertie was away at school or, as now, in Paris.

But then there arose an interesting possibility. Irene's first pregnancy had gone very smoothly and uneventfully. She had felt very little discomfort. There had been virtually no nausea and she had experienced no cravings of the sort that many women feel in pregnancy. So in her case there had been no furtive snacking on chocolate bars, nor gnawing on raw artichokes, nor anything of that sort. Irene had simply sailed through the whole process and, more or less exactly on the day predicted by her doctor, given birth to Bertie in the Simpson Maternity Unit.

Of course it had been an enhanced pregnancy. She had read of the importance of playing music to the baby in utero, and had placed headphones against her stomach each afternoon while resting and played Mozart through them. She was convinced that Bertie had responded, as he had kicked vigorously each time she turned up the volume of '*Soave sia il vento*' from *Così fan Tutte*, and, indeed, after his birth whenever this piece of music was played a strange expression would come over Bertie's face.

There were other enhancements. Irene had changed her diet during pregnancy and had embarked on courses of vitamin pills and nutritional supplements that would ensure good brain development. Although she had previously scorned what she had considered to be the old-wives' tale that fish was good for the brain, she had been won round by recent scientific evidence to this precise effect and had consequently eaten a great deal of fish in the later months. There had also been an intensive beetroot programme in the final weeks before Bertie's birth, and Stuart had remarked on the fact that Bertie as a very young baby had a fairly strong beetroot complexion – a remark which had not been well received by Irene.

This second pregnancy was, if anything, less stressful than the first and Irene actually found herself rather bored by it. That was until she saw a notice in the local health centre advertising special birth and mothercraft classes at a hall in St Stephen Street. Had Irene been more fully occupied she would not have bothered with these, but in her current state she thought that it might be interesting to see what these classes entailed – not that she had anything to learn, of course, about bringing up children. Indeed, it was she who should be imparting knowledge in this area, not receiving it. But the barricades in this life are never in the right place, and so she duly enrolled in a class that was scheduled to run for six weeks, with meetings on Tuesday and Thursday mornings and on the evenings of the same days for those mothers-to-be who were still at work.

The classes were to be run by somebody called Nurse Forbes, and there was a picture of Nurse Forbes on the poster. Irene peered at her. She had a rather bovine face, Irene decided; the sort of face that one used to see in advertisements for butter. In fact, thought Irene, she looked a bit Dutch. The Dutch, she felt, had that rather milky look about them, as if they had eaten too many dairy products. And they probably had, she reflected.

Irene smiled. Poor Nurse Forbes! She probably had not the slightest idea who Melanie Klein was; for her, babies were a matter of bottles of milk and injections and nappy rash and all the rest. Hers would be a life filled with unguent creams and immunisations and breast-milk issues. Poor woman.

And then, shortly after she had seen the poster and studied the picture of Nurse Forbes, Irene had the chance to meet her. It happened after a routine check-up that Irene had with her doctor. This doctor for some reason did not appear to like Irene – a feeling which Irene decided was based on his fundamental insecurity and his inability to engage in a non-paternalistic way with an informed patient.

"I'd like you to have a chat with Nurse Forbes," said the doctor. "If you don't mind, that is. She runs a class, you know. Not that you would need a class, of course. Not in your case."

"On the contrary," said Irene coldly. "I have already decided to sign up for it."

"In that case," said the doctor, "you can see Nurse Forbes straightaway. She's in the building. Speak to the receptionists first. I'm sure that the two of you will get on very well."

Irene had not bothered about the receptionists. She had left the consulting room and walked down the corridor to the door marked Nurse Forbes. She had knocked on the door and, a moment later, a voice had called out: "Come in!"

It was a milky-sounding voice, Irene thought.

84. *No More Nonsense, Nurse Knows Best*

Nurse Forbes was a woman in her early forties. She had been brought up in Haddington, the youngest of three girls, all of whom became nurses. Her mother had been a nurse, as had her grandmother.

That she should become a nurse too had been accepted from the very beginning, and when the time came for her to leave Knox Academy, she had enrolled on a nursing course at Queen Margaret College in Clermiston. In due course she had graduated with distinction, as her two sisters had done. She completed her training in the Royal Infirmary and in that classic of Caledonian-Stalinist architecture, the Simpson Memorial Maternity Pavilion.

Marriage came next – to a man who worked as an accountant in a brewery – and then there had been public service: she had served for a short time on the Newington Community Council, and had been appointed by the Secretary of State to the Departmental Committee on Maternity Services and the Healthy

Eating in Pregnancy Initiative. She was very good at her job.

Irene, of course, knew nothing of this distinguished career when she knocked on the door marked Nurse Forbes. There were so many people who seemed to work in the health centre that it was impossible for her to keep up with them all, and she had great difficulty in working out who was a receptionist, who was a doctor, and who was a nurse. It was most confusing – and irritating.

Nurse Forbes looked up from the report she was reading. Patients were normally announced by the receptionists and she was mildly surprised to see Irene in her doorway. Now, who was this woman? She seemed vaguely familiar, but then she saw so many people. Pregnant, obviously.

"You are Nurse Forbes, I take it," said Irene.

Nurse Forbes smiled. "Yes, I am. Please come in. Did doctor send you?"

Irene winced. She did not like the doctor to be referred to simply as "doctor"; it was so condescending to the patient, as if one were a child.

"Yes," she said. "My doctor sent me." There was a great deal of emphasis on the possessive.

Nurse Forbes invited Irene to sit down. This, she thought, is the typical patient for the area. Thinks she knows everything. Will condescend, if given the chance. But she knew how to deal with people like Irene.

"I'll just take a few details," said Nurse Forbes. "Then we can have a wee talk."

Irene sat down. "I don't have a great deal of time," she said. "I was planning to come to those classes you're running."

"You'll be very welcome," said Nurse Forbes. But she would not. This sort of person tended to be disruptive, and sometimes she wondered why they came at all.

"The classes are quite well-subscribed. I think that people find them quite useful," she said.

"I'm sure they are," said Irene.

"But if there are any particular issues you'd like to raise with me privately," said Nurse Forbes, "please do so now. Sometimes people have concerns that they don't like to raise in front of others."

Irene nodded. "There are," she said. "I do have some questions . . ."

Nurse Forbes raised a hand. "But first we need to go over one or two things," she said. "You know, diet issues. General health matters."

"I have a very healthy diet," said Irene. "You need have no worries on that score. And I take all the necessary supplements."

Nurse Forbes looked up sharply. "Supplements?"

Irene smiled tolerantly. Nurses could not be expected to understand dietary issues. "Shark oil capsules. Slippery elm. Red raspberry. Wild yam," she paused. Nurse Forbes was staring at her. Would she have to explain each of these?

"Why are you taking these . . . these substances?" Nurse Forbes asked.

Irene took a deep breath. It was going to be necessary to explain after all.

"As you may know," she began, "modern foods are lacking in certain important constituents. This is a result of farming techniques which . . ."

"During pregnancy," Nurse Forbes interrupted, her voice raised, "during pregnancy, mother should eat a healthy, balanced diet. She should not – and I repeat not – take non-medicinal supplements, herbal remedies and the like. These may be harmful to both mother and baby. And we do not want baby to be harmed, do we?"

Irene was silent. This would be risible, if it were not so insulting. Here was this . . . this bureaucrat, in her ridiculous uniform, telling me – me – what I should and should not take. And what did she know about slippery elm? Nothing. Nothing at all.

This woman, this ridiculous Nurse Forbes was the state. She was the local, immediate face of the state, presuming – yes presuming – to lecture me as if I were some sixteen-year-old first-time mother who subsisted on a diet of fish and chips. Absurd! They glared at one another.

For her part, Nurse Forbes thought: this woman thinks that she is superior to me, she really does. Nothing I say to her is going to make any difference. But I must be tolerant. There is no point in alienating people, even somebody like this. It's tempting, but it's just not professional. So, count to ten, and take it from there.

"Well, we can return to this issue some other time," Nurse Forbes said quietly. "There is some literature I can pass on to you. But, in the meantime, have you discussed delivery matters with doctor?"

"I have reached a decision on that," Irene replied. "I would like a home delivery, of course. I would like my son, Bertie, to play a part in the delivery of his little brother or sister. I would like him to be the one to welcome the baby to the world."

Nurse Forbes sat quite still. She spoke quietly, as if in shock. "You're proposing that Bertie should actually . . ."

Irene laughed. "Oh, not by himself, of course! With the midwife. Bertie could help to bring the baby . . ."

"But I am the midwife," said Nurse Forbes. "And I forbid it. Birth would be a very, very traumatic experience for a little boy. And, I'm sorry to have to say this, it would be completely inappropriate for a son to attend to his mother in this way. Any boy would be deeply, deeply embarrassed to do this. No, I forbid it."

"Melanie Klein . . ."

"I don't care who your MSP is. I forbid it!"

85. *Poor Lou*

Angus Lordie went with Cyril down the steps that led into Big Lou's coffee house, the very steps down which the late Dr C.M. Grieve, or Hugh MacDiarmid, had tripped and fallen all those years ago when visiting what was then a bookshop. The steps were still perilous, and Angus had once almost fallen; now he was careful to avoid the place where the railings largely disappeared and the step which was cambered in the wrong direction. These snares negotiated, he pushed open the door of the coffee bar and entered the dimly-lit interior, Cyril walking obediently at his heels.

Big Lou was standing in her accustomed position behind the bar, a book open in front of her. She looked up as Angus came in and nodded in his direction. Angus greeted her and walked up to the bar with Cyril.

"I must say, Big Lou," he began, "I must say that you're looking more than usually attractive this morning."

Big Lou glanced up from her book. "I'm looking the same as I always do," she said. "No different." She wrinkled her nose slightly. "Is that smell your dog?"

"My goodness," said Angus. "That's no way to refer to a regular customer! Cyril pays good money here, same as anybody else. And he licks the plates clean, which is more than can be said of most of your clients."

"Malodorous beastie," said Big Lou.

Angus smiled. "Now, now, Lou. Cyril may have the occasional personal hygiene issue, but that's absolutely normal for dogs. They may be smellier creatures than the opposition, that is, than cats. But they are infinitely more intelligent and agreeable in every respect. You should understand that, coming from

Arbroath. You have working dogs up there, don't you?"

"There are some," said Lou. She closed her book and slipped it under the counter. "The usual?"

"If you don't mind. And a dish of warm milk for Cyril, please, with just a dash of espresso in his. Not too much. Just a dash."

Angus made his way over to his table, sat down, and opened the newspaper. The news, he noticed, was uniformly grim, with seemingly endless vistas of conflict opening up in every corner of the world. It was always thus, he reflected: the struggle for resources, the struggle for space, the struggle for primacy. And as we grew in numbers, remorselessly straining the earth's capacity to sustain us, so the levels of conflict rose.

"Bad news, Cyril," he said. "Look at this, boy. Bad news for us; bad news for dogs. We're in it together, I'm afraid."

Big Lou now came across with a cup of coffee for Angus and a dish of milk for Cyril. She laid the dish down on the ground, near Cyril's snout, and he looked up at her with moist, appreciative eyes. Then she put the coffee in front of Angus.

"Lou . . ." Angus had noticed her strained expression and reached out to hold her forearm. "Lou? Are you . . ."

She tried to move away, but he tightened his grip.

"Lou, you sit down. You sit down right there."

She tried to pull away again, but he resisted, and she sat down, opposite him, her head lowered.

"What is it?" he asked gently. "You're greeting." He used the Scots word for crying, instinctively, because that was the word that had been used with him as a child and it seemed to him that it was far more sympathetic. As a little boy, in Perthshire, there had been a girl from a neighbouring farm who had helped look after him. She had comforted him when he had cried, holding him to her, and he remembered how soft she had been, when all around him there was hardness – the hardness of the byre floor on which he had tripped and scraped his knee, the hardness of the shepherds and their smell of tar remedy and lanolin, the hardness of his remote father, with his smell of whisky and the fishing flies in his bonnet. And that girl had cuddled him and said: "Dinnae greet, Angus. Dinnae greet."

For a few moments she said nothing. Angus kept his hand on her arm, though, and she let him. He squeezed it gently.

"Lou? Come on, Lou. Tell me. It's Eddie, isn't it?"

She nodded, but did not speak.

"He's not the right man for you, Lou," said Angus gently. "He really isn't. He's . . ." He tailed off, and Lou looked up. Her voice was strained, her eyes still liquid with tears. "He's what?"

"He's just not a good enough man," said Angus. "You know, other men can tell. Women don't always see it, but men are the best judge of other men. Men know. I'm telling you, Lou. They know. I could tell that Eddie wasn't right, Lou. I could just tell. Matthew too."

She frowned. "Matthew? Has he talked to you?"

Angus nodded. He and Matthew had spoken at length about Eddie one evening in the Cumberland Bar and they had been in complete agreement.

"He's after Lou's money," Matthew had said. "It's glaringly obvious. He's got some stupid idea of a club. He needs her dough."

And Angus had agreed, and added: "And then there's the problem of girls. He goes for younger women. Traceys and Sharons galore. Eighteen-year-olds."

He could not reveal that conversation to Big Lou, but he had been left in no doubt but that Matthew thought of Eddie in exactly the same way as he did.

"I thought that he loved me," said Big Lou. "I really thought that he loved me."

Angus squeezed her arm again. "I think he probably did, Lou. I think that he did – in his way. Because you're well worth loving. Any man would love you. You're a fine, fine woman, Lou. But . . ."

She looked at him, and he continued. "Some men just can't help themselves, Lou. They just can't help it. Eddie's one. He's not a one-woman man. That's all there is to it."

"And then there's the money," said Big Lou.

Angus grimaced. He had hoped that she had not actually paid over any money, but it seemed as if it might be too late. He knew that Lou had a bit of money, the legacy from the farmer she had nursed, but how much would have been left after the purchase of the flat and the coffee bar?

"How much, Lou?" he asked quietly. "How much did you give Eddie?"

"Thirty-four thousand pounds," said Lou.

86. *A Letter to Edinburgh*

Domenica was fussy about the circumstances in which she wrote. In Scotland Street, she would sit at her desk with a clean block of ruled foolscap paper in front of her and write on that, with a Conway Stewart fountain pen, in green ink. There were those who said that writing in green ink was a sign of mental instability, but she had never understood the basis for this. Green ink was attractive, more restful on the eye than an intense black, and she persisted with it.

Such rituals of composition were impossible in that small village near Malacca.

There, she made do with a simple, rather rickety table, which provided a surface for her French moleskin notebook and for a rather less commodious writing paper. But there was still the Conway Stewart pen, and supplies of green ink, and it was with this pen that she now wrote a letter to James Holloway in Edinburgh.

"Dear James," she began, "I know that you are familiar with the Far East and will be able to picture the scene here – the scene of me upon my veranda, at my table, with a frangipani tree directly in front of me.

"The tree is in flower, and its white blossoms have that gorgeous, slightly sickly smell which reminds me of something else, but which I cannot remember. Perhaps you will supply the allusion; I cannot.

"I have at last begun my researches. Ling, the young man who has been assigned to look after me, is proving very helpful, even if he has a tendency to moodiness. I am not sure, though, of his reliability as an interpreter, as he has a strong contempt for everybody to whom we speak and he keeps arguing with them very loudly in dialect before he translates. This leads me to believe that he is distorting the answers and giving me a highly flavoured account of what is being said. Let me give you an example. The following is a transcript from my notebooks. The informant, informant 3, is the wife of a minor pirate, a rather depressed-looking woman with six children, all of them under twelve. Her house is on the edge of the village.

"DM: 'Please ask her to tell me how she pays for the family provisions.'

"Interpreter speaks in Chinese for four or five minutes. Informant 3 is silent. Interpreter speaks again, raising his hand at one point as if to strike informant 3. Informant 3 speaks for two minutes, and then is silenced by a threatening look from interpreter, who translates: 'My husband is a selfish man. He likes to keep the money he earns under his bed. There is a trunk there which is locked with a key which he keeps tucked away in his sarong. That is where the money is. He gives me a small amount each week on Monday and I go to the market to buy provisions. There is never quite enough, but if I ask him for money he shouts at me. People are always shouting at me.'

"Interpreter: 'This is a very self-pitying woman. Her husband is a good man. It must be very difficult to be married to a woman like this. That is all she has to say.'

"DM: 'Please thank her.'

"Interpreter: 'That will not be necessary.'"

"So you will understand, James, how very difficult it is for me to get accurate information. However, I persist!

"But now let us move on from such matters to more intriguing issues. There are, I think, several mysteries here, and I find myself increasingly drawn to them. One of these is the question of what happened to the Belgian anthropologist who apparently preceded me here and whose doings, alas, remain obscure. Nobody seems willing to talk about him, and when I raised him with Ling I met a very unambiguous brick wall. The poor man died while doing his field work, and the other day I chanced upon his grave when I was walking down a path that led to the sea. I found myself in a clearing in the jungle and there, under a tree, was a rather poignant marker which simply said: HERE LIES AN ANT. I found this very puzzling. Why should he be so described?

"Then I had an idea, and yesterday I went down that path again. I had the feeling that there were eyes on me, and indeed at one point when I turned round I'm pretty sure that I saw a quick movement in the bush. I was frightened, I'll admit, but not too frightened to abandon my mission. So I continued, still with that feeling that somebody was not far away. From time to time, I stopped and mopped my brow – the jungle is frightfully sticky, rather like the humid part of the hot house in the Royal Botanic Garden at Inverleith (Edinburgh references are so reassuring, James, when one is in the real jungle; it makes one feel that one could turn a corner and suddenly find Jenners there, which would be wonderful, but too much to ask for, alas!). Eventually, I reached the clearing and there was the grave and its rather sad little marker. So far from home, poor man; so far from everything that Belgians appreciate (whatever that is). Such a very poignant place.

"I sat down near the grave and, rather unexpectedly, the words of a hymn came into my mind. It was the hymn which dear Angus Lordie composed (you know how peculiar he is), and which he once sang at a dinner party in my flat in Scotland Street. If I remember correctly, he called it 'God Looks Down on Belgium' and the words went through my mind, there by that poor man's grave. "God's never heard of Belgium/But loves it just the same" . . . and so on.

"I was humming away to myself when I suddenly noticed a piece of wood lying by the grave. I picked it up and read what was painted on it: HROPOLOGIST.

"Hropologist? And then I realised, and that solved that mystery. Part of the marker had fallen off. No ant lay there.

"HERE LIES AN ANTHROPOLOGIST. What a touching tribute. If I don't return from these parts, that is all I would wish for. That, and no more.

"Yours aye, Domenica."

87. *Stendhal Syndrome*

Some of the members of the Edinburgh Teenage Orchestra had been to Paris before, while others, including Bertie, had not. In fact, Bertie had been nowhere before, except for the trip he had made to Glasgow with his father, and so to be here in the great city, sitting in a bus on his way to the hotel on the Boulevard Garibaldi, was seventh heaven indeed. And when the bus trundled across a bridge and they found themselves close to that great landmark, the Eiffel Tower, there was an excited buzz of conversation among the young musicians. For a few minutes they were lured out of the cultivated insouciance of adolescence into a state of frank delight, experiencing, for a moment, that thrill which comes when one sees, in the flesh, some great icon; as when one walks into the relevant room of the Uffizi and sees there, before one, Botticelli's *Birth of Venus*; or in New York when, from the window of a cab that is indeed painted yellow, driven by a man who is indeed profoundly rude, one sees the approaching skyline of Manhattan; or when, arriving in Venice, one discovers that the streets are subtly different (as was found out by the late Robert Benchley, who then sent a telegram to Harold Ross, the editor of the *New Yorker*, in the following terms: STREETS FULL OF WATER. PLEASE ADVISE). Such experiences may become too much – and awaiting those who lay themselves open to cultural epiphany is that curious condition, Stendhal Syndrome. This afflicted Stendhal on his visit to Florence in 1817, and is brought about by seeing great works of art, there before one, and simply being overcome by their beauty. Shortness of breath, tachycardia, and delusions of persecution may result; in other words, a complicated swoon.

Bertie was not a candidate for Stendhal Syndrome. He was thrilled to be in Paris, and he stuck his nose to the window of the bus and gazed, open-mouthed, at the streets of the elegant city. But he was in no danger of swooning; he was merely absorbing and filing away in memory that which he saw: the old Citroën Traction parked by a small *boulangerie*; the white-gloved policeman standing on a traffic island; the buckets of flowers outside a florists; the crowded tables of a pavement café; these were all sights that Bertie would remember.

And then they arrived at their hotel. This was one of those typical small Parisian hotels, occupying six narrow floors of a building overlooking a raised portion of the Metro. Bertie was put in a room on the second floor with Max, his companion from the flight, and from the window of this room he could look out onto the Metro track and see the trains rattle past. For Bertie, who had always been interested in trains, it was the best possible view, and, as he sat on the end of his bed, he thought of the immense good fortune that had brought him to this point in his life. Now he glimpsed what he had thought existed but which had always seemed to be out of his reach – a life in which he was not constantly being cajoled by his mother into doing something, but in which he was, to all intents and purposes, his own master. It was a heady feeling.

"What are we going to do now?" he asked Max, who was busy unpacking his suitcase into the small chest of drawers at the end of the room.

"Richard says that we have to meet downstairs in fifteen minutes and go for a rehearsal," said Max. "That's all we have to do today. But I'm going to go out tonight."

Bertie looked at his shoes. What time would he have to go to bed? he wondered. Would they insist that he went earlier than everybody else, because he was the youngest, or would he be allowed to go out with Max?

"Go out?" he said timidly.

Max shut a drawer with a flourish. "Yes. Paris is a great place for night life. Didn't you know that, Bertie?"

"Oh yes," said Bertie quickly.

"So I thought I might go somewhere like the Moulin Rouge," said Max casually. "And I've heard that the Folies Bergères is a great place too. Have you ever seen the can-can?"

Bertie was silent. He was unsure what the can-can was, but he was reluctant to appear ignorant – or too young. At least he had known who General de Gaulle was, and Max had not, but then Bertie sometimes wondered whether the things he knew – and he knew quite a lot – were up-to-date enough. He had a set of encyclopaedias in his room, but he had found out that these were published in 1968, and might not be as reliable as he thought. But there was time enough to think about that later. For the moment, there was the Moulin Rouge. Were you allowed to go to the Moulin Rouge if you were only six? he wondered. Or did you have to be at least ten?

"Would you like to come with me, Bertie?" asked Max. "I don't mind if you come along. But you may have plans of your own."

"I haven't really made any plans yet," said Bertie. "And I would like to come with you." He paused. "Are we allowed?"

"Of course not," said Max. "We'll have to slip out the back. But I noticed a fire escape as we came up the stairs. You can get to it from out there, and we can shin down that and then catch the Metro. Easy."

"All right," said Bertie.

"Good," said Max. "We're going for dinner somewhere after the rehearsal and then we come back here. We'll wait fifteen minutes until everyone has gone to bed, and then we'll leave. Boy, are we going to have fun, Bertie!"

They went downstairs a few minutes later and then the whole

orchestra was driven off in a bus to the hall where they were due to rehearse.

At the rehearsal, Bertie found it difficult to concentrate, but the small parts he had been given to play were simple and his distracted state did not show. He threw a glance at Max, sitting with the strings, and the other boy at one point winked at him, as if in confirmation of their conspiracy.

At the end of the rehearsal, as they were packing up their instruments, Bertie went to stand close to Max, so that he could sit next to him on the bus and discuss their outing.

"It's very exciting," whispered Bertie.

"Yes, sure," said Max nonchalantly.

88. *Girl Talk*

They were taken from the rehearsal to the restaurant, which was a large, hall-like establishment, specialising in the feeding of school parties on visits to Paris. The menu, which was printed on laminated cards, was written in English, Italian and German. There was no French. The description of each course was helpfully accompanied by a small picture of what the dish looked like.

To Bertie's disappointment, Max appeared to have found some new friends and sat with them, leaving him to sit with a small group of girls, who made a place for him and seemed to be quite happy with his company.

"You're very sweet, you know," said one of the girls.

Bertie blushed. He was not sure whether it was a good thing to be described as sweet, but he thought that it probably was not.

"How old are you?" said another. "Somebody said that you were only four. Is that true?"

Bertie looked down at his plate. "I'm going to be seven on my next birthday," he said.

"Six!" exclaimed another girl.

Fortunately, the conversation soon moved on to another topic, and Bertie's embarrassment subsided. The topic, it transpired, was the other members of the orchestra, particularly the boys.

"Have you seen that boy called Kevin?" asked one of the girls. "He plays the oboe, or thinks that he does."

"He's gross," said another. "He thinks he's so cool, but he's really gross. Have you seen his ears? They stick out like this. It's really gross."

"He needs surgery," said the first girl. "That's his only chance."

They laughed at this. Bertie, who could see Kevin sitting on the other side of the room, looked at his ears. They did not seem too large to him.

"And that boy in percussion," one said. "I saw him looking in the mirror in the hotel. There's this big mirror in the hall, see, and he was standing in front of it looking at his profile. It was really sad.

"He actually asked Linda out, you know. She couldn't believe it. She said: 'Are you mad or something?' She said to me that she saw the seat he'd been sitting in on the plane and there was a large patch of hair gel where his head had been.

"And what about Max? Do you know him? He sits next to Tessa in the cellos. She says she can't bear him. She says that he's really stupid and that she has to do all the counting for him."

Bertie opened his mouth to say something. Max was his friend, and he did not think he was stupid.

"He's not stupid," he said.

One of the girls glanced at him. "You said something, Bertie?"

Bertie tried to make his voice louder, and deeper. "I said: He's not stupid. Max isn't stupid."

"All boys are stupid," said one of the other girls, and laughed. "Except you, Bertie. You're not stupid. You're sweet."

At the end of the meal, they returned to the hotel by bus and, after receiving instructions about the following day, when the concert was to be performed, they dispersed to their rooms. When Bertie got to his room, he found that Max was already there.

"I saw you sitting with those girls," Max remarked. "What were they like?"

Bertie met his friend's gaze. He was a truthful boy and he thought: would it be a fib, a real fib, not to tell Max what they had said about him? Was it a fib to say nothing when the effect of that would be exactly the same as if you had said something?

"They were quite . . ." Bertie began.

"I think one of them fancies me," said Max casually. "You know that one with the fair hair? You know the one I mean?"

Bertie nodded. It was the girl who had passed on the comment about Max being stupid.

"She's the one," said Max. "Do you think I should ask her out, Bertie?"

Bertie looked doubtful. "I think she may be busy," he said.

"I'll think about it," said Max. "Maybe I'll give her a chance."

Bertie looked out of the window. In the streets below, the cars moved slowly past and there was the sound of an approaching Metro train. "When are we going?" he asked Max.

Max lay back on the cover of his bed and looked at his watch. "It's a bit late, Bertie," he said. "And anyway, do you know the way?"

"To the Moulin Rouge?" asked Bertie.

"Yes," said Max. "Because I don't. And we can't go if we don't know the way."

"I don't," said Bertie, looking crestfallen. "But maybe we could ask somebody in the street."

Max laughed. "I can't speak French," he said. "We can't ask if we don't speak French. I do German, you see. And that's no use in Paris."

Bertie sighed. "So we can't go?"

"Not this time," said Max, slipping out of his shoes and throwing them onto a chair. "Next time we're in Paris, boy will we have fun then!"

It took Bertie some time to get to sleep that night. He was disappointed by the cancellation of the visit to the Moulin Rouge, but he was looking forward to the concert tomorrow and they still had another night in Paris after that. He drifted off to sleep in a state of contentment and pride at being by himself – or almost – in Paris, fully accepted by a group of teenagers, more or less an honorary teenager. It was a fine state to be in.

He dreamed, and in his dream he was in the Moulin Rouge, which was a large room bearing an uncanny resemblance to the Queen's Hall in Edinburgh. He was sitting at a table with one of the girls from the orchestra, who was talking to him, although Bertie did not hear anything that she said. And then, into the Moulin Rouge, came Dr Fairbairn.

It seemed to Bertie that Dr Fairbairn was looking for him, and he tried to hide under the table. But he had been spotted, and the psychotherapist came up to him and pulled him back onto his chair.

"What are you doing in the Moulin Rouge, Bertie?" asked Dr Fairbairn.

"I came here because . . ." Bertie started to reply.

"Because it's a dream, Bertie?" interrupted Dr Fairbairn. "Is that why you're here? Is that why any of us is here? Is that it, Bertie?"

89. Irene Has a Shock

The following day was the day of the concert, which took place in a hall in the UNESCO building. The performance was to be in the evening, which left the day for sightseeing, including a boat trip on the Seine, a trip to the Pompidou Centre, and a walk round Île de la Cité. Bertie, guidebook in hand, enjoyed all of this a great deal, and ticked off each sight against a checklist in the back of his book.

The Edinburgh Teenage Orchestra was one of a number of youth orchestras which had been invited to perform in the UNESCO Festival of Youth Arts. The day before, there had been a concert performed by the Children's Symphony Orchestra of Kiev, and the day afterwards was to feature the Korean Youth Folk Dance Company, which had recently danced in Rome, Milan and Geneva, before admittedly small, but nonetheless enthusiastic audiences. Now it was the turn of Edinburgh, and the orchestra had prepared a programme of predominantly Scottish music, including Hamish McCunn's 'Land of the Mountain and the Flood', George Russell's rarely-performed 'Bathgate Airs for Oboe and Strings' and Paton's haunting 'By the Water of Leith's Fair Banks'.

This programme was well received by the audience of several hundred Parisians. In *Le Monde* the following week, it was to receive a mention in a feature on young people and the arts, in which the writer referred to the fact that while the youth of France appeared to be burning cars at weekends, Scottish youth seemed to be more engaged in cultural pursuits. This, the writer suggested, was the complete opposite of what one might expect, were one to believe the impression conveyed in film and literature.

After the concert, the members of the orchestra were given a finger buffet and listened to a short speech of thanks delivered by a UNESCO official charged with responsibility for youth culture. In the mingling that followed, Bertie attracted a circle of admiring concert-goers, who stood round him in wonderment while he charmed them with his frank answers to their questions. Then, the party over, the members of the orchestra made the short walk back to their hotel. The concert, the conductor declared, had been a great success and he was proud of everybody, from the oldest (a trumpet-player of nineteen) to the youngest (Bertie). Now it was time for bed, as everybody would have to get up at five the following morning in order to catch the flight back to Edinburgh.

When five o'clock came, there was a milling crowd of teenagers in the hotel vestibule. The bus was waiting outside, its coachwork shaking from the vibration of its diesel engine, which made it look as if it was shivering in the cold morning air.

"In the bus everybody," called out one of the adult volunteers who had accompanied the orchestra. "And whatever you do, don't forget your instruments!"

Nobody forgot their instruments – but they did forget Bertie. Max had awoken him and then made his own way downstairs. Bertie had sat up in bed, rubbed his eyes, and then flopped back again. He had been in a deep sleep, and he had not been properly roused. So it was not until nine o'clock that morning, halfway across the North Sea, that somebody in the plane asked the question: "Where's Bertie?"

The question passed up and down the plane, and nobody was able to provide anything but one answer: wherever Bertie was, he was not on the aircraft. And once that conclusion had been reached, messages were rapidly radioed back to Charles de Gaulle Airport. It was possible that Bertie was still in the terminal somewhere and an immediate search should be instituted. But then further questions were asked and it became clear that nobody had seen Bertie on the bus to the airport. He was therefore still in the hotel.

Irene was at Edinburgh Airport to meet her son. When the first of the members of the orchestra appeared from behind the doors of customs, she readied herself for an emotional reunion. But then, grim-faced and apologetic, one of the volunteers rushed up to her and informed her of what had happened.

"He'll be fine," said the volunteer. "It's a charming hotel and they were most co-operative. We shall phone through immediately and tell them to go and check his room and make sure that he's all right. And I'm sure that they'll put him on the next flight back."

Irene stared at the well-meaning woman, mute with incomprehension. Then, when the significance of what had been said was absorbed, she sat down in a state of shock.

"I'm so sorry about this," said the volunteer. "But look, I'm getting through to them right away. I'm sure that they'll have Bertie on the line in no time at all."

As Irene stared dumbly at the ceiling, the volunteer spoke quickly into her mobile phone. Then she paused, smiled encouragingly at Irene, and waited for a response. When it came, her face clouded over. "I see," she said quietly. And then, again: "I see."

"What did they say?" said Irene. "Let me speak to Bertie."

The volunteer put the mobile away. "They said that he's not in his room," she announced apologetically. "They said that he appears to have gone out."

Irene sat back in her seat, her head sunk in her hands.

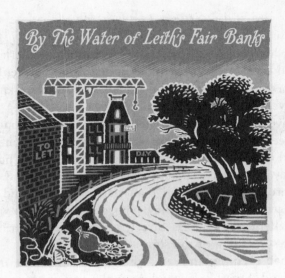

By The Water of Leith's Fair Banks

"I'm sure that he'll turn up somewhere," said the volunteer, looking anxiously about her. "In the meantime, I suggest that we just . . . that we wait."

Irene stared at her. "I can't believe I'm hearing all this," she said, her voice rising in anger. "I can't believe that you could take a six-year-old to Paris and leave him there. I just can't believe it."

"But you're the one who insisted that he go," said the volunteer. "It was explained to you that it was a teenage orchestra and yet you . . ."

"So now you're blaming me?" said Irene. "Is that it?"

The volunteer sighed. She had been at the audition where Irene had insisted on Bertie being given a hearing. She had heard Irene dismiss the argument that Bertie was far too young. If he was incapable of coping with the arrangements, then it was hardly anybody's fault but his mother's.

"Well, now that you mention it," she said, "yes. Yes. I do happen to think that it's your fault. Sorry about that. But I really do. You insisted that he should be included. You really did. But he was far too young. That's all there is to it."

Matthew had seen Stuart several times in the Cumberland Bar. They had exchanged a few words on occasion, but neither had really worked out exactly who the other was. Matthew knew that Stuart lived in Scotland Street and had a vague idea that he might have lived on the same stair as Pat. He also thought that he had seen him with that impossible woman – the one whom Cyril had once bitten in the ankle – and that strange little boy. Somebody had said, too, that he worked in the Scottish Executive somewhere; but that was all that Matthew knew. And for his part, Stuart knew that Matthew had something to do with one of the galleries in Dundas Street, or that he was an antique dealer or something of the sort.

On that evening, though, when Matthew went into the Cumberland, Stuart was standing at the bar ordering a drink, and the circumstances were right for a longer conversation. And this was particularly so when Angus Lordie came in and suggested that they all sit at one of the tables, under which Cyril could drink his dish of beer undisturbed.

The conversation ranged widely. Matthew had seen a picture in an auction catalogue which he was thinking of buying and he wanted advice from Angus. It was a Hornel – a picture of three girls sitting in a field of flowers.

"I don't really like it," he said. "Flowers all over the place."

Angus agreed. "I never put flowers in a painting," he observed. "Not that I'm disrespectful of flowers. Far from it. I have no wish to upset them."

Matthew laughed. "Are you one of these people who talk to plants?"

Angus shook his head. "I have nothing to say to plants," he replied. "Although you may be aware of Lin Yutang's lovely essay on conditions that upset flowers."

Stuart stared at Angus. One did not come across people like this when one worked in the Scottish Executive.

"I have a lot of time for Lin Yutang," Angus went on. "People don't write essays any more, or not many of them do. He wrote beautifully about tea and flowers and subjects like that. He said that flowers were offended by loud conversations. One should talk softly in the presence of flowers."

"Very nice," said Matthew. "I'll remember that."

"And then there's Michael von Poser's essay, 'Flowers and Ducks'," Angus continued. "Another lovely bit of whimsy. But back to Hornel, Matthew. People like him, and I'd buy it. Look at how art has out-performed other investments. Imagine if one had a few Peploes about the house. Or Blackadders. She'll be the next one."

"I had a Vettriano," said Matthew, thoughtfully.

Angus looked down at the floor. That had been an incident in which he had unfortunately put a rather excessive amount of paint-stripper on Matthew's painting, obliterating all the umbrellas and people dancing on the beach. It had been most regrettable, and it was inconsiderate of Matthew – to say the least – to bring the subject up again.

The conversation drifted on in this vein, and then Angus mentioned his discussion with Big Lou that morning.

"Big Lou is pretty miserable," he said. "I saw her this morning."

Matthew, who had been unable to go for coffee that day, frowned. "Miserable? Why?"

"That man of hers," said Angus. "That Eddie character."

"Not my favourite person," said Matthew.

"Nor mine," said Angus. "I never liked the cut of his jib. From the moment I met him. Well, we were right. You and I were absolutely right."

"He's left her?" asked Matthew.

He thought that this would be sad for Big Lou, but only in the short term.

"Not as far as I know," said Angus. "But the penny's dropped anyway. She realises that he's no good. I didn't ask her how it happened, but I suspect that she found out about the girls he gets mixed up with. You know what he's like in that department. But that's not the point. The point is money."

"This club of his?" asked Matthew.

Angus nodded. "He's taken her for thirty-four thousand pounds."

Matthew whistled. Turning to Stuart, he explained the background. "Eddie wants to set up a club. Lou has a bit of money. It was left to her by some old farmer in Aberdeenshire or somewhere. It's the answer to this character's dreams."

"I wonder if it was a loan," asked Stuart. "Would she have any way of getting it back?"

"Fat chance!" snorted Angus. "She can kiss that money goodbye."

Stuart was silent. He was a very fair man, and it caused him great distress to hear of dishonesty or exploitation. That this should happen under his nose, round the corner, to somebody who sounded like a good woman, angered him. It was awful, this lack of justice in the world. We believed that the state would protect us, that the authorities would pursue those who preyed on others. But the truth of the matter was that the authorities could set right only a tiny part of the injustice and wrong that was done to the weak. Justice, it seemed, was imperfect.

It would be wonderful to be able to bring about justice. It would be wonderful to be some sort of omniscient being who saw all, noted it down, and then set things right. But that was a wish, a wish of childhood, that we grew to understand could never be. Except sometimes, perhaps . . . Sometimes there were occasions when the bully was defeated, the proud laid low, the weak given the chance to recover that which was taken from them. Sometimes that happened. "When I was young," he said. "I used to read stories about people who sorted this sort of thing out. The end was always predictable, but very satisfying."

"Sorry to have to tell you this," said Angus. "But the comic-book heroes aren't real. They don't exist."

Stuart laughed. "Oh, I've come to terms with that," he said. "But I have a friend who does exist. He's quite good at sorting things out, I think."

Matthew looked at him. "He could get Big Lou's money back? Unlikely. Eddie's not going to reach into his pocket and disgorge it."

"But this friend of mine has a way of getting round difficulties," said Stuart.

"Is he a lawyer?" asked Angus.

Stuart smiled wryly. "No, he's a businessman."

"Who is he?" asked Matthew. If he was a businessman, then it was possible that he would know Matthew's father.

"He's called Lard O'Connor," said Stuart. "And I could have a word with him if you like. He's very helpful."

91. *Pat and Matthew Talk*

Shortly before seven o'clock that evening, Matthew left the Cumberland Bar and returned to his flat in India Street. He had enjoyed his drink with Angus and Stuart. Angus, as ever, was amusing, and Stuart struck him as being agreeable company. It was good to have friends, he thought. He himself did not have enough friends, though, and he thought that he should make a bit more of an effort in future to cultivate friendships. But where would he find them? He could hardly make all his friends in the Cumberland Bar. Perhaps he should join a club of some sort and make friends that way: a singles' club, for instance. He had heard that there were singles' clubs where everybody went on holiday together. That would be interesting, perhaps, but what if one did not take to the other singles? Besides, the very word single sounded a bit desperate, as if one suffered from some sort of condition, singularity.

But for the moment, Matthew had no desire to find anybody else; not now that he had Pat living in India Street. It was a wonderful feeling, he thought, this going home to somebody. Even if she was not in, then at least her things were there. Even Pat's things made Matthew feel a bit better; just the thought of her things: her sandals, those pink ones he had seen her wearing; her books, including that large book on the history of art; her bookshop bag that she used to carry her files up to the university. All of these were invested with some sort of special significance in Matthew's mind; they were Pat's things.

He walked back along Cumberland Street, past the St Vincent Bar and its neighbouring church, and then round Circus Place to the bottom of India Street. It was a warm evening for the time of year and the town was quiet. Matthew looked up at the elegant Georgian buildings, at their confident doors and windows. Some of the windows were lit and disclosed domestic scenes within: a drawing room in which a group of people could be seen standing near the window, talking; down in a basement, a kitchen with pans steaming on the cooker and the windows misting up; a cat asleep on a windowsill. These were people with ordered, secure lives – or so it seemed from the outside. And that was what Matthew wanted. He wanted somebody who would be waiting for him, or for whom he could wait. Somebody he could share things with. And wasn't that what everybody wanted? he thought. Wasn't it? And how cruel it was that not everybody could find this in their lives.

He reached his front door and went in. He had hoped that she would be there, and his heart gave a leap when he saw the light coming out from under her door. He went through to his room and changed into a pair of jeans and a T-shirt. Then he went into the kitchen and opened a cupboard. He had stocked up with dried pasta; that would do. And there was a good block of parmesan in the fridge and some mushrooms.

He put the pasta on to boil and started to grate the parmesan. Then Pat came into the kitchen while Matthew's back was turned, so that he was surprised when he saw her.

"I'm cooking pasta," he said. "Would you like some? I've got plenty."

He had hardly dared ask the question. He was afraid that she would be going out, and that he would be left by himself, but she was not.

"That's really kind," said Pat, perching herself on a kitchen chair.

Matthew told her of what Angus had said about Big Lou, and Pat listened, horrified.

"That horrible man," she said, shuddering at the thought of Eddie.

"Poor Lou," said Matthew. "But there was somebody there who said that he might be able to help her."

Pat listened as Matthew explained about Stuart's suggestion. It seemed unlikely to her that anything could be done, but they could try, she supposed. Poor Lou. She rose to her feet and offered to prepare a salad. "I can't sit here and do nothing," she said.

"Yes, you can," said Matthew. "Let me look after you."

The words had come out without really being intended, and he hoped that she would not take them the wrong way. But what was the wrong way? All that the words meant was that he wanted to make her dinner, and what was wrong with wanting to make somebody dinner?

Laughing, Pat said: "No, you do the pasta. I'll do the salad." Matthew opened the fridge and took out a bottle of white wine. He poured Pat a glass and one for himself. The wine was probably too chilled, as the glass was misting. He thought of the misting panes in the basement kitchen he had seen round the corner, and of the people standing in their window.

Pat told him about a seminar she had attended that day. He listened, but did not pay much attention to what she was saying. The seminar had been on Romantic art and somebody had said something very stupid, which had made everybody laugh. Matthew did not listen to the stupid remark as she retold it; he was thinking only of how nice it would be to be in a seminar with Pat. He wanted to be with her all the time now. He closed his eyes. I can't let this happen to me, he thought. I can't fall so completely for this girl, because she won't fall for me. I'm just a friend. That's all. I'm just her friend.

And then, suddenly, Pat passed behind him, and brushed against him, her arm against his, and he gave a start and half-turned. She was right behind him and he looked at her and she said: "Oh, sorry . . ."

He took her hand. She looked at him, and then lowered her eyes.

"I'm sorry," said Matthew, reckless now. "I really am. I didn't mean to fall for you. I didn't actually make a decision. It's not like that. That's not the way it works."

"It doesn't matter," said Pat.

"But it does."

There was a brief silence. "But I like you too."

"You do?"

A further silence. The pasta bubbled.

"How much?"

"Lots."

Matthew sighed. "But . . . but not like that."

"That's where you're wrong," she said.

And it seemed to Matthew that all the bells of Edinburgh, and beyond, were ringing out at once, in joyous, joyous peals.

92. *Alone in Paris*

When he woke up that morning and realised that he had slept in, Bertie felt intensely alarmed. But he was not a boy given to panic, and so he dressed carefully, brushing his hair with attention to the fact that he was, after all, in Paris. Then he made his way downstairs, allowing himself at least to hope that somebody from the orchestra might have stayed behind for him or possibly left a note. But the woman at the desk informed him that the Edinburgh group had left. She assumed that Bertie belonged to a British couple staying upstairs and it did not enter her head that he was now entirely on his own.

Bertie sat down in the lobby and wondered what to do. They had obviously forgotten all about him, he decided, but they would remember their mistake when they arrived in Edinburgh and his parents asked where he was. He looked at his watch; that should be happening about now. And then they would come back to fetch him, but would probably not arrive until tomorrow morning. So that, in his reckoning, gave him a whole day and night in Paris, which would be rather interesting. He had quite a bit of his spending money left over, as nobody had allowed him to pay for anything, and he could use that to tide him over. It might even be enough to get a ticket for the Moulin Rouge, should he come across that establishment during the sightseeing that he proposed to do.

Paging through his guidebook and map, Bertie decided that

he would set off to the Louvre. He liked galleries, and he thought that he would possibly spend the entire morning there. Then he would have lunch somewhere nearby . . . He stopped. Although he was sure that he had enough money to tide him over, he did not think that it would run to two meals (not including breakfast) as well as the tickets for the various places that he wished to visit. Would the woman at the hotel desk lend him some, he wondered, if he promised to send it back to her when it came to next pocket-money day? He glanced in her direction. No, he did not think that she looked the type of person from whom one could ask for a loan. Tofu would have had no hesitation in asking, of course, as he was always demanding money from people. But Bertie was not Tofu, and Tofu was not in Paris.

Then Bertie had an idea. When the group had gone to Notre Dame on their sightseeing, they had passed through the Latin Quarter and seen a number of people playing their instruments in the street – busking, explained one of the violinists.

"I did that outside Jenners last Christmas," he said. "I made twenty-four pounds in one morning. Twenty-four pounds! And all I played was 'Rudolph the Red-nosed Reindeer' over and over again. It was dead easy!"

The saxophone which had been borrowed for him was still in his room, and it occurred to Bertie that there was no reason why he should not spend the morning busking in the Latin Quarter. He could play 'As Time Goes By' from *Casablanca*, which people always seemed to like, and he could vary it with some Satie which he had recently learned. He had read that Satie had lived in Paris, and perhaps some of his old friends would recognise his music and give particularly generously. Or Mr Satie himself might pass by, although he must be very old by now, thought Bertie.

Filled with excitement at his plan, Bertie rushed upstairs and retrieved his saxophone. Then, struggling somewhat with the weight of it, he set out from the hotel in the direction of the Latin Quarter. It was heavy going. After a few blocks, Bertie realised that it would take him several hours to walk across Paris with his instrument, as he would have to stop at virtually every corner to rest his aching muscles. He felt in his pocket, where his money nestled, neatly folded. A taxi would be expensive, he knew, but even if it took all his funds, there was the money that he would undoubtedly soon earn from his busking.

He stood on the edge of the road and waited until a taxi came past. He did not have to wait long, and soon he was seated comfortably in the back of a white Peugeot heading for the point on his map which he had shown to a slightly surprised taxi driver. The journey went quickly and Bertie took the money out of his pocket to pay. He was slightly short of the fare requested, but the driver smiled and indicated that the shortfall was not an issue. Then, staggering under the weight of the borrowed saxophone in its heavy wooden case, he walked a few blocks into the network of narrow streets that made up the Quarter.

It did not take him long to find a suitable pitch. Halfway along one street there was a boarded-up doorway off the pavement. With a restaurant next door, a coffee bar a few yards away on the same side, and a student bookshop opposite, it seemed to Bertie that it was an ideal place for him to play. He set the open case down in front of him – as he had seen other buskers do – and, summoning up all his courage, he started to play 'As Time Goes By'.

The first person to walk past was a woman wearing a long brown coat and with her hair done up in a bun. As she went past Bertie, she glanced at him, took a few more steps, and then stopped and turned round. Fumbling in her purse, she extracted a crumpled banknote and turned to toss it into the open case, murmuring, as she did so: "*Petit ange!*"

Bertie acknowledged the donation with a nod of his head – as he had seen other buskers do – and modulated into one of the jazz tunes he had learned from Lewis Morrison, 'Goodbye Pork Pie Hat'. This went down very well with the next passer-by, a visiting Senegalese civil servant, who clapped his hands in appreciation and tossed a few small notes into the case. This was followed by a donation of a few coins from a thin man walking a large Dalmatian. The Dalmatian barked at Bertie and wagged his tail. Again, Bertie acknowledged both man and dog with a nod. It was good to be in Paris, he thought.

93. *Bertie's New Friends*

By twelve o'clock, Bertie's case was almost full of money. Virtually no passer-by – and they were numerous that morning – walked on without giving something. This was not because they made a habit of giving to buskers – they did no such thing – but it was because none of them could resist the sight of a small boy playing the saxophone with such ease and to such good effect. And there was something about Bertie that appealed to the French.

When Bertie eventually stopped and took on the task of counting his money, he found it hard to believe that he had collected so much. Not only would he be able to pay for lunch and dinner that day, but there was enough money to enable him to survive in Paris for several weeks should the need arise.

Tucking the notes into his pockets, now bulging with money, he replaced the saxophone in the case and walked the few yards to the nearby restaurant. Looking at the menu displayed in the window, he struggled to make out what was on offer. It would have been different, he decided, if it had been in Italian – that would have been easy – but what, he wondered, were *escargots* and what were *blanquettes de veau*?

"Are you having difficulty?" said a voice behind him, in English.

Bertie turned round, to find a small group of people behind him, a man and two women. They were too old to be teenagers, he thought, but they were not much older than that. Perhaps they were students, he told himself. He had read that this was the part of Paris where students were to be seen.

"I don't know what the menu says," said Bertie. "I know how to read, but I don't know how to read French."

The woman who had first addressed him bent over to his level. "Ah, poor you!" she said. "Let me help you. Should I read from the top, or would you like to tell me what sort of thing you like to eat and I can see if it's on the menu?"

"I like sausages," said Bertie. "And I like sticky toffee pudding."

The young woman looked at the menu board. "I can find sausages," she said. "But I don't think they have sticky toffee pudding. That is a great pity. But they do have some very nice apple tart. Would you like to try that? *Tarte tatin*?"

Bertie nodded.

"In that case," said the woman, "why don't you join me and my friends for lunch? We were just about to go inside."

"Thank you," said Bertie. "I have enough money to pay, you see."

The young people laughed. "That will not be necessary," said the young woman. "This is not an expensive place. No Michelin stars, but no fancy prices. Come on, let's go in."

They entered the restaurant, where the waiter, recognising Bertie's three companions, immediately ushered them to a table near the window.

"That's Henri," said the young woman. "He has been here ever since the riots of 1968. He came in to take refuge and they offered him a job. He's stayed here since then."

"What happened in 1968?" asked Bertie. "Was there a war?"

They all laughed. "A war?" said the young man. "In a sense. The bourgeoisie was at war with the students and the advanced thinkers. It was very exciting."

"Who won?" asked Bertie.

There was a silence. Then the second young woman spoke. "It is difficult to say. I suppose the bourgeoisie is still with us."

"So they won then," said Bertie.

The young man looked uncomfortable. "It's not as simple as that," he said. "The system was badly wounded."

"And they curbed the powers of the *flics*, eventually," said the first young woman, shrugging, as if to dismiss the subject. "But we should introduce ourselves," she went on. "I'm Marie-Louise, and this," she said, turning to the other young woman, "is Sylvie. He's called Jean-Philippe. We shorten him to Jarpipe. And what, may I ask, is your name?"

Bertie thought for a moment. It seemed to him that the French put in their second names, and he did not want to appear unsophisticated. His second name, he recollected, was Peter, and he did know the French for that. "I'm Bertie-Pierre," he said quickly. It sounded rather good, he thought, and none of his new friends seemed to think it at all odd.

"Alors, Bertie-Pierre," said Marie-Louise. "Let us order our lunch. You said that you liked sausages, so we shall see what Henri can do about that."

They gave the order to Henri, who nodded a polite greeting to Bertie, and then Marie-Louise turned to Bertie and said: "Tell us about yourself, Bertie-Pierre. What are you doing in Paris, all by leetle self? And what have you got in that case of yours?"

"I came here with an orchestra," Bertie said. "The Edinburgh Teenage Orchestra."

"But you are surely not . . ." said Jean-Philippe.

"I'm not a teenager quite yet," said Bertie. "But my mother . . ."

"He is a prodigy," said Sylvie. "That is why."

"Are you a prodigy, Bertie-Pierre?" asked Jean-Philippe.

Bertie looked down at the table. "I am not sure," he said. "Mr Morrison thinks I am. But I don't know myself."

"And who is this Monsieur Morrison?" asked Sylvie.

"He is my saxophone teacher," said Bertie.

"Ah well," said Marie-Louise. "I am sure that Monsieur Morrison knows what he is talking about. We should tell you a little bit about ourselves. We are all students here at the Sorbonne. I am a student of English literature. Sylvie is a student of economics – that is very dull, but she does not seem to mind, hah! – and Jarpipe is a student of philosophy. He is very serious, very melancholic, as you may have noticed. He is in love with Sylvie here, but Sylvie loves another. She loves Jacques, who has blue eyes and drives a very fast car. Poor Jarpipe!"

"I live in hope," said Jean-Philippe, smiling. "What is there to do but to live in the belief of the reality of what you want? That is what Camus said, Bertie-Pierre."

"Camus is very passé," said Sylvie. "How can I love one who talks about Camus?"

"I cannot talk about Derrida," said Jean-Philippe indignantly. "There is nothing to be said about Derrida. Nothing. *Rien*. Bah!"

Bertie listened to this exchange in fascination. This was the Paris he had been hoping to find, and he had now found it. Oh, if only Tofu and Olive could see him sitting here with his new friends, on the Left Bank, talking about these sophisticated matters. Oh, if only his mother could see . . . No, perhaps not.

94. *Deconstruction at the Sorbonne*

Bertie enjoyed every minute of the lunch with his new friends in the restaurant in the Latin Quarter. The conversation was wide-ranging, but Bertie was more than capable of holding his own in the various topics into which it strayed. At one point, when Freud was mentioned, he let slip the name of Melanie Klein, which brought astonished stares from the three French students.

"So!" exclaimed Sylvie. "You have heard of Melanie Klein! *Formidable!*"

Bertie had learned that the hallmark of sophisticated conversation in Paris was the tossing out of derogatory remarks, usually calling into question an entire theory or *oeuvre*. He had been waiting to do this with Melanie Klein, and now the opportunity had presented itself. "She's rubbish," said Bertie.

It made him feel considerably better to say that, and he felt even better when the others agreed with him.

"I'm surprised that anybody still reads her," said Sylvie. "Perhaps in places like Scotland . . ."

Bertie thought quickly. He knew that his mother read Melanie Klein religiously, but he did not want to reveal that now. At the same time, his Scottish pride had been pricked by the suggestion that people in Scotland were less at the forefront of intellectual fashion than people in Paris.

"We only read her to laugh at her," said Bertie quickly. "In Scotland, she's considered a comic writer."

The students laughed at this. "Very good, Bertie-Pierre," said Sylvie. "So, tell me, who do you read at your university?"

Bertie shifted his feet uncomfortably, even though they did not quite reach the floor. "I'm still at school," he said meekly. "I'm not at university yet."

The students pretended surprise at this revelation. "But there you are knowing all about Melanie Klein and still at school!" said Marie-Louise. "Remarkable. Perhaps this is the new Scottish Enlightenment."

Bertie let the remark pass. Jean-Philippe, he noticed, was looking at him with interest. "Tell me, Bertie-Pierre," the student said. "Who are your friends at school?"

"There is a boy called Tofu," Bertie replied. "He's my friend. Sometimes."

"And tell us about this Tofu," asked Sylvie. "Would we like him?"

"I don't think so," said Bertie.

"Ah!" said Jean-Philippe. "And are there other friends?"

Bertie thought for a moment. "There's Olive," he said. "She's a girl."

"Well, perhaps we would like this Olive," said Sylvie.

"No," said Bertie. "I don't think you would."

They were silent for a moment. Then Jean-Philippe looked at his watch. "Well, Bertie-Pierre, time is marching on. We were all going to a lecture this afternoon. Jean-François François, the well-known deconstructionist, is talking at three. Everybody is going to be there. Would you like to join us?"

Bertie did not hesitate to accept the invitation. He had never heard of Jean-François François, nor of deconstruction, but he thought that it would be fun to listen to a lecture with his three friends.

"Time to pay," said Sylvie, signalling to Henri.

Henri brought the bill over to the table and presented it to Jean-Philippe. He glanced at it quickly and then slipped it over the table to Marie-Louise, who shook her head in disbelief.

"Please let me pay," said Bertie. "I have lots of money."

"But Bertie-Pierre," protested Sylvie. "You are our guest!"

"On the other hand," said Jean-Philippe, "it's very generous of you, Bertie-Pierre. And perhaps we should accept."

Bertie extracted a wad of banknotes from his pocket and passed them to Henri. Then, collecting their belongings, he and his friends left the restaurant and made the short journey on foot to the lecture theatre in the Sorbonne where Jean-François François was due to speak.

There was a good crowd already waiting there. Bertie sat near the back row with his friends and watched the scene as the theatre filled up. There was a great deal of conversation going on between members of the audience, but this died down when a door at the side opened and Jean-François François entered the room. There was applause as he made his way up to the podium, but when he reached it he quickly spat out some words into the microphone and the applause died down.

"What's he saying?" Bertie whispered to Jean-Philippe. "I haven't learned French yet."

"Don't worry," said Jean-Philippe. "I'll translate for you. He just said that applause is infantile. He says that only the bourgeoisie claps. That's why everybody has stopped clapping."

Bertie thought about this. What was wrong with clapping, particularly if somebody said something you agreed with? They had been clapped at their concert; was that because the bourgeoisie had been present?

Jean-François François now burst into a torrent of French, pointing a thin, nicotine-stained finger into the crowd for emphasis. Bertie listened enthralled. It seemed to him that whatever the lecturer was saying must be very important, as the audience was hanging onto every word.

"What's he saying now?" he whispered to Jean-Philippe.

"He says that the rules of science are not rules at all," Jean-Philippe whispered back. "He says that the hegemony of scientific knowledge is the creation of an imposed consensus. The social basis of that consensus is artificial and illusory. He says that even the rules of physics are a socially determined imposition.

There is no scientific truth. That's more or less what he says."

Bertie was astonished. He did not know many rules of physics, but he did know Bernoulli's principle which explained how lift occurred. And surely that was true, because he had seen it in operation on the flight from Edinburgh to Paris.

Bertie turned to Jean-Phillipe and said: "But would Mr François say that Bernoulli's principle was rubbish when he was in a plane, up in the air?"

Jean-Philippe listened to Bertie's remark and frowned. Then the frown disappeared and he turned and passed the observation on to Sylvie, who listened with a slowly dawning smile and passed it on to the person next to her. Soon the remark was travelling across the lecture theatre in every direction and people could be heard muttering and giggling. Then a young man at the front of the lecture theatre stood up and shouted out a question, interrupting the lecturer's flow. Bertie could not understand what it was about but he did hear reference to Bernoulli.

Jean-François François hesitated. He pointed a finger into the crowd and began to speak. But he was now shouted down. There were jeers and more laughter.

"Amazing!" said Jean-Philippe, turning to Bertie in frank admiration. "Bertie-Pierre, you've deconstructed Jean-François François himself! Incredible!"

Bertie did not know what to say, but thought it polite to say thank you, and so he did.

95. A Portrait of a Sitting

The portrait which Angus Lordie was painting was not going well. It was not a commissioned work – those paintings always seemed to go smoothly, aided, no doubt, by the thought of the fee – but the result of an offer which he had made one day in the Scottish Arts Club. It was one of those rash offers one makes, more or less on impulse, and which are immediately taken up by the recipient. Most people understand that offers of that nature are not intended to be taken seriously, or are only half-serious, and do nothing about them. Others – and they are in a small minority – take them literally, largely because they take everything literally.

Ramsey Dunbarton, the retired lawyer and resident of the Braids, now sat in Angus Lordie's under-heated studio in Drummond Place, gazing at a fixed point on the wall with what he hoped was an expression that combined both dignity and experience. This was his third sitting, the first having taken place very shortly after Angus had made his subsequently regretted offer to paint his portrait.

"It's very good of you," said Ramsey, sitting back in the red leather chair in which Angus positioned his sitters, "but I hope that I give you a bit of a challenge. One or two people have said that this old physiognomy is a typical Edinburgh one. Perhaps you'll be able to catch that. What do you think?"

Angus was non-committal. He would do his best by Ramsey, but there were limits.

"I wondered whether you'd like to paint me in one of my thespian moments," Ramsey went on. "I played the Duke of Plaza-Toro once, you know. It was at the Church Hill Theatre."

Angus busied himself with his brushes.

"It's not an easy character to play," Ramsey went on. "It requires a certain panache, of course, but the difficulty with parts like that is that one can go over the top. But I hope that I didn't. We still sing a bit, you know. One's voice changes, of course – like so much else."

Angus nodded. He tended to listen with only half an ear when Ramsey was talking. It was like having the radio on in the background, he thought. One picked up what was being said from time to time, but for the most part it was just a comfortable drone.

"Yes," said Ramsey. "The world has certainly changed. And not necessarily for the better. When I compare the world of my youth with the world of today, I have to shake my head. I really do."

"Please don't move your head like that," said Angus. "I'd like you to stay still as far as possible."

"So sorry," said Ramsey. "I was getting carried away. But the world really is a different place, isn't it? And Edinburgh has changed too. There used to be a good number of people who disapproved of things. Now there are hardly any, if you ask me. Everybody is afraid to disapprove."

"Yes," said Angus. "I suppose we've become more tolerant."

"Don't speak to me about tolerance," said Ramsey. "Tolerance is just an excuse for letting everything go. Tolerance means that people can get away with anything they choose."

"Oh, I don't know," said Angus. "I think that we needed a slightly more relaxed view of things."

Ramsey snorted. "Look at what's happened to breach of the peace," he said. "We didn't do any criminal law work in my firm, of course – we're not that sort of firm – but I used to take a close interest in the subject and would follow the Sheriff Court reports in the *Scots Law Times*. It was fascinating stuff, I can tell you."

"A bit murky, surely," said Angus. "Aren't the criminal courts full of people who do nasty things to other people?"

"To an extent," said Ramsey. "But there are some very amusing moments in the criminal courts. I heard some frightfully funny stories, you know."

Angus's brush moved gently against the canvas. "Such as?" he said.

"Well," said Ramsey. "Here's one. It was the Sheriff Court at Lanark, I think, or maybe Airdrie. Anyway, somewhere down there. I don't really know that part of the world very well, but let's say that it was Lanark. The sheriff was dealing with the usual business of the court, and I think that this was a speeding matter. A local butcher was caught doing something way over the odds and was hauled up in front of the sheriff. There he was, in his best suit – there are lots of ill-fitting suits in the Sheriff Courts, you know, taken out of mothballs for each court appearance. Anyway, the sheriff looked down at him from the bench and said: 'How are you pleading?' And the butcher looked up and said: 'Oh fine, sir. I'm fine. How's yoursel?'"

When he finished this story, Ramsey burst out laughing. "Can't you just hear it, Angus?" he said.

Angus nodded. "Very funny," he said. "And then what happened?"

"No idea," said Ramsey. "He was fined, no doubt. But how did we get on to this? Oh, yes, the criminal law. Well, then, breach of the peace: I was always a great supporter of it, because it was so broad. They could deal with any nonsense by calling it breach of the peace. And there were some wonderful examples. This is a bit risqué, Angus, but some of those cases were terribly funny. I always remember a breach of the peace prosecution that followed upon some events that took place at Glenogle Baths. There was this chap, you see, who had been spying on the ladies' changing rooms, and so they got a woman police officer to go to the baths and she found that somebody had drilled a peep-hole in a partition wall. Well, the woman constable looked through the hole at the same time as the accused looked through the hole on his side of the partition . . ."

Ramsey's voice tailed off. Angus, behind his canvas, applied a small dab of paint to a passage he was working on.

He added another dash of colour and stared at the result. Colour was strange; one's life as an artist was one long affair with colour.

And how should we live that life? How should we make the most of our time, make a difference with it?

He paused. Ramsey was quiet. Through the window, Angus saw a gull fly past, a brief flash of white against the blue. Ramsey had stopped talking. Strange. Angus looked past his canvas. The limbs of his sitter were immobile, and the face composed. The eyes were closed. He was perfectly still.

96. *Angus Reflects*

On the following day, Angus wrote to Domenica a letter on which, had the intended recipient held it up to the light, might have been made out the faintest of watermarks – a tear.

"My dear Domenica," he began. "I write this letter seated at the kitchen table. It is one of those cold, bright winter mornings that I know you love so much, and which make this city sparkle so. But the letter I write you will be a sad one, and I am sorry for that. When one is alone and far from home, as you are, then one longs for light-hearted, gossipy letters. This is not one of those.

"Yesterday, as I was painting his portrait, Ramsey Dunbarton, a person I have known for a good many years, died in my studio. He was seated in my portrait chair, talking to me, when he suddenly stopped, mid-anecdote. I thought nothing of it and continued to paint, but when I glanced from behind my canvas I saw him sitting there, absolutely still. I thought that he had gone to sleep and went back to my painting, but then, when I looked again, he was still motionless. I realised that something was wrong, and indeed it was. Ramsey had died. It was very peaceful, almost as if somebody had silently gone away, some-where else, had left the room. How strange is the human body in death – so still, and so vacated. That vitality, that spark, which makes for life, is simply not there. The tiny movements of the muscles, the sense of there being somebody keeping the whole physical entity orchestrated in space – that goes so utterly and completely. It is no longer there.

"You did not know Ramsey. I thought that you might perhaps have met him at one of my drinks parties, but then, on reflection, I decided that you had not. I do not think that you and he would necessarily have got along. I would never accuse you of lacking charity, dear one, but I suspect that you might have thought that Ramsey was a little stuffy for you; a little bit old-fashioned, perhaps.

"And indeed he was. Many people thought of him as an old bore, always going on about having played the part of the Duke of Plaza-Toro at the Church Hill Theatre. Well, so he did, and he mentioned it yesterday afternoon, which was his last afternoon as himself, as Auden puts it in his poem about the death of Yeats. But don't we all have our little triumphs, which we remember and which we like to talk about? And if Ramsey was unduly proud of having been the Duke of Plaza-Toro, then should we begrudge him that highlight in what must have been a fairly uneventful life? I don't think we should.

"He was a kind man, and a good one too. He loved his wife. He loved his country – he was a Scottish patriot at heart, but proud of being British too. He said that we should not be ashamed of these things, however much fashionable people decry love of one's country and one's people. And in that he was right.

"He only wanted to do good. He was not a selfish man. He did not set out to make a lot of money or get ahead at the expense of others. He was not like that. He would have loved to have had public office, but it never came his way. So he served in a quiet, rather bumbling way on all sorts of committees. He was conservative in his views and instincts. He believed in an ordered society in which people would help and respect one another, but he also believed in the responsibility of each of us to make the most of our lives. He called that 'duty', not a word we hear much of today.

"There is a thoughtless tendency in Scotland to denigrate those who have conservative views. I have never subscribed to that, and I hope that as a nation we get beyond such a limited vision of the world. It is possible to love one's fellow man in a number of ways, and socialism does not have the monopoly on justice and concern. Far from it. There are good men and women who believe passionately in the public good from very different perspectives. Ramsey was as much concerned with the welfare and good of his fellow man as anybody I know.

"People said that he had a tendency to go on and on, and I suppose he did. But those long stories of his, sometimes without any apparent point to them, were stories that were filled, yes filled, with enthusiasm for life. Ramsey found things fascinating, even when others found them dull. In his own peculiar way, he celebrated the life of ordinary people, ordinary places, ordinary things.

"I suspect that Scotland is full of people like Ramsey Dunbarton. They are people whose lives never amount to very much in terms of achievement. They are not celebrated or fêted in any way. But there they are, doing their best, showing good-will to others, paying their taxes scrupulously, not cheating in any way, supporting the public good. These people are the backbone of the country and we should never forget that.

"His death leaves me feeling empty. I feel guilty, too, at the thought of the occasions when I have seen him heaving into sight and I have scuttled off, unable to face another long-winded story. I feel that I should have done more to reciprocate the feelings of friendship he undoubtedly had for me. I never asked him to lunch with me; the invitations always came from him. I never even acknowledged him as a friend. I never told him that I enjoyed his company. I never told him that I thought he was a good man. I gave him no sign of appreciation.

"But we make such mistakes all the time, all through our lives. Wisdom, I suppose, is seeing this and acting upon it before it is too late. But it is often too late, isn't it? – and those things that we should have said are unsaid, and remain unsaid for ever.

"I am heart-sore, Domenica. I am heart-sore. I shall get over it, I know, but that is how I feel now. Heart-sore."

He finished, read it through, and then very slowly tore it up. He would not send it to Domenica, even if he meant every word, every single word of it.

Domenica may not have received the letter from Angus Lordie, but she had enough to think about anyway. Her life in the pirate village on the Malacca Straits was becoming busier – and more intriguing – after a somewhat disappointing start. She had at last done something about Ling, the interpreter who had proved to be excessively interventionist and unreliable. Matters had been brought to a head when she had gone with him to see an elderly member of the community and Ling had refused point-blank to interpret what the man had said to her.

"You need not bother with what this old man is saying," Ling had said dismissively. "He is all mixed up."

"That doesn't matter," said Domenica. "You can be assured that I can distinguish between reliable and unreliable material."

"It is a waste of time," said Ling, looking scornfully at the elderly pirate in his rattan armchair. "Stupid old man."

"I don't think that's very helpful," said Domenica. "And I really must insist on making my own decisions as to what is significant material and what is not."

"No," said Ling. "I do not want to waste your time."

Domenica sighed. It was a hot morning and her clothes were sodden with perspiration. She did not want to spend her time arguing with Ling, and yet she was now adamant that she would not accept his decisions as to what she should listen to and what she should not.

"Look, Mr Ling," she said loudly. "I am the one who's paying you. Understand? I decide what we do. And that's final."

Ling's lower lip quivered. "You cannot make that decision when you don't know anything," he said. "I do not wish to be rude to you, honourable anthropologist, but you don't know anything, do you?"

That had been the last straw, and Domenica had dismissed him on the spot. Ling appeared to be taken aback by this, and stormed off, leaving her alone with the retired pirate. She turned and smiled at the old man, who gave her a toothless grin in return.

"Tok Pisin?" he suddenly asked (Do you talk Neo-Melanesian Pidgin by any chance?).

Domenica clapped her hands in joy. "Ya. Mi toktok Pisin gutpela. Mi amamas" (Yes, I speak very good Neo-Melanesian Pidgin, I'm happy to say).

The old man became quite animated, pointing in the direction of Ling's retreating figure. "Dispela man bilong pait!" (This can best be translated as: That fellow's somewhat aggressive, don't you think? Note man bilong pait: pait is fight).

Domenica nodded. "Yumitupela toktok. Dispela Ling autim!" (You and I can talk. We can do without that chap Ling! Note autim, literally out him, to get rid of).

"Ya. Mipela holem long tingting," said the old man. "Mipela roscol boscru."

Domenica had to think about this remark for a few moments. What he had said was: Yes. I remember (a lot). (Holem long tingting, hold on to many things for a long time, is simply translated as to remember. Here it has an additional contextual meaning of recalling things long past, in an almost Proustian sense. If Proust's *À la recherche du temps perdu* were to be translated into Pidgin – which has not yet happened – then perhaps it might be called: Onepela Proust bilong Frans Holem Long Tingting.) Then he had said: mipela roscol, which would normally be translated as: I am a criminal. This puzzled Domenica for a few moments, until she realised that there might be no word in Pidgin for pirate, and that roscol was possibly the closest one could get, if one added to it boscru, which means sailor (boat's crew).

"Yupela roscol boscru? Yupela no damn gut?" she asked.

"Ya," he confirmed. "Mipela Roscol! Yupela man bilong savvy!" (Yes, I am a pirate! You, by contrast, would appear to be a scholar). (This makes one think of the Pidgin translation of the Pirate King song from Gilbert and Sullivan, 'For I am a Pirate King, /And it is, it is a glorious thing to be a Pirate King!' The Pidgin Gilbert and Sullivan has this as: Mipela Rocol boscru luluai, Ya, Ya!/Roscol boscru luluai nambawan ting, Ya, Ya!)

Once they had established that they would be able to enjoy

a good conversation in Pidgin, Domenica sat down with the old man, who introduced himself as Henry, and began to ask him the questions which she had been prevented by Ling from asking. She rapidly established his lineage (his family was one of the oldest ones in the village), his status (he was a widower, his wife having died ten years previously) and his means of support (he had a son in Singapore who was a senior clerk in a firm of merchants and another who was a first officer with a Taiwanese shipping line – both of these sent him money each month).

Henry was happy to talk about all the other households too. He explained about the family who lived next to Domenica – the one with the two sons, Freighter and Tanker. Freighter was a clever boy, Henry said, but Tanker was not. Henry suggested that this could be because he was really not the son of the woman's husband, but the result of an affair she had had with a fisherman from a neighbouring village. Domenica did not note this last piece of information down. Once an anthropologist began to question acknowledged genealogy, then everything could unravel.

After they had talked for an hour or so, Domenica asked Henry about the pirates' work. She explained that she had seen the men going off early in the morning, walking down the path that led to the sea. Was this them setting off to work?

Yes, said Henry. That was exactly it. He paused for a moment and then asked Domenica whether she would like him to take her – discreetly, of course – to watch what they got up to. They could follow them in his small boat, he said. Would she like to do that?

Domenica only hesitated for a moment before she said yes. She had not imagined that she would get mixed up in piracy, but this offer was just too tempting to resist. And she would not actually participate in any illegal activities. That was out of the question. She would simply watch.

"Tumora moningtaim," said Henry. "Samting sikispela. Klosap haus bilong mipela" (Tomorrow morning, then. Around about six. At my house).

98. Poor Lou

"You look very pleased with yourself," said Big Lou to Matthew as he entered the coffee bar that morning. "Have you sold a painting?"

"As a matter of fact, I have," said Matthew, smiling broadly at Lou. "This very morning. A man came in and took a shine to those McCosh bird paintings I had. He said: 'This man is the new Thorburn', and bought all three of them."

Big Lou wiped her cloth over the surface of the bar. "He saw a bargain," she said. "Maybe you should have hung onto them. There must be people who think that about their Hockneys and their Bacons."

"But I don't want to hold onto them," said Matthew. "I want people to know about him. There he is, the finest wildfowl painter to come along for a long, long time. Right on our doorstep. Right outside Edinburgh. All those beautiful paintings. I want people to have them. I don't want to sit on them."

"Well," said Lou. "They've gone now."

Matthew smiled pleasantly. He was pleased about the sale of the paintings, but that was not the real reason for his positive state of mind. He looked at Big Lou, busying herself now with the mysteries of her coffee-making craft. Should he tell her?

"Actually, Lou," he said. "I'm feeling rather happy."

"Aye," said Big Lou, without turning round. "Well, that's good to hear, Matthew."

"Aren't you interested in hearing why, Lou?"

Lou laughed. "I'm going to hear anyway."

"Pat," said Matthew, simply.

"What about her?" asked Lou. "Is she coming over for coffee?"

"No, she has a lecture. She's up at the university."

Big Lou turned round with the cup of coffee. "Well, she is a student, after all," she said. "I suppose that she has to show up there from time to time."

Matthew did not take his cup of coffee to his table, but stayed where he was, at the bar. "Pat and I . . ." he began. "Well, Pat and I are going out together." He paused, adding rather lamely:

"I thought you would be interested to hear that."

Big Lou reached for her cloth and began to polish the bar with vigorous circular sweeps.

"Are you sure about this?" she said.

Matthew seemed taken aback, almost crestfallen. "Sure? Well, yes, of course I'm sure. I've liked Pat a lot right from the beginning. When she first came to work for me . . ."

"That's the point," said Big Lou. "She came to work for you."

"I don't see . . ."

Big Lou put her cloth to one side and leaned over to take hold of Matthew's forearm. "Matthew: that girl is younger that you. She's a nice girl, sure enough, but there she is at the beginning of her time at university. She's just starting. She'll be looking for something very different from what you're looking for. She will be wanting a bit of fun. Parties and so on. What do you think you're looking for? You're almost twenty-nine. You're thinking of settling down. That's when men start to think of settling down. You need somebody your own age."

"There's only eight years between us," said Matthew. "That's nothing."

Big Lou shook her head. "Eight years can be a big difference at certain stages in our lives. It all depends on where you are. There's a big difference between being two and being ten, and between being ten and being eighteen. You see? Big differences."

"I'm not Eddie . . ." Matthew began, and immediately regretted what he had said.

Big Lou looked at him. "I didn't say you were Eddie," she said quietly. "I didn't say that."

She looked at him, and Matthew saw that her eyes were filling with tears. She lifted her cloth and wiped at her eyes and cheeks.

"I'm sorry, Lou," he said, reaching out to take her hand. "I didn't mean it to sound like that. I wasn't thinking . . ."

"I ken fine what he's like," sobbed Big Lou, her shoulders shaking. "I ken he's no a guid man. But I loved him, Matthew. I thought I could change him. You know how it is. You have somebody you think has some good points and you think that those will be enough."

Matthew waited, but Big Lou said nothing more.

"Have you seen him?" he asked gently. "Have you ended it with him?"

Big Lou rubbed at her eyes. "I have. I saw him and told him that I didn't think that it would work. Not after this last business with those girls down at that club of his. He said that I was being unreasonable but that he didn't want to carry on with a woman who would lock him away. That's what he said. Lock him away."

"You're well rid of him, Lou. You really are. And there'll be other men. There are lots of nice men in this town. There are plenty of nice men who would appreciate somebody like you, Lou."

Lou shook her head. "I'll be going back to Arbroath," she said. "There's an old cousin of my father's who needs looking after. I've done that sort of thing before. I can do that."

"But Lou!" said Matthew. "You can't leave us! You can't leave all this . . ." He gestured helplessly about the room. At the tables. At the newspaper rack with its out-of-date newspapers. At the rickety stairs outside.

"I don't want to," said Lou. "But I don't see what else I can do. You see, when Eddie and I got engaged, I made over a half share in the business to him. Now he wants the money for that, and I can't pay him. So he's going to insist on selling the coffee bar. And he can, according to the agreement that his lawyer drew up."

Matthew stood quite still. He had heard about the money that Eddie had persuaded Lou to give him; this, though, was new, and more serious. But then he thought: I have four million pounds. And if one has four million pounds there are occasions when one should use that financial power to make a difference to the lives of others. This, he thought, was just such an occasion.

"I'll buy him out, Lou," he said. "I'll buy him out and we can get rid of him that way."

Big Lou shook her head. "I could never accept that, Matthew," she said. "You're a good boy. I've known that all along. But I can't accept that from you. I just can't."

99. And Here's the Train to Glasgow, Again

For the rest of that day, after his conversation in the coffee bar, Matthew was preoccupied with thoughts of how he could contact Stuart. He knew that Stuart lived in Scotland Street, and he thought it was somewhere near Pat's former flat. But he wasn't sure of Stuart's surname, nor of exactly where he worked, and Pat, who might be expected to know, for some reason was not answering her mobile phone.

He had to see Stuart as soon as possible. Stuart had said that he knew somebody in Glasgow who could help Lou. Had he contacted him? Had he come up with anything? Matthew realised that unless they were able to do something quickly, then Big Lou would sell the coffee bar and go back to Arbroath. He could not allow that to happen – he would not allow it. Big Lou was a feature of his life and, he suspected, the lives of so many others in that part of town. If she went, a little bit of the character of the place would die. One of the new coffee bars would move in, with its standard international décor and its bland sameness. The coffee might be good enough, but these places spelled death to the particular, to the sense of place that a real local coffee bar embodied. They were simply without character, although they might never understand how people could think that. But people did. It was the difference between French cheese, unpasteurised and odiferous (but divine), and the processed rubbery paste that the big food interests passed off as cheese. International business, once allowed to stalk uncontrolled, killed the local, the small, the quirky. International business, thought Matthew, had ruined cheese, will ruin wine, and then will move on to ruin everything. No, he thought, Big Lou's little coffee bar was now the front line.

Eventually, Matthew decided that the only thing he could do was to go to the Cumberland Bar shortly after five that evening and wait to see if Stuart came in. And if he did not, he could ask the barman or one of the regulars; somebody was bound to know where he lived.

As it happened, Matthew did not have long to wait. Shortly

before five-thirty, Stuart came in and walked over to the bar.

Matthew left his seat to intercept him. "Listen," he said. "I've got to talk to you urgently. I've already bought you a drink. It's at the table." He took Stuart by the elbow and led him away from the bar.

Stuart was slightly irritated by Matthew's insistence, but he was in a good humour, as he had been left on his own for a couple of hours. Bertie had been returned safely from Paris that afternoon and had been dragged off for a specially-arranged session with Dr Fairbairn. The psychotherapist had been asked to determine whether there was any psychological trauma that might result from the experience of being left in Paris; Irene was of the view that early identification of trauma helped to reduce its long-term impact. And anything could have happened in Paris; anything. In fact, Bertie had enjoyed himself immensely, and had felt his heart sink when he returned to the hotel after the Sorbonne lecture to discover his mother, and several French policemen, waiting for him. The sight of the policemen had not worried him, but the realisation that his mother had come to take him home had filled him with such despair that he had burst into tears. This had been interpreted by Irene as a sign of trauma.

"My wee boy's just come back from Paris," Stuart remarked conversationally, as they went over to Matthew's table. "He went over there with an orchestra. Then they somehow managed to . . ."

"Oh yes," said Matthew, without any real interest. "Good."

They sat down and Matthew got straight to the point. "You said you knew somebody in Glasgow who might get Eddie to pay Lou back," he said. "Any progress?"

Stuart smiled. "Steady on," he said. "It was just an idea."

"But you do know somebody?" Matthew pressed.

"Yes," said Stuart. "I do."

"Well can we go and see him right now?" said Matthew, looking at his watch. "We could get the six o'clock from Waverley if we rush."

"But hold on," said Stuart. "I'm not sure if I want to go to Glasgow tonight."

Matthew looked at him pleadingly. "Please," he said. "A lot depends on this."

Stuart sighed. "I've just got back from work. I don't want to sit in a train . . ."

"We'll take a taxi," said Matthew. "I'll pay for the whole thing. Taxi there. Taxi back. Same taxi – I'll pay the waiting time. Let's just do it."

Stuart studied Matthew's expression for a few moments and realised that he was desperate. He remembered, too, how he had felt when he had heard the story of Big Lou having her money effectively stolen. If he really disapproved, then he should have the courage of his convictions and do something, rather than just talk. "All right," he said. "Let's get up to Waverley. It'll be quicker by train."

They caught a taxi at the end of Cumberland Street and just made the six o'clock train. As the train drew out of town, Matthew looked out into the gathering darkness of the late autumn evening. There were clusters of light here and there, and beyond them the dark shape of the hills. That was what the world is like, he thought: a dark place, with small clusters of light here and there, where there is justice and concord between men.

A man came through with a trolley and at Stuart's request poured them each a cup of tea. Matthew paid, and they sat back in their seats with the scalding tea before them. The man at the trolley was good-natured. "There you are, boys," he said, handing them little cartons of milk to go with their tea. "That'll keep you going over there in Glasgow. You'll no get ony tea over there!" He smiled at them, and they smiled back. On these small kindnesses, thought Matthew, is everything built. And Scotland was good at that, for all its faults. People were, on the whole, kind, and they were particularly kind in Glasgow, he remembered. Of course one would get tea over there!

"Stuart, tell me about this man we're going to see," Matthew said. "What's he like?"

Stuart smiled. "You'll be able to tell that he doesn't come from Edinburgh," he said.

Grey over Riddrie, thought Stuart as the train wound its way through Glasgow, just short of Queen Street Station. Grey over Riddrie . . . and then? Something about the clouds. The clouds piled up . . . Yes, that was it. That was the first line of Edwin Morgan's poem about King Billy, a Glasgow gang leader who had one of those showy funerals which brought out all the hard men, the troops, the foot-soldiers of ancient gang battles. He thought about the haunting poem each time he saw Riddrie, and remembered, too, how he had learned of it in his final year at school. It had been read out in class by the English teacher and there had been a complete silence when he came to the end, so powerful was its effect. And now, all these years later, here he was going to see just such a man, although Lard O'Connor was not quite King Billy. They were distinguished by a small matter of religious affiliations, apart from anything else.

Matthew and Stuart had only to wait a few minutes for a taxi and then set off for the Dumbarton Road. Stuart could not remember Lard O'Connor's precise address, but he had no diffi-culty in describing the small cul-de-sac where he and Bertie had first made Lard's acquaintance.

The taxi driver knew immediately. "That'll be Lard O'Connor's place, then?" he asked.

Stuart was somewhat taken aback by this, and resorted to his civil service language in reply. "That would appear to be the case," he said. "Assuming that this Lard O'Connor to whom you refer is . . ."

"Listen, Jim," said the taxi driver. "There's only one Lard O'Connor, see? And that's this Lard O'Connor. He's your man. You owe him money, then?"

"Of course not," said Stuart tetchily.

"There's lots of folks do," said the driver. "Lard's very easy on the loans. But not so easy if you don't pay him back like."

"You could say the same thing for the banks," said Stuart.

"Aye," said the taxi driver, "but they don't have enforcers."

"Yes they do," chipped in Matthew. "They call them solicitors."

"You trying to be funny, son?" asked the taxi driver. "Because I'm no laughing."

They travelled in silence for a while. Then the taxi driver, appearing to relent slightly on his shortness with Matthew, asked: "So if you don't owe Lard money, then do you mind my asking why you're going to see him? It's just that you don't look like the typical boys that go to see Lard. No offence, but you're not . . . Know what I mean?"

"We want Lard's help," said Stuart, "on a private matter."

The driver glanced in his mirror. "I hope you two can look after yoursels. That's all I'm going to say."

The rest of the journey was completed in silence, and they soon drew up in front of Lard's front door. Of course they had no idea as to whether he was going to be in, and the whole trip could well have been in vain, but they saw, with relief, that there were lights on.

"He's in," said Stuart. "Look, his lights are on."

"That means nothing," said the taxi driver. "If you're Lard O'Connor you never pit your lights oot. There's too many people want to pit them oot for you. So you never pit them oot. Know what I mean?"

Matthew paid the taxi driver and they walked up Lard's short front path to knock on the door. At first there was no reply, and so they knocked again. A third knock brought sounds of activity within and the door, still restrained by a heavy security chain, was inched open.

"Well!" exclaimed a voice from the other side of the door. "If it isn't my friend Stewie and . . . and who're you?"

"This is a friend of mine," said Stuart. "You haven't met him, Lard, but he's OK." Stuart was not sure that this was the right thing to say, but he had heard people say it in several films, and so he decided that he should say it too.

It appeared to work. There was a metallic sound in the hall on the other side, and then the door was opened entirely. Lard stood there, a great Munro of a man, wearing a collarless shirt, a pair of shapeless black trousers and scuffed leather slippers. In spite of his efforts not to stare, Matthew could not help but gaze in wonderment at the substantial Glaswegian, his stomach hanging over the leather belt that struggled to hold up his trousers.

"Now then, Stewie," said Lard, as he led them through to the sitting room at the back of the house. "How's my friend, wee Bertie? He's a great wee fellow that one, sure he is. Wasted over in Edinburgh. You should send him over here to get a good education. Hutchie's, or somewhere like that. I could have a word with them and make sure they found a place for him."

"That's very kind of you, Lard," said Stuart. "But he's very happy where he is."

"Pity," said Lard. "The problem with Edinburgh is attitude, know what I mean? All those airs and graces like. You don't want wee Bertie growing up to be like you fellows, Stewie, do you?"

"Hah!" said Stuart. "That's very funny, Lard!"

Lard turned round. "It wisnae meant to be funny, Stewie."

"Well, maybe not," said Stuart. "But the whole point of our visit, Lard, is to ask your help. To ask for a favour."

"Aye, that's what everybody wants," sighed Lard. "But you tell me what you have in mind."

So Matthew explained about Big Lou and her predicament, and at the end of his explanation Stuart wondered whether Lard might perhaps be prepared to have a word with Eddie about returning the money and tearing up the business agreement.

Lard thought for a moment. "She sounds like a good wummin, this Big Lou. I don't like to hear about ungentlemanly behaviour towards good wummin."

"So you think you might be able to help?" asked Matthew eagerly.

"I'll go over and have a word with this Eddie," said Lard. "Me and my boys might just give him a wee warning. Just threaten to rain on his parade. It usually works, particularly with characters like this Eddie, who sounds a wee bit sketchy to me, know what I mean?"

"But you won't do anything actually illegal, will you?" asked Stuart.

Lard smiled. "I never do anything didgy-dodgy, Stewie. You know me better than that."

On the way back on the train, Matthew turned to Stuart and said: "What a charming man Mr O'Connor is."

To which Stuart replied: "Helpful, too."

101. On the Doorstep

Angus Lordie did not like to prevaricate, but he had certainly been putting off the visit that he knew he must make to 44 Scotland Street and, in particular, to Antonia Collie, Domenica's tenant during her absence in the Far East. Now he could put it off no longer, and he knew that he must go and present an apology in person. A letter would not be enough, particularly now that a good week had elapsed since Antonia had come to dinner in his flat.

To say that the evening had not been a success would be to put it mildly. We all have our memories of awkward social evenings – occasions when the conversation has faltered, when the guests have disliked one another with cordial intensity, when the soufflés have collapsed or, worse still, congealed. Angus remembered one occasion on which the host had become so drunk that he had fallen off his chair halfway through the meal, and another where the hostess, under the influence of medication, had gone to sleep in the middle of the second course and could only be roused by physical shaking. These were but nothing, though, to his intimate dinner party with Antonia, at which . . . well, he preferred not to dwell too much on what had happened. Human memory, if not reminded of the details, has a useful way of obliterating such events, and Angus did not wish to compromise it in this task.

But he knew that an apology was required, and he would give it. So he brushed Cyril and made him chew one of the canine personal freshness pills which he had acquired on his last visit to the vet. These pills helped; he was sure of it. And just to be on the safe side, Angus popped one into his own mouth and chewed it himself. It did not taste unpleasant; rather like parsley, he thought.

They walked slowly round Drummond Place, with Cyril sniffing conscientiously at the railings every few yards and keeping a good look-out for the cats which prowled around the neighbourhood. It was Cyril's ambition to kill one of these cats, if he could get hold of it, even though he knew that this would result in the most intense fuss and several blows with a rolled-up copy of *The Scotsman*. Indeed, in Cyril's view *The Scotsman* was an artefact which was produced solely for the purpose of hitting dogs, and he always gave piles of the newspaper a wide berth when he saw them in newsagents' shops.

They reached the top of Scotland Street and began the stroll down the sharply descending street towards the door to No 44. Cyril had been used to being tied up to the railings while Angus went in, but after the unfortunate incident in which he had been stolen from the railings outside Valvona & Crolla, Angus now insisted on taking Cyril inside and would never leave him un-attended on the street.

They walked upstairs together, and with heavy heart Angus ran Domenica's bell. One part of him hoped that Antonia would be out and there would be no answer – if that happened, then at least he could tell himself that he had made the effort. But another, more responsible part told him that if he did not see her this evening, he would have to see her tomorrow, or the day after that. And with every passing day the apology would become more difficult.

The door opened.

"Antonia, my dear . . ." He half expected her to close the door in his face, but she did not. In fact, she seemed neither surprised nor outraged to see him.

"Oh," she said. "It's you. I have been waiting for a parcel and I wondered if you were it."

Angus shook his head. "I am empty-handed, as you see. Except for the apology that I bring with me." He was rather pleased with the speed with which he had managed to bring up the subject, and he smiled broadly, largely with relief.

"Apology?" asked Antonia. "Why? What do you need to apologise for?"

Angus was taken aback. "The other evening," he stuttered. "My . . . er . . . my . . ."

Antonia cut him short. "Oh that! Heavens, you don't have to apologise for that! In fact, I found the whole thing rather amusing. Dental anaesthetics can do all sorts of things to people. It's hardly your fault."

Angus had to think quickly. He had no recollection of attributing his condition that evening to the fact of having had a dental anaesthetic, but the excuse sounded like him. Now, should he say anything else; should he confess to her that he had been drunk, or should he leave it at that? It was a difficult decision to make, but he rather inclined to the line of least resistance, which was dental.

But then Antonia said: "But of course you had drunk an awful lot of wine," she said. "So that made it worse, no doubt."

Angus gave a nervous laugh. "Brunello di Montalcino," he said. "Such excellent wine! When the Queen had dinner with the President of Italy, that's what they had."

"In moderation, no doubt," said Antonia drily.

"Hah!" said Angus. This was not as easy as he had hoped. "Oh well! I always remember that great man, Sir Thomas Broun Smith, saying that what a man said after midnight should never be held against him. Such a generous sentiment, don't you think?"

"Yes," said Antonia. "Except in your case it would have to be after six P.M."

Angus, in his embarrassment, looked down at Cyril, who looked back up at him. Cyril was uncertain what to do, but he sensed that things were not going well. Antonia's ankles were directly in front of him, and he wondered if it would help if he bit them. But then there was *The Scotsman* to worry about, and he decided not to risk it.

"Anyway," said Antonia briskly. "It's very rude of me to keep you standing on the doorstep. Do come in and have a cup of tea or something . . ."

"Weaker?" joked Angus. "Well, thank you very much, I shall. I must say, it's always very nice to be back in this flat. Domenica and I used to have such wonderful conversations together."

"She'll be back sooner rather than later," said Antonia. "And then I shall move in over the way. As it happens, the flat opposite is coming up for rent and I've taken it."

"But that's wonderful news," said Angus. He was not sure, though, whether it really was.

102. Antonia Expounds

Antonia was not one to harbour a grudge, and in spite of her acerbic comments about Angus Lordie's unfortunate behaviour at the dinner to which he had invited her, she did not intend to raise the matter again. Domenica liked this rather peculiar man and Antonia felt that she should make an effort to do so too. So, having invited Angus into the flat, she led him into the study and invited him to sit down while she fetched coffee and shortbread.

"How is your book . . . your novel going?" Angus inquired politely as he sipped at his coffee. "The one about the Scottish saints?"

Antonia sighed. "Not very well, I'm afraid. My saints, I regret to say, are misbehaving. I had hoped that they would show themselves to be, well, saintly, but they are not. They are distressingly full of human foibles. There's a lot of jealousy and back-biting going on."

Angus was puzzled. Antonia was talking of her characters as if they had independent lives of their own. But they were her creations, surely, and that meant that they should do their creator's bidding. If she wanted saintly saints, she could have them. "But you're the author," he said. "You can dictate what the people in your book do, can you not?"

Antonia reached out for her cup of coffee. "Not at all," she said. "People misunderstand how writers work. They think that they sit down and plan what is going to happen and then simply write it up. But it doesn't work that way."

Angus looked at Antonia with interest. Some of his paintings had turned out very differently from what he had had in mind at the beginning. Light became dark. And dark became light. Was this the same process? He had thought it was simply mood, but was it possible that the work acquired its own momentum, its own view of things?

"Oh yes," Antonia went on. "The author is not in control. Or, rather, the conscious mind of the author is not in control. And the reason for that is that when we use our imagination we get in touch with that part of the mind which is asking the 'what if' questions. And that is not part of the conscious mind."

"What if?"

"Precisely," said Antonia. "What if. All the time, every moment, your mind is going through possibilities. Any time you look at things. You're busy recognising and classifying what you see. Thousands and thousands – countless thousands of times a day. Your brain is saying: that thing has four legs, ergo it's a table; or that thing has four legs, but it's got fur – it's a dog. And so on. That's how we understand the world. We don't think of it, and you don't see yourself doing it, but it's fairly obvious if you watch a baby. You can actually see them doing it. Watch a baby while it looks at things, and you can see the mental wheels turn round. They sit and look at things intently, working out what they are."

"I see all that," said Angus. "But what's that got to do with . . . ?"

"With writing? Well, a similar process is happening when you write a story. The unconscious mind is asking questions and then exploring possible outcomes. These then surface in the conscious mind, in the same way perhaps as speech surfaces, and become the words that tell the story. And exactly the same thing happens when somebody writes a piece of music or, I should imagine, paints a painting."

"So art reveals the unconscious?" asked Angus. "Do I give myself away in what I paint?"

"Of course you do," said Antonia. "There's nothing new in that. Unless a work of art obeys very strict rules of genre, then it's often going to say: this is what the artist really wants. This is what he really wants to do."

"Always?" asked Angus.

"Almost always. But there is more to it than that. The unconscious mind reveals itself in the story it creates. A writer who writes lurid descriptions of the sexual, for example, is simply revealing: this is what I want to do myself. Yes! That's a thought, isn't it? Some of us are charmingly naive and don't realise that is what we are announcing to the world. We are acting out our own internal dramas. And that, I suppose, is inevitable and is just part of the business of being a writer. People are going to pick over what you write and say: ah, so that's what you're really about! You hate your father or your mother or both of them. You had an overly strict toilet training. You're trying to recreate your first love. And so on."

"And your saints? What does that tell us about you?"

Antonia did not answer for a moment. She looked intently at Angus, and for a moment he thought that he had overstepped some unspoken limit in the conversation. Perhaps there would be more to apologise for; but then she spoke. "The problem with my saints is that I was consciously willing them to repre-

sent something. I wanted them to stand for the triumph of the
will to good. I take it that you know what that is. The sheer
yearning that we have for the good – for light rather than darkness, for harmony rather than disharmony, for kindness rather
than cruelty. That's what I wanted. And instead of being these
. . . these symbols, they've turned out to be distressingly human."

"But surely that's better. Surely that makes them more realistic."

Antonia smiled. "That's assuming that realism is the only goal
we should pursue. Would you say that about painting? Surely
not. So why say it about literature? Why does everything have
to be realistic? It doesn't. Surely we can be more subtle than
that. No, it's not the realism issue with me. I'm reconciled to
these flawed saints, as long as their human failings don't obscure
the ultimate point that I want to achieve."

"Which is?"

"The achievement of a philosophically acceptable resolution.
I want their vision of justice and good to prevail."

"And is that the only possible ending?" asked Angus.

"No," said Antonia. "Things can end badly, as they sometimes do in life. But if they do, then we know that something
is wrong, just as we know it when a piece of music doesn't resolve
itself properly at the end. We know that. We just do. And so
we prefer harmony."

"And everybody lives happily ever after?" asked Angus.

Antonia stared at him. "Do you really want it to be otherwise?" she asked.

103. *Imaginary Friends*

"Now then, Bertie," said Dr Fairbairn, "Mummy tells me you've
been away for a little trip." Bertie, seated on the couch to the
side of Dr Fairbairn's desk, glanced nervously at the psychotherapist. "Yes," he said. "I went to Paris."

"Ah," said Dr Fairbairn. "That's a beautiful city, isn't it? Did
you like it, Bertie?"

"It was very nice," said Bertie.

"Are you sure?" asked Dr Fairbairn. It was very common for the object of dread to be described in positive terms.

"Yes," said Bertie. He paused. Had Dr Fairbairn been to Paris himself? Perhaps he knew Jean-François François; they were quite alike in some ways. "Have you been to Paris, Dr Fairbairn?"

"I have, Bertie," replied Dr Fairbairn. "And tell me, what did you notice about Paris? Did you notice that it has something sticking up in it?"

Bertie thought for a moment. "You mean the Eiffel Tower, Dr Fairbairn?"

Dr Fairbairn nodded gravely, and wrote something on his notepad. By craning his neck, Bertie could see that there were two words: Eiffel Tower.

"I do mean the Eiffel Tower, Bertie. You saw the Eiffel Tower, did you?"

Bertie nodded. "Yes, we all went there. The whole orchestra. We went up the tower in one of the lifts. They have lifts which take you up to the top, or almost."

"And did you like the Eiffel Tower, Bertie? You weren't frightened of it, were you?"

Bertie shook his head. Why should he be frightened of the Eiffel Tower? Had Dr Fairbairn been frightened of the Eiffel Tower when he went to Paris?

"Well," said Dr Fairbairn. "And what else did you do in Paris, Bertie?"

"I went to lunch with some friends I made," said Bertie. "They were very nice. And then we went to a lecture. There was a man called Mr François who gave a lecture. Then I went back to the hotel. And that's when Mummy came to fetch me."

Dr Fairbairn looked out of the window. "And were you happy when Mummy came to fetch you in Paris?" he asked. "Or were you sad to leave Paris?"

Bertie thought for a moment. "I would have liked to stay there a little longer. I would have liked to spend more time with my friends."

Dr Fairbairn turned back from the window. Progress at last.

It was quite unlikely that this little boy had gone out and made friends in Paris; these friends, therefore, were imaginary. And that, he decided, was a very promising line of inquiry. Bertie was a highly intelligent little boy and such children frequently created imaginary friends for themselves. And if one could get some sort of insight into these strange, insubstantial companions, then a great deal could be discovered about the psychodynamics of the particular child's world.

"Tell me about your friends, Bertie," said Dr Fairbairn quietly. "Do you have a best friend?"

There was a silence as Bertie thought about this question. He would have liked to have a best friend, but he was not sure that he did. But if he told Dr Fairbairn that he did not have one, then he would think that nobody liked him. So he decided that it would have to be Tofu.

"There's Tofu," he said. "He's my best friend." He paused, and then added: "I think."

Dr Fairbairn watched Bertie closely. There had been hesitation, which was significant. That was the internal debate as to whether to take him into his confidence. And then there had been the "I think" added on at the end. That made it quite clear, as did the name. Tofu. No real child would be called that. No: Tofu was one of these imaginary friends. And now that he had been declared, some progress might be made with working out what was going on in this interesting little mind. Dr Fairbairn mentally rubbed his hands with glee. There was a growing literature on children's imaginary friends, and he might perhaps add to it. There was Marjorie Taylor's ground-breaking *Imaginary Companions and the Children Who Create Them*. That was a very useful study, but there was always room for more, and it would be especially interesting to see what role an imaginary companion played in the life of this particularly complex young child.

"Tell me about Tofu," he asked gently. "Is he always there?"

Bertie stared at Dr Fairbairn. What a peculiar question to ask. Of course Tofu was not always there. He saw him at school and that was all. There was nobody who was always there, except perhaps his mother, and even she was not there sometimes.

"No," he said. "He's not always there. Just sometimes."

Dr Fairbairn nodded. "Of course," he said. "But when he is there, you know, don't you?"

Bertie's eyes widened. "Yes," he said. "I can tell when he's there."

"But he's not with us at the moment, is he?" asked Dr Fairbairn.

Bertie decided to remain calm. In his experience, the best thing to do was to humour Dr Fairbairn. If one did that, then he usually quietened down.

"No," said Bertie. "He's not here at the moment. But I may see him tomorrow."

Dr Fairbairn nodded. "Of course. And does he talk to you?"

"Yes," said Bertie. "Tofu can talk. He's just like any other boy."

"Of course," said Dr Fairbairn. "Of course he is. He's very real, isn't he?"

"Yes," said Bertie. His voice was small now.

"Does Mummy see Tofu too?" coaxed Dr Fairbairn.

"No," said Bertie. His mother rarely saw Tofu. Sometimes she spotted him at the school gate, but Tofu usually left before Irene arrived, and Bertie did not encourage any contact, as he knew that she had never liked Tofu since he had exchanged his jeans for Bertie's crushed-strawberry dungarees.

"And do you think that Mummy would like Tofu?" asked Dr Fairbairn. "That is, if she could see him."

"No," said Bertie.

Dr Fairbairn was silent. It was classic. This Tofu was a complete projection, and if he could be fleshed out, a great deal would be revealed. But more than that: he could also become a therapeutic ally.

As Dr Fairbairn gazed thoughtfully at Bertie, so too did Bertie gaze at the psychotherapist. When they eventually took Dr Fairbairn off to hospital – to Carstairs – thought Bertie, would he be able to make friends there?

Perhaps not, but then maybe he would be able to invent a

friend. That would keep him from feeling too lonely. He could call her Melanie if she was a woman. That would be nice. Or Sigmund, if he was a man. That would be nice too, thought Bertie.

104. *Lost in the Mists Hunting Pirates*

Sikispela moningtaim – or six in the morning – and Domenica made her way across the compound to Henry's house. A heavy mist had descended, and the trees on the edge of the village were shrouded in white, lending the whole place a distinctly eerie feeling. Domenica shivered. She was cold now, but there was no point in bringing any warm clothing with her as the heat would build up the moment the mist burned off – and it always did that.

The pirates, she had noticed, left for work between seven and eight in the morning, which meant that she and Henry had an hour or so to prepare to follow them. Henry had a boat, she had learned, and they would set off in this and wait to follow the pirates at a safe distance.

Henry came out to meet her. He was wearing a pair of long khaki shorts that reached down to just below his knees, and no shirt. His arms, Domenica noticed, were scrawny, and bore tattoos of Chinese characters. Across his chest there was tattooed a large dragon rampant.

"I hope that this mist won't keep them in this morning," said Domenica, in Pidgin.

"No danger of that," replied Henry. "Pirates actually rather like mist. It gives them the advantage of surprise."

"I suppose so," said Domenica. She shuddered as she thought of the victims' feelings as the pirate boats appeared out of the mists, like wraiths. Since she had arrived in the pirate community, she had tried not to dwell too much on the fact that she was living in close proximity with criminals. There was a certain unpalatability to that, and yet, if one paused to think about it, one had to acknowledge that anthropology, like reporting, involved the observation of appalling or distasteful things. If anthropologists were to refuse to observe those of whom they disapproved, then whole swathes of human experience – polygamy, undemocratic or autocratic authority structures, exploitative or repressive social relationships; all of these would remain unstudied. So there could be no corners into which the inquiring human mind should not probe, and that meant that somebody had to study pirates.

Of course of all of humanity's strange sub-groups, pirates were perhaps in a class of their own. These people, Domenica reflected, were living outside the law and outside society. Being a pirate was as close as one could come to being *caput lupinum*; such a person could in the past have been knocked on the head as if he were a wolf, and it would not be murder. Such days were behind us, of course, but there were still people who were beyond the pale, outside the law, and who were liable to be hunted mercilessly.

Of course, one might say that it was their own fault; that they chose to be pirates. But had they really made such a choice? One thing which her research had uncovered was that many of the people who lived in the village were the offspring of pirates themselves, and indeed came from old pirate families. For many, what they become is not really a matter of choice. We tend to follow the paths that are set out for us in our childhood, and if those paths are the paths of piracy, then it must presumably take a great effort to escape them. And not everyone is capable of that effort. It was the same, she thought, as one of those East Lothian golf clubs where many of the members were the sons of members, just like the pirates. It was all rather sad.

Henry fetched a small can of petrol from underneath his veranda and then indicated to Domenica that she should follow him down the path that led to the sea.

"What are we going to do?" she asked, her voice kept low so as not to alert anybody of their departure.

"We go out to sea," Henry replied. "Then we wait. When the pirates come out, we follow them and see what they get up to."

"But won't they see us?" asked Domenica.

"No," said Henry. "There will be many waves. Our little boat will be hidden in the waves. They will not see us."

"But if they do?" pressed Domenica.

"Bot digim hol bilong solwara," replied Henry casually. "Yumitupela dae pinis. Pinis bot" (lit: Boat digs hole in the sea. You and I die finish. Finish boat).

Domenica digested this information as they reached the end of the path and found themselves at the small cluster of jetties to which the pirate vessels were moored. These were long, black-painted boats to which powerful outboard motors had been attached. Bright paintings had been worked on the prows of these boats – pictures of swordfish, shells and the occasional dragon. Henry's boat, a much more modest craft, had no picture, but was painted in a drab brown, reminiscent, Domenica thought, of the shade with which the Victorians liked to paint the anaglypta in their dreary halls and studies.

Henry held Domenica's hand as she stepped gingerly into the boat. Then he himself boarded, whipped the small outboard engine into life, and untied the boat's painter. In the heavy, mist-laden air, the engine was almost inaudible, like the purring of a cat. Domenica sat forward and watched the water slip past the side of the boat as they cleared the shallows that provided natural protection for the jetties. The water was flat and almost olive-coloured, and as she watched it, a flying fish suddenly launched itself into the air and skimmed the wavelets, a flash of silver against the green. "Pis bilong airplane" (lit: aeroplane fish), observed Henry, pointing at the ripples where the fish had re-entered the water.

They moved away from the coast and soon they were unable to see anything but the all-enveloping mist. Domenica wondered how Henry would be able to navigate in these conditions – was it some sixth sense, the inbuilt feeling for direction enjoyed by pigeons and cats? And pirates? Or was he counting on being able to see something when the mist lifted?

After half an hour or so, Henry cut the engine of the boat, sat back, and wiped his brow with the engine cloth. He smiled at Domenica.

"Do you know where we are?" Domenica inquired.

Henry shook his head. "Yumitupela lus," he said simply. "Lus bilong sno" (You and I are lost. We are lost in this fog. Sno is fog in Neo-Melanesian Pidgin. There is no word for snow, unless, possibly, it is fog).

105. At the Warehouse

Domenica had never panicked in all her years of anthropological fieldwork. She had remained calm when she had been obliged to spend four days in an ice shelter with some hospitable Inuit in the North-West Territories of Canada before weather conditions had allowed help to arrive from Fort Smith. That had been an interesting time, and she had learned a great deal about local counting rhymes and fishing lore. Then, in the New Guinea Highlands, she had been resolute in the face of a demand from some of her hosts that she be sold – for an undisclosed sum, and purpose – to a neighbouring group to whom some ancient debt was payable. Reason – and market forces – had prevailed in that case and the matter had been settled. But even when it looked as if the decision would go the other way, Domenica had been dignified and detached. "If I were ever to be sold," she told herself, "then I would prefer to be sold at Jenners."

Now, drifting in that silent boat with the retired pirate, Henry, she was determined that she would remain cool and collected; not that there was much point in doing anything else. Henry, it seemed, had no idea of where they were, and the persistence of the fog meant that they were unsure of the location of the sun, or of land, or of anything for that matter, apart from the water, which was all about them.

She tried to work out how far they were from the coast. The engine on Henry's boat was not a large one, and they could not have been making much more than four knots. If they had been travelling for half an hour, then that suggested that they could not be more than a mile or two from land, assuming that they had been heading on a course directly out to sea. It was quite possible, though, that they had been following the coast and that at any moment the fog would lift and they would see mangrove within yards. But then there were currents to be taken into account, and they might, in reality, be miles out by now, out in the Malacca Straits and directly in the course of some great behemoth of a Taiwanese tanker. That would be a sad way to go; crushed beneath the bows of the oil industry – tiny, human, helpless.

Domenica sat back and closed her eyes. She had decided that she would simply wait it out and think while she was doing so. And there was a great deal to think about. Had she made the right decision as to the distribution of her estate after her death? The lawyers at Turcan Connell would look after that very well – she was confident of that – but had she left Miss Paul adequate instructions about what would happen to her library of anthropological books and papers? And she could not remember whether she had been specific enough about the conditions she had attached to the legacy to Angus Lordie. That would require attention if she survived.

But of course I shall survive, she told herself. Nobody succumbs this close to the coast, particularly in busy waters like these. At any moment we shall hear a boat and a friendly pair of hands will indicate where safety lies. At any moment . . .

"Bot," said Henry suddenly, cupping a hand to his ear. "Bot bilong roscol bilong boscru. Closap."

Domenica opened her eyes quickly. Henry had heard the pirate boats. She strained to listen. From somewhere close by came the sound of a couple of engines, their droning notes weaving in and out of another, as if in mechanical dance. She looked at Henry. He had now started their own engine, but was keeping the throttle low, to mask the sound, she assumed.

Suddenly, at the very edge of their vision through the fog, they saw a dark shape glide by. A few seconds later, there was another glimpse of the outline of a boat, and then nothing.

Henry swung the prow of their boat round and began to follow. Domenica was not sure about this. Was it a good idea, she wondered, to set off in pursuit of the pirate boats in weather like this? If the pirates did find prey in such conditions, then would there be anything to observe, or would there just be the sound of shouts and, she hoped not, shots? That would hardly give her an insight into pirate activities. It was a basic rule of anthropological observation that one had to be able actually to see something.

Now that Henry had seen the pirate boats, he seemed to have regained his confidence. Domenica looked at him inquiringly, but he simply waved a hand in the air. So she sat back and, as she had done from the beginning of this extraordinary trip, remained calm.

They had travelled for about twenty minutes before the fog began to lift. Domenica peered about her and was astonished to discover that they were very close to the coast and were coming up to a town of some sort. Now they could make out the two pirate boats, some distance ahead, and they were cruising slowly up to a jetty beside a large warehouse.

Henry cut the motor of his boat and waited. The pirate boats had now nosed into the jetty and had been secured by their occupants. Then the pirates clambered out and began to walk into the warehouse. One of the men coughed, and the sound reached Henry and Domenica across the water.

"Roscol bilong boscru smok smok," whispered Henry.

Domenica nodded her agreement. From what she had seen in the village, the pirates were all heavy smokers.

When the last of the pirates had entered the warehouse, Henry started his engine again and they began to inch towards the other side of the jetty. Domenica watched carefully. This was extremely exciting, and she could already imagine her telling this story to Angus Lordie or James Holloway, or Dilly Emslie – to any of her Edinburgh friends, in fact.

"There I was," she would say. "There I was with my good friend Henry, creeping up the jetty to peek through the windows of the pirate warehouse. What would I see within? Chests of booty? Wretched captives tied and gagged by these ruffians? Things that can hardly be described . . . ?"

There is a certain self-conscious pleasure in describing, before the event, one's more distinguished moments, and that is exactly what Domenica experienced, sitting there in the boat, waiting for the adventure to unfold. And it did unfold.

106. An Unexpected Development

Big Lou's coffee bar was not full that morning – it never was – but at least Matthew, Pat and Angus Lordie were there, together with Cyril, of course, who lay contentedly beneath one of the tables. Cyril had one eye closed and one eye open, the latter fixed watchfully on Matthew's ankles, barely eighteen inches away from him. It had been Cyril's long-cherished ambition to bite Matthew's ankles, not for reasons of antipathy towards him – Cyril quite liked Matthew – but because of the sheer attractiveness to a dog of that particular set of ankles. But he knew that he could never do this, and so he just watched with one eye, imagining the pleasure of sinking his teeth into that inviting target.

The conversation had ranged widely, but had been largely dominated by Angus, who was in an argumentative mood. From time to time, Matthew had thrown an anxious glance in the direction of Big Lou, about whom he was still worried. He had not yet had the opportunity to tell Angus about the trip that he had made to Glasgow with Stuart and about their conversation – if one could call it that – with Lard O'Connor. He had felt cheered by the trip, but now, seeing Lou still in a despondent state, he wondered whether he was putting too much faith in Lard's agreement to help. He had tried to convey to him some sense of the urgency which he thought attended the issue, but Lard had been remarkably casual and had told Matthew not to fash himself. Now Matthew wondered if Lard would ever get round to coming over to Edinburgh.

They had finished their first cup of coffee and were on the point of ordering refills when Angus, who was sitting facing the doorway, noticed two shadows on the window which told him that somebody was coming down the stairway from the street. One of the shadows looked extremely large.

"Here comes a substantial customer," he remarked.

Matthew turned round, as did Pat, just at the moment that the door was opened. Lard O'Connor stepped into the room, to be followed, immediately, by Eddie. Matthew gasped.

Seeing Matthew at his table, Lard nodded to him and then walked up to the bar, Eddie trailing behind him reluctantly.

"You're the wummin they call Big Lou?" Lard asked.

"Aye," said Lou. "That's me."

Matthew noticed that as she answered Lard, Big Lou was looking at Eddie. Her expression was a curious one: there was anxiety there, but also an expression that looked very much like regret.

"Hello, Eddie," said Lou. "I hadn't expected to see you." Lard turned to Eddie and gestured for him to come up to the bar. "Eddie wanted to say something," he said. "Didn't you, Eddie?"

Eddie looked helplessly at Lou. Matthew noticed that there was a bruise on one of his cheeks, and one of his eyes, he thought, was badly bloodshot, the surrounding skin discoloured.

"Eddie?" Big Lou's voice was strained.

Eddie looked at Lard, who nodded his head in the direction of Lou.

"Don't keep us waiting," muttered Lard. "You know fine what to say."

"I've come to pay you back, Lou," said Eddie. "I can't manage the full thirty-four grand, but here's twenty-five. That's all I've got left." He reached into the inner pocket of his jacket and took out a folded cheque, which he pushed over the counter towards Lou.

"And?" said Lard, glowering at Eddie. "You have another statement to make, don't you?"

Eddie looked down at the floor. Witnessing his humiliation, Matthew felt almost sorry for him, but then he remembered. Eddie did not deserve his sympathy. "That thing about the coffee bar," he said. "That piece of paper you signed. I've decided to give my share back to you." He paused, and looked over his shoulder, as if looking for an escape route.

"And?" said Lard menacingly.

"So here it is," said Eddie. "I've put it in writing."

"Always get things in writing," said Lard, turning to address Matthew. "Every time. Never rely on gentlemen's agreements. Some people just aren't gentlemen, know what I mean?"

Matthew nodded. "You're right there, Lard," he said.

Big Lou reached out and took the document which Eddie had passed over the counter. She looked at it, nodded, and then slipped it into the pocket of her apron. "Thanks, Eddie," she said.

There was a silence. Matthew looked at Eddie, knowing that he was staring at a broken man. Angus felt that too, and looked away in embarrassment. Pat busied herself with her empty coffee cup. She had never liked Eddie either, but the sight of him being obliged to behave like an errant schoolboy was not a comfortable one.

"One last thing," said Lard. "Then you can go."

Eddie fixed his gaze on the floor. "Sorry," he mumbled. "Sorry, Lou."

"Right," said Lard to Eddie. "You can go now."

Eddie tried to straighten himself up. It was as if he was attempting to salvage at least some shred of dignity, but he could not. He slumped back into his dejected position. For a moment he hesitated, then he turned round and walked out of the café.

"Well, that's that all sorted," said Lard cheerfully. "Now, how about youse fixing me up with a cup of coffee or something?"

Big Lou turned back to her espresso machine and soon had a large, scalding cup of coffee ready for Lard. Heaping several spoons of sugar into the cup, Lard quickly drained it and suggested another one.

"You single-handed here, hen?" he asked Lou.

Big Lou smiled at him. She had no idea who Lard O'Connor was, and why he had intervened on her part, but she felt profound gratitude to him. "Aye, I run the place myself," she said. "But I'm not very busy most of the time."

Lard looked around the café. "You could put in some music," he said. "And maybe one of they fruit-machines. Cheer things up a bit."

Hearing these remarks, Angus shot a glance at Matthew. "Let's hope she doesn't give this chap half the business," he whispered.

Lard did not hear him. He was leaning across the bar, smiling at Big Lou, who was preparing a second cup of coffee for him.

"I don't believe it," said Matthew *sotto voce*. "I just don't believe it."

Lard and Big Lou were now deep in conversation and Lard, reaching out over the bar, had taken Big Lou's hand in his.

"Oh no," said Angus. "Worst fears realised. Close all ports. Prepare to abandon ship."

107. *Wur Planets are oot o' alignment*

Big Lou looked down at Lard O'Connor's hand, resting on hers. Then, very politely, she lifted it with her free hand and placed it back on the counter. Lard O'Connor continued to smile.

"Thank you for what you've done," she said. "But we hardly . . ."

"Aloysius O'Connor," said Lard.

"Thank you, Mr O'Connor. I have no idea how you persuaded Eddie . . ." Lou's voice tailed off. It was hard to utter the name. She had loved him, and in a way she still did. Why had he treated her as he had? She had imagined that she might change him, that he would not need to see those girls, but it had been hopeless. Everybody says that about these things, she told herself. They are just too deeply embedded. And he hadn't cared about her feelings, not in the slightest.

Lard looked grave. "It's amazing what direct talking will achieve," he said. "The trouble with this side of the country is there's not enough direct speaking. All that blethering. No direct speaking."

"Well, you've been very helpful to me, Mr O'Connor."

"Please . . . Aloysius."

"Aloysius."

"That's better."

Big Lou took a step backward. "Well, I have to get on with my work," she said. "Maybe some day we'll . . ."

"Aye," said Lard. "Mebbe."

From their table, Angus, Matthew and Pat watched as Lard left the coffee bar. He nodded curtly to Matthew as he made for the door, and shot a glance at Angus, who quickly looked away.

Lard was almost at the door when he hesitated and looked back towards Matthew. Then slowly he walked over to the table and leant down to whisper to him.

"Tell Stewie everything's tickety-boo," he said. "But wur still a wee bit skew-wiff on this deal, pal. No quite eexy-peexy. Wur planets are oot o' alignment like. So I'll be on your case for a wee bit of reciprocation. Understaund?"

Matthew sat quite still. He looked up at Lard and blinked. He was silent. Lard then winked at him and made for the door.

"That was a most interesting face," said Angus. "I wonder if he might sit for a portrait one of these days. What a mug! Did you see it, Pat? Ever seen anything like it?"

"What did he mean by reciprocation?" asked Pat. "Do you think that . . . ?"

Matthew waved her question aside. Reciprocation could mean only one thing: he would be expected to participate in something illegal – launder money, perhaps, or hide a weapon. He thought for a moment. Could he pay Lard off instead? Could he offer him ten thousand pounds instead of a favour, or would that just whet his appetite for more? And what if Lard got wind of the fact that he had four million pounds in the bank? It hardly bore thinking about.

He looked at his watch. "It's time to get back to the gallery," he announced. "Let's go, Pat."

They crossed the road, Matthew still deep in thought.

"You're worried, aren't you?" said Pat.

Matthew nodded. "It's occurred to me that I've already broken the law," he said miserably. "I incited this awful man to beat Eddie up. If Eddie goes to the police, then I'm implicated."

"Eddie won't go to the police," said Pat. "They would want to know why Lard beat him up. He would have to tell them that he took Big Lou's money."

"But she gave it to him," said Matthew. "Eddie's done nothing illegal."

"He won't go," said Pat. "Eddie probably has other things to hide from the police. There's that club of his. And the girls and the rest. He won't go."

They opened the gallery in silence. Pat was aware of Matthew's anxiety and was worried about what she had to do next, which was to tell him that she was moving out of the flat in India Street. There was a good reason for this, of course, and she could not put off telling him any longer. That afternoon, a friend was coming to help her move her things back to her parents' house in the Grange, and she would have to let Matthew know about this before she made the move.

She waited. One or two people came into the gallery and one of them bought a painting. That seemed to cheer Matthew up, and Pat decided that the moment had come.

"Matthew," she began. "There's something I must tell you."

Matthew stared at her. I should have realised, he said to himself. I should have realised that it could never last. It never does. How long has it been? Three days? Four days?

"I'm going to have to move out of India Street," Pat said. "I'm going this afternoon."

Matthew's face crumpled. "This afternoon? Today?"

"Yes," said Pat. "I'm sorry."

Matthew nodded. Pat noticed that he was looking at the floor, tracing an invisible pattern on the carpet with the toe of his shoe.

"You see . . ." Pat began to say.

Matthew cut her short. "It's all right," he said flatly. "I understand." And he thought: girls just don't like me. Well, they may not actively dislike me – they tolerate me – but they don't find me interesting, or exciting, or anything really. And there's nothing I'll ever be able to do about that. I really like this girl – really like her – but she doesn't like me. And who can blame her?

"I don't think you do understand," said Pat. "What I was going to say is that since you and I . . . well, since you and I are an item, then I don't think that we should be flatmates too. It complicates matters, doesn't it? And I need my space, just as you do."

Matthew stared at her. When people talked about needing space they usually meant that they wanted the maximum space between you and them. This was different. Was it still on?

"You mean that you're not wanting to get rid of me?" he stuttered.

"Of course not," said Pat, moving over to his side. "I don't want that. Do you?'

"No," said Matthew. He looked at her and thought: I have found myself in you. Bless you. And then he thought: what a strange, old-fashioned thing to think. Bless you. But what other way was there of saying that you wanted only good for somebody, that you wanted the world to be kind to her, to cherish her? Only old-fashioned words would do for that.

Now that Domenica had indicated that she was returning to Scotland within a few days, Antonia Collie took steps to conclude the lease on the flat across the landing – the flat once occupied by Bruce and Pat and which had been sold to a young property developer. This person had developed the property by painting it and by installing a new microwave and a new bath before deciding to offer it for rent. Antonia was indifferent to the fresh paint, the microwave and the bath, but keen on the view from the sitting room and the prospect of having Domenica as a neighbour. Negotiations for the lease had been swift and Antonia now had the keys to the flat and could move in at any time she wished.

Antonia, having gone out to purchase one or two things for the kitchen, returned to No 44 to discover a small boy sitting on the stone stairs, staring up into the air. She had seen this small boy once or twice before. On one occasion she had spotted him walking up the street with his very pregnant mother (he had been trying to avoid stepping on the lines and was being roundly encouraged by his mother to hurry up), and on another she had seen him in Valvona & Crolla, again with his mother, who was lecturing him on the qualities of a good olive oil. She knew that he belonged to No 44 and she thought she knew which flat it was, but apart from that she knew nothing about him, neither his name, nor how old he was, nor where he went to school.

"Well," she said as she drew level with him on the stairs, "here you are, sitting on the stairs. And if I knew your name – which I don't – I would be able to say hallo whoever you are. But I don't – unless you care to tell me."

Bertie looked up at Antonia. This was the lady who lived upstairs, the woman whom his mother had described as "yet another frightful old blue stocking". Bertie had been puzzled by this; now here was an opportunity for clarification.

"I'm called Bertie," he said politely.

"And I'm Antonia," said Antonia.

Bertie squinted at Antonia. "I think my Mummy must be wrong about you," he said.

"Oh yes?" said Antonia. "What does Mummy say about me?"

"She said that you wear blue stockings," said Bertie. "But I don't think you do, do you?"

There was a sharp intake of breath from Antonia. "Oh really?" she said. "You're right. Mummy has got it wrong." She paused. "Tell Mummy that you asked me about that, and I said to tell her that I don't wear blue stockings. Will you tell her that?"

"Yes," said Bertie. "If she listens. Sometimes she doesn't listen to what I say. Or what Daddy says either."

Antonia smiled. "That's sad," she said. "But surely somebody listens to you, Bertie. What about at school? Surely your teacher listens to what you have to say."

Bertie looked down at his feet. "Miss Harmony listens sometimes," he said. "But not always. She didn't listen to me when I said that I didn't want to be Captain von Trapp in *The Sound of Music*. She made me be Captain von Trapp."

"I'm sorry to hear that," said Antonia. "But perhaps there wasn't anybody else who wanted to play the part. Maybe that's why you had to do it."

"But there were plenty of people who wanted to be Captain von Trapp," said Bertie. "There's a boy called Tofu. He really wanted to be Captain von Trapp. But she wouldn't let him."

"But I'm sure that he would understand."

Bertie shook his head. "No," he said. "He didn't. And there's a girl called Olive. She wanted to be Maria, but wasn't allowed to be. She didn't understand either."

"Dear me," said Antonia. "But I'm sure everything will go well in the end."

"No it won't," said Bertie. "And now Tofu and Olive both hate me."

Antonia stared down at Bertie. He was a most unusual child, she thought; rather appealing, in a funny sort of way, and she found herself feeling sorry for him. These little spats of childhood loomed terribly large in one's life at the time, even if they tended to disappear very quickly. It was not always fun being a child, just as it had not always been fun being a medieval Scottish saint. Poor little boy!

"Well, cheer up, Bertie," said Antonia. "Even if things aren't going well in *The Sound of Music*, isn't Mummy going to have a new baby? Doesn't that make you excited? You and Daddy must be very pleased about that."

Bertie shook his head. "I don't think that Daddy is pleased," he said. "He said that the new baby is a mistake. That's what he said. I heard him telling Mummy that."

Antonia raised an eyebrow. "Oh well," she said. "Everybody will love him or her. I'm sure they will."

"And then Daddy said we should call the new baby Hugo," went on Bertie.

"That's a nice name!" said Antonia quickly.

"Because that's the name of Mummy's friend," said Bertie. "He's called Dr Fairbairn. Dr Hugo Fairbairn."

Antonia bit her lip. Oh goodness! One should not encourage this sort of thing, but she could not resist another question, just one more question.

"And Dr Fairbairn," she asked. "What does he think of all this?"

"He's mad," said Bertie. "Really mad."

"I see," said Antonia. "Well I suppose that . . ." She tailed off. It was easy to imagine him being angry, he probably did not plan for things to work out this way.

Now Bertie, who was enjoying his conversation with Antonia, came up with a final piece of information. He had been told of his mother's pregnancy one day in the Floatarium. Irene had been in her flotation chamber, speaking to Bertie, who was sitting outside, and that was where she had told him of the imminent arrival of a new sibling. Bertie, whose understanding of the facts of life was rudimentary, had misinterpreted her and had concluded that his mother had become pregnant in the flotation chamber itself.

"Mummy became pregnant in the Floatarium," Bertie now explained. "That's where it happened."

Antonia picked up her shopping bag. This was wonderful. She had a great deal to tell Domenica when she came back. Why did she bother going to the Malacca Straits when all this

was going on downstairs? Anthropology, she thought, like
charity, surely begins at home.

109. In the Ossian Chair

Antonia entered Domenica's flat and thought about her
encounter with Bertie on the stair. It had been a strange experience – amusing, of course, with all those innocent disclosures
– but there was something more to it, and that was puzzling
her. At one level their conversation had been exactly the sort of
talk that one might expect to have with a boy of – what was he?
six, at the most, she thought – and yet there had been another
level to it altogether, and this had made her feel an extraordinary warmth towards him. Yes, that was it: the warmth.

She made her way into the kitchen, dropped her shopping
bag on the floor near the cooker, and sat down in the chair near
the window. It was a high-ish chair, plain in its lines, and covered
with a Macpherson tartan throw. Domenica was not a
Macpherson, but a Macdonald. Why should she have a
Macpherson throw? Was it the sheer prettiness of that particular tartan with its soft greys and wine-red stripe? But then it
occurred to her that there was another reason. Domenica had
many enthusiasms, but one of them, Antonia recalled, was for
the works of Ossian, or, should one say, the works of James
Macpherson. That must be it.

Antonia sat back in the Ossian chair and remembered. It had
been right there – in that very spot – eight or nine years ago –
and she had been in Edinburgh to look something up in the
National Library; something to do with early Scottish monastic
practices, if she remembered correctly; but the memory of what
it was, like the memory of the early Scottish monastic practices
themselves, had faded. After her visit to the Library she had
come here, to Scotland Street, to drink a cup of coffee with
Domenica and to seek solace. Antonia's marriage was not going
well then and she had wanted to talk about that, but had not

raised it in the end because Domenica had been in full flight about Ossian.

"In the scrap between Dr Johnson and Macpherson, I'm on Macpherson's side," pronounced Domenica. "He had seen the subjugation of his world. The burnings. The interdiction of the kilt, language, everything. All he wanted to do was to show that there was Gaelic culture that was capable of great art. And all those dry pedants in London could do was to say: where are the manuscripts?"

"Well, I suppose if one claims to have discovered a Homer, it might be reasonable to ask . . ."

"Not a bit of it," said Domenica. "The poetry was there, passed from mouth to mouth. Not everybody worships the written word, you know. And that Dr Johnson . . . Do you know what he said about the stick that he carried down in London? He said that it was just in case he should bump into Macpherson and would have the chance to wallop him with it! What a thing to say! A typical Cockney bully."

"Macpherson could look after himself. All that money he made . . ."

"No different from the money anybody else made. Better, in fact. Look at the fortunes that were to be made from slave-trading and Jamaican sugar plantations and all the rest. Macpherson's fortune was less tainted than the fortunes of many of those strutting Highland grandees. Why begrudge him his Adam mansion? And, anyway, even if he invented most of the Ossian stuff, it was great literature by any standards. Does it matter whose pen it came from?"

They had moved off the subject of Ossian and on to other controversial cases: to that of Grey Owl, the bogus Indian chief who was really only Archie Belaney from Sussex, or somewhere like that; to Lobsang Rampa who claimed to have been a Tibetan monk, but who was really a man called Cyril Hoskins, from Devon; to Budu Svanidze and his memoirs of his Uncle Joe (Joseph Stalin).

Such conversations! Hour after hour they had passed together – Antonia and Domenica – and much of what had been said had been forgotten, or remembered only in part. When her friend came back, as she shortly would, then they would doubtless have many more such discussions, especially as they would now be neighbours. And they usually agreed with one another in the end, even after great differences of opinion had been discovered.

She thought back to that little boy, to Bertie, and now she saw what it was about him that made him so appealing: he spoke the truth. Candour was so attractive because we were so accustomed now to obfuscation and deceit, to what they called spin. Everything about our world was becoming so superficial. All around us there were actors. Politicians were actors, keeping to a script, condescending to us with their brief sound-bites, employing all sorts of smoke and mirrors to prevent their ordinary failings from being exposed. And rather than say yes, things have gone wrong and let's find out why, they would side-step and weave their way past the traps set for them by equally evasive opponents.

Light, clarity, integrity. Every so often one saw them, and in such surprising places. So she had seen it in that peculiar conversation with the little boy on the stair. She had seen candour and honesty and utter transparency. But you had to be a child to be like that today, because all about us was the most pervasive cynicism; a cynicism that eroded everything with its superficiality and its sneers. And a little child might remind us of what it is to be straightforward, to be filled with love, and with puzzlement.

She arose from the chair and looked out of the kitchen window. The sky was perfectly empty now, filled with light; the rooftops, grey-slated, sloping, pursued angles to each other, led the eye away. When Domenica came back, Antonia thought, I shall do something to show her how much I value our friendship. And Angus Lordie, too. He's a lonely man, and a peculiar one, but I can show him friendship and consideration too. And could I go so far as to love him? She thought carefully. Women always do this, she said to herself. Men don't know it, but we do. We think very carefully about a man, about his qualities, his behaviour, everything. And then we fall in love.

She thought about Angus Lordie, standing as she was in front of the window. And then, at exactly half past four, she came to her decision.

110. *Domenica talks to Dilly*

When Dilly Emslie went upstairs to the coffee room at Ottakars Bookshop, she was concerned that she might not find a seat, as it was busier than usual. What had brought people out on a Tuesday morning was not clear to her; the town seemed bustling, and even George Street was thronged with shoppers. But they were well-behaved shoppers, who did not push and shove, as shoppers did on Princes Street, but moved aside graciously to allow others to pass, lifting their hats where appropriate, making sure that nobody felt that he or she was about to be crowded off the pavement and into the road. Even the motorists, contending for the scarce parking places in the middle of the road, would concede a space if they saw another car about to turn in, gesturing with a friendly flick of the wrist for the other driver to go ahead. It was just as life in Edinburgh should be (*c.*1950).

Dilly ordered a pot of coffee for two and found a table. She looked about her, glanced idly at a magazine which had been left behind by a previous customer, and began her wait. This was not long; barely five minutes later into the coffee room came Domenica Macdonald, smart in her newly-acquired Thai silk trouser-suit, her face and her forearms deeply tanned by exposure to the sun. Dilly rose to greet her long-absent but now-returned friend. She was not quite sure what to say. If she said, simply: "You're back!" it would come out in a surprised tone, because she had half-expected Domenica not to return. And a simpler "Hallo" would clearly be inadequate to mark return after several months in the Malacca Straits. And of course she could not say: "You've caught the sun", because that would be on the same level of triteness as the late President Nixon's words on being taken to the Great Wall of China ("This surely is a great wall."). So she said: "Domenica!", which was just right for the circumstances.

When two friends meet for the first time in months, there is usually a fair amount to be discussed. How much more so if one of the friends has spent those months in a remote spot, the guest of pirates, living amongst them; and yet that was not the first topic of discussion. First there were books to be talked about:

what was new, what was worth reading, and what could safely be ignored.

Domenica confessed that she had read very little in the village. "I had my Proust with me," she said. "The Scott-Moncrieff translation, of course. But I must admit that I got as far as volume four and no further. I also had *Anna Karenina* in reserve, and of course I always take Seth's *A Suitable Boy* with me in the hope that this will be the year that I actually read past page forty. But, alas, I did not. It's a wonderful book, though, and I shall certainly read it one of these days. I carry it, you see, in optimism."

"Rather like *A Brief History of Time*," observed Dilly. "Everybody has that on their bookshelves, but very few people have read it. Virtually nobody, I gather."

The conversation continued in this vein for a while, and then Dilly, reaching forward to pour a fresh cup of coffee, said: "Now, what about the pirates?" She spoke hesitantly, as it was she who had urged Domenica to go out to the Malacca Straits in the first place and she felt a certain responsibility for the expedition. It was, in fact, a matter of great relief to her that her friend had returned safely to Edinburgh.

"Oh yes," said Domenica. "The pirates. Well, they were very hospitable – in their way. And I certainly found out a great deal."

Dilly waited expectantly. What exactly had Domenica seen, she wondered. And had it changed her?

"I spent a lot of time on their matrilineal succession patterns," said Domenica. "And I also unearthed some rather interesting information about domestic economy matters. Who does the shopping and matters like that."

"It must have been fascinating," said Dilly. "And the pirates themselves? What were they like?"

"Smallish, for the most part," said Domenica dryly. "I was a bit taller than most of them. Small, wiry people, usually with tattoos. Their tattoos, by the way, would make an interesting study. They were mostly dragons and the like – more or less as one would expect – but then I came across quite a number with very interesting contemporary motifs. Fascinating, really."

"Such as?" asked Dilly.

"Well, mostly pictures by Jack Vettriano," said Domenica. "*The Singing Butler* is very popular out there. The pirate chief had it on his back. I noticed it immediately."

"How extraordinary," remarked Dilly.

They were both silent as they thought about the implications of this. Then Domenica continued: "Right at the end of my stay I followed the pirates, you know. I followed them all the way to a little town down the coast. They tied up outside a warehouse, a sort of godown, as they call them out there."

"And?" said Dilly.

Domenica smiled. "Well, I crept up the jetty and managed to find a small window I could look through. I had my friend, Henry, with me. He gave me a leg-up so that I could look through the window."

There was now complete silence, not only at their table, but at neighbouring tables, where they had overheard the conversation.

"The window was rather dirty," Domenica went on, "so I had to give it a wipe. But once I had done that, I could see perfectly well what was going on inside."

Dilly held her breath.

The denouement came quickly. "It was a pirate CD factory," said Domenica. "That's what they did, those pirates of mine. They made pirate CDs."

For a moment nobody said anything. Then Domenica began to laugh, and the laughter spread. "It was terribly funny," she said. "I had imagined that they were still holding up ships and so on. But they've adapted really well to the new global economy."

"And the CDs?" asked Dilly. "What sort of pirate CDs were they making?"

"Mostly Italian tenors," said Domenica. "As far as I could see. But I noticed some Scottish Chamber Orchestra recordings and one or two other things." She paused. "I didn't see *The Pirates of Penzance* . . ."

This was tremendously funny, and they both laughed, as did one or two people at neighbouring tables who had heard the joke and who were, strictly speaking, not entitled to laugh.

111. Matthew Bears Gifts

That afternoon, Matthew closed his gallery early – at two o'clock, in fact. He had sold two paintings at lunch time – one an early Tim Cockburn, painted during his Italian period, depicting an Umbrian pergola – and the other a luminous study of light and land by James Howie. He had felt almost reluctant to let the paintings go, as he had placed them on the wall immediately opposite his desk and had become very fond of them. But they had been taken down, cosseted in bubble wrap, and passed on to their new owners. And then, looking out of the window, Matthew had decided that it was time to go shopping.

Matthew had done his arithmetic. The four million pounds which he had had invested on his behalf produced, as far as he could ascertain, a return of round about four per cent. That meant that his income – if one ignored the gallery – was, after tax had been taken off at forty per cent, ninety six thousand pounds per annum, or eight thousand pounds a month. Matthew had no mortgage, and no car; he had very few outgoings. With eight thousand pounds a month, he had an income of two hundred and fifty-eight pounds a day. On average, over the last few months, he had spent about seven pounds a day, apart from the occasion on which he had gone to the outfitters in Queen Street and bought his new coat and the distressed-oatmeal cashmere sweater, now languishing in a dark corner of his wardrobe. There had also been an expensive dinner to celebrate Scotland's victory over England in the Calcutta Cup, an occasion on which Matthew paid for a celebratory meal for six new acquaintances he had met in the Cumberland Bar on the evening of that great rugby triumph. It was only after the dinner had been consumed that one of the guests inadvertently disclosed that they were in fact supporters of England rather than Scotland, but Matthew, with typical decency, had laughed at this and insisted that he had been happy to act as host to the opposition. At which point a further disclosure revealed that one of the party was actually Turkish, and had no idea what rugby was anyway – again a revelation that Matthew took handsomely in his stride. Turkey, he pointed out, might start to play rugby some day; if the Italians could do it, then there was no reason why the Turks should not at least have a try. The Turk agreed, and said that he thought that Turks would certainly be better rugby players than the Greeks. Matthew did not comment on this observation, and for a moment there had been silence. That had been an expensive evening – three hundred and seventy-two pounds, to be exact, which was, for that day at least, an overspend. But the overall position was undeniably rosy, and so Matthew decided that it was time to spend a bit more.

His comparative parsimony towards himself, of course, had not been reflected in what he had done for others. Matthew was a generous man at heart, and he had made handsome donations to a range of charitable causes, with particularly large cheques going to the Artists' Benevolent Fund and the National Art Collection Fund. Matthew had, in fact, been the anonymous donor who had enabled a public collection to purchase, at a price of sixteen thousand pounds, the Motherwell Salt Cellar, a fine example of the eighteenth-century silversmith's art described by none other than Sir Timothy Clifford as "beyond important". He had modestly eschewed publicity on this and had even declined to attend the unveiling of the salt cellar at a special exhibition in Glasgow. There were many other examples of his quiet generosity, including his discreetly settling Angus Lordie's coffee bill with Big Lou after Angus Lordie had consistently forgotten to bring his wallet over a period of eight weeks. That had amounted to a total of one hundred and thirty-two pounds, which Matthew calculated was really only twelve hours' worth of his daily, after-tax income.

After he had locked the gallery, he walked up Dundas Street and turned left into a small lane of jewellery shops and designer studios. He paused outside a jewellery shop and looked in the window. He had no need for jewellery, of course, but then he remembered *I have a girlfriend!* Pat liked necklaces, he thought, although when he came to think of it he realised that he could not picture exactly what sort of necklace she wore. That, of course, was a male failing. Pat had once pointed out to him that men did not notice what women were wearing, whether it was clothing or jewellery. Matthew had defended men, but Pat had then asked him what she had been wearing the day before and he had no idea. And Big Lou? An apron? Under the apron? No idea. And the woman who had come in to look at that small still life an hour ago? Wasn't that a man?

He spent an hour in the jewellers. When he came out, he had in his pocket a black velvet box in which nestled an opal necklace, early twentieth-century, provenance Hamilton and Inches of George Street. Then, on impulse, rather than walking down the street, Matthew made his way up to George Street and to Hamilton and Inches itself. Inside, attended to by a soft-voiced assistant, he purchased a silver beaker on which were inscribed the words of one of the sentences in the Declaration of Arbroath: *For as long as there shall but one hundred of us remain alive* . . . He paid for this – eight hundred and seventy-five pounds – and then went out into the street again.

He walked slowly back to his flat in India Street. It was quiet inside, and it seemed empty, too, now that Pat had left. But he would see her that evening, when they were due to go out for dinner, and that is when he would give her the opal necklace. And the other present – the solid silver beaker inscribed with those stirring words, that statement of Scottish determination, he would give to Big Lou, who came from Arbroath. But it was not just the Arbroath connection which prompted the gift; it was the confidence which Pat had revealed to him a few days ago. Big Lou could not remember when she had last been given a present, by any one. She could not remember.

112. *Giving and Receiving*

It seemed very strange to be back in Scotland Street. Domenica had looked forward to her return and had imagined that she would immediately feel at home, and now she did not. She knew that she would soon adjust, but for a few days everything seemed disjointed and not quite right. The very air, warm and languid on the Malacca Straits, was brisk and fresh here – almost brittle, in fact. And there was also the hardness of everything about her: this was a world of stone, chiselled out, solid, bounded by corners and angles. She had become used to the softness of vegetation, to the malleability of cane, the femininity of palm fronds; so different, so far away.

But if there were difficulties in becoming accustomed to her surroundings again – and these, surely, were to be expected, for what greater contrast can there be between a world of pirates and the world of Edinburgh – there were still compensations in being back at home. There were the consolations of finding that the streets, and the people, were exactly where she had left them; that the same things were being discussed in the newspaper and on the radio, by the same people. All of this was reassuring, and precious, and was good to get back to.

Domenica thought about all this at length and decided that she was happy, and fortunate, to be back. Now she would spend

the next three months writing up her findings and preparing
the two papers that she proposed to write on the community in
which she had been living. She was confident that these papers
would be accepted for publication, as the people with whom she
had stayed had never been the subject of anthropological inves-
tigation before, if one discounted the efforts of that poor Belgian
– and what happened to him remained a mystery. She had tried
to discover his fate, but had met at every point with evasion.
Nobody had anything to say.

But it was good to be back, and in recognition of this Domenica
decided that she would give a dinner party. She had not entertained at all while away, and her social life had been limited to
cups of tea with the village women. She believed that this had
been enjoyable for them as it had been for her, and she had gone
so far as to form a book group in the village, a development that
had gone down well with the women, even if there were very few
books to be had in the village. And she had also laid the founda-
tions of a small credit union, whereby the poorer wives could be
helped by the richer. These were positive achievements.

Pat had agreed to come and help Domenica with the preparations for the dinner, and now they were both in the kitchen
on the evening on which the dinner was to be held. Domenica
had planned an elaborate menu and Pat was busy cutting and
preparing vegetables while Domenica cooked an intricate mush-
room risotto.

"I heard about Matthew," Domenica said, stirring chopped
onions into her arborio rice. "I must say that you could do far
worse. In fact, you have done far worse in the past, haven't you?
What with Bruce . . ."

Pat had to acknowledge that her record had not been distinguished. "I only liked Bruce for a very short time," she said.
"For the rest of the time I found him repulsive."

Domenica laughed. "He was fairly awful, wasn't he? All that
hair gel and that preening in front of the mirror. And yet, and
yet . . ." She left the rest unsaid, but Pat knew exactly what she
meant. There was something about Bruce. Did he have *it*? Was
that it? Yes. It.

"Matthew's such a kind person," Domenica went on. "You'll find him so different from Bruce. "

Pat looked thoughtful. "He gave me this yesterday," she said, pointing to the opal necklace about her neck.

Domenica put down the packet of dried mushrooms she was slitting open and peered at Pat's neck. "Opals," she said. "Look at their colours. Fire opals."

"Do you like it?" asked Pat.

"I love it," said Domenica. "I've always liked opals. I bought myself an opal ring in Australia when I was there ten years ago. I often wear it. It reminds me of Brisbane. I was so happy in Brisbane."

Pat was silent. She began to finger the necklace, awkwardly, as if it made her feel uncomfortable.

"Is there anything wrong?" asked Domenica.

Pat shook her head. "No . . . Well, perhaps there is."

"Do you feel bad about accepting such an expensive present from him? Is that it?"

"Maybe. Maybe just a bit."

Domenica took Pat's hand and pressed it gently. "It's very important to be able to accept things, you know. Gracious acceptance is an art – an art which most of never bother to cultivate. We think that we have to learn how to give, but we forget about accepting things, which can be much harder than giving."

"Why?"

"Possibly because of our subconscious fears about the gift relationship," said Domenica. "The giving of gifts can create obligations, and we might not wish to be encumbered with obligations. And yet, there are gifts which are outright gifts – gifts which have no conditions attached to them. And you have to realise that accepting another person's gift is allowing him to express his feelings for you."

Yes, thought Pat. You are right about this, as you are right about so many other things.

"He gave Big Lou a present as well yesterday," Pat said. "I was there when he did it. A silver beaker with some words from the Declaration of Arbroath engraved on it."

"A somewhat odd gift," mused Domenica. "And was Big Lou pleased?"

"Very," said Pat. "She hugged him. She lifted him up, actually, and hugged him."

Domenica smiled. "It's very easy," she said. "It's very easy, isn't it?"

"What?"

"To increase the sum total of human happiness. By these little acts. Small things. A word of encouragement. A gesture of love. So easy."

Domenica looked at her watch. "We must get on with our labours," she said. "Angus, Antonia, and all the rest will be here before we know it."

"Will Angus have a poem for us, like last time?"

"He always does," said Domenica. "When we reach the end of something."

"But is this really the end of something?" asked Pat.

Domenica smiled, somewhat sadly. "I fear it is."

113. *Domenica's Dinner Party*

One of Domenica's little ways was to give each of her guests a different arrival time, thus staggering them at ten minute intervals. She felt that this was a good way of ensuring that each person got the attention a guest deserves right at the beginning of an evening, even if it should become, as it often did, more difficult for a hostess to devote herself to individual guests later on.

The first to arrive, of course, was Angus, whom she had already seen on her return, even if only briefly. He had been over-excited at that meeting, and had blurted out all sorts of news with scant regard to chronology or significance. He had told her about Cyril's disappearance and miraculous return; about Ramsey Dunbarton's demise; about his new shoes; about Lard O'Connor's appearance in Big Lou's café and the routing of Eddie – it had all come tumbling out.

Then Antonia came from over the landing, and had brought with her a sickly orchid and a box of chocolates as a present. Domenica thought that she recognised the box of chocolates as one that had been doing the rounds of Edinburgh dinner parties over a period of several years, passed from one hand to another and opened by no recipient. She did not reveal this, though, but put the box in a drawer for the next occasion on which she needed to take her hostess a present. It might even be Antonia, should she reciprocate the invitation, but by that time the chocolates would be wrapped in a fresh piece of gift paper and might not be identified. The real danger in recycling presents came in forgetting to remove the gift tag from the wrapping, as sometimes happened with recycled wedding presents.

Then Matthew arrived, wearing a curious off-green jacket, and her friends, Humphrey and Jill Holmes, and James Holloway, who brought her an orchid in much better condition, and David Robinson, bearing a small pile of novels which Domenica had missed and which he suspected she would enjoy. That was the party complete; a small gathering, but one in which everybody knew one another and would be sure to enjoy this celebration of return and reunion.

They stood in Domenica's drawing room, where the friendly evening sun came in, slanting, soft.

"Domenica," said David Robinson. "Please reassure us that you are back for good."

Domenica looked into her glass. "I have no immediate plans to leave Edinburgh again," she said. "I suspect that my field work days are over, but you never know. If there were a need . . ."

"But you've finished with pirates?" asked James. "I really think that we've had enough pirates. Hunter gatherers are fine, but pirates . . ."

Domenica nodded. "My pirates proved to be rather dull at the end of the day. They were a wicked bunch, I suppose. Their attitude to intellectual property rights was pretty cavalier. But bad behaviour is ultimately rather banal, don't you think? There's a terrible shallowness to it."

"I couldn't agree more," said Antonia. "I would have found Captain Hook a very dull companion, I suspect. Peter Pan would have been far more fun." She looked at Angus as she spoke, but Angus, noticing her gaze upon him, looked away.

"Peter Pan needed to grow up," said Matthew. "That was his problem."

All eyes turned to Matthew as this remark was digested. Pat looked at his new off-green jacket and made a mental note to talk to him about it. But she knew that she would have to be careful.

And then, faintly in the background, the notes of a saxophone could be heard, the sound travelling up the walls and through the floor from the flat below. Domenica smiled. "Our downstairs neighbour," she explained. "Little Bertie. His mother makes him practise round about this time. We get 'As Time Goes By' a lot but this . . . what's he playing now?"

Angus moved to a wall and cupped his ear against it. "It's 'The Battle Hymn of the Republic' I believe. Yes, that's it. 'He is trampling out the vintage/where the grapes of wrath are stored' – good for you, Bertie!"

The conversation resumed, but not for long. Angus now stepped forward, glass in hand, and addressed the company.

"Dear friends," he began. "Domenica is back from a distant place. Would you mind a great deal if I were to deliver a poem on the subject of maps?"

"Not in the slightest," said David Robinson. "Maps are exactly what we need to hear about."

Angus stood in the centre of the room.

"*Although*," he began, "*they are useful sources*
Of information we cannot do without,
Regular maps have few surprises: their contour lines
Reveal where the Andes are, and are reasonably clear
On the location of Australia, and the Outer Hebrides;
Such maps abound; more precious, though,
Are the unpublished maps we make ourselves,
Of our city, our place, our daily world, our life;
Those maps of our private world
We use every day; here I was happy, in that place
I left my coat behind after a party,
That is where I met my love; I cried there once,
I was heartsore; but felt better round the corner
Once I saw the hills of Fife across the Forth,
Things of that sort, our personal memories,
That make the private tapestry of our lives.
Old maps had personified winds,
Gusty figures from whose bulging cheeks
Trade winds would blow; now we know
That wind is simply a matter of isobars;
Science has made such things mundane,
But love – that, at least, remains a mystery,
Why it is, and how it comes about
That love's transforming breath, that gentle wind,
Should blow its healing way across our lives."

The Official Home of Alexander McCall Smith on the Web

WWW.ALEXANDERMCCALLSMITH.COM

A comprehensive Web site for new readers and longtime fans alike, with five exclusive content areas:

- **THE NO. 1 LADIES' DETECTIVE AGENCY SERIES**
The original site for McCall Smith's bestselling series. Explore Precious Ramotswe's Botswana through book descriptions, a photo gallery, advice from Mma Ramotswe, and more.

- **THE ISABEL DALHOUSIE NOVELS**
Enter a Scottish atmosphere as thick as a highland mist, complete with a photo tour of Isabel Dalhousie's Edinburgh.

- **THE PORTUGUESE IRREGULAR VERBS SERIES**
Three original paperback novellas introducing the eccentric and ever-likable Professor Dr von Igelfeld, his colleagues, and their comic adventures.

- **ABOUT THE AUTHOR**
Read about Alexander McCall Smith and get updates on tour events and other author activities.

- **JOIN THE COMMUNITY**
Share the world of Alexander McCall Smith with friends, family, and fellow book club members. Print our free Reading Group Guides and sign up for the Alexander McCall Smith Fan Club and e-Newsletter.